NIGHT MAGIC

NIGHT MAGIC

CHARLOTTE VALE ALLEN

·PARRALLEL·

This title first published in Great Britain in 1992 by
SEVERN HOUSE PUBLISHERS LTD.

This edition licensed by Severn House Publishers Ltd.,
produced by Magpie Book Ltd., and published by Parragon
Book Service Ltd in 1994

A copy of the British Library CIP data is available
from the British Library.

ISBN 0 75250 087 2

While the place names used in this novel are actual, the
dwellings on Bulters Island and Contentment Island in
Darien, and the characters who reside in those places, are
entirely fictional

Printed and bound in Great Britain

I am indebted and grateful to Claire Smith for her unfailing support, and to my friends Nina Ring Aamundsen, Philamena Stevanovic, Gloria Goodman, and Dina Watson for their wholehearted enthusiasm.

"Only try to find me out, no matter how I may be disguised, as I love you dearly, and in making me happy you will find your own happiness. Be as true-hearted as you are beautiful, and we shall have nothing left to wish for."

"What can I do, Prince, to make you happy?" said Beauty.

> *Beauty and the Beast*
> *(La Belle et la bête)*
> Madame de Villeneuve

"Love me and you shall see! All I wanted was to be loved for myself. If you loved me, I shall be gentle as a lamb; and you could do anything with me that you pleased."

> *The Phantom of the Opera*
> *(Le Fantôme de l'opéra)*
> Gaston Leroux

1968–1987

1

ON HER THIRTEENTH BIRTHDAY MARISA'S FATHER TOLD
her that being her parent was the single most challenging
and rewarding experience of his life.

"I had my doubts, you know, Keed," he admitted that
day. "The last thing I thought would happen would be
my raising you alone. Scared the living hell out of me—
more than anything else ever did, I promise you. But you
were my girl. We wanted you, Rebecca and I, and I just
couldn't turn you over full-time to a nanny and go on
about my business, pretending I was doing my best by
you. It felt like I was on my knees when she died." He
looked off into the corner of the dining room, his voice
dropping. "I just couldn't believe it, couldn't believe
anyone could die that way at the age of twenty-four.
Twenty-four," he repeated, with fresh disbelief. "We
were such wise-asses, Risa; we thought we were going
to live forever. I at least should've known better. I mean,
I was older. But your mother . . . she was still a kid. She
was so young . . ." His eyes returned to her. "I remember sitting on the landing staring out the window, with
the feeling there was this tremendously heavy *thing*
weighing me down. I couldn't move, the weight of it was
so enormous. And then I heard you come running down
the hall and I turned to watch you, with your arms held
out and your little legs pumping away. Laughing. How

3

could you be laughing? I asked myself. And then I realized death wasn't something that could possibly be real to you, not the way it was to me. You were only a baby, two years old. What could death mean to you? I remember that moment in every detail, remember understanding I had a choice: I could call for Sarah to come get you, or I could open my arms and catch you when you came running. I could make something of what your mother and I had created."

"So you caught me." Risa smiled.

"Damned right, I did! You weren't some accident that happened to us, Keed. You were someone we wanted, someone we'd planned for. And now, here you are, a teenager. I'd sure as hell like to know how that happened, when a few minutes ago you were this titch I could pick up with one hand."

"You'd get a hernia if you tried picking me up now with both!" She laughed.

"To say the least."

"You always go all mushy on my birthdays," she said fondly.

"I thought that's what birthdays are for," he replied, fixing an ingenuous expression on his face.

"Naturally," she agreed. "And I hoped you'd go so mushy this year you'd maybe break down and let me have a dog."

"You are one relentless kid," he told her with a smile. "The answer's the same as it's always been: no. I've explained this to you maybe three or four hundred times. Dogs make me nervous, Risa. I can't live with one. I'm sorry. You're going to have to wait until you're an adult, with a place of your own. Then you can have eight or ten dogs, if you want them."

"Okay," she backed down. "But I had to try."

"Do me a favor, Keed, and give it up. You've 'had to try' one time too many."

"All right, Dad. I'm sorry."

That evening at dinner he gave her the tortoise-shell combs that had belonged to her mother. She only wore them at home, fearful of losing or having them stolen at school. She intended someday to give the combs and other items of her mother's to her own daughter. And she'd give them in just the way her father had given them to her: on each birthday, to celebrate the occasion.

Over the years he told her he wanted her to have a sense of occasion, to know that some times were more meaningful than others. "You have to earn what you most want, Risa. Otherwise, you'll have shoddy values. And you have to know that things can never be as important as people, or occasions." He paused, then said, "I hate the idea I might be spoiling you."

"I'm not spoiled, Dad," she said very seriously.

"No, you're not," he concurred, proud of her.

He hadn't ever segregated her out of the company of his friends because of her youth; he'd encouraged her to speak her thoughts; he'd tried to teach her to be as thoughtful of his employees as she was of him and of her friends; he'd insisted she believe in her worthiness as a person. He'd worked hard to be sensitive to her needs, to be open and accessible the way he imagined Rebecca would have been to their daughter. He took time away from his business in order to be at home with Risa or to take her away on holidays; they played one-on-one basketball together, and raced each other the length of the driveway. It was all by ear, as he liked to say, all from instinct tempered by good judgment. And she wasn't spoiled. Which had to mean he was succeeding as a parent. She did have a tendency to get hold of an idea and pursue it—like the business of wanting a dog, despite his repeated explanations—but he quite admired her tenacity.

The ongoing, concerted effort he put into guiding Risa through her childhood had an unexpected and gratifying reward in his dealings with the women he saw from time to time. He found himself more attuned to their words and moods, and was able as a result to enjoy their company more. He even, early on, considered remarrying. But in the end he managed to find reasons why it would be unwise to upset the status quo. He couldn't stand the thought of anyone or anything detracting from the closeness he felt to his child. He did study the issue closely, to determine if he was behaving too selfishly, and decided that if his devotion to Risa could be deemed selfish, then he'd live with the consequences. He was happy to watch her evolve and grow. As the years passed, it seemed he required little more than this.

On the evening before her sixteenth birthday, he announced, "It's time for some renovation, Keed. This place is starting to fall down around our ears."

"What renovation?"

"I don't know exactly. The kitchen, primarily, which is driving Kitty crazy. She says if we don't get some decent appliances, she may have to resort to dire action. And you know Kitty. That could be anything from serving up nothing but macaroni every night until we beg for mercy, to leaving us altogether. And we don't want to lose her. Plus, my bathroom plumbing's a disaster. I'm tired of having to shower down the hall. So, I guess, mostly it's a complete overhaul for the kitchen—expanding it, bringing it into the twentieth century. And redoing a couple of the bathrooms. I've got someone coming to look things over—as a personal favor to me, you understand."

"One guy's gonna do the whole thing?" She looked around the room as if trying to gauge the scope of the work.

"Not quite. And this 'one guy' isn't just 'one guy.' I've actually persuaded Erik D'Anton to consider doing the renovation. It's not the kind of thing he'd normally do."

"*Persuaded* him to *consider* it? Who *is* he, anyway?"

"A genius," Cameron Crane answered simply.

Risa rolled her eyes and made a face.

"He's stopping by tonight to have a look at the house."

"Why tonight? Why not during the day when he can really see everything?"

"Erik doesn't do business during the day."

"Why not? What is he, a vampire?" She laughed.

"You'll understand when you meet him."

"You're being very mysterious," she accused.

"I'm really not. You'll understand," he said again, "when you meet him."

"Okay. But this is weird."

"I cannot tell you how pleased I'm going to be when that word finally vanishes from your lexicon."

She got up and went behind her father's chair to press her cheek against the top of his head. "No, I'm not going to ask for a dog," she said with a soft laugh. "So don't get nervous." After a moment, she asked, "How do you do business with someone who only works at night?"

"Quite easily, all things considered." He shifted to pat her arm, then got to his feet. "I've got to dig out the original plans for the house. They're in one of the boxes in the cellar, and I want to do it before Erik arrives."

"Okay. Do I get to sit in on the meeting?"

"Of course, if you want to. He'll be here in about an hour."

"Boy, maybe I should go check to see if there's a full moon."

Instead of laughing, her father frowned. "Go casy, Risa. Erik isn't like anyone else you've ever met."

Sobered, she said, "All right, Dad."

Upstairs in her room she looked at the homework waiting to be done. She didn't feel like working and instead turned on the radio before stretching out on the bed with her arms folded under her head. Three more months until school ended. Then, next year, she'd be a senior and they'd really start putting on the pressure for her to decide what she wanted to do after graduation. The problem was she didn't know. There were so many things she thought she might like to do: art college, to study either painting and drawing or fashion design; a music school to pursue her singing seriously; theater school to study acting, or maybe set or costume design. Why did people expect you to know so young what you wanted to do with the rest of your entire life?

Cousin Brucie was raving away on WABC, going at his usual hundred and fifty words per second. She tuned him out, waiting to hear what they'd play. Most of the time she preferred the stations that played jazz or stuff from the twenties and thirties. It was a song by Bread. "(I'd Like to) Make It with You." She liked the song, mostly because David Gates had a decent voice. But she had to wonder about the time and energy, the books and

movies and records all dedicated to the theme of love
and sex and romance. The only boys who ever asked her
out were the mental midgets, the jocks who thought being seen with her would score points for them. She
couldn't stand those guys. The one boy she'd decided to
go out with was Hardy Belmont, who'd used up all his
courage just phoning to ask her. When they were finally
in his car on their way to the movies in Westport, he was
so nervous he couldn't talk. He'd kept staring over at her
and gulping a lot. She'd felt sorry for him, and to help
him out she'd started this totally one-sided conversation
that she thought made her sound like a complete moron.
Poor Hardy. He had the highest grades in the school, but
when it came down to it he was exactly like the rest of
them. He'd only asked her out because of the way she
looked and not because he really wanted to get to know
her.

She couldn't figure out why people got so worked up
about the way she looked. For years now she'd been staring at herself in various mirrors, trying to see what people saw when they looked at her. All she could see was
that her nose was too short and her forehead too high,
and her ears were kind of long, and so was her neck.
She was way too tall—by the time she started eighth grade
she was already five feet ten—and had practically nothing
in the chest department, not to mention arms and legs
that would've been better suited to an ape. The only
things she liked about herself were her hair, which was
long and black and wavy like her mother's, and her eyes,
which she thought were a good shape and an interesting
amber color. Her skin was white as paste, and ten minutes in the sun turned her into glowing neon. She also
had this weird pale line that ran from her navel all the
way down her belly, as if she'd been made in two pieces
and this line was the seam where they'd joined the parts
of her. She was positive nobody else had a seam like
hers, and thought she was probably a freak altogether,
what with her skinny ankles and wrists, and that line
bisecting her dead-white belly. Yet the jocks were forever
calling her up, chuckling and snorting over the phone.

And the girls never wanted to be friends. Except for Meggie. God, but she missed Meggie!

All her life Meggie had lived in the house next door. Then, just like that, she was gone, the family moved to Boston. Sure, they still talked on the phone and wrote letters back and forth, but it wasn't the same. Meggie was already writing about the new friends she'd made and how much better Boston was than Darien. And Risa had no one. The weekends lasted forever; the summer would be endless.

She looked over toward the window, thinking of how, for years, she and Meggie had gone creeping around the old house on Contentment Island, believing it was haunted, terrified the ghostly occupants would come shrieking out at them. They'd crawled around the perimeter of the house on their bellies, trying to get a look inside through the filthy basement windows. Then something would always happen to scare them off and they'd go running, fearfully laughing and breathless, back up the driveway to where they'd hidden their bikes in the bushes, and pedal off back to Meggie's house, or here, to sit huffing on the front steps, laughing and red in the face, exclaiming over their adventure.

A car door slammed. She got up and went to the window to see a tall figure striding toward the front door. Was the man actually wearing a *cape*? Was that what geniuses wore? She wished she could see his face, but a broad-brimmed hat concealed his features. The car was fantastic, sleek and foreign and black, something like a Maserati or a Lamborghini. This was going to be interesting, she thought, hurriedly switching off the radio and straightening her clothes before going to the dressing table for her mother's combs. She'd wear them for luck, although she wasn't sure why. There was a kind of security in the combs, a part of her history tucked snugly against her scalp and holding the hair away from her face.

"Here's Marisa!" her father announced, and she came across the living room with her hand outstretched, a smile on her face, to meet this night-caller, who was standing with his back to her and who began to turn so slowly that it seemed he emerged from the shadows in degrees. It took eons for that turn to be completed, so that her arm grew tired from being extended, and her smile felt exaggerated and unnatural; her entire body ached from the suspense of waiting. The man turned and turned, gradually committing himself to the available light, and in that time Risa was aware of her father watching, and of her inability to look anywhere but at the face being revealed to her. She experienced an odd hesitation in her heart, as if she'd suffered a physical blow, and felt sorrow, terrible sorrow—her own? this man's? She didn't know. She was smiling still. So was her father. But their breathing seemed to have been suspended, as were their thoughts. This man didn't smile, however. His gravity was so pronounced, so habitual, it was like an additional garment he wore.

"Marisa, meet Erik," her father said at last as her hand continued on its route toward the stranger. "Erik, my daughter Marisa," her father said, as her hand was engulfed and held in so fearful and tentative a grip that she could feel the foreign blood pulsing against her fingertips in confirmation of this man's life and reality. Her eyes, she knew, were unblinking as she took in the details of the face before her.

Only his eyes were intact, undamaged. Deep and black, they held her, filled with such a wealth of messages and emotions she couldn't begin to se arate and interpret them. In the briefest fragment of time she recognized fear and great intelligence and even, surprisingly, humor. But above all, she saw the sorrow, as dense and impenetrable as something constructed of lead. Around those eyes, which sat behind heavily rimmed spectacles that seemed to be of clear glass, were overlapping ridges of scar tissue, and multi-toned areas of shiny flesh. His face appeared to have been sewn from many tattered patches of flesh. He had no eyebrows, no facial hair. His mouth too was intact but for a deep scar that began at the left corner and ran in an arbitrary path toward his hairline. Yet the eyelashes behind the lenses were quite luxurious, lending a certain innocence to his gaze. There was something about his nose, something to do with the glasses, but she hadn't enough time to figure it out. She was too mesmerized by the face and by the many faded and tortuous trails intersecting the swaths of polished skin. His hair, as if in defiance of the face it might have concealed, was cut short and brushed straight back from his high, rounded forehead. And it *was* a cape he'd been wearing, she saw when she'd regained herself sufficiently to glance away from his ruined face.

"I'm happy to meet you," she said, her hand still joined to this man's.

He nodded as if unable to speak, his fingers gently closed around her long pale hand.

"A drink, Erik?" Cameron asked, bemused by the silent interchange between his daughter and his friend.

"Thank you." Erik spoke at last, simultaneously releasing Risa's hand.

His voice was deep and very soft, no more than a whisper, so that she instinctively leaned closer to hear his words. "Cognac, if you have it, please," he said, his words lent musicality by an English accent, his eyes on Risa.

She couldn't stop staring, at the same time struggling against an impulse to lift her hands to touch that face. She managed a smile, and stood with her fingers laced together in front of her.

Stupidly, Erik wanted to ask Cameron why he'd failed to speak of his daughter's beauty. She was so young. Her bones were only just emerging from behind the protective cushion of youthful flesh. His hands curled into themselves at his sides and he forced himself to turn away at last from the painful radiance of this child and take the seat his host had offered him upon his arrival. To his consternation the girl came to sit in the companion chair that was positioned at an angle to his, and with her arms crossed on her knees, her body bent toward him, she asked in hushed tones, "What happened to you?"

"Risa!" her father exclaimed, handing Erik a snifter of Armagnac.

"Twenty-four years ago," Erik told the girl in a flat, expressionless whisper, "my parents and I set out for a drive in the car one Sunday afternoon. They died. I didn't."

Risa shook her head and sat back, only to lean forward again after a moment. She could see now that he was wearing a sort of mask. It was formed of the glasses and what had to be a false nose, with flesh-colored extensions on either side that partially hid his cheeks. He'd seated himself deep in the wing chair so that the wings cast shadows over his face.

"I didn't mean to be rude," she said, noticing that his hands were magnificent; elegant and graceful, they moved as if independent of his mental commands. One was curved around the balloon of glass, the other lay on the arm of the chair like some resting but ever-vigilant creature. Each time he spoke his hand came to life, gesturing to underscore his whispered words.

"Of course not," Erik said, assaulted by the very sight of her. Refuse this job! he told himself. It wasn't the sort of work he normally accepted, but Cameron was as close to a friend as Erik allowed anyone to be. He had enormous respect for Cameron—for his energy, integrity, and business acumen. But even so, it would be torture to have to return here and encounter this exquisite child with her curious eyes and direct questions. He'd at last constructed his life so that forays outside his house were at a minimum, because it grew progressively more difficult with the passing of the years to deal with the reactions generated in others by the sight of his obscene face. Cameron was one of the few who were willing to deal with the admitted eccentricity of his terms, of night meetings and business transacted primarily by letter or telephone. Erik accepted work nowadays only to prove to himself that his skills were in no way diminished. He had no need of the money, nor of the acclaim his buildings would have brought had he been inclined to accept it. He had no need of anyone or anything. He had his house, his music, the plans he prepared of fantastic buildings no one would ever see. Why add more horrified portraits to those already lining the walls of his memory? No. He would never again take another risk, he vowed, confronting the eyes of this breathtaking girl, whose beauty was more intimidating than anything else he could imagine. It would be so easy, too easy, to fall prey to those dreams of love, of possession, of heat and bodies and minds in concert were he to subject himself to further exposure. But he would do this job, if only for the chance of seeing her one more time. He'd held her hand for those few seconds, and he did not regret that. Marisa. Even her name had a special taste on his tongue. So very young, and possessed of such daunting beauty. Marisa. He felt like weeping at the wrenching pleasure he derived from studying the fall of her hair, the sweet bow of her upper lip, the fullness of her cheek. Marisa.

2

ONCE THE PLANS HAD BEEN APPROVED AND THE WORK was underway, Risa anticipated Erik's return to the house. Surely, she reasoned, he'd have to come to verify that the workmen were proceeding as they should. But if he did come, it must have been in the dead of night and in secret because neither she nor her father saw him.

"We're in touch by phone," Cameron told her. "It isn't necessary for him to make daily site calls."

"But how does he know everything's being done right?"

"He knows because I tell him so, and because he's made a couple of inspections."

"When?"

"I honestly don't know."

"So he's never going to come back to see how it all turns out?"

Cameron set aside the newspaper he'd been reading to look at his daughter. "Aren't you happy with the changes, Risa?"

"Oh, sure I am. I mean, the kitchen already looks way better. And the sliding glass doors are really neat. I like the glassed-in breakfast area a lot. It's going to be great, like eating in the trees. I just thought," she wound down, "that he'd be around all the time."

"Are you displaying morbid curiosity, Marisa?"

14

"I don't know if I know what that means."

"It means: Are you anxious to have another look at him because you can hardly believe what you saw?"

She pushed her head against the wing of the chair—the chair in which Erik had sat that night and toward which she'd gravitated nightly ever since—to consider this question.

"He was so sad," she said, as if his unhappiness had infected her. "He was the saddest human being I've ever met. I mean, I can understand why, but it made me feel so awful, Dad. Really awful. Have you ever seen him smile?"

Cameron shook his head.

"See! That's what I mean. It's so sad."

"And that's why you'd like to see him again, because it's all so sad?"

"Sort of. I can't really explain."

"He wouldn't appreciate being invited here to be stared at, Risa. That would hardly be a kindness."

"But he must be so lonely. Maybe he'd like to come and have dinner with us. Maybe he'd even smile."

"You want to make him smile?" Cameron was having difficulty following his daughter's logic.

"Maybe I do. It's weird, you know, but I keep thinking about him. Like all the time. Really. I'll be in the middle of math or something and I'll start thinking about him, wondering where he lives, and if somebody looks after him. Does he do his own laundry? And what does he do if something needs dry-cleaning? Who does his grocery shopping? Can you imagine him at Palmer's Market?" She gave a bark of laughter, then clapped her hand over her mouth, appalled at herself. "I didn't mean that. I'm really sorry. But you know what I'm saying."

"I'm not sure I do, Keed."

"Why don't you invite him to dinner, Dad?"

"He wouldn't come."

"I bet he'd come if *I* asked him."

Again, Cameron paused and stared at her. Then he said, "Don't make a contest out of this, Risa. A lot of what you kids think is funny is downright cruel. And it's very goddamned cruel to make fun of a man like Erik."

"I'd *never* do anything like that!" she protested.

"Then why all this business about inviting him to dinner?"

"I liked him," she said quietly.

"What, precisely, did you like?"

"Dad, I don't know! Couldn't you pick up the phone and ask him?"

"If you say or do anything . . ."

"You *know* I never would! God! You're making me sound like one of the stone idiots from school. Go on. Call and ask him. I'll bet if you say it's my idea he'll come."

With his hand on the receiver, Cameron wondered if it was possible that his sixteen-year-old daughter had a crush on a brilliant, disfigured man of thirty-one. And if that was the case, how did he, Cameron, feel about that? Certainly he'd never imagined anyone less than intact for Risa. Did he have the right to make emotional judgment calls for her? Hadn't he always insisted she follow the dictates of her own heart? And besides, she was only sixteen and probably just trying to demonstrate a little kindness. He lifted the receiver, and Risa said, "Tell him if he'll come, I'll cook the entire meal myself."

"Dear God!" Cameron made a face, then smiled and with a shrug picked up the receiver.

Raskin answered the telephone, asked who was calling, then put Mr. Crane on hold while he buzzed the music room on the intercom.

As was his habit, Erik simply picked up the receiver and listened.

"Mr. Crane's on line one," Raskin told him.

Erik remained silent, deliberating, then said, "I'll speak with him," and punched the button for line one.

"Cameron," said Erik, "is there some problem?"

"None at all," Cameron answered, rattled as always by the knowledge that one never opened a conversation with Erik in the traditional way by inquiring after his health. A "how are you" was met with no response at all. One was expected to swing directly into conversation. "Actually, Risa and I are sitting here and she's been after me to invite you to dinner. She's asked me to tell you that if you'll agree to come, she'll cook the entire meal herself."

Erik sharply drew in his breath and held the telephone away from his ear. His free hand fluttered like a startled butterfly, then settled firmly on the edge of the table. He wanted to say no, to say he couldn't possibly subject himself to the agony of swallowing food in front of witnesses. But, closing his eyes for a moment, he could too easily see her exceptional face and her tall, as yet unfinished form, and he felt himself being drawn irreclaimably toward the prospect of seeing her one more time. So dangerous, he warned himself. Too dangerous. A beautiful child, she'll destroy you. And you have no skills for dealing with what you most crave and admire.

"What day, what time?" he asked.

"Let me consult the chef," Cameron said with a laugh, breaking off to speak to his daughter.

Erik could hear her answering voice, the clear treble notes of her reply, and felt himself lurching, sinking, all the hundreds of thousands of tiny cells comprising his being sent into uncertainty by a schoolgirl's few words.

"Friday evening at nine? Would that be convenient?" Cameron wanted to know.

"At nine," Erik confirmed, and with a trembling hand put down the instrument. He couldn't possibly return to his music now. He was too distraught. He called Raskin on the intercom to say, "I'll eat in my room. I won't need you anymore this evening."

"Okay, Erik. I'll make up a tray. I'm not going out, so if you need anything, I'll be around."

Thank God for Raskin, Erik thought, pacing the room, the music now silenced. Poor alienated, shattered Raskin. Who else but I would find him ideally suited for employment? A veteran of an unethical war who screams in his sleep and goes on night maneuvers in a sleeping Connecticut commuter town. A man of vast intelligence, the best education, and keeper of a thousand personal horrors, who can cook and clean, who can type and answer telephones, who has a master's in engineering from Yale to put to good use, who appears perfectly intact and even handsome in the eyes of some, but who cannot function in any effective way in "normal" society. I even envy Raskin, he thought miserably. For all the cracks in his foundation, Raskin is able to deal with the many women who respond eagerly to his bald proposals tendered in bars and other local establishments. Quite often the telephone rings for Raskin and it is some woman with a wish to position herself in open receptivity beneath Raskin's shrapnel-torn body in the hope of pleasure and disclosures. Raskin is most dispassionate in the telling of some of his less salacious conquests. He has an artist's eye for details, a musician's feel for the rhythms of encounter, and a madman's obsession for detachment. How, Erik wondered, would Raskin respond to Marisa?

An interesting proposition, that. Perhaps her curiosity would be such that she'd be eager to see this house and know the lengths to which he'd gone to secure his privacy.

He turned to survey the room, alarmingly able to visualize Marisa in one of the black upholstered chairs with graceful gilt legs and rounded backs that so reminded him of the chests of pouter pigeons. The contrast of her, the very black and white of her, would be sublime in this room. Perhaps she'd even sing for him. Hadn't Cameron said his daughter had quite a wonderful voice, and that she sang frequently for their guests? Cameron's pride in the girl was boundless. Did his indulgence of her run to humiliating business associates for sport? The very notion caused Erik's hands to shape themselves into fists. A mistake, mistake, mistake. Accepting an invitation to dinner as if he were the eligible bachelor in the neighborhood and not a freak who hid behind eight-foot-high stockade fencing topped with barbed wire; a chimera who protected himself with the very latest in security measures that ran to electric eyes and heat sensors, not to mention television monitors and cameras placed everywhere on the property; a miscreation who so mistrusted everyone that even his own home was honeycombed with hidden doorways and listening devices because anyone, even Raskin, might be tempted to sell him out for some obscure or arcane reason.

It was so difficult not to succumb entirely to what he knew to be utter paranoia, but it was right, entirely right, to exercise every possible caution because people would harm you if they could. They didn't see that beneath the harrowing surface lived someone not so very dissimilar to them. No. They believed that the face mirrored a ravaged soul. And perhaps it did. But he had proof of his onetime humanity. He had the photographs of that child, proof of the early ages, the progress he'd made from birth through to the age of seven when—he could still see it, could still hear the smashing, grinding impact roaring in his ears—they'd been crushed, ground to nothing human by a runaway lorry; when the little boy who'd always liked to stand on the back seat as they took their Sunday drives through the countryside so he'd be able to see everything, the full three hundred and sixty degrees of everything, when that little boy ricocheted from window to window like some bit of weightless debris that ended at last flung over the ruined bodies of his parents, the parts of his parents that had, in death, tried to claim him with clutching hands and leaking blood, to drag him down with them into the steaming horror of their irredeemably shattered beings. He could remember how he'd screamed, the cries breaking his chest as he'd begged not to go with them, *Don't take me with you!* he'd implored them, fighting to break free of lifeless curling fingers and lethal bone shards and wetness he knew had been contained within them, those people so giddy and pleased with the lives they wore like expensive clothing. They were the only ones who'd ever loved him, who'd ever truly cared, who'd called him Darling Boy and spun him in dizzying circles from one to the other, always catching him before he fell, always so pleased by their Clever Boy, their Darling Erik, who lived now in a cage of his own constructing, tenanted only by himself and a man others knew only to fear but who, to Erik, made better than perfect sense. If you've viewed the wreckage, if you've been there first-hand to see the meaningless losses, you will only make sense to those others who recognize and empathize with your vision.

And now he was daring to go out, to sit and try to eat while his eyes ravished this child who, all unknowingly, was picking at his exposed innards with her dainty, clear-polished fingertips.

* * *

Risa pored through cookbooks, planning the dinner. On Wednesday after school she went to three different markets to get the ingredients, and on Thursday morning she advised her father of the menu and asked if he'd buy appropriate wines. She took Friday off from school and claimed the kitchen immediately after breakfast.

"This is new and fascinatin'," Kitty observed, sitting in the newly created breakfast area finishing a cigarette and her coffee. "Since when d'you have an overwhelmin' interest in cookin'?"

"Since now," Risa answered, glancing back and forth at the index recipe cards she'd prepared while she assembled ingredients.

"Why?" Kitty asked, exhaling a plume of smoke that drifted upward through her tightly permed, carrot-colored hair. "I've known you most all your life and I never once have seen you show the least bit of interest in cookin' anything more complicated than popcorn."

"You're forgetting that whole year I made chocolate-chip cookies," Risa reminded her. "And eighth grade when I tried practically every recipe in that casserole cookbook."

"That's one very long time between drinks," Kitty said, putting out the cigarette in the new white ashtray—one of four Erik had ordered for the kitchen, along with a service for twelve of white Wedgwood porcelain.

"This is important," Risa told her, impatient with the conversation. She was truly fond of Kitty; she even loved her, but she wanted to concentrate on getting everything right for that night.

"I didn't know better," Kitty said with a knowing smile, "I'd say you were in love."

"Oh, definitely!" Risa snapped back. "Absolutely. He's a hundred years older than me, for heaven's sake."

"Never stopped nobody before." Kitty gulped down the last of her coffee, got up and carried the white cup and saucer to the sink. "I'm not sure I'm that hot about all this white stuff," she said, rinsing the dishes before popping them into the dishwasher. "You sure you don't want me to help?"

"Positive. You go off and have a swell time with Freda. What're you going to do, anyway?"

"Goin' into the city, do a little shoppin', lunch, this 'n' that. Macy's has a sale on. Might pick up some new sheets. We could do with some."

"Well, you have a nice time."

"You sure about all this?" Kitty looked doubtfully at the crowded top of the new center island. "I don't mind givin' you a hand. We're just playin' it by ear, me 'n' Freed."

"I'm sure I'm sure. You're distracting me, Kitty. I almost forgot the chives."

"Chives, yet. Okay, I'm goin'." She came over, reached into her dress pocket, pulled out a rubber band, and in several quick motions fixed Risa's hair into a pony tail, patting it affectionately. "So you can see what-all you're doin'," she said. "Hope it turns out fine. You get in trouble, I'll be at Freed's for another hour or so. You can call me."

"I won't get in trouble."

"I'd sure like to see this fella you're doin' all this for."

"Good-bye, Kitty. Have a terrific day in the city, Kitty."

Kitty laughed, picked up her handbag from the counter by the door, and, with a skeptical shake of her head, went clicking off down the hallway on the three-inch-high stiletto heels she wore day and night. Some twenty-odd years earlier, a young man Kitty had been dating had so extravagantly admired the look of her legs and slender ankles in her high-heeled shoes that she'd not only made love to him with the shoes on but she'd never once, since then, considered any other footwear. Even her slippers were mules with heels, and decorated in front with bits of marabou that wafted in her wake as she traveled about the house of an evening. Her shoes had been a source of amusement to Cameron from the outset, and he'd occasionally stoop to catch one of those drifting feathery bits on the tip of a moistened finger and smile and make some whimsical remark about bordellos.

With Kitty gone, and everything assembled, Risa took a deep breath and sat down for a few minutes to review the index cards one last time before she actually began creating the meal. For appetizers there'd be a tray with a good ripe Brie and imported crackers, as well as a crystal dish of carrot and celery sticks. Then, while her father and Erik finished their drinks, she'd set out the vichys-soise—one of her all-time personal favorites. After the soup, she'd bring out the main course: breasts of chicken with shallots and mushrooms in a heavy cream-and-cognac sauce, rice, and French beans. This would be followed by the salad of Boston lettuce, endive, and watercress with a chive dressing. And for dessert, a chocolate mousse, followed by espresso she'd serve in the new white demitasses, with neat little snippets of lemon rind tucked next to the cup. Erik would have to like it. Everybody liked chicken. But what if he didn't like mushrooms? God! She hadn't even thought of that. Meggie, for one, loathed and despised mushrooms. Of course Meggie also loathed and despised books of any kind on any subject, the Beatles, one-on-one basketball, and all classical music. Well, if Erik didn't like them he could push them aside.

Looking up from the cards, she sighed. Food every-where. Maybe Kitty was right; maybe she did need help. But no! She'd promised to cook the dinner, and she'd do every last bit of it herself. It would be perfect, and he'd smile and compliment her.

Momentarily forgetting the work to be done and the cards in her hand, she thought about poor Erik and his ruined face, and wondered how he looked under the mask. She decided it must be very bad, especially in view of the condition of those areas that showed. Again, she felt that desire to place her hands on his face, to touch those shiny patches of skin. They'd be soft and cool. His eyes were so grief-stricken, so uncertain. It made her throat constrict and her heart hurt to think of him. Imagine Kitty saying she was in love! It was all Kitty ever thought about, what with her romance novels and her soap operas and her movie-star heroes. Kitty professed to know all about love, claimed to have tried it all, done everything, and had, at the age of forty-one, long since satisfied her curiosity. She knew everything she needed to know about men, thank you very much, she said. And one thing she knew for sure was that there weren't but a handful, Mr. Crane included, of course, worth the powder to blow them away.

Risa thought she probably said stuff like that because no man had ever wanted to marry Kitty, so she was let-down about the way things had turned out in her life. After all, it was only logical that a woman so old who didn't have a husband would be a little bitter on the sub-ject of men. Although, according to her father, when Kitty had first come to them fourteen years before to look after the widower and his baby, every time he'd gone out to the kitchen there'd be some man sitting at the table with a cup of coffee and his eyes on Kitty as she bustled around, flashing her legs in her outrageous high heels.

Kitty was very pretty, although the permanent had been an admitted mistake. "They went 'n' gave me an Afro!" she'd railed upon her return from the hairdresser. "All I wanted was some body, and look what that fool woman went and did!" She'd taken herself off to her room and spent three hours under the shower, shampooing her hair over and over, trying to get rid of some of the curl. She ran the hot water tank dry and her hair came out almost exactly the same. "It'll just have to grow out," she'd said with a sigh. "But, Lord, that tees me off! White people don't look right with Afros. And will you look at this color! Be six or eight weeks at least before this tones down some. I *love* goin' around havin' people think I *chose* to look this way!" She slammed around the kitchen for a few days, then gradually calmed down, only occa-sionally pausing to put one carefully manicured hand to her hair and mutter, "Still tight as bedsprings, damn it!"

Taking a deep breath, Risa got up and went to the closet for Kitty's apron. As she tied it on she wished fervently that she had a proud full chest, like Kitty's. Kitty really did have a terrific figure, although she wore her clothes way too long, insisting, "Women my age look plain foolish in these mini things. Bad enough I got me an Orphan Annie hairdo!"

Risa couldn't help thinking it would make all the dif-ference if she, too, had a terrific figure. But she wasn't sure how, or why, or to what.

3

Cameron was both amused and puzzled by his daughter's behavior. By eight-fifteen on Friday evening she'd posted herself by the living-room windows, and turned every few moments to look out. In between times she dashed to the kitchen to check the various pots on the stove. Back at her post by the windows, she absently smoothed the skirt of her dress—one Cameron couldn't recall having seen before. It was an unexpectedly somber garment of lightweight black wool with long sleeves and a full skirt, relieved by a round white collar. Her hair was parted in the middle and held back from her face by Rebecca's tortoise-shell combs. She looked pale, yet had a flush to her cheeks as she stood chewing on her lower lip for a moment before suddenly darting across the room to start a record going on the stereo.

"If I'd known this was going to make you so nervous, I wouldn't have agreed to it," Cameron said after half an hour of this performance. "You look on the verge of collapse."

"I'm fine. There's just a lot to think about," she said, again going to the window. "I honestly don't know how Kitty does it, getting it so everything's finished at the same time."

"It's only a meal, Risa, not a career. If it doesn't come

24

together perfectly, no one's going to condemn you. Why don't you sit down for a few minutes, try to relax?''

"I can't. I've got too much to do."

"Well, standing there isn't going to make him arrive any sooner. If Erik said nine, he'll arrive on the button, not a minute before or a minute after. He's almost frighteningly punctual."

"What do you know about him?" she asked with sudden eagerness. "Do you know anything about him?"

"Not a whole lot. He was recommended to me for a job by an old friend of mine who taught Erik at Princeton. That was about six years ago. He was damned good, so I recommended him to a few other people. We've stayed in touch. He'd call to thank me for the referrals, that sort of thing. I know he lives here in town. He has a local number. But I couldn't tell you where. He has a post-office box and his mail goes there. He has an assistant, man named Raskin, who does the fetching and carrying, handles the correspondence, the telephones and so forth. He's also Erik's professional associate. As for Erik, his work is inspired and unique; his jobs are always completed exactly to specification, on time, and on budget. Beyond that, I know very little."

"But you must know more than that. Where does he come from?"

"I believe he grew up in England, although I don't think his parents were English. His degrees are from Princeton, so I'd imagine he lived for some time in New Jersey. French, I think, his parents were. I recall hearing somewhere that his father was a brilliant violinist, but I'm not up on classical music, so I couldn't swear to that. I know Erik plays some instrument, piano perhaps."

"Maybe he'd play for us."

"Don't ask him!" her father said quickly.

"Why not?"

"Just, please, don't! I have a suspicion that simply coming here tonight is as much as he can handle."

"You'd think he'd get bored," she said, almost to herself, once more looking out the window. "Only going out at night, never seeing anyone. It must be awful." As she gazed out at the driveway, she heard an echo of Erik's soft compelling voice saying, "They died. I didn't." She shivered and rubbed her hands up and down her arms. Eight fifty-five. Her stomach was kind of shaky, unsettled, and she thought she probably wouldn't be able to eat. Her whole body was stiff. She wished he'd get there. He'd smile for her; she was certain he would. And she knew he'd be someone else altogether when he did.

"Was his throat, his voice box, you know, injured in the accident? Is that why he whispers?"

"So far as I know, there's not a thing wrong with his larynx. Listen, Keed, I want your promise you're not going to hold an inquisition when the man gets here."

"I'm only curious," she defended herself.

"I hadn't noticed." He laughed and held his hand out to her. "Come here a minute, Risa; talk to me."

She placed her hand in his and stood looking down at him.

"Your hand's like ice." He gave it a squeeze. "Marisa, maybe I'm being a silly old fart, but you've got the symptoms, you know."

"What symptoms?" she asked, resisting the urge to turn toward the windows.

"You're acting like someone in love."

"Oh, crap, Dad!" She laughed, her color heightening. "That's what Kitty said. The both of you have been single too long. You two have one-track minds."

"That's what Kitty said, huh? No flies on our Kitty. Well, maybe that's true and we're looking too closely. But go carefully, Risa. I think you've got a crush on this man, and it's only going to make you unhappy."

"Supposing that was true, why would it make me unhappy?"

"Because nobody at sixteen knows her own mind. You're a long package of exploding hormones and sudden impulses. And neither of those things has anything to do with good judgment. Erik's a grown man with a strange life and a lot of problems. He's not about to take up with a teenager."

At that moment there came the sound of tires on the gravel and Cameron released her hand to look at his watch. "On the dot," he said, sounding pleased. "I'd dearly love to know how he does that."

When he looked up again it was to see that Risa seemed fixed in place, on her face an expression bordering on agony. She appeared on the verge of tears. Then, in an instant, she drew a deep breath, turned and ran off to the kitchen, calling over her shoulder, "Don't forget to turn the record over when it gets to the end of the side. I'll be in in a couple of minutes."

In the kitchen she splashed cold water on her face, then hung over the sink wondering if she was going to be sick. She felt nauseated and strangely afraid. The water she drank from her cupped hands seemed to calm her stomach and she dried herself with a towel before turning her attention to the stove. As she turned the heat off under the rice she had an overpowering desire to run up to her room, hide under the bedclothes, and cry. Her emotions were so tangled, so unfathomable that she wished she'd never instigated any of this.

Her father was showing Erik into the foyer as she returned to the living room to position herself near the fireplace. She was perspiring and her stomach had started dancing again. Erik was there! In his broad-brimmed hat and flowing cape he came over the threshold into the living room, his movements balletic. She hadn't before noticed the way he moved, the sinuous extension of his legs as they drew his torso forward. He was a tall, muscular man who gave the impression of great power. His face was not so startling to her this time, yet his graveness had precisely the same impact as it had at their first meeting. His eyes settled on her and she couldn't look away. They had the effect his hands might have had had he placed them on her body. Wide behind the heavy-rimmed glasses, they held her, unblinking and black. And then his hands rose from beneath the protective cover of the cape and she laughed in delight at the appearance of the pink roses in a paper cone that seemed to materialize in the space between them.

"For you," he said, in that voice that pushed so gently and pleasurably against her ears.

"Thank you." She stepped forward to accept the roses and stood admiring their still-damp color. "I've never been given flowers before,'' she told him. ''I'd better go put them in water.''

How splendid she was, pellucid skin and golden eyes, abundant black hair slipping forward as she bent to inhale the bouquet of the just-maturing blossoms. She moved before him like the slowly unspooling frames of a film, indelible impressions, each a minute shock to the system; low-voltage spasms of electric gratification generated by the engine of his impossible longing. For a few moments, he yearned to envelop her, to absorb her into his very cells. Madness! He shook off the cape and surrendered it into Cameron's waiting hands before accepting his host's offer of a drink. As he seated himself in the wing chair and watched Cameron fill glasses, he thought how ridiculous this was, how truly ridiculous. He was playing out a role, acting out some part they'd assigned to him—the visiting business associate; as if he were ordinary, undamaged, a man to whom they were well accustomed.

''It's good of you to come, Erik. I know you rarely socialize.''

''I never socialize,'' Erik answered, more abruptly than he intended. He had, after all, a certain fondness for this man; a fondness that had grown considerably since meeting Marisa. He took a sip of the neat Glenfiddich, allowing it to slide over his tongue and ease its way down his throat. Setting the heavy-bottomed crystal glass down with care, he tried to think of something he might say to soften his remark. ''Your daughter,'' he began, then shifted direction slightly. ''It's generous of you to invite me.''

''Had I thought for a moment you'd come, I'd have invited you a lot sooner.'' Cameron gave his guest an open, honest smile. Erik nodded, his hands poised *en pointe* on the arms of the chair. He breathed cautiously, traces of Marisa's faint fragrance tingling in his nostrils as he had a fleeting vision of placing his lips in the curve of her neck while her body flowed like a river into his. The vision created a sudden constriction in his lungs and he reached again for his drink. His free hand reassured itself by stroking briefly the pocket flap of his black cashmere jacket.

''Okay!'' Marisa said with an edgy little laugh, coming to sit in the companion chair beside Erik. ''Ten minutes until dinner. What're you drinking?'' she asked of both men.

"Glenfiddich," her father answered, noticing she'd grown animated and less pale with Erik's arrival.

"Can I have a taste?" she asked Erik, holding her hand out for his glass.

Erik looked inquiringly to her father, who said, "I have no objections. Risa's been tasting my drinks since she was about three."

Erik gave her the glass and watched as she held it to her mouth, took a swallow, then looked at the ceiling while she decided whether or not she cared for the taste.

"It's interesting. Thank you." She returned the glass to Erik. "I'd rather have wine. Have you actually seen the work they've done on the house?"

"I have," Erik told her, his eyes on the impression her lips had left on the rim of his glass, his entire body surging in response. Looking up at her, he lifted the glass in such a way that he was able to drink from precisely the same spot. Foolish, but it thrilled him; a cool kiss.

"Are you pleased?" she asked him.

"Are you?" his deep whisper inquired.

"Yes. Yes, I am," she said decisively. "Every time I sit down for breakfast, I feel great knowing nobody else has a room anything like it. It's like being right outside and yet completely protected."

Again Erik nodded.

"It's a treat being able to use my own bathroom again," Cameron put in, feeling as if he were eavesdropping. There was a silent communication taking place between these two that excluded him utterly. It both fascinated and discomfited him. After all, this was his daughter, his baby, not some woman he scarcely knew. And that, he realized all at once, was a substantial part of what so discomfited him: the understanding that Risa had attained womanhood, but he hadn't noticed until this moment. Yes, she was still shedding the last soft vestiges of her childhood, but she had a woman's height and grace and lure. He was able to see, with quite alarming clarity, how another man—this man, this one man most certainly—might find her highly appealing.

She got up to turn over the record—one of the Mozart piano concertos, Cameron could never remember them by number—and both men watched her lift the cover on the turntable and with the very edges of her fingers take the LP by its outer rim and deftly flip it over.

"I'll organize the first course now," she announced, "if you'd like to come to the table."

"We haven't finished our drinks yet, Risa," Cameron pointed out.

"Bring them with you," she said airily, as if she'd done this dozens of times before. "It'll be another minute or two before we're ready to start."

"Then why," suggested her father indulgently, "don't we just sit here and enjoy our Glenfiddich until those two minutes are up?"

"Oh, Dad!" She was reassuringly childlike again as she capitulated. "All right. But have some of the Brie, then." She dropped to her knees beside the coffee table to cut the cheese, then offered the tray to Erik.

He thought he'd choke if he tried to swallow any food. Yet how could he refuse anything she offered? She smiled at him as he took one of the pieces she'd cut and he felt the powdery surface of the cheese between his fingers as he noted the golden clarity of her eyes and the all but invisible down on her cheeks. His eyes wanted to close; too much, this proximity. Why had he come here? Why was he subjecting himself to this socialized torture? And how could she look at him that way, so unflinchingly, as if he were someone other than Erik D'Anton, social pariah? He couldn't eat. How could he? But he had to. He could scarcely return this yielding overripe morsel to the tray, or push it down between the cushion and the side of his chair. As she held the tray out to her father, he slipped the cheese into his mouth, bit into its melting, faintly acrid core, chewed quickly, then swallowed. At once he drank the last of the Scotch, allowing it to carry away all the remnants of the unwanted tidbit. There was an entire meal still to come. He might very well asphyxiate in an effort to appease this determined child.

"Okay!" she said. "Now you have to come to the table." She rose and went to push apart the doors to the dining room, standing aside in order that they might appreciate her artful table arrangement: Erik's white porcelain and Dansk stainless-steel cutlery set on white linen, Rebecca's bridal-gift Waterford goblets fracturing the light, and in the center an arrangement of still-green forsythia branches and tall white candles in polished silver candelabra. She'd placed one of Erik's pink roses diagonally across each of the plates.

Erik's hands drew together in a devotional attitude, inspired by appreciation of her work. "Lovely!" He turned to look at her with approving eyes.

She waited a moment, hoping he might smile. But he didn't. She seated them, then went to the kitchen for the tray with the vichyssoise. "So far, so good," she said to herself before pushing through from the kitchen.

It all went far more easily than she'd imagined. Somehow, incredibly, everything came together, and she didn't drop anything in her lap or, more importantly, on her father or Erik.

"This is wonderful, Risa." Her father beamed at her. "I'm proud of you, Keed."

"It's splendid," Erik told her across the table, although he could do no more than sample each dish. He was so moved—by her, by the effort she'd made in preparing this sumptuous meal, and by her very presence so close by—he was incapable of ingesting more than a few bites. He drank the wine gratefully and watched her as she ate, and as she glanced over to smile at her father, or even better, at him. He couldn't think what to do. There was no point to promising himself he'd never return here. The thought of her would bring him back if other invitations were not forthcoming. A mistake, mistake, mistake.

But if he were to leave here and not return, he had to know before he left if she could sing. He felt a spark of hope. If she sang and was no better than mediocre, he'd have some hook upon which to hang his departure. He'd be able to discount or discredit her. And so, as she was shepherding them back to the living room for coffee, he ventured to say, "I understand you sing rather well. Would you sing for me?"

Her face creased becomingly with indecision. "Dad's always bragging about me. I'm nowhere near as good as he says. You really don't want to hear me sing."

"Yes," Erik said firmly. "I do."

"Honestly?" Her luminous eyes questioned him.

"Yes."

"Well, okay, if you're sure. Let me just go get the coffee. You two sit down and make yourselves comfortable."

Comfortable? Erik repeated the word to himself as he resumed the wing chair. It was a concept almost entirely alien to him. The only times he felt even remotely close to comfortable were when he worked, or when he involved himself with his music.

After serving the espresso, she went to the grand piano—Rebecca's Steinway—and sat down, at once turning with a self-deprecating grin to say, "Remember, you asked for this." She stared at the keyboard for several moments, rubbing her knuckles as she decided which number to do. Then she spread her fingers over the opening chords of "Sweet and Lovely."

Erik's hands pushed themselves between his knees, which in turn locked tightly, almost painfully, against them, as her wondrous voice oozed over him like warm lotion. Rich as Cornish cream in the low register, clear as early morning air to the E above high C, with quirky phrasing and powerfully intimate intonation, she was a natural. Perfectly pitched, she did admirably eccentric things with the melody line, sang a chorus and a half of good jazz over a perfunctory rendering of the piano chords, and stopped.

Risa turned to acknowledge the applause her father always offered, then looked to see Erik's response. He stood suddenly and took several steps forward, halted, then continued across the room until he was standing directly in front of her. Uncertainly, she held still, for a second wondering if he was going to strike her as his hand, the fingers slightly spread, approached the side of her face. The hand brushed against the hair falling over her shoulders, then pulled back and, with a flourish, he revealed to her the silver dollar standing upright between the first two fingers of his left hand.

Enchanted, she accepted the coin. "You do *magic*!" she laughed. "How terrific!"

"No," he corrected her, grave as ever, "*you* do magic. May I?" he asked, indicating the piano bench.

"Sure." She shifted to the far end of the bench, curious to know what he'd do.

His majestic hands lowered themselves to the keyboard where they lingered for a moment before bearing down to produce the chords that simply had to accompany her.

"Oh, that's wonderful!" she sighed, watching his effortless fingering, the great span and agility of his left hand.

"You come in here," he said, leading out of the introduction and offering her a slight pause in which to insinuate herself into the music. She slid in on cue, his sweet complicitous partner, and sang the song again, even more fluently now that she no longer needed to bother with the accompaniment.

Cameron sat listening to the two of them, watching the way Erik seemed to be breathing in time with Risa, as if he'd achieved something of lifelong importance, and experienced a unique gratification when Erik actually smiled. It seemed an entirely involuntary gesture, perhaps even one of which Erik was unaware. And dear Risa, who'd planned this evening with the hope in mind of making this very thing happen, missed it. She was so lost to the music that she failed to see the transformation she effected in Erik. For several long moments, he was a young, happy man. Then the music was ended and Erik was getting up, saying, "I must go," as he rushed toward the foyer to throw open the closet door and retrieve his hat and cape.

Taken aback by the swiftness of this departure, Risa and Cameron followed after him.

"You don't have to go yet," she protested. "It's still early. And I don't have school tomorrow."

Erik paused in his flight, the cape over his arm, hat in hand. "I must go," he whispered urgently, and looked at Cameron as if for assistance.

"Say good night, Risa," Cameron told his daughter, automatically draping his arm across her shoulders.

"I wish you didn't have to go," she told Erik. "I love the way you play; I loved singing with you. I know tons of other old songs. Maybe you could come again, we could . . ." She trailed off, knowing nothing she could say or do would prevent his leaving.

"Good of you to come, Erik." Cameron shook the man's hand.

"Please come again," Risa said. Then, impulsively, she took a step forward, put a hand on Erik's shoulders, and kissed his cheek.

He reacted as if she'd struck him. His hand went at once to his cheek. He turned, flung open the door, and in seconds was in the sleek black car, driving away.

Risa stood in the open doorway with her father watching the taillights of the car disappear down the driveway, saying, "He didn't have a good time."

Again Cameron put his arm around her shoulders. "He had a great time," he said consolingly. "Probably one of the best times of his life. C'mon, Keed. I'll help you clear up." He closed the door.

"Dad, I feel so *bad*," she said, her face twisting. "He didn't have a great time at all. You're just trying to make me feel better."

"No, I'm not. He smiled, Risa; a great big happy smile."

Her eyes went wide, "He did? When? Where was I?"

"You were singing."

"He did, honestly and truly?"

"Smiled his heart out."

"He smiled and I didn't *see* it? Oh, damn! You promise?"

"Cross my heart."

"D'you think I sang all right?"

"As good as Sarah Vaughan."

"Did you *hear* the way he played? *God!* Wasn't he *great*?"

"You were both great. The dishes're waiting, Risa."

"Okay. I'll be right there. I have to get the coffee cups."

She went into the living room, collected the cups, then stood looking at the piano. He'd sat so close to her their bodies had touched; he'd been so close she'd been able to smell his many aromas—soap, and shampoo, a hint of tobacco. And his clothes had been so soft; the brush of his sleeve against her bare hand had been like a caress. They'd sat right there together on that bench. He'd smiled, but she hadn't seen it. She'd kissed his cheek and it had been as soft and as cool as she'd known it would be. If only he'd stayed a little while longer.

She felt somewhat queasy with mixed disappointment and elation.

Erik picked up the intercom and waited for Raskin to answer.

"Yes, Erik?" came Raskin's even-toned, very Eastern voice.

"Raskin," said Erik, "tell me about your evening with the insurance secretary."

"The one last December?"

"Yes."

"All of it, or just the key parts?"

"The key parts."

"Okay. Let me grab a cigarette. Hold on a minute."

While he waited, Erik settled on the floor with his back against the wall, positioned so he had a full view of his entire bedroom.

"I'm back. Okay. After we left the bar we went in my car and I took her home to her place. She lived in one of those condos in Stamford on Strawberry Hill. We had another drink in the living room, a quick one, then we went into her bedroom . . ."

As Raskin's voice buzzed in his ear, Erik touched his hand to his cheek and mentally transposed the players so that it was he, not Raskin, and it was lovely Marisa, not some nondescript secretary, who came together skin to skin on the cool sheets. Her hair was liquid ebony pouring through his fingers; her mouth opened to emit loving murmurs; her long limbs enclosed him. Marisa, angel. She'd touched her precious mouth to his cheek. She'd kissed him. Marisa.

4

FOR DAYS ERIK'S FACE BURNED WITH THE IMPRINT OF her kiss. His hand lifted repeatedly, his fingers gingerly examining the area. He remained for long hours at a stretch in the music room, the speakers throbbing from the powerful thrust of Corelli and Vivaldi, Mozart and Handel, Beethoven and Chopin. When he grew weary of the confining legitimacies of the classical compositions, he switched to lengthy periods of Bill Evans or Charlie Parker, Wes Montgomery or Oscar Peterson, Dizzy Gillespie or Charlie Byrd. He walked the room from side to side, corner to corner, in a turmoil. His brain seething, he waged war against the instinct that urged him to return to that house to see the child again. His eyes haunted by too many images of her, he fought his terrible need, his impossible longings. The flames of the candles dimmed as his frantic passage created drafts in the vast underfurnished room.

Pausing for moments, his eyes searching the deeper darkness of the perimeter, he'd imagine the door opening to reveal her figure on the threshold, and the potential for all but fatal joy promoted by his imaginings destroyed his taste for food and drink. The trays Raskin brought remained untouched, and silently Raskin removed them after a time, only to replace them later with fresh offerings.

Back and forth, back and forth, he paced out the

nights, music howling in his ears and candle wax dripping silently to form unheeded sculptures. Once when a tape ended, he sat down at the piano and spread his hands over the keys, but couldn't begin to play. The sound of his yearning had no melodic line. He was helpless in the face of what he craved, yet powerless to give it meter and rhyme. Another time, determined, he was able to play four bars of introduction and opened his mouth to sing, but had no voice. She'd come to stand between his intent and his ability to make good on that intent. How could he push whispered words into the tallow-scented air when all he truly wished to hear was the schoolgirl's self-taught brilliance? If only she'd been ordinary! If only, when she'd emitted her first notes, they'd been slightly less than true, even a little less felt. But no. She sang with divine purity, unimpeachable clarity.

What should he do? None of Raskin's stories contained clues that might assist him. And there was no one to whom he could speak of his heart's folly. He'd been rendered voiceless and heartsick by a child who could be harmed, it seemed, simply by the admission of his hopeless passion for her. She might, yes, be able to look at him without evincing horror; she could even place her acid kiss upon his patchwork cheek, but she could never respond with anything less than outraged contempt to an invitation to enter the inner sanctum of his life and feelings.

And why should she respond otherwise? What, after all, did he truly know? His experience of women was predicated completely on hearsay. He was the invisible partner in Raskin's conquests, the uninvited third party whose unseen presence and weightless flesh followed in Raskin's wake. Through his compliant employee he'd gained access to the world of erotic pleasures, to acquiescent limbs, billowy breasts, and moistly yielding chasms. But he could stake no claim on any direct contact, ever, with the exception of one child's lips grazing his startled cheek. And it burned, it scalded, it seared. His hands groped the smoky air, his fingers spread wide to catch any stray wisp of possibility. Nothing. Opening, closing, his pathetic hands searched the limited atmosphere, settling at last on the hated face where they pulled and punished the dismal ruin that was all that remained of Darling Erik's childhood beauty. The mask set aside, his fingers probed the bony mass and puckered ridges of what had, long ago, been a young child's promising future.

I *can't* go back! I must *never* go back! he roared inside the cavern of his skull. Kindness and pity and the sudden laughter of a beautiful young girl were not the guaranteed precursors of love. He would never be granted access to the resilient sweep of her embrace. No one so beautiful could ever conceive of leaving the daylight world to which she had a natural claim in order to be smothered by the midnight secrecy of his illicit caress.

Oh, but to see her again! To note the way the flesh dimpled and acceded to the flexing of her lissome limbs; to hear her draw in her breath and see the rise and fall of her chest as it filled, then expelled exotic sounds that caused his skin to swell and shudder as if it might burst from the effort to contain such undeserved pleasure. What could he do? he asked the walls, the ceiling, the floor. What should he do? he asked Rachmaninoff, Respighi, Poulenc. One way or another, he'd die from this breach of common sense. Either she'd murder him with her young girl's good intentions, or he'd expire from the mammoth effort of attempting to suppress more emotion than he'd ever thought to feel.

He could not go back; he dared not go back. He'd held so long, so tenaciously to this life he was doomed to live, he couldn't now surrender it for the sake of these unworthy and adolescent yearnings for a girl half his age. She had smiled for him; she'd cooked and sung for him; she'd made it seem she sincerely wished to have more of his company; and she'd kissed him. With her eyes fully open, her hand placed trustingly on his shoulder, she'd leaned across the abyss to press her lips to his noisome face. It was once; it was done; he would not go back.

Four days of intermittent sleep, four endless nights of parading back and forth before the arras he'd embroidered with the silken threads of his besotted longings, and the need was beaten down to a manageable level. Leaving the music room, he walked through the dark house, breathing the refreshing air through nostrils still thick with the scent of the girl, to climb the stairs to his room. Throwing off his clothes, he closed himself into the unlit bathroom to sink into soothing hot water and soak away the countless coils of tension. He could not go back.

Days, then weeks, passed and the anticipated telephone call didn't come. Risa couldn't understand it. She'd been so positive, so utterly convinced he'd call. But he didn't. And she tried to imagine why not. Perhaps the meal hadn't been the success she'd thought; or her singing had been too amateurish; she shouldn't have given in to her impulse to kiss him. She'd never forget his reaction, the way he'd looked—as if she'd struck him. He'd fled from her, roaring away in that unearthly black vehicle, its taillights like spots of blood on black velvet. There were too many things she could see now she shouldn't have done. Yet she'd been so certain he liked her. Her father assured her Erik had actually smiled. But she hadn't seen it for herself, and her father had always made his best effort to ensure her happiness. Her father was prejudiced in her favor, blind to her many faults and shortcomings. God! She couldn't believe Erik didn't intend to call, and couldn't bear the idea, rapidly becoming a conviction, that he wouldn't.

"Daddy, phone him," she asked Cameron one night just before school ended for the year. "Or give me the number and let me phone him."

"What for?"

"We'll ask him to dinner again. You said he enjoyed himself. Maybe he's embarrassed or something to call us, so we'll have to call him."

"Risa, what's the point of this? You can't force people to do things just because you want them to."

"But he wants to come back. I know he does."

She was, her father thought, inches away from hysteria. If one telephone call would keep her from going over the edge, what harm could there be to it? "All right, Risa. I'll call him."

"Oh, thank you." She sat down at his feet as Cameron reached for the telephone after looking up the number in his address book.

Raskin asked who was calling, then went off the line for quite some time.

"What's happening?" Risa asked, tugging at her father's trouser cuff.

"Nothing. I'm on hold."

At last Raskin came back on the line. "I'm sorry, Mr. Crane. Erik says if there's any problem with the billing for the job, don't pay it. He's not available just now to talk."

"It's not about the bill. There's no problem with that. I was calling to ask if he'd care to come to dinner."

"Erik isn't seeing anyone at the moment, Mr. Crane, but I'll give him the message. Anything else?"

"I don't think so. Thank you."

"Good-bye, Mr. Crane."

Cameron hung up and turned to Risa.

"Well?" she wanted to know. "What?"

"Erik isn't seeing anyone at the moment."

"What does that mean?"

"I think it's fairly clear."

"But did you *talk* to him? Did he actually *say* that *himself*?"

"I spoke to Raskin. I have no reason to believe he'd lie to me, Risa."

"Oh!" She lowered her heard and sat looking at the carpet. "Did he say how long it was going to be before Erik was seeing people again?"

"I didn't ask, and he didn't say. You really should forget about this," he said gently. "I told you at the outset Erik isn't like other people."

"I know," she said dully, still looking at the carpet. "Thanks for trying," she said after a time. "I guess I'll go to bed now."

She got up and kissed him good night then trudged upstairs to her room. Erik didn't want to see her. That's what Raskin had really been saying. Something she'd said or done had offended Erik, and now he never wanted to see her again. But what had she done? If only she knew that, she might be able to fix it, smooth things over. It made her frantic to think she'd messed up without even being aware of it. How could she have been so stupid?

And that's what she was all right: stupid. She hated herself for thinking she was so clever when all the time she'd been an idiot, a stupid idiot. All at once she disliked herself so intensely, so violently she felt like doing something wild, something painful to punish the idiot inside her. She yanked at her hair but the pain was tolerable. She pinched her arms but that, too, was tolerable. Whirling around, she tried to think what she might do to herself that would be commensurate to the degree of hate she felt. Nothing. What could she do? She could drown herself in the bathtub, or swallow an entire bottle of aspirin. But then she'd be dead, and if she were dead there'd be no chance, ever, of seeing Erik again.

Why, she wondered, did that strike her as such a terrifyingly empty prospect? She scarcely knew him. But, oh God, all she had to do was think about how it had felt to sit beside him on the piano bench, his thigh hard against hers, his broad long-fingered hands pressing into the keyboard, his elbow just touching her wrist, and she could barely breathe. Did love feel this way? Was it something so immense and painful that it made you think about things like failure and death? Did people in love go around suffering all the time? She'd always believed love was something light, the consistency of beaten egg white, the weight of one of Kitty's bits of marabou. Love was something that made you feel good, not stupid. So how could this possibly be love? No, no. She'd liked him because he'd brought her pink roses—she'd pressed two of them between the pages of Anne Sexton's *Love Poems*, with the collected works of Shakespeare on top to weight them down—and he'd played for her while she sang; and he'd made a silver dollar appear in her hair. She'd liked him because his sensuous whisper made the muscles in her belly contract, and because he moved like someone in a dream, and because she'd believed with every ounce of her being that she was the one person in the entire world who could somehow make him smile. What an idiot! Who did she think she was, anyway? He probably thought she was just some smart-ass kid, too tall, with no chest, and delusions about her abilities and power.

But she missed him, and she thought about him even

more now than before. Just this morning at breakfast, after her father left for the office, Kitty had come to sit with her in the lovely breakfast area Erik had created, and said, "Reese, you're really draggin' yourself around here these days. You feelin' okay, hon?"

"I'm just tired. Too much studying for the finals."

Kitty had shaken her head. "That's crap. You could ace them exams without ever crackin' a book, and you and I both know it. It's that fella, right, the one you turned the kitchen into a disaster area for?"

"What is it with you and my father? The two of you are forever on my case about Erik. I've met the man exactly twice in my whole life."

"Once can sometimes be enough to do it."

"Do what?"

Kitty finished lighting a cigarette before answering. "To turn on all your electric lights and charge up the batteries real good."

"What?"

"Look," Kitty said, taking hold of Risa's hand. "I'm gonna say this one thing, then I won't go bringin' the subject up again. If you get to the point where you're considerin' gettin' seriously involved, you come to me and we'll have us a talk about it, make sure you know what's what and how to protect yourself."

Risa stared at her, then slowly pulled her hand free. "You'll be the *first* to know," she said angrily. "And thanks a lot for this heart-warming little chat."

"Don't be bitchy!" Kitty cautioned. "You got more goin' on inside your head right now than you know how to handle. And I can surely sympathize with that. But don't chew me out just 'cause I care enough about you to want to be sure you know which end is up."

"I'm sorry, Kitty," she said tearfully. "I didn't mean it."

"Yeah, you did," Kitty said, her eyes narrowed against the smoke. "But I can take it. You better get goin' now. You're gonna be late."

"I really am sorry," Risa insisted.

Kitty softened. "You'll miss the bus. Scram on outta here."

"Your hair's looking good again," Risa said by way of additional apology.

"Yeah," Kitty agreed. "And about goddamned time, too."

Sitting now on the side of her bed, gazing down at her shoes, Risa reviewed that morning's conversation and the grinding embarrassment she'd felt. Kitty had been talking about sex, for heaven's sake; about her, Risa, getting into bed with some man. Not some man. Erik. Her face went hot, but the idea held a very definite appeal, and she thought her father and Kitty and Meggie would have screaming fits if they knew she could picture herself taking her clothes off for Erik, of all people. Yet why not Erik? The way he played . . . She let her head fall to one side and closed her eyes, seeing and hearing once more the marvelous music he'd made—for her. How could he do that and not want to see her again? It didn't make sense. But obviously he wasn't going to phone or come back. It felt like a death, as if someone she loved with all her heart—her father, for example—had suddenly died. The ache inside was paralyzing in its enormity. It made her eyes fill and created spontaneous sobs she tried to stop by covering her mouth with her hands. She was such a moron! she told herself, furious. Why was she carrying on this way? She'd have to stop or her father and Kitty would decide to do something about her, like sending her to a psychiatrist, or having her locked up in some place like Silver Hill or something. And no doubt a psychiatrist would confirm her incredible capacity for sheer outrageous stupidity.

She told herself she'd have to stop thinking about him. Yet even as she thought it, she couldn't imagine how she'd do it. It was as if Erik had taken control of her brain, as if it were *his* voice and not her own that narrated her thoughts as they sped past the receptors that translated some items into action and others into immobility. And when she slept, things happened that made her waking self giddy with shame as well as with a small perverse pride in the accomplishments of her sleeping self. Because in her dreams she marched through the front door of Erik's house—wherever it was—and claimed him, in clearly stated terms demanding that he capitulate to what they both knew to be the truth. And he acceded, his magical hands creating brilliant effects. He revealed himself to her, then deluged her with a pleasure that swamped her senses and left her weakly subservient to his desires, and her own. In her dreams their conversations underscored their every action as he whispered into her ear the tragic tales of his lifetime and his unabridged aspirations for the future they'd have together. "Help me," he whispered. "Save me," he begged. She held him secure in the anchor of her arms, and without pain found herself the able channel through which he might pass to safe harbor. In these dreams they were both rescued by the truth, which—as only happens in dreams—was effortlessly acknowledged. "I do love you," she told his astonished eyes. "I love you," her body insisted to his. "I don't care about the way you look or about the need to live a life of nights with no end. Let me be with you and I'll never again ask for sunlight. I'll swim with you in tidal pools at midnight. I'll sing all the songs I ever knew, for you. I will be your home, your shelter, your haven. You're all I want, all I will ever want."

She fell asleep finally with her clothes on, and had to hurry the next morning not to miss the bus. Somehow she got through the last days of school, and somehow she wrote the exams, although afterward she couldn't remember even one of the questions. Then summer spread itself before her in all its heated lassitude and she lay on a chaise out on the back lawn, blinking at the sunlight glinting off the waters of the Sound while she allowed the brutal sun to punish her hapless flesh for her many and critical inadequacies. She burned herself day after day until her skin cracked and split, and finally Kitty came marching out the back door to drag her physically off the chaise and into the house.

"I don't know what-all you think you're doin'," Kitty ranted, "but if you think I'm gonna sit by and watch you tryin' to incinerate yourself, you're plain crazy. Now you get up to your room and take a long cool shower. After that, you put on plenty of Noxzema. If you don't come down here with a good thick layer of that glop all over you from head to toe, I'll come up there and do it myself. And if I catch you outside there one more goddamned time, I'll take my belt to you like maybe somebody shoulda done a long time ago. Now you git!''

Risa just stood there, radiating heat and giving off a faint smell of burned flesh. Her visible grief undid Kitty, who gathered the girl into her arms and stroked her overhot naked spine as she murmured, ''It'll be okay, Reese. You'll see. Everything's gonna be okay.''

Risa nodded dumbly and bent her head to the smaller woman's shoulder. ''I feel so bad, Kitty,'' she confessed. ''Nothing I do will make it stop.''

''Time'll see to you,'' Kitty crooned. ''You need to find something to do with yourself, something to take your mind off what's troublin' you.''

''I've tried! I've tried everything I can think of, but nothing works. I feel as if I want to die.''

''I don't want to *hear* that!'' Kitty said sharply, taking hold of Risa's upper arms. ''I don't *ever* want to hear that! Maybe you don't think of me as much more than the hired help around here, but I'm kind of possessive about you, girl. And I care one whole lot about your life. It's all out there in front of you, and there's nothing that's happened that's so bad it should make you want to think about dying.'' She paused, then asked, ''Is there?''

Risa had to admit she was right.

''Well, all right then,'' Kitty said, greatly relieved. ''Git on upstairs and do like I told you. When you come down, you'll have some nice fresh lemonade and we'll watch the soaps. That'll keep your mind off what's distressin' you so.''

Risa gave her a shaky smile and went off to do as she'd been told. But while she stood under the shower, she couldn't help thinking she'd be happy again if only Erik would call or come to visit. It wasn't such a lot to ask, was it?

5

ERIK HAD ONE LAST PROJECT TO WHICH HE WAS COMMIT-
ted. His decision was to finish this job and refuse all
future offers. The making of this decision and the rec-
ognition of his final existing responsibility allowed him
to take up work again at the drafting table in the attic
office.

Almost the first thing he'd done upon purchasing this
house was to gut the entire area under the eaves and redo
it according to his needs. The only items he'd left intact
were the two round stained-glass windows set at either
end, facing north and south. The Victorian caprice of
installing two very fine windows in an area where they'd
never be appreciated, and the excellent quality of the
glass itself, prompted him to respect the original builder's intent—whatever that might have been. Since these
windows were placed high in the end walls, and were
comprised of cut pieces of deep hue—a blood red, an
emerald green, an eggyolk yellow, and a royal blue—they
admitted little direct light but did, in the early morning
and late afternoon, project wheels of color that were ka-
leidoscopically pleasing to his eye.

He and Raskin had undertaken to do the work themselves, and had placed fiberglass insulation between the
ceiling joists, then a layer of soundproofing and, at last,
covered everything over with Sheetrock, which they'd

spackled and seamed for hours on end until their arms quivered from strain and their necks were stiff and kinked from work done entirely above their heads. The walls were given a similar treatment. Wearing face masks, they sanded the wide-board pine floors, then coughed for days afterward in spite of their precautions. With the floors stripped and the Sheetrock joins sanded smooth, Raskin spray-painted the room a matte black, per Erik's instructions. The floor was given three coats of the darkest stain, then sealed.

When Erik was satisfied with the results, the drafting tables and file cabinets, Raskin's typewriter, the Xerox copier, and the telephones were put into place. A handsome old Oriental carpet in predominantly navy tones with hints of red was laid in the center of the floor; overhead fans were installed to assist the new central air-conditioning that operated through the existing floor ducts; and then Erik positioned the high adjustable stool upon which he sat to do his work so that his back would be to the room.

With the office completed, Erik next went to work on the remaining two floors and the cellar. The six original bedrooms were restructured into three; the three upper bathrooms were gutted and done over with new fixtures and fittings. On the main floor the old parlor and sitting room were merged to form one very large room. The several pantries were eliminated to create the huge kitchen where Raskin prepared the meals. The dining room, paneled in gleaming mahogany, was left intact with its brass wall sconces and crystal chandelier. The front hall was done away with altogether, the walls taken down so that the front door opened directly into the living room, which was painted charcoal gray and outfitted with two custom-made sofas upholstered in black glove leather. The only adornment anywhere in the house consisted of the two portraits in the living room that hung on either side of the fireplace: the one of his parents, and the one of Erik and his mother, done when he was five.

Everything in the house was in shades of black or gray, so that no matter where Erik might choose to stand or sit, he could effectively disappear into the background or upholstery. Only the Oriental carpet in the office, the stained-glass windows, and the kitchen appliances had any color. And one corner of the kitchen was the sole area where direct light was allowed to enter. Erik didn't question Raskin's choice of color in bed linens, but his own were navy—the darkest shade available.

The cellar now housed the music room, which ran beneath better than half the ground floor. Beyond it was a tidy area where the washer and dryer, a large freezer, the hot-water tank and furnace were situated. The oil tank was buried in the ground at the side of the house, and the air-conditioning units were concealed behind shrubs planted exclusively for that purpose.

There were speakers and intercoms throughout the house, even in the bathrooms, so that Erik could summon Raskin, or listen in on him, should he care to, or have music instantly if he felt the need. As well as all this, there were several concealed doors and passages of which Raskin was unaware; one Erik had devised that led from the music room along an old tunnel he'd discovered during the renovations. It ended at the tumble-down boathouse—about which he intended to do nothing at all, since it was structurally sound despite its ramshackle appearance—and allowed him to go late at night to sit and gaze at the moon or the water, or to get into the boat moored in clement weather to the rickety dock. He did install an electric winching system that made it possible to shift the boat easily and quickly, so that if he felt a sudden need to be out on the Sound, it could be accomplished in minutes.

Sometimes, deep in the night, with the motor barely ticking over, he'd tour the waterfront, gazing at the houses along the shore, occasionally seeing figures pass before lighted windows. And once, he'd had the rare opportunity of watching a nude woman standing on the balcony outside her bedroom, backlit as she slowly drew a brush through her hair.

Another of his doors lay beneath the carpet in the office. Should he care to, he could flip back the end of the carpet, open the trap door, pull the carpet back into place above him, and vanish down the narrow ladderlike stairs that brought him to a sliding panel at the rear of the walk-in linen cupboard on the landing.

The third door was at the side of the closet in his bedroom. By pulling forward a piece of the molding, he could open the door to enter the secret room he'd created during the initial stages of the renovation. Six feet wide by ten feet long, with an air vent cut into the floor, this was where Erik frequently spent the night when he couldn't sleep. There was a deep armchair, a small table, and several items of extreme importance to him: his mother's photograph album, his father's violin and mother-of-pearl dress studs, his books on magic, his props, and a gun. He never touched the gun. It remained in its box, positioned precisely at the far right-hand corner of the table, beside a supply of bullets. Periodically, he'd raise the lid to look at its gray, oiled and loaded, finality. Then he'd close the box and return to practicing his sleight of hand. He worked with coins, and flowers, and silk scarves. Card tricks bored him. He preferred to make things appear and disappear, and could spend four or five hours at a time moving coins between his fingers, or stuffing his curled hand full of varicolored squares of silk that were gone when he flung his opened palm into the air.

Often, when restlessness overcame him, he'd strip off his clothes and in the dim candlelight work his body through a rigorous series of exercises that maintained both his flexibility and his strength and muscle tone. He'd subject his body to an hour or two of calisthenics, of bends and stretches and twists; of handstands, shoulder presses, and leg lifts that left him trembling and sufficiently exhausted to sleep.

At times he would simply sit in the chair with the photograph album in his lap, one hand flat over its leather cover, the other moving back and forth with a cigarette from his mouth to the ashtray at the front of the table. When he did dare to look at the pictures it was invariably an act of self-punishment. He'd be contained initially as he admired the lovely child his mother had been, as he examined his parents' laughing faces in their wedding portraits. Then he'd come to those first shots of the infant Erik and he'd begin to seize up inside, so that by the time he got to the candid and posed shots of the small boy in short pants cavorting on the front lawn or clinging to his doting mother, he'd be in a state of fulminating rage. None of this was directed toward the innocent trio who played for all eternity on the fraying pages, but rather toward the ogre he'd grown to be.

He couldn't think now how he'd managed to survive his university years and the feigned acceptance of some of his classmates. He'd believed then, and still did now, that the most honest of those young people had been the ones who'd let their horror show, who'd covered their mouths or clutched their chests at the sight of him. But he'd been younger then and still knotted in the last skeins of his unfeasible optimism, his ill-founded hope that someone, somewhere, one day, would be blessed with eyes that saw beyond the surface of things. Time had proved him wrong and had rotted the optimism, crushed the hope. The last brave thing he'd done had been placing the advertisement in the "Help Wanted" section of the New York *Times*. There'd been a deluge of responses, and he'd sifted through them, discarding the majority at once. But Raskin's letter had been unlike any of the others. It was one written by a man Erik recognized, a letter penned from desperation, and without pretense. "I need a job," Raskin had written. "I've got a master's degree in engineering from Yale. I'm a Vietnam vet. I don't care where I live, so relocating's no problem. But I prefer to work in quiet surroundings, with only one person to answer to. I can cook and type. I can drive anything that has four wheels and a motor. I'm single and intend to stay that way. I'll do anything reasonable for fair pay, and I'm free to start right away."

Erik had telephoned and asked him to come to the old Riverside house for an interview. Raskin seemed unfazed by the front door that clicked open to admit him, or by following instructions issued over the speaker to seat himself in the living room. He'd sat with a cigarette and calmly answered Erik's questions, unconcerned by the television camera in the corner of the ceiling or by the heavily draped interior of the house. Erik knew, watching and listening to the then twenty-eight-year-old Ras-

kin, that luck had provided him with someone ideally
suited to his many needs. When Erik had asked, "Have
you any questions?" Raskin had looked directly into the
camera and said, "Do I ever get to see you? Or do you
have a real problem with that?"

"You may see me," Erik had replied, and descended
the stairs to enter the room, halting just inside the doorway.

Raskin's expression had remained unchanged. "That's
what I figured," he'd said. "The war?"

"No."

"No problem. Do I get the job?"

He got the job, and for over two years now Raskin had
been his cushion against the world, his bearer of news to
and from the outside, and his personal raconteur. Upon
seeing Erik enter the office and go to his desk now, Raskin's only comment was "I was starting to think I'd have
to do this job without you."

Erik drew over the plans, seated himself on his stool,
referred to the specifications, then set to work; his back,
as ever, to Raskin, his face to the wall.

Somehow Risa managed to get through the summer and
returned to start her senior year at the high school, grateful for the daily distraction of other faces and voices, and
facts to be studied and remembered. The days passed
with relative ease; the evenings remained as difficult as
before.

While the autumn weather held warm in the evenings,
she'd walk the length of the back garden after dinner to
stand for a time where the land left off some eight or ten
feet above the water. She'd then sit on the dock with her
legs dangling and watch sailboats returning to shore. An
occasional motorboat would roughen up the water and
send choppy waves splashing against the pilings beneath
her. Sea gulls complained like hungry babies as they
swooped and soared, scouring the surface of the Sound
for food of any kind.

Often she'd look across the inlet to the old house on
Contentment Island, which appeared now to be lived in.
Sometime in the course of the past eighteen months,

someone had bought the house and fixed it up before installing high fencing that blocked all but the upper stories from view. As the evenings grew chill, she'd see smoke rising from one or two of the several chimneys. People not only lived there, they used the fireplaces and even kept a good-sized motor launch tied up outside the old boathouse. In a way, she was glad about the house. Despite the games she and Meggie had played as children, scaring themselves witless, she'd always thought it was a fine, dignified house, and she'd never understood why people hadn't seen its potential. Well, someone finally had, and although she couldn't help smiling when she thought of the way she and Meggie had gone creeping around over there looking for ghosts and terrified of encountering any, she was pleased to see the place returned to life.

For the most part, as she sat nightly on the dock, she wondered about Erik—not so urgently or despairingly as she had, but with an ongoing hurt at her very core that felt as if it would never diminish. Every time the telephone rang, she thought it might be him. Each day's mail was liable to bring some message. A knock at the front door could signal his arrival. But his silence remained absolute. She'd said or done something to wound or offend him, and he'd decided never to see her again. The feeling she had when she thought this bordered on agony. It came accompanied by a squeezing sensation in her chest that made it hard for her to breathe and equally as hard to sleep.

Her nights had grown long and noisy with the imagined dialogues she held with Erik. When she did sleep, it was only for an hour or two before something, some thought or idea, awakened her. Restless, she took to late-night rambles through the house, often sitting in the dark living room or in the moonlit breakfast area. She'd go from room to room, familiar with the various settling creaks and tiny shifts of the house, the noises of the furnace and refrigerator. She was comforted in a minimal way by her unlimited access to the house, to its sleeping cadence, its particular smells.

In early December, in the course of one of her nocturnal strolls, she came across her father's address book open on his desk in the den. Grabbing a pencil and a piece of notepaper from the drawer, she flipped through the pages, found Erik's name and number and made note of them. Then she carefully folded the paper and tucked it into the pocket of her robe where her fingers toyed with it ceaselessly as she continued on her way to her frequent night post in the kitchen.

She was there at the kitchen table, staring up through the denuded branches of the chestnut tree one night in early January, when she decided she simply had to talk about what was happening to her. And the one person she could talk to was Kitty. It was almost one-fifteen, but Kitty regularly stayed up late to watch the Carson show or some old movie with Clark Gable or Spencer Tracy. Risa pushed silently away from the table and went along the hallway at the rear of the house to where Kitty had her rooms.

As she came down the hallway she was relieved to see Kitty's door ajar and an orange slice of light falling through from inside. Risa went toward the light and was about to tap lightly on the door when caution took hold, prompting her to lean forward to look inside through the gap of some six or so inches. Inside, a scarf draped over the bedside lamp was responsible for the orange-tinted light that fell in an appealing crescent over half the bed. And there in that crescent lay Kitty with Risa's father. They were talking quietly. Cameron's head rested against one of Kitty's ample breasts, his hand idly stroking the other. It was, in an instant, manifestly clear to Risa that this was only a part of a long-ongoing conversation the two of them in the bedroom had been having for years.

She backed away and returned upstairs to her room, wondering why she hadn't figured out the situation ages ago. Her father's good-natured bordello comments, his indulgence of Kitty, which had prompted the remodeling of the kitchen, which was, in turn, directly responsible for the advent of Erik into Risa's life. She was neither upset nor angry. She merely wished they'd told her about this, let her in on the fact that neither one of them was so lonely or love-starved as Risa had imagined them to be. In fact, when she thought about it, it made a good deal of sense that her father would spend his nights with Kitty. After all, she was right there, and familiar; she was pretty, and sexy too, in a kind of no-nonsense way. And she was, as she said herself, very involved with this family. The thing was, she was a whole lot more involved than anyone had ever let on. But that was okay. She was really, honestly, glad the two of them had each other. What moved her to tears was the understanding that she was on the outside of just about everything. Cameron had Kitty to talk to; the two of them had been talking about her, Risa, for years and years, obviously; both of them had discussed her stupid behavior, the weird way she'd been carrying on for all these months. That part was unfair. She should have been informed that there was one voice speaking in the household, and not two as she'd thought.

Curling up on her bed, she held the worn-smooth paper with Erik's number in the palm of her hand. No matter what happened, she had to hear him tell her personally that he didn't want to know about her, that he didn't care.

The next afternoon she got off the school bus at the end of Tokeneke Road and went into the variety store near the corner of the Post Road to use the pay phone. Her mouth dry, lips parched, she dialed the number, then waited with her heart thumping as the ringing on the other end began. When a man's voice answered, she said, "Is that Mr. Raskin?"

"Yes, it is."

"This is Marisa Crane. Could I speak to Erik, please?"

"Please hold, Miss Crane," he said, and went off the line.

She waited, sweating, repeatedly moistening her lips. He *had* to talk to her. She didn't know what she'd do if Raskin came back to say Erik wouldn't accept her call. He was gone for ages, and her hand grew slick around the receiver as she glanced about, hoping to God nobody else would decide to want to use the telephone.

There was a click, and then he was there. "What is it?" came Erik's peremptory whisper.

"Erik," she said, hunching closer to the mouthpiece of the wall-mounted phone, "what did I do wrong? Why don't you want to come back? Do you hate me?"

A pause. And then there was the sound of laughter devoid of any humor, laughter bitter and disbelieving and breathless; it went on for several merciless seconds. Ashamed, Risa's eyes filled as she listened to the cruel sounds he made. When a lull came, she said quickly, "I'm sorry. I shouldn't have called. I'm sorry," and hung up.

Clutching her books, she tore out of the store and started running toward home. A stitch in her side, she slowed to a fast walk as she got past the entrance to the turnpike. Blind to everything but her self-inflicted humiliation, she fled toward home, down Old Farm Road, slipping on the icy road, oblivious to the bitter cold. All she wanted was to get into her room and turn on the radio really loud to some acid-rock station to drown out the hateful echo of her pathetic little voice asking, "What did I do wrong?" She wanted to die, and wished it were something that could be accomplished just by willing it to happen.

She knew she'd never be able to face Kitty or her father over dinner. They'd guess from looking at her that she'd done something truly idiotic. God! *Why* had she done it? What on earth had made her think she could do a thing like that? The way he'd laughed, the breathy hollowness of the sound rushed inside her head. Maybe she'd go ahead after all and take a whole bottle of aspirin. Or better still, she'd sneak into her father's bathroom and steal all his prescription bottles. He had things in there like Percodan and Nembutal. Pills like that could put you to sleep forever.

"My stomach's upset," she told Kitty upon reaching home. "I'm going to skip dinner, just do my homework and go straight to bed."

"You comin' down with something?" Kitty asked, touching the back of her hand to Risa's forehead, which was cold and clammy.

Without knowing in advance she was going to do it, Risa looked into the older woman's bright-blue eyes and said, "Kitty, how come neither one of you ever bothered to tell me? Did you think I'd mind, or that I'd make a fuss? Is that why?''

''What . . . ?''

''I know about you and Dad,'' Risa said unemotionally. ''I don't mind a bit, honestly. I only wish the two of you trusted me enough, thought I was intelligent enough, to be told.''

''Oh, hell!'' Kitty exclaimed and grabbed for a cigarette. As she held it to her lighter, her eyes on Risa, she asked, ''Is that why you're not coming down to dinner tonight?''

''That has nothing to do with anything. I don't feel like eating.''

''Are you telling the truth, Reese? Or are you tryin' to make the best of things?''

Standing there, holding her schoolbooks to her chest, Risa began to cry.

''It's the truth, honest to God. If you want to know, I'm glad the two of you aren't alone. I always worried about Dad being on his own.'' She bent her head over her books and started to go, then turned back and lifted her head. ''I've always loved you, Kitty. It's okay, really.'' She swung around then and made good her escape.

Dumping her books on the desk, still in her coat, she sat down in the slipper chair by the window. To hell with it! she thought. She'd go clean out her Dad's medicine chest right now and, with luck, she'd be dead before dinner. She was on the verge of getting up when the telephone in her room rang and she turned to stare at it. Her father had arranged for her to have her own line years ago, believing that all teenagers tied up telephones for hours on end. But in her case the only person who'd regularly called her unlisted number had been Meggie. And since the start of this school year, not even the jocks were bothering anymore. So who could be calling? Another ring. She put out her hand and, puzzled, picked up the receiver.

''Be on your dock at eleven,'' Erik instructed. ''I will come for you.''

There was a click, and then buzzing. He was gone.

6

ERIK, WHAT DID I DO WRONG? WHY DON'T YOU WANT to come back? Do you hate me?

Hate you? Hate *you*? It had never occurred to him that she'd construe his determination to remain away in those terms. It had never occurred to him that she might call, or that the sound of her name on Raskin's tongue could send him into such an immediate state of distress; it had never occurred to him that she might actually care, or take it personally, that he hadn't responded to their second invitation to dinner. And his shock was such that his only immediate reaction was the hurtful laughter that—he'd heard it in her sad, injured voice—had spewed so automatically, so laden with irony, from his mouth.

She'd spoken softly, asking her questions timidly, directly into his ear, causing shock waves to travel through his body, and he'd rewarded her with mocking laughter. For close to ten months he'd managed to survive without the sight or sound of her, although he hadn't for a moment ceased thinking of her. He had even, at last, been able to return to the piano and his music; he'd been able to sing in the secret seclusion of the music room. He'd been well on the road to learning to live again his peculiar brooding life of solitude. And then she'd come seeking him, wanting absolution or explanation. He'd laughed, and she'd flown away.

What did this girl *want* from him? he asked the curtained walls of his lightless bedroom, where he'd come to speak in private over the telephone, away from Raskin's hearing. Why was she pursuing him? What did she hope to achieve with her schoolgirl's persistence?

His hands smoothed his hair, ground together briefly, then flew, spread-fingered, to reassure himself that the mask was in place, that he was fully clothed, everything properly buttoned and fastened.

He'd made her weep, he was sure of it. There'd been such a telltale catch to her voice as she'd made her small forlorn apology. She'd gone off shedding tears because of his unfeeling spontaneous reaction to the absurdity of her innocent questions. Do I hate you, Marisa? Hate? I adore you, revere you. I would drop my life down at your feet and allow you to dance upon it, if the fancy took you. I want you as I've wanted nothing else, nor will I ever want again. You're in my mouth, my ears and eyes and throat. My hands crave your hair, the bends of your elbows, the acquaintanceship of your flesh and the bones it conceals. Just your name, the sound of your voice in my ear, and control is lost. I am rendered deaf and blind, dumb and senseless with the pleasure your very voice gives to me. You're the living embodiment of every lovely thing ever created. And you ask do I hate you. I could *never* hate you, dearest child. It's me. I'm the one toward whom I direct my considerable hatred. This face, this grim joke of fate, is what I hate. But you? Not ever, never you. If I die as a result of loving you, I will never be capable of bearing you the least malice.

It was all in aid of very little, this additional period of excoriating deliberation because he was, and had been, a victim of her youth and beauty and piercing sweetness from the moment his eyes had initially focused upon her. He'd separated himself for months on end from the one person, the knowledge of whose very existence renewed his hopes and revived his near-dead spirit. Life until first sight of her had been a tedious, sometimes self-indulgent, routine through which he was obliged, by the sheer questionable tenacity of his instincts, to travel. From the night they'd met he'd been fueled by emotions more powerful, more consuming even than the loathing he felt for the boy who'd fought against being a fellow traveler on the long black journey embarked upon by his mother and father those many years ago; emotions more potent than the contempt he had for that feckless child who'd fought to retain his life without the least notion of what that life would come to mean.

She might very well cast him aside, abandon him, once her girlish curiosity had been satisfied. But there'd never been a question of choice. She had the power to turn him any way she chose, to deprive him of all rational thought. She turned him into a creature made entirely of nameless and dimensionless need simply by her being alive in the world, and within his grasp. He could only surrender to something greater than his fear; could only close his eyes and submit himself to the boundless depths of his incapacitating need for her.

So he capitulated, as he'd known all along he would, and called Raskin on the intercom.

"Is the shoreline accessible?"

"There's no ice," Raskin answered. "Do you want to take the boat out tonight?"

"Have it ready, please."

"Okay, Erik."

She was able, after all, to dine with her father that evening. As they ate, she was overtaken by a keen sense of finality. She might eat in this room, at this table, with her father, another ten thousand times in the days and years to come, but the Marisa who came to sit with him would be someone else. Everyone in the household would, from now on, have some secret to withhold. She was prepared to do anything, anything at all, should Erik ask it of her. She hadn't understood that a few hours earlier when she'd climbed off the school bus to go to the telephone at the variety store, but she could see now that she'd already pledged herself to whatever was to happen when she'd picked up the receiver and asked for Erik. As she smiled across the table at her father, and answered his questions about her day, and chatted easily about inconsequentials, she wondered if there was any way he could possibly divine that he was seeing the Marisa he'd always known for the last time. The Marisa who returned to eat with him at breakfast and again at dinner tomorrow, and all the tomorrows thereafter, would be altered irrevocably. Just how, precisely, she didn't know. But she would be changed. For the first time in her nearly seventeen years of life she'd seen what she wanted and she'd undertaken the initiative to have it. She felt aged at having been bold enough to make her wishes known, and too lacking in knowledge of the world and its esoteric inner workings to be able to gauge the full extent of the possible consequences. All she knew was that she would be at the water's edge at eleven, and that nothing whatever could prevent it. Were she suddenly taken seriously ill, were her father and Kitty to learn of her plans and lock her up somewhere, she'd still find some way to be waiting for Erik when he came for her.

Picturing his hands, those masterful, free-sweeping birds of fancy that acted out what the man could not or dared not say, she felt herself loosening, softening, her flesh accumulating new texture and density. Anything! He could do anything, and she would offer no protest. Her eyelids started to lower in anticipation of the many possible outcomes this meeting might have.

"You look sleepy, Keed," her father said. "You're not getting enough rest."

"I'm not tired," she told him. "I don't need a lot of sleep. I was just thinking, that's all."

"Thinking about sleep, from the looks of it." He laughed, then cleared his throat. Solemn all at once, he said, "Kitty told me about the conversation the two of you had."

"And?" She looked at him, thinking how familiar he was and yet how many areas of his life there were about which she knew almost nothing. She knew that face, clean-shaven and appealing, with its enviably arched eyebrows and its gray-green eyes, its squared chin and slanted jawline; she knew the kindness and concern that glowed out at her in all its parental benevolence.

"And? You tell me," he said, a bit fearfully.

"I told Kitty, and now I'll tell you: I wish you'd had

enough respect for my native intelligence to let me know about it. I mean, Dad. What did you think I'd do, throw a fit or something, insist you drive her out into the snow?'' She laughed indulgently. "I'm not a little kid. I'm almost seventeen, for heaven's sake. I know what's what. And anyway," she wound down, "I like Kitty. Are you going to marry her or anything?''

He had to chuckle at the way she put the question. "I don't think so. Neither one of us is interested in that. We're friends, Risa. That's really what it comes down to. I have no real say in her life, and she has none in mine. From time to time, when there's a need, Kitty and I spend a few hours together and talk—for the most part. If it bothers you in any way, it can be over, just like that." He snapped his fingers.

"Why should you give up something you enjoy for me?" she asked earnestly. "I don't know if I'd be willing to do that for you, Dad.''

"Wow!" He rocked back in his chair, his eyes appraising. "That's getting pretty deep.''

"I'm trying to be truthful, and that's as truthful as I know how to be. I think that's the way things are, the way people are, when it comes right down to making choices. Nobody really decides for anybody else. I mean, you're a grown man. You're fifty-one years old, Dad. Are you going to start letting me make your decisions for you? Are you going to invite me to sit behind your desk at the office and start running your business? I don't think so. Oh, sure, you'd try to do something about the situation if I made a fuss. But that would just make you ticked off at me, and make me feel guilty. I don't want either of those things to happen.''

"Risa," he said, "when did you get so smart?''

"I don't know about smart. I mean, I read about what's happening in the world, about the way women are starting to demand equal rights, and I agree with that. The thing is, I know how I'd feel if it was me we were talking about, and not you.''

"Still," he said, thinking it through, "this does change things.''

"Not so far as I'm concerned. If you want to come

down to talk to Kitty at midnight, it doesn't have a thing to do with me. Not one single thing. I mean, you've gone to all this trouble for a pretty long time to keep me from knowing. Just because I know now doesn't mean the two of you are going to start carrying on in public, does it?''

"And would it bother you if Kitty and I *were* seen together in public?''

"Would it bother *you*?'' she asked cannily.

"Oh, brother!'' he said slowly. "You've got me every way to Sunday on this one. I don't know the answer to that, Marisa. For better than thirteen years Kitty's been a damned good friend. We've had an understanding that what goes on inside this house doesn't necessarily have anything to do with what goes on outside. She and I have both seen other people. Somehow we always manage to wind up back together. If anyone had told me years ago that I'd come to admire and care very much for an opinionated, stubborn yet flighty, hard-soft Southern woman who dotes on daytime television programs and who likes to do crossword puzzles in bed, I'd have laughed myself silly. But here we are, and I'm fonder of her than I can say. She makes me laugh, Risa. And she's got more common sense than most people I could name. She listens well, and she *hears*. And, most important of all, she cares about *you*. It's one of the major attractions she has for me. To be truthful, there are plenty of willing women around. But there's only one I know who cares for you almost as much as I do. It's reassuring to know that, God forbid, should anything ever happen to me, Kitty would be here to look after you.''

"I hardly need looking after, you know. I mean, I'm not eight years old.''

"In the eyes of the law, you're still a child for a while yet. It'd be irresponsible of me, Risa, if I didn't consider your well-being in all eventualities. I told you: We wanted you, Rebecca and I. I made a promise a long time ago that I'd be your father to the best of my abilities. That includes considering the future.''

"Okay. But nothing's going to happen to you. And I'm not a little kid. So don't worry about it. Okay?''

"Have I ever told you how much I like you, Marisa?''

"Only six or seven million times." She smiled.

"Well, don't ever forget that I do. I like the hell out of you."

"Me, too, you, Dad. Why don't you pretend I never found out?"

"That's easier said than done. But I appreciate your understanding. I truly do."

"Oh, Dad," she said, starting to choke up. "Don't *thank* me. You're my *father*. I love you. I'm going up to do my homework. Okay?"

"Sure. Don't stay up too late, though, Risa. You really do look kind of worn out."

"I feel fine." She stopped behind his chair to kiss the top of his head, then stood for a few seconds with her hand on his shoulder, feeling grieved, as if she were in some way saying good-bye.

She'd taken a very hot bath, washed and dried her hair, and then dressed herself in everyday clothes when she realized that if she encountered her father or Kitty on her passage either into or out of the house, she'd have to explain being fully dressed at that hour of the night. So she removed her day clothes and pulled on a freshly laundered soft flannel nightgown, a long one with buttons down the front and ruffles at the cuffs, in white with a pattern of sprinkled violets. Over this she put her robe. Before leaving the house, she pulled on her coat, wound a scarf around her neck, stepped barefoot into her boots, then slipped out the kitchen door. The night was cold but very clear and she stood on the dock with her hands in her coat pockets, her face uplifted to a sky alive with stars, and waited.

It was only minutes before a boat slid alongside, and there was Erik, one gloved hand holding fast to the dock to steady the boat, the other assisting her over the side. Without a word he returned to the wheel, the noise of the motor gained in volume, and the boat swept in a slow half-circle away from the house. The wind clawed at her face, making her eyes water, but she stood where he'd left her, waiting to see where they'd go. Not far. Just across the inlet to the old boathouse where he cut the motor, tied the boat secure, then nimbly hoisted himself up and turned, his hands reaching for her.

As if she weighed nothing at all, he drew her up, then turned away, expecting her to follow. He opened a trap door at the far end of the boathouse and she went with him, scarcely able to see in the disc of light cast by a flashlight he held out in front of him. Frightened and exhilarated, with the sense that she was trailing some mythical figure and not anyone real, she hurried after him along a damp narrow tunnel that went for quite some distance. Then he opened another door, stepped inside, and waited for her to enter.

Accustomed now to the darkness, she moved into the huge candlelit room, slowly turning to take stock of her surroundings while Erik closed and bolted the door through which they'd come. This had to be the cellar of the old haunted house, she thought, and yet it didn't seem possible. There, positioned close to the far wall, was a gleaming black grand piano. And over there, along the near wall, were shelves filled with all sorts of equipment: tape decks, tuners, amplifiers, and other electronic items she couldn't identify. Speakers were mounted on the walls in all four corners of the room. There were two lonely yet elegant antique chairs, a single small table, and the candles—dozens of them, some massed in candelabra atop the piano, some on the shelves housing the equipment, others placed at random on the floor near the walls. The light from the many flames created an underwater, rippling effect with their slow-waltz motion. The silence was so complete she could hear Erik's quick breathing, and her own, as he removed his hat and cape, then came to her side indicating that she should give him her coat and remove her boots. Obediently, she took off the coat and scarf, then set her bare feet down into the surprising warmth of luxurious carpeting.

"Where are we? Is this your house?" she asked.

"This is my music room," his deep tuneful whisper informed her as he draped her coat and his cape across one of the chairs.

"It's wonderful," she said inadequately, aware of the

pulse beating strongly in her throat as he straightened from his brief domestic chore to stand gazing at her.

He was dressed in black again, perhaps the same suit or its twin. His shirt front was so white it seemed to glow in the uneven illumination of the room. With exquisite slowness he began to peel off his gloves. His every move seemed choreographed as part of some never-ending ballet; even the slightest gesture had an impressive grandeur. She felt imperiled, yet reckless, and drew deep breaths as if about to take a plunge into cold dark water.

He dropped the gloves on top of his cape, then moved toward her to stop perhaps a foot away, his head tilting slightly to one side as he looked at her, his eyes large and inner-lit behind the heavily framed glasses.

"Sing for me," he whispered, and held out his hand to lead her over to the piano.

Her hand again caught in his tender yet tentative grip, she allowed herself to be directed, and sat at his side on the bench where he turned once more to say to her, "Anything at all. The music will be there."

She took him at his word, certain in this mystical environment that he could do anything, no matter how improbable. Without pausing to consider if he'd derive some personal thinly coded message from her choice, she began "Mean to Me." Why must you be? and he was already there underscoring her voice, her life, with chords of an unearthly force and lyricism that compelled her to open her throat more, to place even more of her lungs' accumulated power into the words, their sound and meaning. In perfect synchroneity they became the embodiment of the music.

At the end, with Erik's graceful fingers still poised over the keys, she allowed her head to come to rest on his shoulder, content. And as if they'd been together this way a hundred times before—she with her head on his shoulder, he with his hands on the piano—his fingers bore down to make more music, and he opened his mouth to sing for her, a song of his own composing, with a voice so pure and refined, so intimate and meaningful, that she had to close her eyes in order to appreciate it fully: a ballad built on the dreams of a lifetime, filled with vivid images that told her everything about his naked, barren existence. He sang for her his lullaby, his slumber song, his night music, and she absorbed his warmth and his fragrance as his arm moved against her side making melodies, and his voice delved into the deepest recesses of her mind and thoughts, possessing her.

I love you, Erik, she thought, wanting never to have to leave here. *I'll never in my life love anyone else the way I love you.*

The song at an end, he sat feeling the dear weight of her head on his shoulder, wishing he were an ordinary man so that he might take her in his arms and claim her as his own. Here she was, beautiful Marisa, with her hair falling over his arm, her long pale hands folded serenely in her lap; so very close, yet separated from him forever by his accursed and pernicious disfigurement.

"Come," he said at last. "I must take you home."

In one sudden motion he was gone from her, gathering their outer clothes from the chair before enfolding her in her coat. His cape slicing the air like that of a matador, it settled around his shoulders as he pulled on his gloves, then pushed back the bolt of the door to the tunnel and drew her into it.

Before leaving her on the dock, he kept hold of her hand for a moment, whispering, "Tomorrow," and then the boat turned and cut away back across the inlet. "Tomorrow," whispered in her ears as, in a trance, she made her way across the snow-glazed lawn to the house.

7

NIGHTLY HE CAME FOR HER, EITHER IN THE BOAT OR, when the shoreline was ice-encrusted and inaccessible, in the otherworldly sleek black car. Nightly they sat together at the piano and made music. And nightly, after an hour or two, he returned her to her home before dissolving into the darkness and leaving her to wonder if all this was nothing more than some fabulous extended dream.

Week after week, through the end of January, past February, and into early March, they managed to steal time together in the subterranean music room. For Marisa, the expense of so much energy and the withholding of so much more, combined with the lack of sleep and her general disinterest in food, finally took its toll. She simply slid out of her seat in English class one afternoon, and when she regained consciousness she was tucked in bed in a private room in Greenwich Hospital, being fed intravenously.

She lost track of time. People came and went—nurses, doctors, her father and Kitty. She slept for the most part, able, it seemed, to stay awake only for minutes at a time. She was fairly sure it was real and not a dream when her father sat on the side of her bed holding her hand and telling her, "We have to take better care of you from now on, Marisa. I had no idea you were so run down.

Anemia combined with malnutrition's no laughing matter, Keed. You're going to start getting a lot more rest, and paying more attention to your poor tired body."

She seemed to remember promising him she'd be good from now on, and she would take the pills and anything else they wanted her to do. But she slept for such long periods of time, and so deeply, that everything had an unreal quality.

The first night Erik drove to the top of the driveway on Butlers Island to discover Marisa wasn't there waiting, he experienced such a spasm of dread he could scarcely think. When there was no word from her the next day or the one after that, he got Raskin on the intercom and said, "I need you to go to the Crane house and find out in whatever way you can what's become of Marisa."

Raskin said, "Sure, no problem," and reported back later that evening that the girl was ill and in the hospital.

Profoundly frightened and guilt-ridden, positive he was responsible for whatever illness Marisa might have, he climbed that night into the Lamborghini and went streaking off down I-95 to Greenwich. Making his way through back doors and fire exits, he located her room and went to stand at the side of the bed gazing down at his beautiful child in the slim strips of light entering through the gaps between the curtains. His fear for her well-being and his dreadful guilt reduced him to tears. He stood and wept silently over her, praying for her recovery, and cursing himself. She was a child and needed her rest, yet he'd deprived her of it for months for his own selfish purposes. And if she should die he'd be entirely to blame.

"Don't die!" His lips shaded the soundless words. "Please, don't die."

She was so pale, so utterly without color, so still she scarcely seemed to be breathing. And then, stunningly, her eyes opened. She looked at him and smiled, and with agonizing slowness lifted her arms to him, whispering, "Erik!"

How could he help himself? He bent into the circle of her arms, to breathe his abject apologies into her ear, to press his lips lightly against the frail flutter of the pulse in her temple. "I love you, love you," he whispered, his tears dropping into her hair. "More than life, I love you." But her arms had gone limp; she'd returned to her deep-dreaming sleep. With the greatest of care, he disentangled himself, stood a moment more gazing down at her, then turned and left that place of acute angles and antiseptic odors and echoing corridors.

He was killing her, he told himself as he took the car speeding over the highway toward home. His love had never been intended to harm her. They could not go on as they had been. He was draining the life out of her body with his unquenchable thirst to have her near him. He had no right to harm her; he had no wish to do so. In order to save her, he had to allow her to return to the normalcy of her life before him. The only way he could do that was to remove himself altogether from the arena of temptation.

"Pack!" he told Raskin over the intercom. "We are leaving at once!"

"To go where?" Raskin asked equably.

Where? Erik asked himself, trying to think. "London," he said. "Make arrangements, book passage on one of the Cunard ships. We'll leave for New York tonight. We must be on a ship tomorrow."

"I'll take care of it," Raskin assured him. And true to his word, by late morning of the following day he and Erik were installed in adjoining staterooms on a Norwegian ship—no Cunard sailings being available—bound for Southampton.

Throughout the voyage, Erik remained in his stateroom, pacing its abbreviated length and alternately grating his hands together or tugging at his face, in a state of sorrow and renewed self-hatred.

On the day before they landed, when he came to bring Erik's dinner tray—Erik refused to permit a deck steward to enter the stateroom—Raskin ventured to say, "I know I'm out of line, Erik, but it's not your fault the girl is sick."

"How would you know that?" Erik rounded on him, his whisper razor-edged.

"I know that," Raskin said, cool as ever, "because,

number one, that girl wanted to be with you. She *chose* to be, whether you believe that or not. And, number two, people get sick sometimes, Erik. It's not necessarily anyone's fault. It just happens. And lastly, number three, I think you're making a mistake running away. I know my opinions probably don't interest you one bit, but that girl cares about you. And your running off this way can only hurt both of you.''

''Leave me alone!'' Erik said irritably. ''And take that with you!'' He pointed at the tray. ''Just leave me alone!''

''No offense intended,'' Raskin said, retrieving the tray.

''None taken,'' Erik relented. ''Just, please, leave me alone.''

''I'm right next door if you need anything.''

''I need nothing,'' Erik declared flatly. ''Nothing!''

The first thing Marisa did upon returning home from the hospital was to call Erik's number. A woman answered, saying, ''Answering service,'' and for a moment Risa couldn't think what to say. She'd been so geared for the sound of Raskin's voice that she was totally thrown.

''Is Mr. D'Anton available?'' she asked at last in her most grown-up voice.

''Mr. D'Anton is in Europe,'' the operator told her.

''For how long?''

''Indefinitely. But we are taking messages.''

''Oh.''

''Is there a message?'' the woman asked rather impatiently.

''Yes,'' Risa told her, angry that Erik could have gone away without letting her know. ''Tell him Marisa Crane called and that I said he should come back *at once*!''

She put down the phone and stood looking at her outheld hands, which were trembling quite violently. How could he *do* that? How could he leave without so much as a word? Was it some game he'd been playing with her throughout the winter? God! She was furious. Well, to hell with him! she told herself, going to her desk to look over the pages and pages of assignments she'd have to complete in order to catch up on the three weeks of school she'd missed. *Go to hell, Erik! You can stay away forever, for all I care!*

Pulling the chair out from the desk with an angry yank, she sat down and started in to work.

For two weeks, every time her thoughts started to shift toward Erik, she'd swear under her breath and refuse to allow it. She would *not* think about him. She'd do her work, get through the rest of the year until graduation. She couldn't think beyond that point, but concentrated instead on the immediate present.

Her dreams, however, were something else altogether. Each night while she slept the hours were crowded with endless and overlapping scenes with Erik. And once—a dream she had great difficulty shaking in her waking hours—she opened her eyes to see him at the foot of her bed, a tall silent shape somewhat darker than the surrounding darkness. He came around the side of the bed and lifted away the blankets, revealing her nakedness, and stood for a very long time staring at her. Then he laid himself over top of her, his weight no burden at all. Reverentially, she held him, deeply elated by his presence in her arms. Scarcely moving, they joined together, his body merging with hers, and her flesh grew molten and swollen, before she was overtaken by a lengthy series of downflowing inner waves accompanied by her whispered outpouring of affection for him. He gave her unimaginable pleasure, then began to lose substance in her arms. She tried, but could do nothing to prevent his leaving her. In the end she was alone, naked and very cold on her bed, weeping with confusion and frustration.

The other dream that returned to her waking self was the one in which she was sitting at her desk, working on a trigonometry assignment when she heard the door open, and turned to see Erik entering. He came to stand halfway between her desk and the door and, his eyes riveted to hers, his hand lifted to remove the mask. She knew what was coming and steeled herself, prepared to show no reaction to what she was about to see. The mask was taken away to show a livid configuration of scars down the center of his face in the area where his nose should have been but where there were only two skeletal holes concealed by a vestigial trace of elevated flesh.

"It's not so bad, Erik," her dreamself told him. "I don't mind, honestly."

The Erik of her dreams elected not to believe her and with a cry of mingled pain and fury he spun about and vanished.

"*Don't go!*" she called after him. But it was too late, and she was left to wish she'd thought to say words other than the ones she'd chosen.

Maybe, she thought, during the few minutes when she looked up from her schoolwork to permit herself to think about him, nothing she could ever say or do would either be completely satisfactory to Erik or guarantee he'd stop running away from her. What did she actually know about him? Almost nothing. But that wasn't true. She knew everything she needed to know, everything he required her to know. Hadn't they used music to effect their communication? Hadn't he told her through his many compositions all he wished her to know? And hadn't she responded in kind with renditions of songs that spoke for her? What more did he want? She'd offered everything she had, but it hadn't been enough. She couldn't do more.

The net effect of all this was to make her feel aged, and a little jaded, and determined to preserve herself at all costs. That, of course, was her waking philosophy. The Marisa who dreamed had another agenda entirely. That Marisa sensed she was temporarily powerless to do anything and so must bide her time. Eventually she'd be able to do the one thing that would put a stop forever to his doubts, to his need periodically to flee from her: She would, upon his return, give to him one ultimate gift. She would give him her body. It was, she believed, a gift of such scope and immensity that he couldn't afterward possibly harbor any doubts about her love. Luckily, her two selves were unaware of their separate pacts and so she was able to go about her daily business; she was able to talk with her father and with Kitty, to eat with them and even to be present when her father's business associates and their wives came to dinner. She played hostess to her father's friends and marveled over her newfound maturity. Yet, every so often, something nagged at the edge of her attention; something having to do with her stay in the hospital, and the strong impression she had that Erik had come to her in the night and told her he loved her. But that was impossible. It couldn't have happened. It had to have been something she'd imagined in her delirium. Yet it had seemed so real. She could almost feel again his substance, could almost smell him and feel the dampness of the tears that had fallen into her hair; she could swear she'd heard him whisper "I love you." But it must have been some dream manufactured by her ludicrous and childish longings.

Erik did nothing in London. He remained secluded in the suite at Claridges, picking at the room-service food Raskin regularly arranged to have delivered and staring sightlessly at the television set he kept on almost constantly. He sat in one of the armchairs, or paced the length of the sitting room, or threw himself face-down on the bed, where he lay for hours at a time, not asleep, but reviewing his near-disastrous acts and berating himself for the inimical behavior inspired by his affliction. His accursed face, his long years of living behind a mask that only partially shielded him from the probing eyes of strangers, had taken him far beyond the bounds of reasonable thought and decorum. The loathing he felt at being trapped behind an image in no way representative of the man he truly was threatened to devour him. And as he lay prone on the hotel bed, his fingers clawed at the bedding and the mattress beneath, as if hoping to dig their way to freedom so that his hands—these two independent and resourceful entities—might find some better life, free of the six-foot-three-inch appendage they were presently obliged to carry about with them.

"There are messages," Raskin said one evening, sitting himself down in one of the chairs. "Are you interested? I checked in with the answering service."

"I am not interested," Erik said, his voice muffled by the pillows banked around his head.

"There's one I think you might want to know about."

"What?" Erik asked, his body almost vibrating in its attempt to stifle his raging self-loathing.

"Marisa Crane called almost two weeks ago. She said to tell you you should come home at once." Raskin sat with the piece of hotel stationery upon which he'd noted the message, waiting.

First, Erik's body seemed to go very still. Then his arms, which had been at his sides, began to extend outward from his body to the perimeters of the bed. They traveled upward until they were stretched parallel to his torso, his fingers hooked over the edge of the mattress as if, at any moment, the entire bed might levitate and he wished to save himself from falling.

"Everything else is routine," Raskin went on after a time. "Business mainly. Nothing I can't handle with a couple of calls."

Erik remained unmoving, his hands still clinging to the top of the bed, his body a long arrow.

"Personally," Raskin said conversationally, as if having a pleasant chat with someone in full control, "I've had a nifty time, what with seeing the shows and several of the more interesting female employees of this establishment. You, on the other hand, are having what I would say has to be one of the worst times known in the history of mankind. What the fuck are you doing, Erik?" A note of exasperation sounded clearly in his voice. "D'you need an engraved invitation? Or do you want me to haul my ass out of here and stop volunteering my impressions?"

When Erik failed to answer, Raskin said, "I know my own feelings on the subject of women and attachments. But that's me, and I'm not you. You've got a chance to have something you seem to want. Why not have it?"

With a roar, Erik leaped from the bed, tearing off the mask. Pushing his face against Raskin's, his whisper a maniacal shriek, he demanded, *"Who could want to see this? Who?"*

Without losing a beat, Raskin calmly said, "I've seen worse. I've seen guys with their eyes hanging out of their sockets and their faces half shot away. I've seen guys with their arms and legs blown off, with their guts piled in their laps. I've seen them without ears or noses, or mouths, Erik. I've seen little kids incinerated, and grandmothers eviscerated. I've seen paraplegics and quadriplegics. I've seen guys who scream nonstop, and other guys who're quiet as can be right up to the moment they go out with a gun and start shooting pedestrians. You can't show me one fucking thing I haven't seen a thousand times before and don't see most every night of my life in my sleep. You're worse-looking than some, and not as bad as others. This whole thing is bullshit. Either go crazy once and for all, or go home and take this girl off the hook. But don't leave both of you suspended in mid-air. It's not decent. I may be a lot of things, and crazy's definitely one of them, but I'm not stupid, Erik. I have all kinds of respect for you, for your work, for your music, too. This whole scene's not worthy of you. So your face got wrecked. Too bad. You want to let it wreck your head, too, that's your choice. Personally, I think it's a waste." He got up and said, "Let me know what you want to do. I'll be in my room."

"*How dare you!*" Erik thundered at Raskin's retreating back. "How dare you presume to equate me with some filthy unethical war?"

"Because," Raskin said without inflection, turning back, "you *are* a war, Erik; an entire one-man war of epic proportions. You've got more dead and wounded inside you than any six battalions. Inside, outside, it's all the same. War's war. One way or the other, everybody gets fucked up. Or dead." With that, Raskin continued on his way to his bedroom, leaving Erik stranded with his rage and bewilderment.

Unable to leave it at that, Erik stormed after his employee, heaving open the bedroom door to demand, "Why are you saying these things to me?" Quivering, he hung in the doorway with his clenched fists held in front of his chest.

"Because," Raskin said, "believe it or not, I like you, Erik. Now what're you gonna do, try to beat up on me?"

Erik was defeated. Gradually, his fists unclenched; then his arm fell to his sides; his outraged energy drained away and he sagged against the doorframe.

"I'm your friend, whether you like it or not," Raskin told him. "And as long as you've got work for me to do, I'll stick around. I know a few things," he said without cockiness. "Not a hell of a lot, but a few things. And I know you're crazy for this girl. She wants you back, Erik. Don't be an asshole. Let's go home. I hate the fucking weather here. And half the time I can't understand what these English girls are saying. The accent throws me." He offered Erik a conciliatory smile.

Erik suffered through this proclamation of friendship. He was so accustomed to rejection he wasn't sure how to handle a straightforward declaration of caring. *No one liked him.* People never had. Certainly not the aunt who'd undertaken his guardianship after the death of his parents. She'd been unable to look at him once the surgeons had stated they could do nothing more to improve his appearance. She'd shipped him off to boarding school where he'd suffered a thousand indignities at the hands of "well-bred" little boys who found him a suitable object for their hostility and humor. There'd been no one for more than twenty-five years who'd wished to be seen in public with him, and most definitely no one, except for Raskin, who'd been at ease in private with him. Except for Marisa. Marisa whom he'd almost killed with only a small measure of the enormous love he had for her. Marisa who'd left an imperative message, insisting he come back to her at once.

And here was Raskin saying he cared, giving advice, being a friend and telling him he had every right to care and be cared for by others. Could this be real? Would it actually be all right for him to return home and dare to open his heart to this girl?

"Tell me about your night with the waitress while we pack," Erik said finally.

"Sure," Raskin said. "Let me just grab a cigarette."

8

BY THE END OF HER SECOND WEEK AT HOME, MARISA was irate. She was so angry with Erik that she thought if she ever did see him again she might just kill him. She wanted to hurt him, to go at him with her fists and beat him bloody. *Why* was he doing this to her? She'd done nothing to him, not a single thing. And was she out of her mind or hadn't they sat side by side nightly for months, touching but not touching as their voices blended and they told each other of their autobiographies through music? She got sick and he ran away. It made no sense. Unless, she thought slowly, he'd decided for some reason that it was his fault she got sick. Could that be it? Could he really have pushed and pulled at the facts, distorting them to make them suit his reasoning? With a terrible need to know, she went downstairs one evening to talk with Kitty.

She related to Kitty the hypothetical scenario of a story she was supposedly writing for English class.

"Oh sure," Kitty said knowingly, puffing away at a cigarette. "Some men'd do exactly that. Most men can't deal with it if a woman gets sick. They come unglued. They're rotten with physical things, men. Most of them expect a woman to be a hundred percent all the time. The least little thing goes wrong and they either assume it's their fault, or they head for the hills so they won't have to deal with it. Not a lot of really grown-up men in the world, Reese. Mostly, they only play at it. What kinda story you writin', anyhow? Doesn't sound like the sort of theme I used to get handed in high school.''

"It's our choice of topic," Risa lied easily. "I thought this might be kind of interesting."

"Well, it's different, that's for sure. You finally gettin' interested in the opposite sex?" Kitty teased.

"Maybe. And maybe not. It's only a story, Kitty. No big deal."

"I wonder," Kitty speculated. "You're different lately. Nothin' I can put my finger on. Just different."

"I'm older, that's all."

"Hmmn. So you say."

"Kitty," Risa changed the subject, "how'd you ever come to be a housekeeper? Surely that wasn't what you set out to be."

Kitty gave an amused laugh and ran her hand through her now grown-in hair that was back to its normal light-brown color. "Hell, no!" she replied. "Way back, I was gonna be a movie star. That didn't last too long, thank the Lord. Then, for a time, I was mighty taken with the notion of nursin'. You know, tendin' some grateful young man who'd reward me with marriage and a life of luxury. But when I thought on, considerin' blood and bedpans and bedsores, I decided I didn't have the stomach for it. At which point, I thought it might be okay to be some-body's secretary, 'cept that I couldn't learn to type to save my life, and I figured an office job'd be too borin' for words. Then, I went and got married when I was nineteen and figured I wouldn't have to give it another thought."

"I never knew you'd been married!" Risa exclaimed.

"You never asked. Sure, I been married. I figured everything was settled and I'd be right where I was for the rest of my days. 'Cept that after a year or so, we couldn't hardly stand the sight of each other. We went ahead and stuck it out for another year. Savin' face, you know. But it wasn't ever gonna work, so we moved apart easy as pie and I got a job waitressin' for a time. This 'n' that, gettin' through, livin' a not bad life, when there was this ad one day in the paper—I always liked to read the ads to see what was bein' offered—put in by this man with an invalid wife, needin' somebody to come cook and clean and help out. It raised my curiosity. I don't know why, but I went ahead and answered that ad, got the job, and decided it suited me down to the ground. I could run the whole house with none of the grief of ownership, and still had me plenty of free time for socializin'. So I stayed with them, the Wendells, for near on four years, until she died, poor thing. And then I was sittin' one night, lookin' through Mr. Wendell's alumni magazine—used to tickle me, those things—and there was your father's ad. Widower with baby girl, needs carin' woman to tend to house and child. Kinda got to my heart, and I thought, what the hell! So here we are.''

"That's what it said? 'Widower with baby girl, needs caring woman to tend to house and child'?''

"Word for word,'' Kitty confirmed. "Touched me, that did. I had this picture of some poor young man, left helpless with this needy infant. It wasn't quite like that. Your daddy was older'n I thought he'd be, for one thing, but it wasn't too far off, neither. I liked the man right away. And I took one look at you and thought, I'll have my hands full, but it'll be okay. And it was. You were way easier than most kids, no trouble at all, 'cept when you got hold of the notion there was somethin' you wanted and you wouldn't turn that notion loose no way. But I've always admired folks with gumption, and you were a tyke with plenty of that, for sure. Your daddy and I kind of drifted together natural-like after about a year or so. It bother you, my sayin' that?''

"No. It doesn't bother me a bit. I'm glad you answered that ad, Kitty. And thanks for helping with my theme.''

"Anytime,'' she said. "I like havin' my opinion solicited. Makes me feel right important.''

"I bet Freed asks your opinion all the time.''

"Oh, sure. Half the world's lined up wantin' to know what I think about this and that.'' Kitty laughed and put out her cigarette. "You want anything? Some tea, a Coke?''

"Nothing, thanks. I want to get back and finish writing this thing.''

"Come on down anytime,'' Kitty invited.

"You're great," Risa told her, and gave her a kiss. "I don't know what I'd do without you."

"It's what everybody says," Kitty joked to hide her delight.

Risa returned to her desk having almost managed to convince herself there actually was an English composition waiting to be written. It took her a few moments to remember that she'd gone down to Kitty seeking confirmation of her sudden insight. And she'd received it. She had no doubt now that Erik had fled either from guilt or from fear, but in no way from a lack of affection for her or from some inclination to play bizarre games. He'd run away because he cared too much. Believing this, she was comforted. All she had to do was wait for his return. She knew exactly what the next step would have to be.

She hadn't long to wait.

The next day, she'd been home from school less than an hour when her private telephone began to ring. Instantly excited, she raced over to hear Erik's voice whisper, "Tonight at eleven. I will come for you with the car."

She was ecstatic. She'd been right. He did care; he did want to see her; he wasn't able to stay away. She'd never been happier, more filled with elation at the prospect of seeing anyone.

It was difficult for her to contain herself during dinner. Her father was in a mood to talk. She tried to accommodate him, but was so preoccupied with thoughts of her forthcoming reunion with Erik she could barely pay attention to the conversation. She absolutely couldn't eat, and merely pushed the food around her plate until she'd put in enough time at the table and excused herself on the pretext of having to finish her homework.

Upstairs, she took a long time bathing, washing and drying her hair before selecting a long pink silk nightgown with hand embroidery on the front panels and a high neckline. Over this she put on her new white dressing gown, then stood before the full-length mirror to study the results. She thought she looked too young but acceptable, and wished again that she had a more voluptuous body. Her feet were too big, too white and bony. Perhaps Erik wouldn't notice, she thought, as she placed dots of perfume behind each ear and at the base of her throat.

At last it was time. Stealthily, she crept through the house in her coat and boots, let herself out, and walked up the driveway to discover the car was already there. Like a resting panther it sat quietly rumbling, its lights off. As she approached, the door opened and she climbed into the passenger seat. At once the headlights went on, Erik put the car into gear and they raced toward his house. Neither of them spoke. She sat back and breathed in his enticing scent, holding her hands together in her lap.

Upon arriving at his house, he flew from the car to open her door, offering his hand. She placed her hand in his and was drawn into the interior of the house, along unlit corridors, down to the music room. Once inside, with the door bolted, he took her coat, mutely urged her to remove her boots, then came to stand nearby, his hands attempting to convey with their silent language what he couldn't bring himself to say. They stirred in the air between them, approaching then retreating, until she reached to take hold of them, stilling their distressed communication.

Holding fast to his hands, confronting his apprehensive eyes, she asked, "Why did you go?"

He couldn't reply; he could only turn his face away as his shoulders rose helplessly.

"I didn't get sick because of anything you did, Erik. But you thought it was your fault, didn't you?"

"I asked too much of you," he said, plainly angry with himself, his face still averted.

"Look at me," she said softly, and waited for him to do so. When he turned back to her, she said, "You haven't asked a thing of me. You could've asked for whatever you wanted anywhere along the line and I would've given it to you. Don't you know that?"

He shook his head, but his hands took a firmer grip on hers.

"Don't you want me, Erik?" she asked him bluntly.

He responded by throwing back his head and making an anguished sound low in his throat.

"Don't you?" she asked again, uncertainly.

His hands freed themselves and he shifted away, presenting his back to her.

"Erik?" She put her hand on his shoulder, and when he refused to turn, she stepped around in front of him. His head at once lowered self-defensively. "Erik?" She stepped closer.

With another of those eerie cries, his arms opened and wound themselves around her, to hold her pressed to his chest. She sighed and rested inside his embrace, feeling the heat of his body and hearing the ragged unevenness of his breathing as he kept her face safely hidden from his against his shoulder.

For many minutes he held her captive, not daring to demonstrate his ineptitude. Everything he wanted stood within his grasp but he lacked the courage to take it. She might express willingness now, but revealing his features would put an end to this closeness. And he had no alternative but to reveal himself. It was one of the last barriers remaining between them. Once he'd shown himself, she would either leave him for all time, or she would stay. It was that elemental, that simple. He believed she would leave him, and he was using these minutes to brace himself for that parting.

At last, he opened his arms and backed away from her. Then, as she watched, his hands went to his face and removed the mask. Not daring to breathe, he stood waiting for her reaction.

She looked at him and felt the pain begin in her belly and rise, spreading to fill her. "I love you," she whispered, distraught. "I've seen your face in my dreams and it didn't frighten me." Words, just words, she thought. Not enough. More was needed. She placed her hands on his poor dear face and kissed his mouth, then looked at him again. More, she thought. And put her lips to his damp eyes, to his temples, to his cheeks and chin, to the deep scar that commenced at the corner of his mouth, and then, once again, to his lips. "I want to make love with you, Erik," she whispered.

"*I can't!*" he cried, his hands on her shoulders, attempting to hold her away. "*I can't!*"

"Why not?" she asked. "Is it because I'm too thin and bony?"

"You're perfect, *perfect!*" he cried, his arms now winding protectively over his face.

"I know I'm not," she said unhappily. "I don't have much of a chest, and my neck's too long; my feet are too big. Is it because you think I'm too young? I'm not, really. Lots of girls at school have been doing it for ages. I hear them talking about it. Compared to them . . ."

"No!" He put a stop to her litany of doubts, his arms flinging themselves wide, one hand still clutching the mask. "It has nothing to do with *you*," he whispered fiercely. "Nothing! It's *me*. Don't you understand? I can't! I don't know *how*."

"Oh!" She paused to think about that, then said, "It doesn't matter to me. I don't know how, either. But don't you *want* to?" She was beginning to feel embarrassed at pushing the issue. "All you have to do is say so, if you don't want to."

He answered by pulling her forward to kiss her, tasting the minty interior of her lips and tongue; kissing her until her arms had gone tight around his neck and her long body was pressing urgently into his. They were generating a heat that threatened to incinerate both of them. But he couldn't get past either his reservations or his conviction that it would be wrong, morally and in every other way, to inflict his unskilled body on her. His hands explored the length and breadth of her back, the nape of her neck, her arms, as he drew air into his starving lungs before again seeking the eager welcome of her mouth. How did he dare to know such pleasure? he wondered. How could she give of herself this way to him? How could she, with such satisfied sighs, surrender to his hands' investigation and his mouth's ravening appetite? How was it she didn't pull away when he ventured to kiss the delicate column of her throat, or the supple curve of her neck? Why did she tolerate his hands as they traced the embroidered patterns that lay over her small round breasts? Yet she did surrender; she didn't pull away; she not only tolerated his hands but reached to loosen the robe and undo the several buttons at the neck of her

nightgown in order to offer her naked flesh into his disbelieving hands. Trembling, he was granted access to her
breasts, to the delectable weight of them on his palms.
Exalted, he found the courage to look at her, to touch
with hesitant fingertips the exquisite buds that sought to
blossom against his inquisitive hands. She held her hand
over the back of his head as he bent to pay homage, as
he rested his cheek against the gentle rise of her tremu-
lous breast, hearing the steady thudding of her heart beneath his ear. Could this be? he wondered, daring to
place careful kisses on her bared breasts. Was this actually happening? Was this miraculous child offering her
naked self to his close scrutiny, and behaving as if the
gesture not only pleased her but was also pleasurable?
Did she actually emit soft sighs and shiver responsively
to his tongue touching the stiffened tips of her nipples?
She made no move to run from him, but remained as if
rooted in place, prepared to accept whatever he might
offer. It brought him to his knees before her. With his
face pressed into the slight swell of her belly, he thought
he might literally die from the munificence, the enormity
of this gift. He could reach down and stroke her elegantly
arched foot, learning the circumference of her ankle, its
bony prominence, the silken rise of the underside of the
arch, the spaces between her strong, well-formed toes.
His hands could rise slowly up the length of her legs,
curtained in silk, discovering the rounded thrust of her
knees and, higher, the gradual alteration in the texture
of the skin as knees gave way to thighs. And, beyond,
the bones of her hips jutted hard against his palms, her
belly warm and fresh as milk under his cheek, against
his lips.

When he simply had to know, beyond any point of
resisting, all of her, and allowed his questing hand to
shape themselves to her shape, molding themselves to her
haunches, he was moved beyond measure to feel her
yielding more, then more, beneath his hands. She
touched his face, his neck and shoulders. Pliant, she was
opening like the sky at sunrise, offering him the definitive
gift of knowledge and experience. Hesitantly, yet unable
to deny his need, he delved between her thighs to find

the sleek moist core of her body. At this, the message she delivered to his head and shoulder grew more urgent. It could only mean she had no objection to the progress he was making in charting the topography of her physical landscape. It had to mean she approved of his preliminary incursions. And, as if to ease any lingering doubts he might have had, she hoarsely whispered his name while her hands clutched at his shoulders and he stooped to kiss her ankles, her knees, her thighs and hips, her belly from side to side, while his fingertips went on with their investigation of her most secret self. Stirred beyond his wildest conceiving, he was lost to sensation.

It was she who, as if caught finally in the heart of an inferno and consumed by the flames, tore off her robe and nightgown, to stand completely naked to his searching hands and mouth. With her eyes closed and her senses wide open, she encouraged his voyage of discovery. He remained kneeling before her as his hands swept back and forth, touching, seeking, testing, while he attempted to taste every area of her body, his teeth at one moment grazing her hipbone and, in the next, closing with extreme caution over her nipple. He immersed himself in her body with a dedicated fascination that erased from her mind everything but the idea of perpetuating, perhaps forever, this immensely arousing assault.

It was also she who, finding it near impossible to remain upright for very much longer—her knees kept seeking to buckle beneath the pleasure—began to grope for access to his body, finding buttons that opened to admit her hand to an expanse of broad, muscled chest; finding the means with which to remove him from the clothes concealing his upper body so that she had the warmth of his smooth skin to savor, and was able for some time to content herself by feeling through the sensitized skin of her fingertips his every reaction to her slightest inquiring touch.

When she was very nearly mad with a need to bear the weight of his body upon her own, it was she who finally whispered, "Erik, I have to see you. I want to. Please, let me see you."

Which put an end to the first part of their mutual investigation and led to the next.

9

He was deeply reluctant, returned to his senses both by her overt and perplexing interest and by his instinctive timidity and countless qualms. The fact of his face was one matter, the reality of his body another. He couldn't accept the validity of her claim to want to see him. Nowhere in his imaginings had his nakedness played a part; and the niceties of disrobing had never been detailed in any of Raskin's chronicles. His body was scarred too, though not as terribly. To show himself, even when nearing the pinnacle of the greatest pleasure he'd ever envisaged, seemed exceptionally risky.

"Don't be afraid, Erik," she encouraged him. "I'm not."

And that not only appeared to be the truth, it also struck him as phenomenal. She was fearless, his heavenly child. She was predisposed to all eventualities. She shamed him with her courage. So, there in the candlelit music room, he tacitly agreed to meet her display of fortitude with one of his own. Separating himself from his entranced involvement with her succulent body, he got to his feet and turned his back to shed the last of his clothes with unsteady hands.

"Don't turn away from me," she entreated him. "If you do, I'll be afraid again."

"Were you afraid?" he asked, turning in surprise.

"Of course I was," she admitted. "I've never done any of this before either, don't forget."

He'd neglected to give this fact due consideration. He was actively engaged in the process of deflowering a virgin. That he, too, was a virgin seemed scarcely relevant. He was, after all, a grown man of thirty-two and had, for several years now, listened avidly to Raskin's recountings of his dissolute activities. Nevertheless, he was daunted by the passage of her eyes over his body. Chagrined at being seen in so enflamed a state, he covered himself with his hands. Where her eyes touched him, he burned, with both desire and agonized embarrassment.

"No, let me see you," she said softly, moving his hands aside.

Then, to his delirious stupefaction, she put her hand on him. His own hands, startled starlings, beat against the air for a moment before coming to rest in her luxuriant hair.

The feel of him was unexpected, wonderfully silken and smooth. Her awareness of his vulnerability overjoyed and frightened her. This was undeniably real, inescapably real. She was wholly involved in something about which she knew nothing at all, and could only rely on instinct to guide her. Her instinct told her that he was as frightened as she. And she could see it in the way he tolerated yet appeared to relish her caress like some great barely tamed animal holding still out of sheer blind faith in her unspoken promise not to harm him.

Suffering the almost insupportable exhilaration of her touch, he forced himself to be brave, to allow this to occur, and worked to keep his eyes open, despite their need to shut down his sight. Twenty-five years before, his mother had scooped him up to kiss him on the top of his nose before depositing him on the back seat of the automobile. It had been his last close contact with the body and flesh of another. Now he was being rewarded—for no reason he could think of—by this gracious child, this indulgent, loving child.

Looking into her eyes, searching for signs, he could find only caring. There was no hint of anything but welling fondness in eyes that gazed unswerving into his. His fear began very slowly to lessen.

"I think you're beautiful," she said, and held her arms open to him.

In one sweep, he held her clasped to the length of his body, experiencing for the first time the heady power that came with learning the symmetry, the inescapable logic of why their bodies had been made as they had. She fit to him as if she were the missing other half of his person. He hadn't known until this moment that a woman's body could be such a source of completion, that the texture of her skin, her contours, and hollows, might have been created solely for the purpose of filling all the empty spaces in him that had craved substance for so many years.

"You feel so good," she sighed, fitting herself even more closely to him. "I never thought it would feel as wonderful as it does."

Freed finally of everything that might have held him back, he lowered her to the carpet in order to trace the length of the veins running from her wrists to her shoulders and across her upper chest, to warm his knuckles in the shallow caves beneath her arms; to enclose with his two hands her ribcage and then her waist; to rest each cheek and then each finger in turn against the tightened tips of her breasts, lost to her softness and increasing warmth. It was a miracle; she was his miracle, this long lovely creature with her newly acquired skills of kissing and stroking, with her satiny limbs and beguiling inner heat.

She set about her own exploration, intrigued by the way her slightest caress caused his muscles to bunch reflexively. His body was hard everywhere, arms, chest, shoulders, buttocks, thighs, hard hard. His belly jerked against her palm as if flinching, but she soothed him, gentled him, understanding that she had the ability to do this, to calm his fears so that she might, again, hold him between her hands, wondering if it really could be possible for him to place himself inside her. She doubted that her body could contain him entirely. But she had to know, had to see to completion what they'd begun. It would be the final proof of her love for him, the very essence of the gift she'd planned to give to him. The more he fondled her, the proportionately stronger her need and determination became to fit him within her. Yet he seemed so engaged with the other parts of her she feared distracting or accidentally upsetting him.

"Erik," she whispered, her hands closed around him, "put yourself inside me."

His eyelids lowered, he shook his head in agitation. "I'm afraid to hurt you, Marisa. I can't bear to hurt you."

"It doesn't matter," she insisted, spreading herself beneath him. "It doesn't matter." What she couldn't speak of, because she wasn't sure she understood it, was a mounting kind of craziness she was feeling that would only be quelled by the kind of hurt he was so fearful of causing her. She thought perhaps she was losing her mind. Her body had taken charge, moving with independent rhythms, opening in readiness for a satisfying attack. She directed him forward, her eyes holding his, and then lifted to meet him. She'd never dreamed it could be possible to be this naked or this vulnerable. And perhaps it wasn't possible after all, she thought, her fear returning. She could feel him hesitating, could read the misgivings in his eyes. "Don't be afraid, Erik," she insisted. "I want to love you. You have to do it."

His eyes half closed, he collected himself, drawing upon her plentiful reserve of courage, and pushed cautiously against her, his slight effort aided by her heated moisture.

She knew at once the truth of his fears. It would hurt; it did. He withdrew, then slowly pushed forward again. More hurt.

"Oh, God!" she whispered, feeling deficient, defective.

At once he withdrew, his eyes flying open.

"No! Go on!" she urged. "We have to go on!"

Holding still for this, keeping herself receptive in mind and body, was far more difficult than she'd imagined. The pain seemed to return her to sanity, and to separate her from Erik. It appeared that in order to join with him she first had to suffer through yet another separation, one that would occur even while she was as close to him as it was possible to be. She was all at once chilled, but her body was growing wet with the perspiration generated by their slow exertions. Once more he approached her. She held her hands to his hips and watched him closely as he made progress inside her, on and on, never ending, as sweat rolled down the sides of her face and a groan gathered strength in her throat, but she labored to suppress any expression of the pain she underwent. At last, it seemed they'd succeeded. She'd managed to bring him entirely inside her. And there he rested, pulsing within, surrounded by the flesh she knew he'd torn in his entry. They were separate, but joined. She lay beneath him thinking nothing could ever hurt more than this, and fearing there might be additional pain still to come. Why had she ever thought love to be painless? Why had she daydreamed of lightness and feathery things when the reality was of a transition made with tearing and with blood?

He leaned on his elbows, his body astonishingly embedded deep within hers, and looked at her exquisite face, searching for a way to bring her back from the torture he knew—could feel in every part of him, and in her—he'd inflicted upon her.

"I love you so," he confessed, humbled. "If you live a thousand years, you will never outlive my love for you. Do you want this to end? Tell me what I must do, Marisa?"

It brought her back to him. This was Erik, dear gentle Erik, who'd choose to put his hands in fire before he'd knowingly, intentionally, hurt her. This was Erik, and she had a peculiar need to revolve somehow around the center of his being. Her muscles inside clenched involuntarily and Erik's face was illuminated by the surprise of heightened sensation. Abandoning words, he sought her mouth as he began to move resolutely within her.

There was no further pain. Relieved and grateful, she held him as he rocked against her, witnessing the emergence of another Erik. His features cleansed, his expression beatific, he strove toward the conclusion his body indicated was expected and necessary. In the arms of his beloved child, aware of every aspect of her being—the shift of her hips, the tightening musculature of her arms and thighs—he labored to get to the end of something close within his reach. And then, in a dizzying explosion of interior lights, with a heart out of control and love beyond all bounds, he lost himself finally and forever in the darkness of this womanchild's body.

For many minutes he went away to a place he hadn't known existed but to which he was destined to want to return daily, nightly for the remainder of his life. Deadened, yet not unaware, he dragged his weight somewhat to one side in order not to crush his darling Marisa while he regained control of his breathing and of his senses. Then, concerned for her welfare, he hastened to ask, "Are you all right? Have I hurt you?" He stroked her forehead and cheeks, desperate for her reassurance.

"It did hurt," she admitted, and then smiled for him. "We did it!" she laughed, and hugged him in congratulation. "We *did* it, Erik!"

"But I hurt you," he persisted.

"I'm pretty sure," she said with newfound confidence, "that it only hurts that way once. Next time'll be fine."

"Next time," he repeated, awed. She would not flee from him, from his abusive body, but would return to bestow more gifts upon him. "You'll come back?"

"Well, of course I will. What did you think?" she wanted to know, holding his face between her hands. "Did you think I'd run away and never come back? You did, didn't you? That's just what you thought. Don't you *believe* me, Erik? *I love you!*"

"How can you?" he asked, curious to understand this magical circumstance. "How can you possibly?"

"Because you're good and kind, because you brought me pink roses and made a silver dollar come out of my hair. Because you write wonderful music, and I adore the sound of your voice. And *now*," she added momentously, "I know I love the way you touch me."

"You do?" He seemed like a small boy who'd been given a present beyond his comprehending when it wasn't even a holiday or a special occasion.

"I do," she declared. "But I think I need to move. My legs are going all pins and needles."

At once, and again with great care, he withdrew from her. She gave a startled cry, unprepared for the final pain, and they both looked at the blood streaking her thighs.

"I am so sorry," he cried, his hands hovering over her, "so terribly sorry."

"It's all right, but I think maybe we need a towel."

"Don't move! I'll fetch something."

He disappeared into the shadows and in a few moments returned with a small white linen napkin. Kneeling between her legs, he applied the hastily dampened cloth to her skin, cleaning away the evidence of their communion.

He sat back on his heels holding the cloth in both hands, looking at its stained surface with renewed horror. He'd given her unthinkable pain and here was the proof. How could she tolerate this? How was she able to speak of returning to him, of doing this again?

"Erik," she said quietly, watching him, "you're supposed to be feeling terrific, not unhappy."

"Is that how you feel?" he asked, unable to fathom her ongoing display of fondness.

"Well, I'm definitely not unhappy. Give me that," she said, holding out her hand for the napkin. "It's on you, too," she said, and began sponging him clean.

Amazed by the intimacy they'd achieved, as well by her lack of self-consciousness, he allowed her to tend to him while a disbelieving tape rolled inside his brain, insisting that none of this could be real. It struck him then that if he spent every minute of every hour of every day for the rest of his life working at it, he'd never fully comprehend another person; he'd never be able to predict with any real accuracy the things that person might say or do or feel. Certainly, he doubted—although he did intend to try—he'd ever know this girl's mind as well as he'd know her body. Were he never to see or touch her again, he'd remember every line of her, every slope and curve; he'd be able to summon instantly the fragrance of her, the heft of her hair as it slipped through his fingers, the faint down on the lobes of her ears, the set of her shoulders, the knobs of her spine, even the shape of her toes.

Risa studied him as he sat on his haunches in front of her, his gravity in no way diminished. If anything, it seemed more pronounced in the aftermath of their awkward lovemaking. All she'd ever wanted, from their first meeting, had been to make him smile, to see him show some sign of happiness. She'd believed the experience they'd just shared was bound to achieve that. She'd been mistaken. In all the time they'd spent together she'd never seen him quite so shrouded in the darkness of his thoughts and feelings as he was at that moment.

"Do you feel happy, Erik?" she asked, her own mood rapidly descending to match what seemed to be his.

He raised his eyes to her as if puzzled by the question. "Happy?" The word had no meaning for him. "Happy" belonged to the realm of small children and those beyond the points of thought or caring. "Happy" lived in storybooks and silly films. "Happy" wasn't a state of existence one could realistically think to achieve within one's lifetime in a world full of cringing strangers. And yet what was this odd emotion staking its claim on him? It lacked the bulk and urgency of his other emotions; it felt cloudlike and pastel-tinted and terribly frangible, as if the slightest negative occurrence might cause it to shatter. Could that be happiness? he wondered. Or could it be the influx of excruciating tenderness that overwhelmed him every time his eyes came to rest on this glorious, generous girl?

"I don't know that I believe in happiness," he confided, scarcely able to credit that, without benefit of clothing, they were actually conversing.

"I believe in it. I know I feel it now. Don't you feel good?"

"I don't have words for what I feel," his mellow whisper conceded.

"But it's not bad, is it?"

"No, not that. We must dress. I must return you home."

"Wait!" The flat of her hand on his chest stopped him.

"Don't rush me away, Erik, please. I want to be with you a little while longer."

"Why?" He understood none of this.

"Because no matter how much time I get to spend with you, I always want more. That's the way I think it is when you care about someone. Don't you agree?"

His head gave a slow shake. It saddened her. "Poor Erik," she crooned, and sat up on her knees to embrace him. "That's the way it is for me, anyway. Wouldn't you like to be with me all the time?"

"I would like to keep you here forever," he said, again inundated by multiple sensations at having her skin-to-skin with him.

"And what would we do?" she asked playfully, her face in his neck.

"I don't know," he told her.

"We could sing together," she prompted.

"Yes. But for now you must finish school, complete your education."

"School's boring," she protested. "Maybe I'll just get through to graduation in June, then come live here with you."

"You're too young to think in those terms."

"What terms? I want to *be* with you."

"Perhaps someday that will come to pass."

She yawned against his shoulder and he sat smoothing her hair for a minute or two, then said, "I must take you home now, Marisa. It's very late."

Sleepy, she stopped resisting and put on her nightgown and robe, then watched him conceal himself once again in his clothes. As she dressed, she wondered if it would always be this way, that they'd be profoundly close for long moments, then entirely distant for hours and days. And even in the same room together, only a few feet apart, they were somehow disconnected. "It's weird to think I have to go to school in the morning," she said lazily. "I feel way too old to be someone who's still in high school."

Holding her coat in his hand, his mask back in place, he turned and came toward her. Getting to her feet, she reached to hold his face in her hands, her heart suddenly lifting. "Erik!" she exclaimed. "You're *smiling*. You *are* happy! I made you smile."

Wrapping her in her coat, shy again with these new emotions, he had to have her in his arms one last time. "You are so dear, Marisa, so very amusing. Come now." He unbolted the door and led her by the hand to the front of the house and out to the car.

In minutes they were at the top of the driveway and he was hurrying to open the passenger door for her.

"Tomorrow?" she asked, offering him a final kiss, drugged by the softness and warmth of his lips.

"Tomorrow," he agreed. And then he was gone.

Instead of going to school the next day, she took herself off to the Family Planning Clinic in Stamford where she took another irrevocable step into adulthood.

Returning home with her newly filled prescription and the flat packet of birth-control pills, she was so looking forward to nightfall she was unaware of anything but her own anticipation. To be with Erik, to have his hands on her, to talk with him and, perhaps, see him smile again was all she wanted. She ate hugely at dinner—everything looked good, smelled better, and tasted terrific—which prompted her father to say, "I can't believe you're the same kid who sat here last night and played hide and seek with the peas and made castles out of her mashed potatoes."

"I'm hungry." She laughed.

"More like ravenous. Looks as if you're trying to make up for years with one meal."

"Not exactly, but maybe."

"I've been giving some thought to the summer, Risa," he began. "I was thinking since you're graduating we ought to do something to celebrate, take a trip maybe, or a cruise. What would you think of that?"

Her chewing slowed and she tried to answer carefully. "What did you have in mind?"

"I don't know. Europe? We haven't been for a few years. Or a Mediterranean cruise, something along those lines. Maybe you'd like to go to southeast Asia, Hong Kong."

"You're talking about a long vacation."

"Three weeks, a month. You don't like the idea?"

"Oh, I do. It's just that I hadn't thought about being away. I mean . . . I . . ."

"What?" He asked, sensing she was trying to spare his feelings.

"I want to stay here for the summer, Dad."

"Every summer of your life you've complained non-stop of boredom. Now, I'm offering you a chance to get away and you want to stay here. Why? What's going on, Risa? Something's definitely up. I'm getting it in bits and pieces. First you don't eat at all and you're moping around here like somebody died. Then you're high as a kite and eating everything but the tablecloth and the cutlery. Would you care to enlighten me?"

She put down her knife and fork, debating telling the truth. If she did, she'd get Erik in trouble. No matter how tolerant her father might be in most areas, she knew he still thought of her as his little girl, and finding out that she was in love with Erik would probably send him into fits. She hated to lie to him, so she did the next best thing. She sculpted the truth somewhat, to make it fit her needs.

"Erik's been giving me music lessons," she told him. "It's going really well, and I'd hate to have to interrupt it at this point."

"Erik's been giving you music lessons," he repeated doubtfully. "Since when? For how long? And when exactly do the two of you get together?"

"I thought you'd be mad or say no, so I didn't say anything. It's been a while now. I go to his house almost every night. He picks me up and then he brings me home."

"Every night? Well, now that explains quite a few things. I'm not sure I care for this, Marisa. I don't know that I like the idea of a young girl alone every night with a man so much older."

"Dad, you said yourself Erik isn't like other people. I mean, can you see him coming here in the afternoons, or me going there? He doesn't do things in the daytime. You know that. And he'd never harm a hair on my head. You know that, too.''

"I think I'm going to have to have a chat with him," her father said.

"You don't believe me? You don't trust me?" she demanded, getting red in the face.

"Now, calm down. I didn't say either of those things. I'd just like to talk to Erik."

"Dad," she said evenly, "if you upset him and he stops my lessons, I'll never forgive you. I mean that with all my heart. I will absolutely never, as long as I live, forgive you."

He abruptly sat back in his chair, shocked by the passion of her outburst. "Since when did music lessons become so important to you?" he wanted to know.

"Since Erik said I was good." Her defiant tone giving way to one of pleading, she said, "Please, don't call and upset him, Dad. Please?"

"Marisa, are you sure that's *all* that's going on?"

"What else could there be?"

"I don't know, but I don't think I care for this. I don't like the idea of my daughter sneaking out of the house at night for so-called music lessons."

"Are you saying I'm *lying*?"

"I'm not saying that at all. I just don't think I'm hearing the whole truth."

"Then you *are* calling me a liar. I've never once in my entire life lied to you. Why would you think I'd start now?"

"Because you've never before in your entire life done anything like this—sneaking out every night for God knows how long to be with a man almost old enough to be your father."

"He is not! And besides, that has nothing to do with anything!" God! She wished she hadn't said a word. But he'd forced her into it. What else could she have said to get out of being away from Erik for maybe as long as a month? "Why are you *being* this way?"

"If it's what you say it is, neither one of you should be in the least upset by my having a talk about it with Erik."

"I don't mind your talking to him. I just don't want you accusing him, the way you've been accusing me."

"I've accused you of nothing," Cameron said heatedly. "I'm merely trying to get to the truth."

"I've *told* you the truth!"

"And *I've* told *you* I have misgivings."

"Why? About what?"

"I've told you that, too: about your spending hours every night alone with a man so much older than you."

"What d'you think he's going to *do* to me?" she challenged him. "And how d'you know I'm not the one who might be up to something? Why do you automatically assume the worst about Erik? I'll tell you why!" she stormed. "Because of the way he looks! Because you think he's a freak, that's why! If he looked like everyone else you wouldn't mind one bit."

"That is not true!" Cameron defended his position. "That is not only not true, it's unfair and insulting. I have no objections to Erik, on any grounds. What I do object to is the secrecy of this whole business, the underhanded way the two of you have agreed to get together without my knowledge or consent."

"You seem to forget I'm not a child anymore. I'm perfectly capable of making my own decisions."

"I don't deny that. But you're also very impulsive, and inexperienced in the ways of the world."

"Well, if I have to come to you for permission every time I get an idea, how am I going to *get* any experience? I can't believe you're talking to me this way, as if I'm stupid, as if I haven't got a brain in my head."

"You are not stupid; you have a very fine brain. What I'm trying to get across is that you haven't lived long enough to know that people sometimes have hidden reasons for the things they do."

"And which one of us is supposed to have those, me or Erik?"

"Christ!" he sighed, wearied by the argument. It was so rare an incident and so unexpected that he found himself halfway willing to surrender and halfway determined to exert the full strength of his parental authority. "What the hell kind of father d'you think I'd be if I just smiled and said yes to every goddamned notion that comes into your head? It's like that damned dog business all over again that you kept on at me for years about. Marisa''— he softened his voice—"this has to be discussed by all the parties concerned. Since I suspect you'll head directly to the telephone to tell Erik what's transpired here, I suggest you ask him to come over tonight so we can thrash this out. In fact, I'd like you to do that now, if you would.''

"He's only going to tell you the same things I have."

"Good. Then I'll be satisfied."

"Shit!" she muttered under her breath as she dutifully went upstairs to call Erik.

10

ERIK FELT REMARKABLY WELL. HE'D SLEPT FOR FIVE hours, a sleep so deep and so crowded with sensation and dreams of Marisa that he'd awakened in the early morning brimming with renewed energy and rekindled optimism. He was also taken, immediately upon waking, with the idea of buying for Marisa something as rare and marvelous as she herself was.

After he'd bathed, reluctantly washing her scent from his skin, he dressed, then got on the intercom to Raskin.

"I would like you to do an errand for me."

"Sure. What?"

"I want you to drive into the city and buy something at Cartier. A necklace, I think. In gold, a fine chain, with a small pendant. Diamond. A good size, but not too large. Nothing ostentatious."

"No problem. You want me to go now?"

"If you wouldn't mind."

"I'm on my way." Raskin hung up, smiling to himself.

Alone in the house, Erik ate some bread and butter standing by the counter in the kitchen while he watched the sunlight that, through the filter of the tree branches outside, darted by inches back and forth across the far corner of the room. Like something alive but penned by the dark boundaries of the kitchen, the light hesitated, then shifted, hesitated once more, then held still. Fascinated, Erik watched as he drank his coffee. Then he poured himself another cup and carried it up to the office where he had to stop to admire the brilliant primary-colored reflections thrown across the walls and floor by the sun insistently cutting its way through the stained-glass window. Altogether, he felt most unusual. And touching his fingers to his face, he found his mouth upturned into what Marisa had called a smile. Odd, yet today everything seemed to please him. The coffee tasted exceptionally flavorful; the light seemed less menacing; and his facial muscles were creating peculiar effects. He lit a cigarette and that, too, had a better than usual taste. Most peculiar of all, the problem that had been so irksome regarding the cement-canopied entryway to the office building in Greenwich appeared suddenly solvable. All that was needed to accommodate both his client's preferences and his own dissatisfaction with the concept of a covered entrance was to arch the canopy somewhat higher and extend its perimeters no more than a foot on either side. Simple. Yet he'd been unable to see it before, and had been stalled on the design for quite some time. Now it was viable. And his inspiration had come somehow as a result of studying the trapped light in the corner of the kitchen. Structurally, he could see the change represented no difficulty. And aesthetically the building was now all of a piece.

Quickly he sketched new front and side views of the entry, noting the dimensions and calculating the stress factors created by the additional weight of concrete. Extra steel rods at either end would secure the castings. So simple. Having penciled the details in the margins, he set the views aside for Raskin to copy to scale. All that remained were the electrical, mechanical, and heating/ventilating requirements for a building of this size: boiler capacity, ductwork estimates, the usual gutworks. Once Raskin drafted the last of the views, the project could go to the modelmaker. Then the client would see the plans, the model, and go over the presentation with Raskin, who did this part of every job for Erik. A client knew in advance all queries and problems would travel with Raskin back to Erik, who would either settle them—usually by telephone—or alter the design to suit, although he required a good reason to doctor his designs.

But this was, as he'd promised himself, the last project. It had become yearly more difficult to deal with referrals who didn't understand the special circumstances under which he'd agree to work. He detested having to explain himself, and seldom did. Raskin undertook to inform potential clients of the terms, and if they agreed, initial contact was made. But there were clients who'd been known to grow peevish at having to deal with their architect secondhand, who felt if they were spending the money to have a building designed it was their right to have direct communication.

Erik loved the work, loved the challenge of creating buildings to suit the needs of different people. But the contact, however minimal, with querulous, demanding businessmen with no comprehension of the fine points either of architecture or engineering, made his work difficult and robbed it of pleasure. So much of the time what was wanted by these men was a monument to their personal potency, the bigger the better, good taste not an issue. There was no shortage of potential clients. His designs were successful and much admired. His buildings were of clean lines and pleasing angles, with their interior square footage used to provide the most natural light and warmth. He thought it highly ironic that his best concepts made the most use of the sun—including two Connecticut low-rise office buildings predominantly fueled by solar energy—when there was nothing he could think of that would draw him out of doors before sundown.

The sun was his enemy, daylight his torment. He was imperiled in the light of day, put at risk by the exposure of his gruesome features. He had once—and still shuddered to recall it—caused a serious but fortunately not fatal accident on the turnpike when, driving home from an unavoidable meeting in Stamford with the banker and lawyer who were the executors of his parents' estate, he'd moved into the outside lane to pass a slow-moving car driven by a young woman with long blond hair accompanied by a young man also with long blond hair. The young man saw Erik and began wildly gesticulating and yattering at the young woman, who looked to her left to see what he was raving about. Upon seeing him—Erik had felt the peripheral scorching her eyes caused his flesh— she'd evidently forgotten she was in a moving vehicle and plowed into the car ahead of her. The resulting crash involved some four or five cars, so far as Erik could determine in his rearview mirror as he swung back into the center lane and kept going. As he left the turnpike at the Darien exit, he hoped no one had been badly injured. Then he'd amended that, hoping the stupid young blonde and her hippie boyfriend had been ground to mush in the collision. He despised them for their ignorance, their lack of sensitivity and so revised his wish for their death to the hope that they'd both been left with injuries that would result in their spending the remainder of their days with disfigured faces. It would be, either way, a very long time before they were quite so quick to point and gape.

Daylight was his nemesis, his undoing, but his respect for its power was limitless. And, he thought with a pang, his Marisa lived in the light. She was a child of the sun; her skin was fragrant with it even now, in the last of winter. Her voice, when she sang or spoke, was redolent of daytime. It contained the sounds of birds, of the breeze, of sun-dappled water washing over smooth rocks. It was the whish of leaves lightly brushing together, the diffusion of sunrays through cumulus cloud clusters, the push of a bird's wings against the oppressing air. She was all that was good of the daylight world. So how could he dare to imagine having her near him always in the protective penumbra of the exclusive little world he'd constructed with such obsessive care?

Ah, but he did imagine it. Descending to the music room, where he lifted a tape from the shelf and fitted it to the reel-to-reel player, he not only imagined it, he craved it as he'd never before craved anything. With her voice and his music emerging from the four speakers, he sat in one of the black-and-gilt chairs and shut his eyes to appreciate the sound. He did so admire her natural interpretative skills, her instinctive inclination to sing slowly, hauntingly, a song traditionally chanted up-tempo. Her rich lower register gave new resonance to a song he'd previously considered trivial. *I want to be happy. I won't be happy till I make you happy too.*

With her voice surrounding him, with the feeling he was somehow contained by her sound as he'd in actuality been contained by her demonstrative limbs, he permitted himself to dream. And what he dreamed was of a new life, a life infinitely improved and made more tolerable by her presence within it. He visualized her moving through the rooms of his house, pictured her taking possession of the house the way she'd assumed ownership of his heart. Knowing it was foolish and likely improbable, he saw himself drawing perfumed baths for her, then being accorded the privilege of sitting close by to watch as she immersed herself in the steaming scented water; he saw the two of them eating together beneath the tinkling crystals of the dining-room chandelier; he followed after her as she traveled from room to room, subtly altering forever his perception of his home by leaving faint traces of herself everywhere; he felt her by his side at the piano, and even at the drawing board and, most significantly, he saw himself standing guard over her sleep, vigilant in his love.

It electrified him to review what she'd given him and to absorb its enormity. He'd been accorded the unprecedented privilege of becoming her lover. His entire body suffered a frisson at the recollection of the feel of her beneath his hands, the taste of her on his tongue. She had actually allowed him to penetrate the interior of her body, allowed him to divest himself of a lifetime's longing while, in the process, consigning himself to a lifetime's caring. It had been real, oh yes. She had offered, and he had dared, to immerse himself in sensation. So real had it been that even now, with his eyes closed and her voice in his ears, he could feel again the impossibly deep inward sweep of her waist, the taut thrust of her breasts, the tight heat of that yielding interior corridor. Real! Dear God, too real! So real that just recalling it filled him with the need to hold her again, to touch and taste and feel her again; to know her better, deeper, and to find ways in which to return to her some measure of the stunning pleasure she'd so liberally given to him. He knew, from years of Raskin's uninflected tales, the ways in which love could be made. And while before he'd been nothing more than an unseen specter at the proceedings, he had now an opportunity to be an active participant, an eager accomplice in the act of making love. He couldn't think how he'd get through the hours until he could see her again. There were so many things he wished, all at once, to say to her, so many long-suppressed thoughts and memories he might at last share.

He wanted to give her everything within his power to give: knowledge and music and diamonds, secrets and stories and love. Love. Was he a fool? he wondered, suddenly opening his eyes to the realization that the tape had come to an end and so had his fevered conjecturing. Was he placing far too much store in the as-yet-untried emotions of a schoolgirl? Perhaps he was nothing more than a convenient means by which a headstrong girl had chosen to rid herself of her tedious virginity. No. That was not Marisa. She was different; she knew her own mind. And, heaven only knew why, but she'd chosen him. It was scarcely credible, but she had chosen him.

When Marisa telephoned that evening and said, "My father would like you to come over, Erik. He wants to talk to you," Erik's hand closed tightly around the red-and-gold Cartier box in a reaction of complete and immediate fear.

"Why?" he asked, his body coated with sudden perspiration.

"He was suggesting he and I go away to Europe this summer and I had to give him some reason why I didn't want to go. So I told him you've been giving me music lessons. It was the only thing I could think of in a hurry, Erik. I haven't told him anything really, and I won't. But I had to say *something*. Now he's furious with me and wants to talk to you. I'm sure it'll be all right, and I'm really sorry to drag you into it, but I couldn't think of anything else to say. Are you mad at me?"

His fear abating somewhat, he answered, "No."

"You are. I can tell."

"I am not angry with you," he said stiffly. "Tell your father I will come at ten."

"Please don't be mad at me!" she implored him. "I love you so much, Erik. I couldn't go away and leave you for three weeks or a month. I *had* to say what I did."

"I understand," he told her, and hung up.

He was filled with apprehension, all but drowning in it. Cameron had it within his power to separate them forever if he chose. Marisa was a child, an underage child. Her father could dictate the course of her life with impunity. The man could do anything he wished with regard to his child, and Erik would have no way or any right to stop him. Please don't take her away from me! he thought desperately. I will do anything you ask, but please don't take her away.

He had to forearm himself, had to think of what he would say. Pacing back and forth the length of his bedroom, he tried to calm himself enough—the red box still in his tight grip—to think clearly. Cameron was bound to want to know why, if Erik had consented to giving his child music lessons, he hadn't bothered to confer with Cameron on the matter. What to say? It simply happened. He hadn't thought any harm would come of it, but of course he'd been completely in the wrong and did apologize most humbly for causing any distress. Obsequious, toadying, but appropriate. He would prostate himself, if necessary; he would pave entire city blocks with apologies, and promise anything at all if Cameron would only forgive this breach of manners and custom.

He longed to be able to approach the man and say, Sir, I love your daughter. I would marry her tomorrow were that within the bounds of acceptability. I would give up my life for her. And, sir, I believe with every fiber of my being that your daughter reciprocates that love. Please don't act rashly and sever something that represents my very ability to continue living. For a few hours I was permitted to feel complete, unimpaired in any way. It was a gift, sir, of such magnitude I haven't the words to articulate for you its scope. For a brief time I was a normal man, an ordinary man, able to give and receive love.

Don't take that away. Don't deprive me of the only possibility for peace I've ever known.

So rattled and fearful was he that he decided to confide in Raskin.

"What should I do?" he asked over the intercom, the red box turning, turning in his fingers.

"That's a tough one," Raskin replied. "I think the only thing you can do is wait and find out what the man wants to hear, then say it. Don't volunteer anything. He'll let you know what he wants you to say. Just be cool, Erik. Say too much, and you'll blow it."

"Thank you," Erik whispered fervently. "That is good advice. Thank you."

"The necklace what you wanted?"

"It's exactly right. Thank you." Erik put down the phone and at last gave up his hold on the Cartier box. Setting it on the chest of drawers, he backed away to stand staring at the box as if his entire future hinged on the successful giving of this diamond token. The meeting with Cameron Crane would, in fact, determine his future. Of that he had no doubt. And should the meeting go well, Marisa would soon have in her hands the first of many tangible offerings Erik hoped to make to her.

Marisa came running up as he pulled into the driveway.

"I've been waiting for you," she said, the wind driving the hair across her face. "Don't worry. I'm sure everything will be all right."

He was too fearful to speak, and so afraid of losing her that he simply had to hold her for a moment, hoarding her embraces so that their recollection might sustain him in desolate days to come.

His fear was so palpable she couldn't help being aware of it. "It'll be all right, Erik," she promised, pressing quick kisses on his face. "Let's go in."

Taking his hand, she towed him inside, pausing to turn off the overhead light in the foyer, a gesture that touched him deeply. She was real; she was his; she was concerned for his comfort. She even knew to release his hand once inside, and stood waiting like a well-trained hostess to take his cape. He gave it into her hands, then turned, squared his shoulders, and entered the living room.

Cameron got to his feet, offering his hand and a drink.

"Cognac?" he asked Erik.

"Please."

"Relax," Cameron said. "Have a seat."

Erik forced himself to sit down in the wing chair. He was sweating again. His hands went at once to the arms of the chair and waited there like sentries.

"Here you go!" Cameron gave Erik his cognac, then went to his usual chair. Both men tasted their drinks, their eyes on each other. Then Cameron said, "Risa tells me you've been giving her music lessons."

Erik nodded, concentrating on Raskin's advice: Volunteer nothing.

"I have to tell you," Cameron continued, "not only did I have no idea of Risa's interest in furthering her music studies, I was also completely unaware these lessons were taking place."

Again Erik nodded. Risa came in to sit in the companion chair.

"Suffice it to say, I'm angry with Risa for neglecting to apprise me of the situation. I can understand why you'd choose to give these lessons at night, given the circumstances. What I really can't fathom is why neither one of you thought to tell me. Unless"—he directed his eyes to Risa—"you were under the impression that I did, in fact, know."

"He thought you knew, Dad," Risa put in. "It's totally my fault."

"Is that true, Erik?" Cameron asked him.

"No," Erik replied in his alluring whisper. "We didn't discuss it. I was remiss, and for that I apologize."

It was Cameron's turn to nod. "I'm sure you can appreciate my concern, Erik. A young girl going alone nightly to the home of a grown man, a home whose address I don't even know."

"I will rectify that at once," Erik volunteered, his hands flying to his inner jacket pocket for the notebook and gold fountain pen he always carried. Setting the notebook on the arm of the chair, he quickly printed out the address in his draftsman's lettering, then tore the page from the book and handed it to Cameron.

Cameron looked at what Erik had written, then began to laugh. "I'll be a son of a bitch!" he chortled. "You bought the old Terwilliger place across the way. *You're* the one who finally rescued the poor old ruin."

Unutterably relieved, albeit still on his guard, Erik's facial muscles relaxed some and he said, "Yes."

"Well, if that doesn't beat all," Cameron crowed. "And here I was worrying that Risa here was going off every night into the sticks somewhere, when all the time she was right next door. Why the hell didn't you tell me that, Risa?"

"You didn't ask." She smiled at her father, then turned to look at Erik.

"My God, that place had to be empty a good ten years. You had your work cut out for you there."

"It took some time," Erik allowed. "Five months."

"Well, I'll be," Cameron said, taking a last look at the page before folding it away into his pocket. "Just do me a favor, the two of you. See if you can't hold these lessons at a more reasonable hour, say nine o'clock. Risa's only got a few more months of school, and then you can sing all night, if you want. But for now, let's agree to an eleven-thirty curfew. Okay?"

"Sure," Risa said at once, looking to Erik.

"Of course," Erik agreed. "And I do apologize for the misunderstanding."

"Not at all. Let's forget the whole thing. Now, tell me. I understand you've submitted a plan for Farrell's new building."

It *was* going to be all right. Erik's loss of tension was so great it left him feeling sleepy, barely able to pay attention to the ensuing conversation. Risa sat back in her chair, crossed her legs, and let one foot swing lazily back and forth as she listened. Riveted to the sight of her schoolgirl's knee socks and bare knees, Erik responded to Cameron's questions, not daring to look at her face. He knew if he did he'd give the game away; his feelings were bound to transmit themselves to her father. And he couldn't do anything to jeopardize their now-sanctioned visits.

He stayed just over an hour, then excused himself on the pretext of work waiting to be done.

"I'll walk Erik to his car, Dad," Risa said, and contained herself until they were well beyond her father's seeing or hearing before winding her arms around Erik's neck, whispering, "I was looking forward all day to making love with you tonight. It was all I thought about the whole day long. Now it'll have to wait until tomorrow."

"Marisa, there are things to consider . . ."

"I've taken care of those things," she interjected. "I cut school today and went to the Family Planning Clinic."

"You did what?"

"I went and got birth control pills. Now we don't have a thing in the world to worry about. Unless I got pregnant last night."

He was jolted. "I never gave it a thought," he reproached himself aloud. It was something Raskin hadn't ever covered in any of his tales. As far as he knew, neither Raskin nor his women ever took any precautionary measures. Erik's only knowledge of their necessity was derived from his reading.

"Well, why would you? It's not as if it's something you've ever had to think about before, is it?"

"No," he replied honestly.

"So, okay. *I* thought about it, and it's taken care of." She held her mouth to his to be kissed and he somewhat distractedly obliged her. Then he pulled away. "You must go back inside, Marisa. It's too cold to be out here without a coat."

Her response to this was to pull his cape open and enclose herself within it. "Do you feel me trembling?" she asked him. "I wish I could come home with you now. I was a little sore this morning, but I kind of liked feeling it. All day I kept thinking about the way you touched me. I'd go off into these little dreams and start remembering everything we did, and I'd get this jumpy feeling in the pit of my stomach. I want you to touch me again. I love you so much."

"Perhaps," he ventured, "it's only making love you love."

"Don't say that!" she told him, stung. "It's *you* I love. I know the difference. Thinking about you today," she whispered against his ear, "I could hardly sit still, Erik. It made me all wet."

"Christ!" he exclaimed, automatically holding her closer while his own body rose in response.

"Give me another kiss and then I'd better go."

He touched his mouth to hers, then shifted out of her reach. "Please, hurry back inside. I will come for you tomorrow at nine."

"Say you love me, Erik."

Ah, he thought, she was capable of subtle torment. "I love you" came his whisper. And then he was driving away and she was running back to the house.

11

WITH RASKIN OUT FOR THE EVENING, ERIK BROUGHT Risa in through the front door and invited her to view the house. As she inspected each room, he drank in whatever praise she offered. When she commented on the softness of the leather covering the living-room sofas he felt much as he did when she placed her hands on his face. When she appeared not in the least bothered by the funereal lack of color, but opted instead to admire the dining-room chandelier and the spaciousness and clever planning of the kitchen, he was humbled. And when at last they stood together in his bedroom, having completed their tour of inspection, she pronounced his room "Sensational. It feels like sleep, like the way it is when you're tired beyond belief and all you want is to sink into bed, and you do, and it's just the best thing ever," it was the highest praise he'd ever received.

There she stood in her student's clothing—white button-down shirt, Shetland cardigan, short pleated skirt, knee socks and Bass loafers—looking at his bed, saying, "It's the biggest bed I've ever seen. Did you buy it so there'd be room for me?" She smiled so lovingly, holding out her arms to be embraced, that he could no more have resisted her than give up breathing.

"You're quite sure about this?" He had never taken anything for granted and was not about to begin now.

In answer, she took off the cardigan, then her hands went to the buttons on her blouse. But he stopped her, asking, "May I do that?"

"Yes, you may," she replied and stood in place while his eager hands tried to contain their excitement, flexing then curling several times before commencing the delicious task of baring her body to his eyes. "But," she added after a moment, "only if I get to do the same."

"Wicked girl!" came his whisper.

"Wicked you!" she returned happily.

He couldn't help wondering as he slowly opened the front of her blouse why he'd never considered that intimacy, in particular physical intimacy, could be sufficiently elastic to contain humor and conversation. All he'd learned from Raskin was of the act itself, its variables and permutations. He'd heard everything about the graphics, but nothing of the freedom, the euphoric loss of restraint. Perhaps, he realized with a sympathetic pang, it was because Raskin knew nothing of these things. Raskin either feared closeness or failed to hope for it, for he'd never once referred in the telling of his many encounters to anything beyond perfunctory conversation between perfunctory drinks followed by business-like lovemaking. His tales lacked emotion, Erik now saw; they were titillating only by dint of their aspects of conquest and sportsmanship and athleticism. Poor Raskin, Erik thought, reclining on the bed beside his adorable lover. Fortunate Erik.

As before, he was drawn into a prolonged and extravagantly pleasurable minute examination of her flawless body. In the faint light from two thick candles placed on the dresser top, he watched the way her nipples tightened and elongated at his touch; he studied her face as his cautious fingers made her writhe and reach for him. His actions upon her affected her breathing and her body temperature; they turned her moist, especially when he touched her just there. At this point, just here, his seeking fingers created a visible and quite violent reaction in her. And this in turn created a matching response within him that prompted him to learn to what extent he might augment and prolong this reaction of hers. It had to be possible, he reasoned, to take her to a place parallel to the one he'd discovered in their first encounter. And the route to that unthinkable ecstasy was precisely here. How astonishing to find himself possessed of the ability to please her, when the process itself so thrilled him! He could close his eyes and lose himself to her taste and texture, drinking from her as if from some jeweled chalice, greedy yet never incautious in the pursuit of a no longer elusive secret.

If someone had suggested to her, even three days ago, that she might one night lie naked on a bed while a man she felt she loved more with each passing moment kissed her between the legs the way he'd kissed her mouth, she'd have laughed and declared it was the most ridiculous thing she'd ever heard. But it was happening, and it wasn't in the least ridiculous. It was terribly serious, and she liked it so much she thought she might very well have some sort of seizure. Her hands of their own accord held Erik's head close to her as he delivered this lengthy kiss, and her eyes rolled closed in order that nothing should distract her from her pinpoint focus on the flame he'd lit and was now stoking to a bonfire at the very center of her being. Her knees, independent and determined, bent and parted; her belly quivered; her entire body quaked, her chest and neck now caught fire; and her breathing apparatus had gone completely haywire so that she could only draw in occasional sips of air that were exhaled on encouraging murmurs over which she had no control. His hands continued to search her flesh like homeless creatures seeking to nest, examining every part of her, challenging its potential as a new dwelling. She abandoned herself to him, entrusting her very soul into his keeping.

The longer it went on, the more her body responded and the more heated it became; the more sensitive to touch and pressure. Until, all at once, there was an utter interior silence, a space in which all thought and movement ceased. Then Erik delivered the final spark that set her ablaze. She went rocketing, selfless, into the heart of the conflagration, gasping with shock as a tide of exultation capsized the vessel that had always contained her.

Erik was awed by their achievement, by the visibility

of the pleasure he'd managed to give her. He lay with his arms wrapped around her hips, his face hidden against her belly, feeling the love she transmitted through the hand that stroked his head. In this lull, he had a sudden and dire insight. Marisa was taming him, crashing through the defenses he'd spent so long structuring. With her love, she was domesticating him, bringing him in from the wild. And out of his love for her, he was going docilely, albeit guardedly. He was so undone by his feelings for her that he could no longer maintain the barricades with which he'd secured himself for so long. She loved him, and one day she would leave him. When that happened, when he found himself armorless and alone, he would die. He'd have nothing left to protect himself from marauding strangers, no means of escape. And he'd have no Marisa. He wouldn't wish to live without her.

"What's the matter, Erik?" Her hand now lay on his shoulder. "What's wrong?"

He had no words for the vast emptiness of the horizon he'd glimpsed off in the future. He could only succumb to his horror of that eventual day.

"Erik." She slid down through the loop of his arms to cradle his head against her breast. "Tell me what's wrong."

Ashamed of his weakness—he'd fought most of his life against his easy inclination to tears—he sat away from her, rubbing his fists into his eyes.

"Is it me?" she asked. "Did I do something wrong?"

He couldn't speak of his feelings for fear of appearing an ingrate or a fool. "It's just that I care so very much for you," he was able to say.

"And that makes you cry? Come here." She pulled him back into her arms and caressed his patchwork face. "Be happy, Erik. I care just as much for you. I may be young, but that doesn't mean I don't know what I want or how I feel. I want to spend my whole life with you."

"You can't know now what you'll want for all of your life," he told her, pressing his lips to the alabaster mound of her shoulder. "You may think now it's what you want, but one cannot guarantee anything, especially not emotions."

"*I* can," she insisted with the charming arrogance of her youth. "I know I want to be with you forever. If I could, I'd marry you tomorrow. And if the other night did get me pregnant, I'd be glad."

To her dismay, he cried, "*No!* Don't *say* that! It was imbecilic of me to take such a risk with you. We'll have to pray you don't become pregnant as a result of my ignorance."

"But why?" she wanted to know, cowed by his adamance.

"I will *never* put a child into this world to know the humiliation and horrors I've known."

"But, Erik, a child of ours wouldn't have to grow up the way you did—however that was. I know so little about you, about your life."

"Please, I'd prefer not to discuss it."

"It's all so weird," she said, half to herself, drawing up her knees and winding her arms around them, her eyes on his brawny back. "One minute we're so close, and the next we couldn't be farther apart. I wish I could understand how this happens. Sometimes, I feel so lonely with you. I don't know why that is."

He peered over his shoulder at her to see that she did, indeed, look forlorn. At once, he melted.

"I'm sorry." He placed his hands on either side of her face and raised her head in order to look into her eyes. "I am most truly sorry. I have no right to burden you with my thoughts, my fears."

"But you *do*," she said ardently. "Love gives you that right, Erik. It's not a burden. It's an honor. If you hold back on your feelings, then I'll have to do the same. And neither one of us will have anyone to tell our true feelings to, so we'll both be lonely."

"Oh, my sweet girl, dear little girl, I don't want you to be lonely." His facial muscles made their smiling contractions again, and he was rewarded by the sight of a smile lifting the corners of her delectable mouth. "My angel," he crooned in his low whisper. "My lovely Marisa."

"I love the way you say my name," she told him, falling back against the pillows. "And I *love* what you just did. It was like holding a prism up to the sun right in front of your face so that all the rainbows fall in your eyes. Is that how you feel when you shudder inside me? Is it like rainbows in your eyes?''

"It's rather more like *being* the rainbow," he said, straightening her legs before bending to touch his cheek against her instep. "So very lovely," he sighed, his hands reverently skimming over her knees and up the length of her thighs, then reaching beneath her to turn her over onto her belly so that he could dip his tongue into the twin indentations at the base of her spine while his hands, uncontrollable scavengers, went seeking treasure underneath. These two eager explorers roved over her body, locating new areas of reaction, ways of probing and teasing that had Marisa lifting and pushing back into him. The more overt her reactions, the more potent he became. He hadn't ever felt quite so powerful or so aware of his physical strength and the need to be gentle. He vowed he would never hurt her in any way, and kept this firmly in mind as she moved against him, her arms spread to the sides of the bed. She repeated his name over and over, nearing another peak. Sensing this, he turned her again, lifted her easily and brought her down in his lap with her legs on either side of him.

With an instinct and intent that galvanized him, she reached to guide him as he lifted her forward. "It doesn't hurt," she reassured him, before opening her mouth over his, all eagerness and heat.

Locked together, he held her to his chest, amazed by her resiliency and zeal. There was nothing, it seemed, she couldn't do, his brilliant womanchild; nothing she wouldn't do. Unlocking her legs from around him, he eased her down again, maintaining the heartening connection. Then, fluidly, he swung to one side so that she lay above him, her knees tight against the outer sides of his. "How does it feel?" he asked, monumentally concerned.

"Wonderful." She raised herself to smile down at him, then playfully tilted her head so that her hair fell across his chest. "How does it feel?"

"Wonderful," he echoed, his hands on her hips hold-

ing her steady as he rose higher into the liquid core of
her body. "And how does this feel?" he asked, watching
her face closely as he slipped his hand between their bodies to press cautiously against her.

In response her muscles clamped around him inside;
her face cleared as all thoughts fled from her mind and
she rose and fell to perpetuate the feeling, to commence
a ride that at each descent stabbed her with pleasure.
Lowering the upper half of her body to his chest, her
fingers interlaced with his, she kissed his forehead, his
eyes, and then his mouth, deeper and deeper, accelerating the motion until she felt, in an instant of separation
and awareness, his body being overtaken by spasms as it
completed its journey within her. Only a moment and
then she was paralyzed, trusting him to know she needed
him to pull her with him over the edge. *"Please, Erik!"*
she cried, lost to dependency. And he climbed to meet
her, keeping her oscillating on the brink for perilous seconds before hurling her off into space.

He returned to himself slowly, opening his eyes to find
Marisa sharing his pillow, her eyes gazing into his.

"I was watching you sleep," she said, tracing the out-
line of his lips with the tip of her forefinger. "You sleep
so nicely, like a little boy. I looked at you all over," she
said with bold impishness. "I love looking at you. Tell
me all the things you like to do."

"I don't understand." His forehead furrowed.

"Well." She smiled, the eternally patient teacher. "Do
you like to swim? Or play basketball? Do you dance? I
love dancing."

"I don't know how to dance."

She sat up and gaped at him. "You don't know how
to *dance*? I don't believe it! You have to know! You move
like a ballet dancer, for heaven's sake!"

He laughed. A pure stream of untainted laughter
gushed from his throat.

She punched him lightly on the arm, asking, "Why're
you laughing?"

"A ballet dancer," he scoffed. "It's too absurd."

"But it's true. I've never seen anyone move the way

you do. Your beautiful hands, and the way you seem to drift from one place to the next. I know absolutely you can dance.''

"No, I cannot.''

"Then I'll teach you. There has to be a radio or something in here.'' She jumped off the bed and stood peering into the shadows.

"There is a switch on the wall to one side of the dresser,'' he told her, amused and curious to see what she'd do. "Push it and a panel will slide back. There is a radio behind the panel.''

She did as he said, then stood fiddling with the tuning dial, found a station and turned, beckoning to him. "Come on, Erik. I'm going to prove to you you can dance.''

He got up good-naturedly and went to stand in front of her.

"Okay. Now put this arm around my waist, and hold my hand with this hand. Great. Bend your elbow a little. Perfect. Now, on the beat all you have to do is step forward, toward me, then to the side, then back, then to the side again.'' Following her instructions, they moved through the four steps. "Just don't look down,'' she said. "Hold me closer and put your cheek against mine, and we'll do it again.''

It was easy. After eight bars, he attempted a turn, completed it successfully and received her effusive congratulations. "Didn't I *tell* you? *Of course* you can dance. You've got that perfectly. Okay. Now don't move! Let me find a different station, and I'll teach you something else.'' She fussed with the tuning dial until she found a station playing what sounded like a Strauss waltz. "You can do this, for sure,'' she promised him. "It's just one-two-three, one-two-three.'' She started out leading, then stopped to say, "We can't do a waltz cheek-to-cheek. This one we do at arm's length, looking deeply into each other's eyes.'' Again, he laughed, but gamely submitted himself to her instructions. In a minute or two, he'd taken the lead and was waltzing her around the room, dancing as if he'd been doing it all his life. And laughing completely spontaneously.

"This is great!" she exclaimed. "Every night when I come I'll teach you a new dance. I *love* dancing, don't you?"

"I love *you.* And I must take you home. It's eleven-twenty."

"I wish I could stay and sleep beside you, wake up early and watch you sleep. I wish I *never* had to go home, or go back to school. I learn so much more from you than I do at school. I'm so happy with you."

"I wish you could stay, too," he said, gathering her clothes and his own from the floor. "But for now, we must get you home."

"Why do you whisper, Erik?" she asked, pulling on her undergarments.

He stopped dressing and looked over at her. The air was suddenly filled with tension and static. "Would you speak loudly if you were trapped behind this face?"

"Oh, Erik!" At once distressed and apologetic, she went to put her arms around him. "I'm sorry. I only thought it might have been because of the accident. I'm sorry."

"It's of no importance. I must learn not to foist my bitterness on you."

"I understand." She kissed his shoulder, then went back to her dressing. "I really do understand, you know."

He didn't reply, and she had the wits not to force it. Privately she believed she truly did understand. And she'd make it up to him for all the awful things that had happened in his life. She'd make him forget he'd ever been unhappy.

Before they left the room, he went to turn off the radio, then picked up the Cartier box from the dresser. He studied the box thoughtfully for a moment, then held it out saying, "This is for you, Marisa."

"You bought me a present?" Her eyes were wide. "You really do love me, don't you?"

"Yes."

"Oh, my God! It's a diamond. Erik!" Her widened eyes filled with tears. "I wish I could wear it," she said mournfully. "But I'd never be able to explain this to my father."

"You'll wear it when you come here," he suggested.

"Yes, I will. Thank you." She flung her arms about him and hugged him hard, then went to put the box back on top of the dresser. Returning to take hold of his hand, she said, "I can make you happy, Erik. I can show you what it is. It's not very hard. You'll see."

He held her hand to his mouth, then whispered, "Come now. It's late."

12

Just over two weeks after their initial lovemaking, Risa got her period. It saddened her because despite Erik's protestations she'd secretly hoped she'd get pregnant. Now that wasn't going to happen and it meant she'd lost the opportunity to prove to him that a child of his could have a full and happy childhood. It also meant they could not make love.

When she explained this to him he looked at her in something like wonderment. Whatever basic knowledge he had of women came from books he'd read. To have this living, breathing, healthy young woman tell him matter-of-factly that her body was in the process of renewing itself was a revelation and a furthering of their already intense intimacy.

"Do you feel ill?" he asked her. "Shall I take you home?"

"I feel fine. We could go to the music room, if you like."

"Yes," he agreed, and gingerly took her hand to direct her downstairs.

As in the early months of their nightly visits, they sat together at the piano.

"Sing for me," he whispered.

"What would you like to hear?"

"Anything at all."

122

"I'm in a silly mood, Erik," she cautioned him. "Can we do silly songs?"

"Is this what happens to women?" he wondered quite seriously.

She laughed, delighted, and said, "No, not at all. I'm just in a happy, silly mood. Okay?"

"Yes, of course."

She sang "Shuffle off to Buffalo" and "Yes, We Have No Bananas" and "Abba Dabba Honeymoon," then said, "I want to ask you something."

His head tilted to one side.

"I'm afraid I'll make you mad."

"Perhaps you will," he said. "But ask."

Turning more toward him on the bench, she held her open hand gently to his face. "It's funny," she said softly, "but I know your face. I mean, when I look at you what I see is the face you were meant to have. I know how you look. Your eyebrows are kind of feathery, and your beard isn't heavy, not the kind you'd have to shave twice a day the way Dad does. Your nose is straight and not too long, and there's a very nice little groove here"— she touched the space between the bottom of the mask and the top of his upper lip—"and your chin is strong and a bit square." She paused. His features revealed no reaction. "I don't mean to be unkind. I just want to understand. You know?" Still he showed no emotion. "Couldn't they have done more for you, Erik? Was this the best they could do? Oh, God! Please, don't be mad at me!"

When he spoke, it was with the dispassion of someone highly skilled after years of lecturing on one subject. "There is," he told her, "just so much skin on the human body that can be used for grafting purposes. The only skin entirely compatible with facial skin is that which is located directly behind the ears." He turned his head and pulled his ear forward to illustrate graphically. "There is not very much of it," he explained, as she studied the stripped-looking region. "When the facial trauma is such that more grafts are required, the surgeons are obliged to raid other parts of the body. In my case," he went on, slowly turning away from her, "they had to use what skin they could. And since the grafts all came from different areas and each area has its own tone and texture, we have the resulting patchwork effect. As for the nose, it could have been reconstructed. But without natural skin or bone. *Plastic*, in essence. The chances were I'd have looked even more grotesque, so there seemed no point. Besides, I'd come to loathe those surgical procedures. A few months recuperating, then they'd bundle me off back to hospital to put me under one more time, make a few more grafts, bring me round and hold a basin in front of my mouth while I vomited blood. Twenty-two procedures in all, and then I refused to go back. I was very young." He gave one of his embittered laughs. "I thought it wouldn't matter. Because, you see"—he turned back to her—"I looked *so much better*." Another derisive laugh. "It's all a matter of comparison. This face is nowhere near the horror of the face that emerged after the collision. I find that rather amusing." Again, he turned away. "Wonderfully amusing."

"I'm sorry," she said softly, wishing she hadn't questioned him.

As if he'd failed to hear her, his fingers moving noiselessly over the keyboard, his voice lower still, he said, "Quite often it comes back to me, the terror of those few seconds, the deafening noise of the crash, the frantic weightlessness as I fly about the interior of that automobile, the screams, and the blood. So much blood, gushers of it, sheeting across the seats, spattering on the shattered glass, and over me. The *smell* of it, the slippery *ooze* of it; its sticky thickness. Mine and theirs. And I feel the demented pounding of my heart as I see them, those monsters who'd been my mother and father. Only a few seconds and my heart is trying to escape from my body, trying to escape those bodies holding me down, spilling their poisonous liquids over me, looking to take me with them to their black world, their reeking haven. But I will not go; I refuse to go; I push against them, strike them with my fists, screaming all the while my refusal to go with them." He went silent, listening to the echo of his steady heartbeat in his ears, swallowing to rid himself of the taste in his mouth so like blood. The sounds of the crash gradually diminishing, his eyes returned to the present to gaze at his fingers splayed on the keyboard. Then he lifted his heavy head to see Marisa shedding tears. She sat very still, her eyes never having left him, and wept. Still caught up in that long-ago scene, he studied her, finding it hard to connect her tears to the tale he'd just told.

At the beginning, in the immediate aftermath of the accident, the few remaining family members had wept, copiously and long, including his Aunt Dorothy. She'd believed then that members of the medical profession could work miracles and so it was bound to be only a matter of time before Erik was once again the perfectly beautiful child he'd been prior to that Sunday afternoon. But it was not to be, and Dorothy was dutiful in arranging his frequent returns to surgery. She packed his bag and saw him into the Daimler, then stood at the front door until the chauffeur had driven out of sight. And turning every time to look out the Daimler's rear window, Erik had seen his aunt make a face before going back inside the house.

It was Henry, the chauffeur, who oversaw the admitting procedures, who made sure Erik was safely installed in his hospital bed, who placed a large caring hand on the small boy's head, saying, "There's a good lad," before regretfully leaving. Only Henry had sought to offer consolation, had been in the least sympathetic to the child's undiminished fear. "You'll be right as rain in no time, and home again," Henry said every time, producing some boiled sweets from his uniform pocket before marching away in his military fashion. Erik several times heard him tell one or the other of the nursing sisters, "Look after the lad now, won't you?" or "Have a care to leave a night light for the boy. He finds the dark worrisome."

Erik had had, in those early days, a terror of darkness. Very quickly he'd discovered that it was his ally, and not something to fear. And when his body had mended, wide awake when the rest of the household lay sleeping, the boy had gone down the wide staircase to turn cartwheels on the Aubusson carpet, to walk the countertops of the kitchen barefoot, pretending they were high wires, to dance about on the wet early-morning lawn—all acts of useless defiance directed toward Aunt Dorothy who so prized her carpet, her immaculate countertops, and who railed against hapless guests who chanced to set foot upon the closely cropped grass.

Twenty-two surgical procedures in three years, and then his aunt had shipped him off to boarding school with no concern for the type of reception he might meet in this upper-class jungle of smug, vicious little members of the peerage. These future dukes and earls and lords were masters of creative cruelty, geniuses at the art of torment, and set about the task of demoralizing and victimizing the new boy, the monstrosity, with manic determination. Erik's only recourse had been to seek knowledge in the school library, reading up on ways to defend himself and strengthen his body, and perfecting his skills in the dead of night when the wearied little shits, exhausted from a day's active abuse of one small child, slept sprawled in their tidy beds. He imagined acts of vengeance, dreamed of a moment of triumph when he would make them all see how truly badly they'd behaved. But, of course, it never came. He dared not take on singlehandedly dozens of opponents who'd happily have ground him into the dust. So what he did instead was concentrate on music, picking up his instruction from the point at which his father had left off. To evade the other boys he spent hours in the music room after lessons, attempting ever more difficult pieces, practicing scales and exercises and committing to memory entire concertos, and not merely those composed for piano but ones for trumpet, or violin, or harp, as well as others intended for bassoon, or flute, or cello. So that when they found him, as they inevitably did, and began their poking and taunting and physical assaults, he played fully orchestrated suites inside his head, conducting whole orchestras while playing solo piano, or flute, or contra bassoon. The blows fell upon him but he paid them no mind, lost to the swelling crescendos only he could hear.

No one, not even the masters, had cared. Only Henry, when he came with the Daimler to collect Erik at the start of each school holiday, expressed the least interest in his well-being. And because of Henry's position as employee, Erik was not permitted to spend any of his time at home in the older man's company. Aunt Dorothy frowned on fraternization between the classes, and Erik must always remember, she told him repeatedly, that he had been born into a family of high standing and must behave accordingly. Which did not include socializing or even conversing with the chauffeur.

When, at seventeen, Erik was leaving for New Jersey to attend the American university that had been quick to accept him, Henry drove him to the airport, saw Erik's bags safely into the hands of a porter, then went with him to the check-in desk. Before leaving him at the departures lounge, Henry had taken hold of Erik's hand and held it in both his own. ''I hope life is good to you, Erik,'' Henry had said. ''God knows, you deserve it.'' Then he'd touched two fingers to the brim of his peaked cap, and marched out of Erik's life forever. He remained in Aunt Dorothy's employ for another six years, then retired to a small inherited cottage in Surrey, where he lived four more years before he died. Henry was the only one to whom Erik had ever written, the only one who'd remembered Erik's birthday and sent a card each year. Henry alone, with his limited contact, had provided sufficient proof of his caring to give Erik the courage to try to make a life for himself.

And now there was Marisa, this tender-hearted girl who could weep over the small fragment of his history Erik had elected to offer. This girl represented his salvation, yet he was so mired in a lifetime's anger that all he could do was hurt her repeatedly in order to prove the truth of her caring. It was wrong of him, and as cruel in its own way as the things those boys had done all those years before.

''It was hateful of me to do that to you,'' he said now ''Please forgive me.''

''I forgive you, Erik. It wasn't hateful at all.'' She accepted the handkerchief he gave her and blotted her eyes. ''I want you to feel you can tell me anything. I'm just sorry your life has been so unhappy.''

He had to wonder how much proof he was going to require before he accepted that her caring was in no way synthetic, not generated by curiosity or, worse, by some perverse streak.

"It's something I seem unable to stop myself doing," he tried to explain.

"I know," she said. "It's hard to trust people."

She truly did understand. It staggered him. Placing his arm around her shoulders, he drew her to him, appalled at the way the past was constantly interfering with his present contentment. "I do trust you," he told her, for this evidently was the truth. "I simply have no experience of exchanging confidences, of holding extended conversations, of talking at all."

"But the best of it is the talking part, Erik. You could tell me absolutely anything and it would only make me love you more. I like to think you'd want me to come to you when there are things I need to talk about."

"I would, I do."

"I'd do anything for you, anything. I wish you'd believe that." She sat back from him, her hands fastening to his forearms. "I don't know *why* I love you, not really. I mean, I don't have just one reason, and I don't know how it happened. I only know that I do, and it's very real. When you came to dinner that first night, all I could think was: I could make you happy. And I know I could; I can. I know you wonder all the time why I would pick you to love. I know you do wonder about that, because every time we're together, I can feel you asking questions; I can almost *hear* you. But what you don't understand, what I can't make you see, is that I'm on the inside of me, too, and can't see the outside. Just the way you're on the inside of you. Nobody ever sees their own outside, Erik. That's the part *everybody else* sees. So you see me, and you have your picture of me. And I see you, and I have my picture of you. And I'd bet you anything that if we could actually have those pictures and hold them in our hands to show each other, neither one of us would believe for one single minute that that's the way either one of us actually looks. *Because we don't see ourselves!* Do you get it?"

"My God, you're incredibly bright!"

At once she smiled. "You think so?"

"I think one day you're going to be a woman to reckon with."

"Right! Whatever that means."

"You know precisely what it means."

"I guess. I *wish* we could make love."

"Is it out of the question?"

"I don't know. I don't know if people do. Have you noticed it's something they never write about in books—whether or not people do it at times like this?"

"It'll wait." He kissed her forehead.

"It's only a few days." She rested in his embrace for several long moments, thinking. Then she announced, "I have an idea, a wonderful idea. In fact, it's a sensational idea. Let's go upstairs!"

Feeling rarely childlike, caught up in her sudden enthusiasm, he let her hurry him upstairs to his room, then stood and watched, bemused, as she locked the door. Then, turning, she said, "Take off your clothes!"

"Oh, now, just . . ."

"Come on, do it." She tugged at his jacket. "You'll like this, I promise."

Doubtfully, he began to undress while she stripped down to her underpants and then folded back the bedclothes. "I love watching you undress," she said, waiting for him. "I love seeing your body, the way you move. And best of all, I love touching you. Come here and lie down with me."

He obeyed and she curled up against him, whispering, "*You're* not having a period. So *I* can make love to *you*. Now you'll know what it's like when you do this to me."

Then she gave herself over to an examination of his body that was as intense and prolonged as any he'd made of her. She took her hands and mouth over his body, kissing and stroking, probing and caressing until she was playing him in the way the boy he'd once been had, in self-defense, played entire symphonies in his head in order to save himself from going mad with loneliness and despair.

She tracked the passage of the slim raised scars that

traversed his body, the one that ran horizontally across the base of his belly, another that lay across his right hip, the twins that sat precisely down the center of both thighs, the slick, slightly raised scar that began inside his left shoulder and went halfway down his back. And as she ran her tongue over the evidence of what had to have been unimaginable pain, she concentrated on healing him. Her hands and lips and tongue could erase the evidence of his torment; she could, with her personal magic, make him whole—if not in the eyes or minds of others—to himself. Can you feel how I love you? she silently intoned. Do you feel it? Can you tell? You must see it, know it! Believe in us! she willed through her ministrations.

Rapaciously she tended to him, without permitting him to touch her. She dined on him, a lavish banquet. She gorged herself on his flesh and displayed for him her newly acquired skills and some she was only just discovering. And throughout she gauged his reactions by the sound of his breathing, through the tremors that shook him. She showed him the way along a lengthy winding path toward rapture, determined he should know a happiness as great as her own. Her determination was blended with sorrow for the little boy who'd been so torn apart, so mangled, and so ultimately deprived by what had started out to be a jolly Sunday outing. She would make up for his years of hiding and isolation; she would be his deliverance. And in return, he would allow her to be with him, to hear his music, to learn the many things he had to teach her, and to sleep away her nights at his side.

When it was done, she lay with her head on his chest listening to the antic drumming of his heart, her arm possessively enclosing him, as she vowed, "I'll always love you, Erik. You'll never have to be alone again."

Decimated, he could only hold her while tears leaked from his eyes. One day, he reminded himself, just as she'd come so unexpectedly bringing with her his life, so she would leave again, taking it away. But until that day, he would treasure each moment of the time he spent with her. He would learn to trust her and to trust the part of himself that loved her, because he knew without question that it was the best part of him—the salvaged remnants of the battered boy.

For quite some time he could do no more than weave his fingers through her abundant hair while he underwent ever-milder aftershocks that at last ebbed and left him utterly at peace and even, quite possibly, happy.

13

AT THE END OF MAY MARISA BEGAN TO GET PANICKY.
"I'm so far behind in my work," she told Erik over the
telephone. "I'll never pass my finals. And if I don't
graduate, Dad'll go crazy. I haven't even looked at the
last of the novels we were supposed to do for English.
I'm months behind in French. And forget math."

"Bring your books," Erik told her. "Raskin can help
with the mathematics. I will work with you on the French
and English."

"But I don't even know Raskin," she protested. "I've
never even met him."

"He'll be happy to help you."

"And how can you help with the French and English?"

"First of all, what is the novel you didn't read?"

"*Northanger Abbey*, by Jane Austen."

"Fine, bring your copy with you. I have another here
somewhere."

"And what about the French?"

"I was born in France," he reminded her. "My father
was French and always, in private, spoke to me in
French. For the first seven years of my life, I was completely bilingual. I am still fluent."

"You honestly wouldn't mind?"

"I would be delighted and so, I'm sure, would Raskin.

132

You may come now, if you like. I'll send Raskin to collect you."

She was about to question this when, turning the window, she saw it was still daylight. "Let me check with Dad at the office, and I'll call you right back."

Cameron had no objections. "That's very decent of Erik," he said. "Don't take advantage, Keed. And make sure you say thank you."

"No, Dad. I thought I'd spit on his shoes as I was leaving." She laughed. "I can't get over the way you think I'm such a ninny I don't even know how to say please and thank you, as if you and Kitty haven't been going, *'What do you say, Risa?'* to me my whole life long."

Cameron laughed. "Give Erik my best. And by the by, don't you think we should do a little something, make some kind of gesture to show we appreciate all the time he's devoted to you?"

"Definitely. I was planning to buy him a present."

"Well, good. For now, why don't you take one of the bottles of that Armagnac he likes?"

"Great! I will. I won't be late, I promise."

"See you later, Keed."

She called Erik back, and he said Raskin would come at once.

Five minutes later, she was waiting outside with her books in a big canvas carryall and the bottle her father had suggested. She'd long been curious about Raskin, having pictured him—based solely on their short telephone conversations—as a big, burly man with black hair and bulging biceps. She was therefore mightily surprised when a black Mercedes pulled up and a slim, good-looking, sandy-haired, hazel-eyed man jumped out and came around to open the door for her before extending his hand and saying, "Hi. It's about time we met. I'm Raskin."

"Hi." She shook his hand. "Do you have a first name?"

"Everyone does," he hedged.

"Well, if you're going to call me Risa, which you are, then I need to called you something more personal than Raskin."

He smiled at her, all but assaulted by the combination of her exceptional beauty and her warm, unassuming manner. He fully understood at first sight of her why Erik was so hopelessly in love with the girl. She had a directness and a lack of pretension that were so in contrast to what her tall, cool beauty led one to expect that it turned him somewhat tongue-tied. It was flabbergasting to think that this was the girl who loved Erik, the girl who'd left that imperious message demanding Erik return home at once, the girl who was regularly making love, and obviously liking it, with Erik. Fucking unbelievable! he thought. "Call me Hal," he told her, hefting her bag of books onto the back seat of the car.

"Hal," she repeated as he climbed into the driver's seat. "I'm happy to meet you finally. I really hope it's not an imposition, Erik's asking you to help me with my math."

"Not a bit. I minored in math, and at one point—before the war—I even thought I might prefer teaching to engineering."

"You were in Vietnam?"

He nodded, his jaw going tight, his eyes on the road.

"I'm sorry," she said inexplicably, and he glanced over to see she actually did look sorry. For some reason, her saying these two words made him feel absolved in a way. And he thought if she could do that for him with just two words, she must be working miracles with Erik. Certainly since her advent into his life Erik had changed, not in ways anyone else might perceive, but subtly. He no longer barked commands over the intercom, but requested that Raskin do this or that, and often thanked or commended him on jobs well done. Erik still worked facing the wall, still clung to darkness and almost never went outside in daylight. But his bearing had changed; he exuded well-being. He was loved. And by this girl. Raskin could understand Erik's reactions. He wasn't entirely sure he understood what motivated Risa, though. But he was confident he'd know soon enough. For one thing, Erik had to be extremely sure of her to trust her alone with Raskin, knowing as he did Raskin's predilection for women and his abiding determination never to become involved in any binding fashion with one. He'd never harmed a woman physically. He was not an abusive man. He simply felt murderous when a woman harbored expectations of him. He was incapable of forcing his attention span to spread beyond a few hours, or a night. If you cared, you got killed.

"Is this your car?" Risa asked him.

"It's Erik's. Everything is Erik's."

"Does that bother you?" she asked incisively.

"It's the only way I'd have it. He enjoys the cars, their style, their power. To me, they're just hunks of machinery that'll get you from point A to point B. I'm not interested in possessions. They only bog you down."

He pulled the car to a stop at the front of the house so that it was nose to nose with the Lamborghini, then jumped out to give her a hand out of the car, saying, "Erik's finishing up some work. So we'll go over the math first, if that's okay with you. I've got fresh coffee made. We have a couple of hours, then I'll whip up some dinner while you and Erik work on your French and good old Jane Austen."

She made a face. "I can't even get past the first page. Her stuff's so boring."

"Old Jane grows on you, if you let her, if you can see the humor."

"You like Jane Austen?"

"I don't hate her," he said, going ahead to carry her book bag into the kitchen. "Will you be okay here?" he asked her. "If not, we can shift to the library."

"I didn't know there was a library."

"Oh sure," he said, reaching for two cups. "Coffee?"

"Yes, please."

"The library's in the living room. Press a couple of buttons and the two walls opposite the fireplace open up to show you all the books. Erik loves gadgets. The whole house is filled with them. Buttons to open the doors by remote control, buttons to turn the appliances on or off, buttons for the telephones and intercom, buttons to switch over from heat to air-conditioning, buttons to turn on the TV or the radio or to activate a tape." He smiled like a proud father speaking of a brilliant but erratic son.

"There must be a thousand miles of wiring in this house. Cream and sugar?"

"Yes, please. How long have you worked for Erik?"

"What is it, three years? About that." He carried the cups over to the table and sat down opposite her.

"Thank you," she said, her eyes on him as she tasted the coffee. "It's very good. I love coffee. It's as if you can taste the country it came from when you drink it. I imagine people in bright printed clothes in Jamaica. Or dark-skinned Italians walking between rows of coffee plants. Or maybe South Americans, Colombians, say, all in white, with white bags over their arms, picking beans."

Raskin laughed. "That's some imagination you've got."

"Yeah," she laughed with him. Then quietly she asked, "You love Erik, don't you?"

The question rocked him.

"I know you do," she went on. "I know how much you do for him, and you wouldn't do half of it if you didn't love him. I was wrong about the way I thought you'd look but I wasn't wrong about the way you are. You've been good to him."

"People should be," he said, quite dangerously moved by her and her candor. "Erik is unique and pretty amazing, all things considered."

"Yes," she agreed. "I think so, too."

Raskin smiled at her. "I know that. Now let's crack these books."

"It's social satire," Erik was explaining. "You have to take everything she says and turn it, hold it in such a way that you can see she's mirroring the manners of the time, the fads and fancies. And making mock of it all. She's painting you a portrait, then laughing and saying, 'Can you believe how ridiculous these people are, how trifling and petty their concerns?' "

"I don't get any of that. It just puts me to sleep."

"Concentrate," he insisted. "If you can write rational answers to the examination questions, you'll come through beautifully. You simply have to understand her point in writing the things she does. Satire," he said again, "subtle and devilish."

She chewed on the eraser of her pencil, listening. He was enjoying himself in his role as tutor. He'd already reviewed the French with her, and at the sound of his perfect accent, she'd fallen in love with him all over again. It seemed as if there wasn't anything he didn't know. He'd read every book ever written, studied every subject ever taught. And he was able to simplify anything in order to make it readily comprehensible to her. He'd brought her upstairs to the bedroom to work, leaving the kitchen to Raskin. They were sitting together on the floor with their backs against the end of the bed and books and notes strewn across the carpet. A cluster of candles provided the only light. Tossing aside her pencil, she suddenly lunged at him, biting his neck and laughing.

"I can't *take* anymore!" she cried. "No more Jane Austen or I'll lose my mind."

She toppled him to the floor, chewing at his lapels and growling. "No more! No more!" Snorting and tossing her hair, she flopped down on top of him, snuffling with her nose against his neck, tickling his ribs. "I never want to hear that woman's name again as long as I live! And if you don't promise right now to let me off the hook at least for the rest of tonight, I'll be forced to tickle you to death."

Laughing and trying to fend off her groping fingers, he managed to say, "No more. I promise."

"Thank God!" she groaned, and collapsed atop him, letting her arms and legs go any which way.

His laughing subsiding, he pushed the hair back from her face, then ran the tip of his finger across her eyebrow and down her nose to her lips. Lulled by her apparent torpor, he was startled when her mouth shot open and her teeth closed around his finger. She began growling again and shaking her head around his captive finger, like a puppy with a stick. Again, he began to laugh. From someplace very distant, the memory came to him of wrestling with his father in a room where sun poured in through wide-open windows, bathing them in light and warmth, and giddy laughter floated along with the dust motes caught in the light. From his remembered vantage point on the floor, he could look over and see his mother's slender legs in the doorway, and hear her contributing laughter. It was a happy memory from long ago, returned to him intact by Marisa's playfulness.

Then the playfulness took a shift, and she was drawing each of his fingers in turn into her mouth, then licking between his fingers and across the palm of his hand. Instantly, matters turned flammable. His hand closing over the back of her head, he directed her mouth to his, immediately needful. Fumbling at their clothes, they made a hurried connection, and moved in greedy haste, Erik withholding and withholding until he knew she was on the verge of leaving him for the self-contained world of her private pleasure. Then he raced to meet her, to be with her and not left behind to imagine how it must be inside Marisa's world. It was suddenly started and as suddenly completed. Then they looked at each other and laughed. They were still laughing when Raskin announced over the intercom that dinner was ready any time they cared to come down.

"Can he hear us over that thing?" Marisa wanted to know.

"I hope to God not," Erik chuckled, biting her dear cleft chin. "I like to think you're my well-kept secret."

"Don't be crazy, Erik! He knows all about us."

"Why do you say that?" he asked, at once alert to possible menace.

"Of course he does," she said reasonably. "I mean, you send him out to buy me a diamond necklace; you send him out to buy fresh flowers for me every day; you ask him to tutor me; you and I disappear into this bedroom for hours at a stretch. He knows, and he approves, too. He really cares about you, you know, Erik. He's a good friend to you. I like him."

"I suppose you're right," he said, relaxing again. "I have moments of supreme stupidity when I think I'm invisible to the world and everyone in it."

"You may be to most people, but you're certainly not to me, or to Hal."

"Hal?"

"That's his name: Hal."

"I'm well aware that's his name. I'm just rather stunned that he told it to you."

"Why?"

"Because Raskin never tells anyone his name. It's some sort of protective device. The women he sees only know him as Raskin."

"Does he see a lot of women?" she asked, looking around for her underpants.

"Legions. Quite often they ring up, asking for him when he's not in. They usually stop after a time. They always sound so hope-filled the first time they ring, asking may they speak to Raskin. And they're invariably crushed when I say he's not available. More often than not, they don't bother to ring a second time. But some few do. He never sees any woman more than once."

"That's because he's afraid," she said, smoothing down her skirt. "He doesn't want to care about anyone, not counting you. It might have been the war, but I'll bet it was something else that didn't have a thing to do with the war. That has to be it, otherwise he'd be in touch with his family at least once in a while. And he isn't, is he, in touch with them, I mean?"

"Not that I know of."

"See! Something happened. I really do like him. He kind of reminds me of this big dog Meggie's family used to have. I can't remember what kind of dog it was, but he was huge and ferocious and he'd bare his fangs and snarl when kids came over to play. And Meggie's dad was always grabbing hold of his collar and dragging Charcoal—that was his name and he was a Rottweiler, I think—off to chain him up outside. But this one time Meggie dared me to go pet Charcoal, and I was scared silly, but I thought to myself, That dog's all show. So I went and let him smell my hands and petted him a bit, and then the big stupid pooch lay down and rolled over with his legs in the air, wanting me to scratch his stomach. Wait a minute, Erik. Your shirt's caught in your zipper." She deftly corrected the problem, then said, "Hal's like Charcoal. He just wants someone he trusts to scratch his stomach."

Erik smiled and kissed the top of her head. As they started out of the room, he said, "I don't recommend you try it. Aside from the fact that I'd probably detonate from sheer jealousy, Raskin might very well stab you in the hand with a bread knife or a pair of scissors."

"Hah!" she scoffed. "You men like to think you're so complicated and hard to understand, but you're all just big stupid pooches."

"For that compliment," he said at the top of the stairs, bowing from the waist, "I thank you from the bottom of my heart."

"Yeah!" she laughed. "Let's go eat. I'm starving."

It was the first time she'd sat down to a meal in Erik's home, and the first time the three of them dined together. It was just fine. She felt safe, protected, with not one but two men to look after her. Raskin was a good cook and had prepared halibut steaks broiled with lemon and butter, new potatoes, and slivered carrots, with a green salad and garlicky hot rolls. The three of them ate in hungry silence. Then Risa set down her knife and fork and said, "That was divine!" which, for some reason, set both Erik and Raskin to laughing loudly.

"What's so funny?" she asked, but neither of them was able to answer.

"It's just funny," Raskin said after a minute or two. "You're funny." He looked to see if Erik disapproved, but Erik was laughing wholeheartedly, nodding in agreement.

"She is," Erik declared when he was able to draw a breath, "*divinely* funny." Which set them off again.

Risa sat looking at the two of them, failing to get the joke, and finally said, "You're both batshit. I'll make the coffee." And she got up to start clearing the table, leaving the two men mopping their eyes and pounding the table.

"Batty as bedbugs," she told them, taking away their plates and depositing them on the counter. "Out to lunch, mentally AWOL, looney tunes. Brother!" She shook her head in pretended disdain, perfectly happy.

14

WITH THE HELP OF ERIK AND RASKIN, RISA MANAGED to get through the final exams. The talk all around her at school was of the parties everyone seemed to be planning. Several of the jocks even ventured to ask if she'd care to go to one or another, but she declined. She found it singularly odd to be in the midst of so many very young people. She herself felt, in many ways, far older and infinitely more mature. She intended to go only to the graduation ceremony. Otherwise, she was glad finally to be free of high school. She was also free, at last, to spend some time looking for the perfect gift to give Erik. In view of how pleased he'd been by her father's bottle of Armagnac, he was bound to go wild over a gift she'd give him—if she could only find something wonderfully unique.

Kitty said she had no objection to Risa's taking the car for the day, but couldn't resist asking, "Don't you mean to go to any of the parties your friends're bound to be havin'?"

Risa hoisted herself up to sit on the edge of the kitchen island to finish her morning coffee, saying, "You know perfectly well I haven't had one single friend since Meggie moved away. And I hardly ever hear from her anymore."

"You're never home to hear from anyone," Kitty said

mildly. "Seems like you spend every free moment with that Erik fella. He must be somethin' pretty special for you to be runnin' over there every chance you get."

Kitty was fishing, Risa knew. She'd been dropping hints about Erik since the night Risa and Cameron had argued about her purported music lessons.

For her part, having never laid eyes on the man, but well able to make a four out of two twos, Kitty had long since figured Risa and this fellow had something substantial going. Cameron was mostly closemouthed on the subject, only telling Kitty, "I trust him with Risa. He's no ordinary man."

"He's *very* special," Risa confirmed now, in part fairly desperate to discuss Erik with Kitty, who, being another woman, would understand; and in part very afraid Kitty might not understand and, because of her closeness to Cameron, might carry whatever Risa said back to him. "In fact," she continued casually, "I'm going shopping today to buy him a present for being so good to me."

"Oh?" Kitty's eyebrows lifted inquiringly, cigarette smoke hanging in a cloud around her head and shoulders.

"Your hair looks really good now," Risa said, able to see why her father would be attracted to Kitty. "I like your natural color, and this length, way better than all those little red curls."

"I always thought dirty-blond hair was a true curse," Kitty said, "but I'm fed up with payin' these women a fortune to mess it up. It'll probably go yella," she said, holding a strand out to look at it, "like my mama's before it turned pure white. I wouldn't mind the pure white, understand; it's the yella that gives me the shudders. The color of nicotine, my mama's hair was, before it finally turned." She let her hair drop and returned to the subject at hand. "So, you're off shoppin' for a gift for this special fella. And what d'you reckon you'll get him?"

"I wish I knew. Nothing ordinary, like shirts or ties or any of that boring stuff."

"How about cuff links? I always admire a man with a handsome set of cuff links."

"It's possible."

"Or maybe a cigarette lighter. Does he smoke?"

"Sometimes."

"What about cologne, or aftershave?"

"That's so boring. That's the kind of stuff you buy your father, not someone like Erik."

"Well, now," Kitty said, getting more of a picture from Risa's replies than Risa knew. "There's wallets, or key cases, or even a briefcase, if you're out to spend the money." Risa was shaking her head, so Kitty thought on aloud. "Okay, then. How about a tie clip, or maybe a money clip? Or what about . . . ?"

Kitty went on reciting suggestions, but Risa had an idea. Maybe it was vain of her, or presumptuous, but she'd latched on to the notion that Erik would really like a photograph of her. She could easily have one taken, then buy a good silver frame for it. As Kitty's voice hummed beneath her thoughts, she visualized the scene: She'd give Erik the package; he'd open it, and be totally knocked out. Or maybe he wouldn't like it at all. There were no photographs in his house, only the two portraits in the living room. What if it upset him? But why would that upset him? She knew she could never have a portrait of Erik to carry about with her, but she couldn't help believing he'd like one of her. And there was a photographer right in Darien who'd probably be able to take her picture on the spot if she walked in off the street and asked.

"You're not listenin' to a word I'm sayin'," Kitty complained, waving the smoke away from her face before putting out her cigarette.

"Sorry. I was thinking."

"Is there anything you want to tell me?" Kitty asked, folding her arms on the tabletop and looking meaningfully at Risa.

"Yeah," Risa said with a smile. "But I'm not going to. I'd better get going."

"I take it you've come up with an idea."

"I think so. I should be back in a couple of hours. You want anything while I'm out?"

"Where you gonna be?"

"Just in town."

"I'm low on cigarettes, if you wouldn't mind pickin' me up a carton. Wait and I'll fetch you some money."

"That's okay. You can pay me later." Risa was in a hurry now to get to town to see the photographer, and then go looking for the right frame.

Halfway into town, she wondered if she shouldn't go back and change clothes. She decided not to. She didn't want this photograph to be too stagey, too "dressed." A casual portrait would be better, and the cotton dress she had on would be fine.

She was in luck. The photographer had had a cancellation and could take her right away. All he had to do was set the lighting, if she didn't mind sitting on the stool in the studio for a few minutes while he did this and that, checking every so often to see how the lights were falling on her.

"I think this is going to be nice," he told her. "Just head shots, right? You sure you don't want any background?"

"Nothing."

"Okay." He spent several minutes positioning the camera, turning dials, then came over to hold a light meter in front of her face. Back behind the camera, he looked at her through the lens and said, "You're a beautiful girl. These're gonna be beautiful shots."

She smiled reflexively, ready to dispute this observation, but he said, "Hold that!" and began making exposures, telling her to turn this way, then that, until he'd shot an entire roll. "I can have contact sheets ready for you to look at by tomorrow morning," he said, removing the exposed film from the camera and giving it a toss before catching it in his hand. "Normally, it'd be at least a week, but I'm kind of anxious to see these. I don't too often get the chance to shoot someone as photogenic as you. You don't have a single bad angle, not one," he complimented her, while she collected her shoulder bag and walked with him to the reception area. "I think you'll be very happy with these pictures."

After leaving the photographer's studio, she got into the car and began systematically visiting the antiques shops in town, in search of a frame. She found exactly what she wanted in the third place, an extravagantly ornate Victorian sterling-silver frame that would take an eight-by-ten print. She paid in cash, then waited while the proprietor lovingly wrapped the gift in several layers of tissue.

She almost forgot Kitty's cigarettes and had to go back to the variety store to get the carton of Kools. While she was waiting for her change, she noticed a row of imported cigarettes and on impulse bought a pack of Gauloises for Erik and, as an afterthought, some English Rothmans for Hal. She loved having people to buy things for. She daydreamed on the way home of someday shopping for Erik, deliberating over silk ties or dressing gowns; she even saw herself in a supermarket selecting imported cheeses or prime cuts of meat for him. She thought she could be very happy spending her days seeing to his needs, and spending her nights at his side in the music room, or in his bed. To sleep an entire night in that big bed with Erik was something she badly wanted and which she was determined to have, if she could just think of some way to work it out.

As she pulled into the driveway, the front door opened and Kitty came running out. Risa knew at once something was wrong. It showed in Kitty's face and in the graceless way she ran in her high heels over the gravel toward the car. Oh God, Risa thought, something's happened to Erik!

"What is it? What's wrong?" she asked, scrambling out of the car.

Kitty's face ashen and drawn, she dragged Risa into her arms and held her tightly to her cushiony breasts. "It's your daddy, Risa. They called right after you left. I been phonin' all over town tryin' to find you."

"What? What's wrong with him?"

Kitty's arms went even tighter around her, and she sought to free herself but Kitty held on with surprising strength. "There's no easy way to tell you," Kitty said, her lips against Risa's ear, her perfume and cigarette aroma rising richly into Risa's nostrils. "One of the secretaries was late gettin' to the office. She parked in the lot and was hurryin' inside when her eye was caught by your daddy's car sittin' with its motor runnin'. And when she took herself a closer look, she saw him slumped behind the wheel. She figured somethin' was wrong and went for help, but it was too late."

"Too late?"

"He's dead, Risa. Looks like he had a heart attack and it took him." She could feel Risa's denial in the way she began to turn her head back and forth, and struggled to escape Kitty's embrace. "Don't fight against it," Kitty told her. "I know it's gonna be hard for you, but don't fight it. Your daddy loved you better than anything in this world, and you're a lucky girl in that, 'cause he showed it to you. Now you're gonna have to begin lettin' him go. But I want you to know I'm here for you if you need me. D'you hear me?"

"*I have to call Erik!*" she cried, and broke free to go running into the house.

Trailing after her, Kitty watched Risa fly to the telephone and dial a number, wait, then ask to speak to Erik. Shaking, all but palsied, she waited. And then, gripping the receiver with both hands, she wailed, "Erik, I *need* you!" Something was said, then Risa put down the receiver and rushed into the living room to position herself by the windows, gripping the draperies as she stared out.

Kitty backed away to stand near the dining-room doors where she lit a cigarette, her eyes never leaving the girl. She'd guessed there was strong feeling on Risa's part for this Erik fella, but she'd seriously underestimated how strong it was. And it struck her as a downright pity that she was finally going to get to meet this Erik under such tragic circumstances. She stood quietly, smoking her cigarette, until she saw Risa start, her hand pulling so hard at the curtains she nearly brought them down. Then she ran to the foyer to open the front door.

Shifting slightly, Kitty had a clear view, and watched as Risa, sobbing out, "Erik, my father's dead!" threw herself into the arms of the man who entered. He reacted overtly, seeking to shelter her with his body. Kitty let her cigarette fall into the ashtray, her eyes on the two in the foyer, unable to believe that this was the man to whom Marisa had given her heart. A pitiful-looking creature with a face you might see in some side show, or in the aftermath of a five-day drinking spree; a man who'd suffered some truly terrible accident once upon a time; a man whose eyes slowly lifted to connect with Kitty's.

She'd never forget the moment, never forget the way those eyes beseeched her, begging her to understand how powerless he was to resist the love—Kitty could almost reach out and touch it, it was so real—that he had for this girl. Maybe at some other time she'd have given in to her immediate reaction to the sight of his face. But now, because she knew she herself would grieve for a long time to come over the loss of Cam, she could only give her unspoken approval to this man who'd come at a moment's notice because Risa claimed to need him.

"I'll make some coffee," Kitty said, and left the two of them there.

In the kitchen, with the percolator plugged in, she stood with her hands braced on the counter looking down at the floor, trying to take everything in. Cameron was gone; Risa had herself a lover whose face would cause most hearts to stop for a beat or two; all kinds of changes would be coming now. And she was too old, and knew too much about too many things to make rash judgments just on account of a man's face. Because whatever he might look like, that man had a heart full of love for a seventeen-year-old girl who'd just lost her daddy.

When she returned to the living room and set down the tray of coffee things, Risa was with Erik on the sofa. Upon seeing Kitty, Risa got up to volunteer herself into Kitty's arms. "Kitty," she whispered, "please . . ."

"There, there," Kitty consoled her. "Everything's gonna be all right. I'm Kitty," she introduced herself to Erik, keeping one arm around Risa's waist. "And you're Erik. It's right decent of you to come so quick."

Erik rose to take the hand she offered, stricken with gratitude for the woman's kindness. "Please sit with us," he said in a tuneful whisper that captured Kitty's complete interest and attention.

"This is the lull before the storm," Kitty said, seating herself without thinking in Cam's favorite chair. "There's gonna be a whole lot needs doin'."

"Where is he?" Risa asked, on the sofa again close to Erik. "Can I see him?"

"They took him over to Norwalk Hospital," Kitty told her. "There's gonna have to be an autopsy so they can say the cause of death. I called his lawyer and the lawyer's tryin' to get hold of your Uncle Harmon to get permission."

"Why can't *I* give it?" Risa wanted to know.

" 'Cause you're not of age, honey."

"Well, then, why can't you give it?"

" 'Cause I'm not kin, Risa. It's gotta be a member of the family."

"I want to *see* him!" Risa reached for Erik's hand. Her grip was fierce. "I want to see my father, to say good-bye." Her voice cracked, and she broke. Erik held her while she cried, his eyes again on Kitty.

"I will help in any way I'm able," he told the woman, deeply saddened by the loss of the only man outside Raskin who'd ever treated him simply as another man.

Kitty nodded, knowing the only way Risa was going to get through the next few days was with this man's help. It was real odd about his face, Kitty thought, but the more she saw it the less it seemed to bother her. Maybe it was because there were other things about him that were downright attractive—that voice, for one, and the build on him, for another, and his hands, which were just plain beautiful. She didn't think she'd ever seen another pair of hands that were their equal. And his eyes. He had the eyes of a boy, but filled with a grown man's wisdom and apprehension. And one thing was absolutely certain: All you had to do was look at the way he sought to comfort Risa, the tender way he stroked her through her tears, and any fool could see he might not look too fine, but his feelings were all in the right place.

"I'm glad you're here for her," Kitty told him. "Have some coffee."

The church was jammed with friends and business associates who'd come, some of them, from as far away as California and Vancouver, even two from London; there were former classmates from St. Paul's, and men he'd gone to college with. His brother Harmon and his wife Tenny, along with their two sons, Harmon Junior, and Rolly, had flown in from Boston. There were two distant cousins from upstate Connecticut, and Great-Aunt Patience who, at eighty-seven, was still fit and trim but quite deaf.

An audible murmur started up at the back of the church when Risa entered on Erik's arm, with Raskin and Kitty close behind. Lost to her grief, Risa was unaware. But the other three were not. Kitty automatically drew closer to Raskin, and the two of them cast stony glances to each side, quieting the perturbed whispers.

They made it all the way to the front of the church in the ensuing silence when suddenly, loudly and very clearly, Great-Aunt Patience demanded, "Who *is* that creature?" Her question fell like a grenade into the center of the silence that held for a few seconds before the whispering started up again and people all around tried shushing the elderly woman.

Risa had stopped dead, her hand fastening around Erik's. Turning slowly, she scanned the crowd until she located the source of the disturbance. Casting a look of sheer hatred at the old woman, Risa turned back and slid into the pew. Seated, she leaned close to Erik to whisper, "I love you. *I love you!*" Then she straightened and stared straight ahead.

The morning was hot, the sky deeply blue and dotted with amorphous clouds. Risa blinked against the sun, clinging fast to Erik's hand, trying to make what was happening stay real. Things seemed to come back and forth, in and out of focus. They were putting her father in a box into the ground. He was never coming home again, never going to call her Keed, never going to argue or praise her. She'd never again sit with him to eat a meal, or race him to the end of the driveway, or leap up to knock his shots away from the hoop fixed over the garage door. Without a hint of warning, or any meaningful last words, he'd gone away for good and always. She knew it was only his body, not her actual father they were burying, and she couldn't stop wondering where he'd gone, if there was some place people went when they were finished with their lives. She knew it was infantile and stupid, but she wanted to believe he was with Rebecca, that the two of them were up there, looking down at her from the sky.

She didn't hear a word that was said, not by any of the several people who eulogized her father, or by the minister. Her only anchor was Erik's hand, which remained joined to hers throughout the entire grim event. At one point she turned to look at Erik and then at the crowd of faces, all of which, she saw, were directed towards them. Her hand going tighter around Erik's, she realized what an enormous act of courage he had undertaken in escorting her on this day. He'd come out into the merciless glare of morning, subjecting himself to the eyes of dozens, solely for her sake. And she was infuriated by these so-called friends of her father's who were paying no attention to his last rites but were instead gawking at the man she loved. How dare they? she wondered, enraged. Her anger robbed her of her tears. Lifting her chin, straightening her spine, she sat staring them down, her hand linked with Erik's, and wished them all in hell.

After the service, the crowd evaporated. Only the minister and Uncle Harmon came to talk with her, to express their condolences. Not even Aunt Tenny or her cousins came near. Raskin and Kitty stood a little ways off, smoking and talking quietly.

"We've got to get back to Boston," her Uncle Harmon said apologetically. "If there's anything at all you need, Marisa, please call me."

"There's nothing I need, Uncle Harm. Thank you for coming."

Her uncle offered his hand to Erik, then turned to go. Touched by his humanity, Risa ran after him to give him a hug. "I'm glad you came, Uncle Harm. My dad always thought the world of his little brother."

"He was a good man," Harmon told her. "I loved him and I'll miss him."

And then it was over. Raskin and Kitty returned to the house with Erik and Risa. The two of them went off to the kitchen to put together some lunch, leaving Erik with Risa in the living room.

"What you did today was wonderful, Erik. I'll never forget it. I know it was awful for you. And I hate those people, those idiots!"

"They couldn't help it," he said, trying to be charitable, but still feeling flayed by the hundreds of eyes that had picked over him like vultures on a carcass.

"Oh yes, they could," she disagreed heatedly. "I hate them all, every last one of them, including that senile idiot, Aunt Patience. God!" she said, forgetting her anger as she looked around the room. "What am I going to do, Erik? What am I going to *do*?"

"Things will sort themselves out," he promised. "For now, take one step at a time."

"I keep thinking I'm so lucky to have you, then I get scared something's going to happen to you, too, and I won't have anyone."

"Nothing's going to happen to me," he said, holding her.

"I feel so *guilty*, Erik. When Kitty came running out the other day, the only thing in my mind was: 'Something's happened to Erik.' I never once thought it could be Dad. As if he wasn't even important enough for me to think about."

"You know that's not the truth, Marisa. You loved your father, and he knew it."

"You think so?" She searched his eyes. "D'you honestly think so?"

"I know it. There's no need for you to feel guilty."

"Erik, would you ever marry me?"

"This is not the time to discuss something like that."

"I'm not saying tomorrow. I'm asking would you?"

He lifted the hair back from her face, then with one finger caught the tear that spilled from her eye. "Oh yes," he said very softly, "I would."

15

THREE DAYS AFTER THE FUNERAL, AND AFTER THREE nights of sleeping alone in her room because Erik insisted it would be most disrespectful to her father if she failed to observe a proper period of mourning, Risa and Kitty drove to the lawyer's office in Greenwich for a reading of her father's will.

The lawyer, Archie Henderson, an old friend of Cameron's who had been to the house for dinner many times with his wife, greeted Risa by saying, "I can't believe he's gone. It must be tough on you, Marisa. I want you to know I'm available at any time if you need help."

She thanked him politely, disinclined to be affable since he was one of the ones who'd stared so blatantly at Erik.

After offering coffee, which neither Kitty nor Risa wanted, Henderson sat down behind his polished desk and opened a file. "Your father," he began, "made some changes in his will only a few weeks before he died." He paused to look at both women above the tops of his reading glasses. "He was very concerned for your future, Marisa; most concerned you be secure in the event anything untoward should happen to him. He told me he had put a lot of thought into the changes he made. I hope you agree with his thinking." Removing the blue-jacketed

152

will from the file, he said, "I'll skip the standard boiler plate and go directly to the main points.

"First of all, since his death has occurred while you are still legally in your minority, Miss Katherine Hemmings is appointed your guardian. She is also appointed co-executor and trustee of the estate together with myself, in conjunction with the Connecticut Fidelity Bank. It was your father's wish that the ownership of the dwelling on Butlers Island in the town of Darien, county of Fairfield in the state of Connecticut, should pass into the hands of Katherine Hemmings with the proviso that the minor child reside in this dwelling for as long as she so wishes.

"There are several charitable bequests, including two to alumni associations of the schools your father attended. In addition to the foregoing, it was your father's wish that Miss Hemmings be the recipient of an annual income of twenty-five thousand dollars, this income separate from and in no way to be used for the maintenance of the minor child. Along with this, Miss Hemmings is to receive title to one vehicle, a 1969 Ford Fairlane station wagon currently registered in the name of the deceased.

"The rest, residue, and remainder of the estate is to be held in trust for Marisa, with one third of the total capital payable on her eighteenth birthday, another third payable on her twenty-first birthday, and the balance to be paid on her thirtieth birthday. Any and all expenses for the minor child shall be paid for by the trustees from the interest income earned on the capital investments, and no reasonable request by the minor child for access to the capital shall be denied by the trustees or co-executors.

"There is a final term which does not directly concern either of you," Henderson said, once more opening the file to remove a sealed envelope. "Your father asked that this letter be delivered to Mr. Erik D'Anton. I've spoken with Mr. D'Anton's assistant on the telephone and have been told it is acceptable to Mr. D'Anton that you be given this letter, Marisa, to give to him. Have you any questions?"

Studying the envelope back and front, Risa answered, "No, none."

Kitty said, "What happens if Risa doesn't want me for her guardian?"

At this, Risa's head shot up. "Of course I want you!" she exclaimed. "Did you think I wouldn't? Don't you want to?"

"Sure, I do, hon. I was just coverin' all your bets, that's all."

"My bets don't need covering," Risa said, standing. "Thank you very much, Mr. Henderson. May I have a copy of that?" She pointed to the will.

"If you wish. I can have my secretary Xerox it while you wait."

"You don't have to do that. Just mail it to me."

In the car driving home, Kitty said, "I didn't know a thing about the house or the car or the money, none of it."

"Kitty, I'm glad he did that. Don't worry about it. If he hadn't left you those things, I'd've given them to you myself out of the estate. You've been good to both of us. And you've been so nice to Erik. I love you with all my heart for that. I really do. I guess you've figured out how I feel about him."

"I guess so," Kitty agreed. "I hate to change the subject, but you and I have to do somethin' about your daddy's things. Truth to tell, I find it truly distressin' to keep comin' on things of his. I'm havin' a whole load of trouble even wearin' my mules, what with hearin' Cam make some wisecrack in my head every time I slip 'em on. The other mornin' I must've lost me an entire hour just comin' across his shirts waitin' to be ironed. I figure we should clear everything out and give it to the Goodwill or the Sally Ann. How d'you feel about that?"

"Will you help me?" Risa asked, feeling all at once too young to cope.

"Well, sure I will. We can do it this afternoon, after lunch. I already went ahead and got some boxes from the market."

"I'm not hungry."

"You're gonna eat!" Kitty said firmly. "I'm not havin'

you collapsin' again, the way you did last winter when you starved yourself half to death. You think your daddy would like you to quit eatin'?''

"No."

"So, okay. We'll have us some lunch, then we'll get his room cleared out."

It started out well enough. The two of them took all the clothes from his closet and put them on the bed. Then, while Kitty removed the hangers and began folding sports jackets and trousers into the boxes, Risa started going through the chest of drawers. She dumped his underwear into a carton, followed by his socks, then returned the empty drawers to the chest. But then she came to the sweaters, some of which still bore his scent. Burying her face in Cameron's favorite cashmere pullover, Risa burst into tears almost at the same moment Kitty, holding a suit in her arms, began quietly crying.

Kitty looked over at Risa. The two of them laughed, chagrined, then cried even harder.

"This is truly the worst thing I've ever had to do," Kitty admitted. "I loved your daddy, you know, Risa. I dearly loved him."

"I know," Risa told her, gulping down sobs. "I know you did. Kitty, how're we going to live without him?"

"We'll muddle through somehow. Let's sit down here a minute." Kitty put aside the suit before taking the sweater from Risa's hands. "Set yourself down here with me and let's have us a serious talk."

Sitting on the floor surrounded by half-filled boxes, Kitty took hold of Risa's hand. "We need to have us a heart-to-heart," she said, "so we both of us know where we stand."

"Okay," Risa sniffed, mopping her face on her sleeve.

"I'm not your mama, but I'm your friend. And I want you to think of me as your friend when I ask you for a straight answer, Risa. Are you sleeping with your Erik?"

Risa flushed darkly, but replied, "Yes."

"That's what I thought. Are you takin' any precautions?"

"Yes, I am."

"Okay, that takes care of that. Now I know it's early days yet, but have you given any thought to what you're gonna do next? I know you planned to take a year off. Is that still your plan?"

"Yes, it is."

"And after that, what'll you do?"

"There won't be any 'after that,' Kitty. As soon as Erik feels the time is right, I'm going to marry him."

"You don't think you're just a tad young?"

"I'm over the age of consent, and less than a year away from majority."

"You're talkin' as if you think I'm gonna be against you, Reese. This is me, Kitty, and we're talkin' friend to friend. Remember?"

"I'm sorry."

"That's okay. Now when d'you figure Erik's gonna think the time is right?"

"I don't know. We haven't actually discussed it. I just asked him if he'd marry me, and he said he would."

"You asked him, huh?"

"Yes, I did. He would never dare ask me. He'd be too afraid. But it's what we both want."

"You sure do know your own mind, always have done. Have you thought about what kinda life the two of you're gonna have? You saw what it was like the other day. Are you gonna be able to handle that for years to come?"

"Yes! What you don't seem to understand is that Erik never goes out during the day. And what he did coming to the funeral was the bravest, most wonderful thing anybody's ever done for me—not counting you or Dad. Erik loves me, Kitty. And I love him. I don't care what other people think. I only care about Erik."

"There may come a day when you have to care, Risa. There's a lotta people in this world who're gonna wanna know why a beautiful young girl like you's throwin' herself away on a man that looks the way he does. Now before you go gettin' yourself all riled up, it's not me we're talkin' about here. Anyone with eyes could see the two of you love each other. But not everyone's *got* eyes, if you catch my meanin'. And if, as you say, the man don't go out in daylight, what kind of life d'you imagine the two of you leadin'?''

''A very happy one.''

''Doin' what, exactly?''

''I don't know, Kitty. I mean, I guess I'll do things other married women do—cooking and cleaning, having babies.'' She spoke aloud of having babies and heard again Erik's adamant refusal even to discuss the possibility. She'd dared to mention it just last week and he'd simply turned and glared at her. His anger, when roused, was formidable and frightening. She understood it but didn't wish to anger him further. She'd give him room to grow accustomed to the idea and, in time, he'd be bound to agree.

''I wonder how we're gonna work this out,'' Kitty mused. ''I can't see you'll be spendin' a whole lotta time around here. And I sure don't much like the idea of rattlin' around alone in this big ole house.''

''Why don't you get Freed to move in with you? You said she's only got a crummy little apartment in Stamford.''

''Freed *loves* that crummy little apartment. No. I've been thinkin' maybe it's time for me to head back home. Oh, not right away. But if you're bound 'n' determined to marry Erik, then maybe I'll plan on goin' home. I still got some family, and you won't be needin' me.''

''But I will!'' Risa threw herself against Kitty. ''Don't go away! Even if I do marry, Erik, I'm still going to need you. You're the only family I've got left, Kitty. I'd die without you. I'd have no one to talk to woman to woman. Please don't think about going away. You always said you hated it there. You said you wouldn't be home a week and you'd be wanting to come back here. That's what you've always said.''

''I guess you're right,'' Kitty agreed, satisfied. She'd been wanting and needing confirmation of Risa's caring. ''Don't fret yourself. I'm not gonna go off and leave you. I just want you to promise me one thing.''

''What?''

''I want your word that no matter how late it gets to be, you come home nights and you sleep in your own

bed. I'm not gonna interfere with the two of you, but I'm
still responsible for you. And there could be trouble—
I'm not sure what kind, but some trouble—if word got
out I was lettin' you run wild. You can spend all the time
you like over to Erik's. And he can come here any time
he wants. But you've gotta promise me you'll sleep right
here under your own roof, until such times as the two of
you get legal.''

"Get legal?" Risa smile and wiped her eyes again on
her sleeve. "God! You've got some of the corniest expressions. And," she went on, her eyes glistening, "if
you're so hot on 'getting legal,' how come you didn't
mind all that secret carrying-on with Dad?''

"That was different. We were both adults, with not a
helluva lot to lose. But you're a young girl with her whole
life yet to live, in a town that loves gossip almost as much
as it loves booze, religion, and real estate, in that order.
Now! What say we get on with the job at hand?''

That evening, after they'd taken the boxes to the Goodwill drop-off, and after Risa had left to spend the evening
with Erik, Kitty walked slowly up the stairs and along
the hallway to Cameron's bedroom. She stood for a time
staring at the bed, and then at the empty closet, before
going inside and through to the bathroom. She'd saved
this job for last because she'd known it would be hardest
of all—disposing of the very personal items Cam had
touched daily.

With the wastebasket positioned on the toilet seat, she
opened the medicine cabinet and one by one cleared the
shelves, holding each item for a moment or two before
carefully placing it in the basket. His scented shaving
soap and brush, his heavy-handled blade shaver, his
toothbrush, his several combs, and his nail scissors; his
styptic pencils, the Ace bandage he'd used now and then
for the tricky knee he'd got playing hockey back when he
was a boy at St. Paul's, and his prescription pills.

It was the bottles of aftershave and cologne that finally
did her in. She removed the tops of each and smelled
them in turn, then replaced the tops tightly, and tearfully
put the bottles into the basket.

She remembered to clear the area around the tub and to retrieve the soap from the shower stall, then went out carrying the basket. In the kitchen, she slipped the contents into a plastic trash bag, sealed the top with a twist tie, then took the bag out the rear door, headed for the garbage bin. But at the last moment she had to stop and open the bag to root around inside and find the cologne. With the bottle safely tucked into the waistband of her skirt, she resealed the bag and dropped it into the bin before returning inside.

With a glass of Cam's Glenfiddich, she sat in his chair in the living room, periodically holding her wrist to her nose, breathing in Cam's scent.

Without warning, Risa would begin to cry. She'd think of something, remember an occasion with her father, and go to pieces. She kept apologizing until Erik drew her onto his lap and held her head against his chest. "Don't go on saying you're sorry, Marisa. I'm the last person on earth who needs an explanation for the way you're feeling now. When my parents died, I was not *permitted* to grieve. Aunt Dorothy wouldn't *allow* it; it simply wasn't *done*. One was expected to get on. It never entered her mind, the hateful bitch, that I was a small boy who'd lost a great deal. I will never forgive her her cruelty. It is only fitting that you should grieve. Your father was an honorable man with great integrity. No one can ever replace him, or fill the gap he's left. You must *never* apologize, *not to anyone*, for having loved enough to feel the loss."

It was the longest speech she'd ever heard him make. Eased and thoughtful, her tears gradually subsided, leaving her so wearied she fell asleep.

He sat unmoving for hours while she slept in his lap, respectful of her sorrow. He felt an immense sense of responsibility for her, as well as a kind of fraternal kinship. They had both now lost their parents. Two orphans, one aged seventeen and the other thirty-two. It was strange to think that one could be orphaned at any age and the pain would be identical. Age wasn't the factor that determined grief. It was the knowledge of what had

gone from your life forever and could never again be
duplicated. He envied her her freedom to mourn. It was
a necessary right that had been denied him by a mean,
self-indulgent woman with entirely superficial values
who'd failed to see beyond a small boy's outer injuries to
the deeper, more harmful ones underneath. That she still
lived, with her Aubusson carpet and immaculate countertops and untrod-upon lawns, filled him with outrage.
But he buried it. He had the satisfaction of knowing she
would die as she had lived: alone. And no one would
mourn her passing. But he, Erik, had found someone
who did care. In spite of the quite considerable odds,
he'd been blessed with this dear sleeping child who
claimed to want to marry him and be with him always.

Marisa slept on as if drugged and, at last, Erik lifted
her and carried her out to the car. She stirred briefly
when he was setting her down on the passenger seat, then
sank back into sleep.

He rang the doorbell and Kitty came.

"She's quite worn out," he told her, his whisper softer
than ever. "If you'd be good enough to direct me, I'll
carry her up to her room."

Kitty smiled, then turned to show him the way to a
bedroom that was exactly the one he'd imagined Marisa
would have: with a canopied four-poster bed, swagged
white curtains over the windows, and a menagerie of
stuffed animals loitering on the pillows.

Easing Marisa down on her bed, Erik backed away,
blinking in the offensive overhead light.

"Why not go down and fix yourself a drink?" Kitty said.
"I'll get Reese squared away and be down in a tick."

He thanked her and made his way down to the bar in
the living room to pour a balloon of Cameron's good
Armagnac before going to the wing chair. Settled, he
looked over to see the glass on the table beside the chair
where Cameron had always sat. And a bottle of Royall
Lyme bay rum. Noting all this, Erik sighed. More had
been lost here than he'd known. This woman had loved
Cameron. No wonder she was kind. Marisa's father
wouldn't have cared for an unkind woman.

"We saw Cam's lawyer today," Kitty said, pausing to

retrieve her Glenfiddich before resuming her seat. "Cam left a letter for you." She pulled an envelope from the waistband of her skirt and leaned forward to give it to him. "Reese was gonna give it to you, but I guess she forgot, what with one thing and another."

Erik took the envelope.

"If you want to be private when you read it, I can go make us some coffee to go with our drinks."

"No, no. Please, don't go. I would like to share this with you."

"Now why would you want to do that?"

In answer, he raised his eyes to hers, then indicated the bay rum.

They sat in silence for a time, their eyes on each other. Then Erik said, "Not long after I left Princeton, one of my professors recommended me for a job to an old friend of his. I was most apprehensive, but my professor's old friend was an exceptional man. He accepted my terms without equivocation; he accepted me without equivocation. Nothing he ever said or did was in any way judgmental or insincere. I trusted him, and in return he made further recommendations that resulted in establishing my credentials.

"Over the years, we'd talk now and then on the telephone, and he was always interested; he always had time. He was a rare man, generous and tolerant. And had I known how to go about it, we might have been friends. But I didn't know how, and so our contact was limited to occasional telephone calls. Until one day a year or so ago when he rang me to ask if I'd consider doing some minor renovations to his home. I agreed at once, and came here for the first time to discuss the matter with him." His hands lifted, signaling his inability to say more. Then he picked up the envelope.

The letter read:

Dear Erik,

I decided tonight after you came here to explain about the so-called music lessons that I've been avoiding admitting to something I've probably known since the night you came to look over the house more than a year ago. I know you love Risa, and I know she loves you. I don't have the right to make my daughter's decisions or to stand in the way of what she wants. So I thought I'd put it in writing, in case I never get around to saying it in person, although I have every intention of living to play with my grandchildren, that the two of you have my blessings. If fathers could handpick their sons-in-law, I'd have a hell of a hard time finding anyone I'd enjoy more as a son-in-law of mine. Risa's impulsive and hard-headed and stubborn sometimes, but she's funny and good-hearted and sharp as a tack. Look after her, and be happy the two of you.

With my love,
Cameron

Unable to speak, Erik handed the letter to Kitty.

Then the two of them sat and drank in the dark and shed tears for their friend.

16

THROUGHOUT THE SUMMER RISA ALTERNATED BETWEEN looking forward to the future and feeling morbidly guilty about the past. She'd reached a point where she was angry with her father for abandoning her so abruptly, and angry at being saddled with the ongoing chore of making her own decisions. It had been quite all right for her to make decisions while her father was alive because, always, in the back of her mind, was the thought that she'd have him to come home to, should anything go wrong. He'd be there to support her in every way. Now he was gone, and from one day to the next she couldn't think what to do with herself. Some days she was so bogged down in anger and frustration she didn't leave her room, and consoled herself by talking to Erik on the telephone. He was endlessly patient and compassionate, which only served to compound her guilt. She was wasting his time, taking him away from the important work he had to do now that his office building in Greenwich was in the construction stage.

She had entire catalogs of doubts and misgivings and could, at any time, launch into very vocal diatribes that were in essence recitations of her many sins of omission and failings. Everyone was far too tolerant of her, she thought, growing irritated with Kitty and even with Erik for allowing her to go on and on the way she did, while

163

one or the other or both of them sat and listened. Then she'd sink into shame, disgusted with herself for her misuse of people who loved her.

Mid-August she received a telephone call. It was the photographer.

"I came across these contact sheets and realized you never did come in for your prints. You still interested? There's some awfully nice shots here."

The call roused her from the apathy in which she'd been mired for weeks.

"I'll come right over now and have a look," she told him, then went to ask if Kitty minded her using the car.

"I don't mind. But how come you don't drive your daddy's car?"

"I'm *never* going to drive that car. We should probably sell it and get something else because I can't bring myself to go anywhere near it."

"You shoulda said so. I'll look into it." Kitty handed over the keys to the station wagon.

The photographer had gone ahead and made prints of half a dozen shots. "They were so good I couldn't resist," he told her. "Course, if you'd prefer some of the others, I'll be happy to print them."

"No, these are fine. Thank you so much." She paid him and went directly home, planning to give Erik the picture that same evening.

After a lengthy search of her room, she located the frame she'd bought in her book bag, along with the unopened envelope containing her diploma. Since her father hadn't been there to attend, there'd been no possibility of her going to the graduation exercises. The school had, in due course, sent along her final report card and the diploma. She hadn't been sufficiently interested even to look at these items. But she couldn't think why or when she'd put the envelope or the picture frame in the bag.

Pleased with the final results, she carried the framed photograph downstairs to show Kitty, who took hold of it and examined the picture asking, "You do this for Erik?"

"D'you think he'll like it?"

"Sure he will. I don't suppose you got any spares? I'd love to have me one of these."

"You would?"

"Uh-huh. Thought I'd keep it for target practice on my bedside table." Kitty laughed. "You got any more?"

"Yup. You really think he'll like it?"

"Lord, but you're thick sometimes, Reese! Course he will. That man would like anything you gave him, no matter what. And this is special, sure enough. Way better than some ole money clip."

"Great, because I'm going to give it to him tonight. In fact, I think I'll get dressed up and make it an occasion."

"You do that," Kitty encouraged her. "I'm gonna go see Freed, maybe go out for a drink or two."

Risa was quiet a moment, then said, "We're starting up again, aren't we? We've living our lives without him."

"Honey, it's supposed to be that way."

"I guess. But I keep feeling guilty."

"Well, don't! Just remind yourself your daddy wouldn't have wanted you to stop livin' because he did. And," she added, "for all you or I know, he's probably havin' a helluva good time wherever he is."

"I like to think that, too." Risa kissed Kitty's cheek before going off to her room to decide what she'd wear.

Taken by the idea of creating an occasion, she telephoned Raskin to say, "I'm going to bring over a bottle of champagne from the cellar. And I've got a present for Erik. Let's make it a little party. What d'you think?"

"Sounds good. I'll defrost some Cornish hens I've got in the freezer, and stuff their tiny bodies with a bunch of good things."

"It's going to be fun."

"I'll even wear a tie." Raskin laughed.

At nine, Erik came for her in the boat. As he pulled up to the dock, putting his hand out to assist her over the side, he said, "How very lovely you look!" and had to admire her for several moments before looping one arm around her waist and steering the boat away from the dock.

Upon arriving at the boathouse, instead of going

through the tunnel to the music room, he directed her onto the grass, leading the way to the rear of the house where, on the seldom-used terrace, Raskin had set up a table and chairs. Candles had been placed here and there, and Dave Brubeck was pouring out through speakers in the kitchen.

"This is so nice," Risa said, giving Erik first the Dom Pérignon and then the gift-wrapped picture.

"What is this?" he asked of the gaily wrapped package.

"It's a present, for you."

He appeared not to understand, but stood holding the beribboned offering and staring at her.

"I'll put the champagne in the refrigerator," she said, taking it back from him. "You open your present."

Stepping inside, Risa saw Raskin, with an apron on to protect his suit, bending to check the progress of the hens in the oven. Straightening, he watched her stow the bottle in the refrigerator, saying, "You've outdone yourself. You look most elegant," and walked in a circle around her to get the full effect of the white, full-skirted dress with a square neckline, tucked bodice, and flowing sleeves she'd bought to wear to her graduation. Her only jewelry was the diamond pendant Erik had given her. She'd pinned her hair into a loosely coiled topknot from which tendrils escaped down the sides of her face and the nape of her neck. "One hundred percent," he declared. "After seeing nothing but granny dresses or half-naked females in micro-minis at the supermarket, you're a breath of fresh air from some other time and place."

"You look swell, too. A suit and tie and everything. This is going to be terrific."

"Only if you get out of here and let me attend to my hens and my wild rice and the rest of it."

Erik held one of the candles close to the photograph and gazed at Marisa's gift. There, on matte finish paper, captured for all time in her exquisite girlhood beauty, was his beloved child. It was the only gift he'd received since the age of seven, and that alone would have been sufficient to move him. But that she'd chosen to give him her image was monumentally significant. How could she have known it was the one thing he most wanted? How had she guessed that he had a need to be able to see her face when she wasn't with him?

"Do you like it?" she asked, having waited several minutes for him to say something while he stood holding the frame with one hand, the fingers of the other flitting uncertainly in the air above it like a bird before a dish of seeds, hungry but wary.

"I cannot begin to tell you what this means to me," he said at last, holding the frame before him with unsteady hands, unable to take his eyes from her portrait. "I will treasure this always."

"Oh, you wait," she said lightly. "We'll have dozens of pictures, albums full of them."

His head turned and he gazed at her, as if reminding her of the unlikelihood of that.

"I know," she said softly. "But somehow we'll figure out a way to fill a few albums. Do I get a kiss or anything? The whole point of giving people presents, you know, is that they get so excited, they're so totally blown away by them, that they want to jump up and down and kiss the giver. Things like that."

"Do you get a kiss?" he repeated, thinking he would like to be able to open his body and invite her to step inside, then magically close around her so that they need never again be apart. "I think so," he said and, still holding the frame, put one hand to her cheek while he touched his mouth to hers. "You are my miracle," he whispered, the back of his hand skimming over her cheek. "You are the dream of my lifetime. Nothing will ever be of importance unless you're with me to share it."

"I know that," she laughed. "But do you like it?"

His face made its smiling contortion, his eyes absorbing her. "I like it more than you could ever imagine. And after dinner I have something I would like to show you."

"What?"

"After dinner," he repeated.

"Erik," she said, turning inside his arm to look out at the Sound. "Will you marry me on my birthday?"

"Yes."

"Will Hal be your best man, and could we have Kitty give me away?"

"Yes."

"And will you promise to love, honor, and cherish me until death us do part?"

"Yes."

"Okay!" She laughed, turning back to him. "Could we have the honeymoon after dinner?"

"I think it could be arranged." He kissed her again. "It will be *divine*," he whispered.

"What is this 'divine' thing?" she asked him. "Why does that word send you and Hal into silly fits?"

"I will explain after dinner."

"God! After dinner's going to last for days."

"Possibly. Any objections?"

"I've promised Kitty I'll sleep at home every night until you and I 'get legal.' That's what she calls it. Isn't that quaint?"

"I rather like it. And I'll make sure you're home before your carriage turns back into a pumpkin and the white horses devolve into scampering rodents."

Erik disappeared after dinner, telling Risa he would see her upstairs in ten minutes. Meanwhile, she sat on at the table on the terrace with Raskin finishing the last of the champagne. It had been a superb dinner and she praised Hal's culinary skills, asking, "How did you learn to cook?"

"Self-defense. Either learn or die of starvation."

"Maybe you'll teach me some of your secrets."

"I thought you already knew how. You cooked for Erik, as I recall."

"That was one time, and I nearly had a nervous breakdown over it. Would you? Teach me, I mean."

"I'd be glad to. Any time."

"You wouldn't leave if Erik and I got married, would you, Hal?"

"Not unless you or he wanted me to."

"Neither one of us would want that," she told him.

"Then, fine. Long as you're happy."

"May I ask you something?"

"You can ask. I don't promise I'll answer."

"Did you have an unhappy childhood, Hal?"

He let out a howl of laughter, then went suddenly serious and looked at her assessingly, saying, "What is it about you? There's this thing you do where you zero in on people. It could get you in trouble, kid."

"I didn't mean to pry. It's just a feeling I have about you."

He smiled wolfishly, then tapped his fingers in a tattoo on the tabletop. "You don't scare easily, do you?"

"Oh yes, I do. Very easily."

"You want to know about my childhood, Risa? I'll give you the abridged version. My father liked to beat people up. He especially liked to beat up my mother. He beat her up so well he finally killed her one night. And then I killed him. The jury decided it was justifiable homicide committed by a minor, acquitted me, and the court awarded custody of me and my older sister to our grandmother, our mother's mother. Some years later my sister got married to a man who liked to beat people up. And to save myself from killing him, I gave up my engineering career, enlisted, and was one of the first to go to Nam, to kill a whole bunch of other people instead, to get the murder out of my system. While I was in Nam, my sister hanged herself from the back porch of her house in Bridgeport. The husband took off for the hills. Five months into my tour of duty I got myself wounded, got an honorable discharge, and was shipped home. My grandmother had died, so that was the end of the family. Three months after my discharge, I came to work for Erik. End of story. Any questions?"

"How did you kill him?" she asked in a hushed voice.

"You don't want to know that. And Erik's waiting for you."

"I'm sorry, Hal."

"Yeah," he said. For the second time, he felt that odd sense of absolution. What *was* it about this girl? he wondered, watching her leave the terrace.

Erik had rigged up a small lamp and positioned it so that no light shone on him. He invited Marisa to sit with him on the bed, then he opened the photograph album across his lap.

"This is Philippe," he told her, one long finger pointing. "And this is Lavinia. And this is Erik." His finger moved over individual shots of his parents as teenagers, then turned the page to show shots of the two together. Then his fingertip moved to the picture of an infant. "Lavinia met Philippe when she was eighteen and he was twenty-two." He turned pages as he spoke. "She was in Paris on holiday with two friends from school. He was first violinist with the Paris symphony but hoped for a career as a soloist. They met through mutual friends and were immediately drawn to one another. That was in 1933. By 1935 Philippe had had a successful solo debut and he asked Lavinia to marry him. They were married in March of the following year, and in September of 1937 Erik was born." His hand slowly turned another page. "Early in 1938, Philippe began to fear there would be a war. He convinced Lavinia it would be wise for them to leave Paris and relocate in England. Since England was her home, her birthright, she readily agreed, and they left with their child.

"Philippe's career was flourishing, and by 1944, despite the war, he was performing regularly, giving concerts throughout England and making successful recordings. Things were going very well indeed.

"Then, on a Sunday afternoon in November of 1944, they died in an automobile accident. This is a photograph of Lavinia's family taken in 1932 at the family home in Gloucestershire. These are her mother and father, and *that*"—his voice quivered and his pointing finger went rigid—"is Lavinia's older sister *Dorothy*." He spoke the woman's name as if it were a poisoned pellet on his tongue.

Turning the final page, he said, "This is Lavinia and Philippe and Erik at Christmas 1943. They were very happy," he said almost inaudibly, and gently closed the book.

Risa reached to turn out the light, then sat with her head on his shoulder. "Why do things have to be so sad?" she said quietly. "It's all so unfair."

"Nothing is fair."

"Erik, I do love you—very much. I wish I knew some magic words to say that would wipe away the bad part and make you happy."

His hand lifted and moved to the side of her head, then reappeared before her holding a pink rose.

With an excited cry, she accepted the flower. "I love your magic! It's so incredible when you do things like that." Sitting up on her knees, she took the album and the rose and set them on the floor beside the bed. Then, presenting her back to him, she said, "Unzip me, please."

His hands worked the zipper, then slipped inside the loosened bodice to close over her breasts. The feel of her was a warm recurring dream, one that brought constant delirium.

Covering his hands with her own, she said, "Wait a minute! You have to tell me what that 'divine' business is all about."

With a soft laugh, Erik let his head fall forward against her bare back. "One of Raskin's women," he explained. "Everything from martinis to lovemaking is, to her, divine."

"Oh, swell! Here I am, in the ranks with Raskin's women."

"Not ever," he said, placing kisses down the length of her spine, his thumbs gently abrading her nipples.

Pulling her arms free of the dress, she swung around to clamp her mouth over his.

17

ON HER EIGHTEENTH BIRTHDAY, THE TWENTY-SECOND of February, 1970, Marisa and Erik were married, by the minister who'd conducted the service for her father, at her home on Butlers Island. The others present were Kitty and Raskin.

Risa wore the pale-pink suit Kitty had helped her select. In her hair were her mother's tortoise-shell combs, around her neck was Erik's diamond pendant, and in her pocket she carried the blue handkerchief Raskin had thought to give her just prior to the arrival of the minister.

At the appropriate moment during the ceremony, Erik and she exchanged the rings he'd designed and had made by a goldsmith in Manhattan—each band formed of two irregularly curving interlocked circles of white and yellow gold. Erik was nearly immobilized by anxiety and could scarcely utter his "I do." Risa felt dizzy and disconnected, as if this were something she was dreaming, rather than an event she'd long been anticipating.

When they'd signed the certificate, Raskin produced a bottle of champagne and Kitty brought a tray of glasses. There were toasts to the bride and groom. The minister kissed Risa's cheek and wished her well. He gave Erik's hand a hearty shake, then went on his way.

As agreed beforehand, Risa and Erik left soon after

172

the minister to go to Erik's house on Contentment Island. Her things had been moved over during the previous week and she had, earlier that day, carried a small suitcase up to the third bedroom.

There was a note taped to the front door. It read: "Please be sure to look in the dining room, also in the refrigerator. A few surprises from Hal and Kitty."

With a laugh, Risa took Erik's hand and went running with him to the dining room. The table was set for two. In the kitchen was another note that told them at what temperature to set the oven and for how long. The refrigerator held two bottles of champagne and a pair of tulip glasses whose stems had been tied with white ribbons.

"This is great!" Risa said, relaxing for the first time in days. "I'm not hungry yet, are you?"

Erik shook his head, his eyes on his ring.

"What's the matter?" she asked, approaching him.

With his right hand he took hold of her left, so that they were side by side.

"We're married," she said. "We are actually married. I am a missus!"

"We are. You are," he said, as if numb. Despite wanting it with all his heart, and despite having achieved his greatest wish—to have her as his wife—he was stricken by a sense of foreboding so potent he could barely function. When you got all you'd ever wanted, something was bound to happen to strip you of it, to bring you to your knees and force you to rue the day you'd ever had the audacity to wish for anything. If the Fates didn't actually take away your life altogether, they'd make certain it was barely worth living. And today's ceremony, the realization of the only dream he'd ever nurtured, was tempting the Fates to the maximum. It was challenging them to wreak havoc, to whip up hurricanes or tidal waves or earthquakes.

"Erik?" She touched him lightly on the arm.

He shrugged off his foreboding and looked at her, at once and always heartened merely by the sight of her.

"My plan is that we each go now to prepare ourselves,'' she said. ''And in thirty minutes, we will meet in your room. Do you like my plan?''

''I am captivated by the potential of your plan.''

''Okay. So let's go. I've got a lot to do in half an hour.'' She kissed him on the chin, then went running off.

He remained where he was, battling his trepidations, telling himself that to succumb to them would taint Marisa's happiness. This nameless fear might, if he gave in to it, put down such deep roots he'd never be able to weed it out. This was the point at which he was obliged to have faith, to believe that even an ambulatory horror deserved a measure of contentment.

Squaring his shoulders, he ran his hands over his hair, took several deep breaths, then started through the house to his bedroom. He had less than half an hour to assemble everything.

With her hair protected by a plastic cap, Risa showered quickly, then placed dots of perfume behind her ears, in the bends of her elbows and knees, and between her breasts. Then she brushed out her hair and slipped on the white silk gown and robe Kitty had insisted on buying her for this night.

''You're gonna look like an angel,'' Kitty had said. Then with a laugh, she'd added, ''You'll drive the man wild.''

She and Kitty had shopped for two weeks, making several trips into Manhattan to find the many items on Risa's list. They had even, after much deliberation, ordered announcements from Tiffany's.

''You gotta do it right,'' Kitty had told her. ''You can't make it seem like this is something you're sneakin' off to do. And, besides, wait till you see the presents that come pourin' in. Three toasters and five silver serving spoons, two irons, and heaps of mismatched towels, not to mention crap people got given and they've been dyin' to get rid of. It'll take you months to return half of it, and years to figure out what to do with the rest. You gonna buy a present for the groom?''

''No. I thought I'd steal his car and leave town. Of course I am!'' Risa had said somewhat indignantly.

"You mind if I ask what you have in mind?"

"No, I don't mind. I'm going to buy him this." She pulled from her bag a page torn from a magazine.

Kitty looked at it and whistled. "That's gonna cost *thousands*!"

"It's not as if I get married every day."

"That's a good thing," Kitty teased. "It'd be very damned expensive."

Not bothering with slippers, Risa now gathered up her offerings, then went to tap on Erik's door. It clicked open and she stopped just inside the room, taking in the sight and scent of the many vases of pale-pink roses around which Erik had arranged dozens of candles. Music came from the speakers concealed in the ceiling, a violin concerto she thought was Paganini. Erik was waiting for her, his hands in the pockets of a black silk dressing gown.

"This is wonderful, Erik!"

She came toward him with her arms full of packages, the white silk swirling around her like fog, her long black hair shimmering over her shoulders as she moved. He wondered for a moment how any of this had come to be, then shoved aside his doubts and speculations, determined to savor every second of his wedding night.

"Come sit here with me so I can give you your presents." She beckoned him to join her on the end of the bed, where she let the packages fall from her arms.

"You are so beautiful," he whispered. "There are times, like now, especially now, when I have the feeling that were I to reach for you, my hands would find only empty air."

"I'm real," she laughed, and leaned forward to kiss him. "This one first." She selected a package and held it out to him.

His hands took the small square box and turned it this way and that as if performing a prelude to some conjuring trick. "I think you plan to make up for every birthday and Christmas I've ever missed."

"I intend to try. Open it. There's a lot of stuff here for you to look at and I'm dying to see how you like it all."

"You are very generous," he said hesitantly.

"Open it, Erik. The suspense is killing me."

His hands, she thought, were incapable of any hurried or ungraceful gesture. Like a surgeon's, they deftly stripped away the wrappings to reveal the box inside. He glanced up at her questioningly, then lifted the lid.

"Everything after this is sheer anticlimax." She laughed softly. "Do you like it? What do you think?"

He gazed at the gold Rolex wristwatch, then removed it from the box to hold it in his hands, turning it over and over, his fingers examining the band. "It is magnificent. I am overwhelmed. Thank you."

"If you don't like it, we can take it back and get something else."

"No, no. I like it *very* much."

"Great! Now open this one."

The second box contained a bottle of cologne. It had a gold-rimmed white label with "Erik" written by hand on it.

"I had it made for you," she told him. "Smell it."

The scent was evocative of winter and woodsmoke, with an underlying warmth of sandalwood. "You had this made?" he asked.

"Just for you. No one else anywhere has this fragrance, only you."

"Extraordinary! I like this very much, too."

The third box, large and quite heavy, held an imperial quart of Glenfiddich.

"A present," she said softly, "to you, from my dad."

The fourth, small and compact, contained a gold Dunhill cigarette lighter.

The fifth and largest of all and lined with tissue revealed six custom-made white silk shirts, with his monogram embroidered in white silk thread on the pockets.

And the last box offered up Cameron's gold-and-onyx cuff links.

"That's from Dad, too," she said. "I know he'd have wanted you to have them. I hope you don't mind."

"Mind? I am honored. These are exceptional gifts, every one of them. Thank you." He assembled the packages and the discarded wrappings and shifted them from the bed to the top of the dresser. This done, he returned across the room, his hands signaling her to stand but not move. He faced her from perhaps three feet away. One hand placed itself palm outward before her eyes, then twisted from the wrist like a small acrobat and opened again with a long strand of lustrous pearls draped across his slightly spread fingers. The clasp was of platinum and diamonds, and he opened it to fasten the pearls around her neck. She was about to speak, but a finger to his lips kept her silent. Once more he held up his hands, showing them front and back before he slid them into the sides of her hair, pulling back with his fingers curled shut. Turning over slowly, his fingers uncurled one at a time to reveal a diamond earring on the palm of each hand. Another signal and she held out her hands. He turned his hands so they lay on top of hers, depositing the earrings on her outheld palms where they sat refracting the candlelight and shooting off small sparks.

Again, he motioned her to keep silent and she obeyed, captivated by this performance. His left hand danced for a moment before her eyes, then his right, the fingers opening and closing hypnotically, Then, startlingly, he clapped his hands together before folding them open to show a bracelet of small gold links each set with a diamond. Plucking the earrings from her palms, he secured the bracelet to her wrist, then dropped the earrings into the pocket of her robe.

"The show is over," he whispered, with a finger tracing a line from the underside of her chin down her throat to the hollow at its base where it remained for a moment before continuing on its way down the outside of the robe to the sash at her waist. A flick of his finger, the sash was undone and the robe fell open. She turned her shoulders, and the garment slithered away like a substanceless ghost. The violin concerto was reaching a crescendo, and she asked, "What is the music, Erik?"

"It is Paganini's Violin Concerto No. 4 in D Minor. Played by my father with the London Symphony Orchestra."

"He was wonderful, wonderful."

"He played as if God whispered in his ears. He was a genius."

"That's what my father said about you," she told him, undoing his dressing gown.

"Your father overstated my abilities." His hands at her waist, he was gathering the fabric of her nightgown under his fingers, drawing it slowly higher and higher.

"No, he didn't," she disagreed, feeling the air wind itself around her calves like a sinuous cat. "I'm very excited. I feel all shaky."

He nodded, feeling precisely the same way as he lifted the gown over her head and dropped it to one side. He paused for a moment to rid himself of his dressing gown, then, without touching her, his hands wafted over her silhouette as his eyes followed their passage. "My wife," he whispered. Such rare and gemlike words, so exceptional a concept. "My wife." Tall and proud and long of limb; passionate and funny and giving; narrow of waist and hip, with small perfect breasts and yielding thighs; fragile ankles and elegantly arched feet, finely formed toes. "Beautiful," he crooned, his hands at last closing around the supple flesh of her upper arms. "How I love you! Do you know how I adore you?"

"I know." She let him draw her closer and closer until their bodies met. Standing on her toes, extending herself fully, she pushed forward, rubbing luxuriously against the length of his broad sinewy body. Then she slipped down to rest her cheek against his belly, her hands on the backs of his thighs. She dipped her tongue into his navel, then kissed him on each hip, her hands shifting down to his knees and then kissed him on each hip, her hands shifting down to his knees and then up again. She was aware every time she caressed him in this fashion that it stupefied and somehow shattered him. But she had to show him in whatever way she could that however much he claimed to love her, her love for him was equal and no less deep. So it was a great pleasure and another, albeit transitory, gift she could give him to stroke and kiss him until he had to ask her hoarsely, please, to stop because she was driving him nearly mad with her devoted attentions and questing mouth.

He had to lift her onto the bed and duplicate her attentions, losing himself to her flesh while the roses exuded their perfume into the atmosphere and the candle flames darted in the sudden currents created by their shifting, sighing consummation.

Raskin looked around and said, "Let's get the hell out of here. Come on. I'll buy you dinner."

Kitty also looked around. "All right. Why not, seein's how we're all decked out in our finery."

Raskin had the Mercedes, and showed her into the car, asking, "How d'you feel about someplace with live music?"

"I feel just fine about that."

They went to a steakhouse where a trio played in the bar so that couples could dance in the small area provided. Because it was a weeknight, the dining room was only about half full and the bar was fairly well deserted. The hostess gave them a secluded table off in a corner of the dining room, then waited to take their drink orders.

After she'd gone, Kitty opened her purse for her Kools, and smiled as Raskin at once held his lighter to her cigarette.

"You're one sharp cookie." She grinned at him.

"You're pretty sharp yourself," he replied. "This is the first time I've seen you decked out in your 'finery.' You should do it more often." He gazed admiringly at her, wondering why he hadn't before noticed the size or depth of her blue eyes, or how very pretty she was, especially this evening with the hair swept back from her face and coiled into a knot at the nape of her neck.

"For who? For what?" she said matter-of-factly.

"Maybe for me."

She regarded him with raised eyebrows. "You?"

"Sure. Why not?"

She took a breath that swelled the cleavage revealed by her handsome gray suit. "Why not?" she repeated, then paused to take a puff of her Kool. "Well, how old're you, for one thing?"

"Thirty-two."

"And I'm forty-two. That alone should answer your question."

"Nope." He shook a Kent from his pack. "That's not going to do it."

"All right, then. How about this: I doubt there's a single woman in all Fairfield County who hasn't encountered you in one place or another."

"So?"

"You don't think you're spread maybe a little thin?"

"I'm not spread at all," he countered. "You don't get spread when you never spend more than one night with a woman."

"And you're thinkin' I might like to be another of those one-night women?"

"You're different."

"Maybe *I* like to think so." She smiled. "But I doubt you do."

"You have no idea what I think," he said evenly, his grayish eyes holding hers.

"Your eyes change colors," she said, distracted. "A while back, they were quite blue. Now they've gone near most gray."

"I'm a chameleon," he laughed. "Yours are always blue. Very very blue."

"I do believe you're tryin' to flatter me."

"No, just telling the truth."

The waitress came with their drinks, said she'd be back shortly to take their dinner orders, and went away.

"Why'd you want to sleep with a woman ten years older'n you?" she asked bluntly. "You got a hankerin' after saggy flesh?"

He laughed boldly. "You're not saggy. You're a lot more trim than most of the women I see. And from where I'm sitting, the view is very nice."

She looked down at her breasts, then said, "I think we've exhausted this topic. Let's see if we can't find somethin' else to talk about."

"That won't be easy. I've kind of made up my mind to talk about you."

"Well, you'll just have to change it, won't you?"

"It's going to be an awfully quiet dinner."

"You'll survive," she said. "Tell me something. How

d'you figure things're gonna work out with the three of you all livin' together in the one house?''

"I figure it'll work out fine. It's a big house, plenty of room to get away from each other. Unless Erik decides otherwise, I'm satisfied with the arrangement. Risa's been halfway living there for months now. I don't see things'll change all that much now they're married.''

"You like my girl?" she asked.

"You think of her as your girl?''

"I surely do. I've looked after her near all her life. She's as much mine as ever she could be.''

"I like that," he said solemnly. "I like hearing you talk about her that way.''

"Why?''

"I just do.''

"You got any kin?" she asked. "Any people hereabouts?''

He shook his head.

"I got a few left back home. Not one I'd give you a nickel for, though.''

"Back home where?''

"Memphis. I been gone so long now I can't even hardly remember the place. I left there twenty-four years ago. Better'n half my lifetime. Where-all d'you hail from?''

"Bridgeport." He smiled sardonically. "The armpit of the universe.''

"As I recall, a lot of folks I once knew used to say that very same thing about Memphis. Me, I didn't mind it that much. I just didn't wanna spend my entire life there.''

"Come dance with me," he invited suddenly. "I bet you're a terrific dancer.''

"I don't mind," she said by way of consent.

Alone together on the dance floor, he pulled her close. She hesitated for a moment, resisting, then gave in. They danced without speaking for a time, well-matched and comfortable together. When, without breaking, the trio went into a second number, he put his lips to her ear and said, "You *are* a terrific dancer. You feel good, and you smell better.''

"It's not gonna work," she told him.

"Oh, sure it is. You made up your mind about half an hour ago."

"I've been known to change my mind on a regular basis."

"But you won't."

"Now, what makes you think that?"

"Because you're lonely, too," he said simply.

That took her aback. He kissed the side of her neck, and she thought he was probably right.

"There's a condition," she said.

"Name it."

"There's gotta be a second time. After that, I don't much care one way or the other. But I'll be damned if I'm gonna get put on your list as another one-night woman."

"I might surprise you." His hand dropped down to her hip. "I've met most of them, but I haven't met you before."

"You sure do have all the lines."

"No line," he said, pulling back to look her in the eyes. "I mean it."

"My Lord!" she said softly. "I believe you do."

18

ERIK HAD TURNED THE THIRD BEDROOM OVER TO RISA, telling her to do whatever she liked with it. Her immediate reaction was to blurt, without thinking, "It could be a nursery, Erik."

"I think not," came his frosty reply.

"Someday," she offered.

"I think not," he repeated.

"Okay," she backed down. "Don't be angry with me."

"I am not angry with you."

"You're way beyond angry. You're furious."

"Let's, please, not pursue this discussion further." He stepped out into the hallway, leaving her alone.

"Okay," she said to herself, turning to survey the room. "Okay."

Since it was the one room in the house Erik had all but ignored during the renovation, she was free to start from scratch. The walls had only been primed, and carpet had never been laid. After deliberating for a time, she decided that if she couldn't persuade him to consider the room's future use as a nursery, she'd go for vivid colors and create a room of light. She thought she might be able to tempt Erik into an appreciation of the sun. So she bought and put up herself a wallpaper with brilliant green palm fronds on a white background, and painted

183

the wood trim a matching green. The carpet was white, as were the bed linens and the spread. She filled the room with potted plants and wicker furniture, including what she thought was an attractive, even enticing, grouping of two white wicker rockers positioned on either side of a round white table.

To open the door to this room after the darkness of the rest of the house was like entering into a cool spring morning. When it was finished, with her clothes hung away in the walk-in closet—Erik's closet being surprisingly too small to accommodate her wardrobe—she went up to the office to invite him to inspect the end result of her labors.

He actually covered his eyes when she opened the door, and she hurried to draw the curtains, but he stopped her, saying, "No, don't. Let me have a moment." When his eyes had adjusted to the assaultive light, he was most complimentary. "It's lovely, Marisa, truly lovely."

"Would you sit here with me sometimes?"

"Sometime," he said, intentionally vague. "Of course."

He kept his back to the window. She saw this and doubted he'd ever voluntarily spend any time in there with her. It crushed and defeated her. "I know you're busy," she said, swallowing her disappointment. "I just thought you'd want to see."

"Marisa," he said, well aware of her letdown, "please don't be upset. It's been too long, too many years of living the way I have to change my habits now." Reaching for her hand, he said, "There is something I'd like to discuss with you. Now might be a good time."

"Let's get out of here, then," she said, and started for the door.

"Don't!" he cautioned kindly. "Don't fly away from your charming creation simply because I don't fit in here."

"Sure you do!" she disagreed. "You fit in because I say you do, not because you say you don't."

"Please believe that it is my fondest wish to do what gives you pleasure. I'm simply not able to do all I would like. I'm not defying you. I'm engaged full-time in an effort to be worthy of you.''

''You already are. You were to begin with. It *kills* me when you say things like that!'' As if to illustrate, she held her fists to her chest. ''Oh, hell!'' she cried. ''Why am I doing this to you? Come on, Erik.'' She grabbed his hand and began towing him to the door. ''Let's talk in your room. I apologize for all that. It was stupid.''

''This is *our* room,'' he corrected her, once they were inside and seated together.

''And so is that jungle next door. Every goddamned room in this house is *ours*. Sometimes I'm so stupid I hate myself.''

''You are never stupid. You are simply very young. And that brings me to what I wanted to discuss with you.'' He reached into his pocket and brought out a pack of Sobranie cigarettes, taking his time to light one with the gold Dunhill. He held on to the lighter while he repositioned the ashtray. As on every other day of his life, he was wearing a black suit and a white shirt, with an immaculate dark-gray silk tie.

''In very short order,'' he began, ''you are going to become utterly bored by spending your days and nights in this house trying to find things to do to occupy your time. Please, don't speak for a moment. Hear me out.

''Raskin and I have talked, and we've come up with an idea. If it is of interest to you, both of us will be pleased to work with you to implement the idea.''

''What is it?''

''You have a talent for line drawing, and you're good at mathematics. What we are proposing is that Raskin and I teach you how to draft, with the thought in mind that eventually you will take over from him and make my presentations to prospective clients. We would, during the coming months, teach you how to read and interpret specifications and plans. Then, if you agreed, you could accompany Raskin when next he makes a presentation.

''I had planned,'' he went on, ''to give up my work, you see. It wasn't that I dislike it. In fact, I like it tremendously. But I'm unable to deal anymore on a direct basis with the clients. With both you and Raskin to assist, I'd be free to do the work and oversee by remote control, as it were. It would also simplify matters and reduce the workload if it were divided among three. Does this appeal to you at all?''

''I don't know,'' she said truthfully. ''I'll have to think about it.''

''We all need work of some kind, Marisa. It's what, for many of us, validates our existence. I don't think you're any more capable than I of sitting idle for months on end, amusing yourself with shopping excursions or new recipes. Not that I don't very much enjoy your cooking and the things you buy. But you really should have something to do that challenges your intellect and stimulates your imagination. If you choose not to go along with this suggestion, I'd ask you to consider attending one of the colleges nearby. You're too young to immerse yourself completely in the workings of this household, with no outside interests to divert you.''

''Are you trying to force me to be emancipated?'' she asked with a smile. ''It sounds as if I'm going to be equal whether I want to be or not.''

''It's just common sense,'' he said, failing to see the humor.

''It was a joke, Erik,'' she told him, going over to kneel on the floor in front of him with her arms folded across her knees. ''Joke. Funny. We all laugh. Ha ha.''

He smiled at her, his hand cupping her chin. ''Ha ha,'' he whispered. ''What do you think?'' he asked, turning to extinguish his cigarette.

''I'm sure you're right. Could I come up and have a look at some of what you and Hal are doing, so I can get an idea what it's all about?''

''Certainly.'' He returned the Dunhill to his jacket pocket. ''Any time you like.''

''How about now?''

''Good.''

Hal showed her a set of his drawings, explaining that his specialty was mechanical engineering while Erik's degrees were in architecture and electrical engineering.

''Between us, you see, Risa, we can cover everything, including things most other architects would have to subcontract for. Another hand to help with the drafting would be very welcome, and it's not hard at all. It's just a matter of rendering to scale and being able to draw straight lines with the help of a few set or T-squares."

"It looks kind of interesting." She wandered over to look at the model on top of the drawing file cabinet. "Who does these?" she asked, put in mind of the doll's house she'd had years ago.

"A model maker in Stamford. He does good work, doesn't he?"

"It's wonderful, with the little trees and tiny cars and pushpin people."

Erik, at his drawing board, dropped his head on his arm and laughed.

She marched across the room and pounded her fist on his arm. "What's so funny now?" she demanded as Raskin also started to laugh. "Is this another of those dumb-ass 'divine' things?"

Erik sat up and swiveled on his stool to put his arm around her waist. "Pushpin people," he said. "That's very funny, Marisa."

"Well, how'm I supposed to know what to call them?"

"Precisely! From now on they shall be termed pushpin people." He hugged her and she bent forward until her forehead was touching his and she was smiling into his face. "Don't make fun of me, buster! Not if you want me to come work for you."

"You think you'd care to try?"

"I guess. Will I get one of these nifty drafting tables for my own?"

"Oh, most assuredly. Raskin will ring up and order one for you at once."

"Yes, he will," Raskin said from across the room. "With a nice high stool of your very own, and all kinds of nifty mechanical pencils, and erasers, and everything else you want or need."

"Maybe this is a mistake," she said, looking over at Raskin, then back at Erik. "The two of you will do nothing but tease me from morning to night."

"Erik doesn't work before four in the afternoon,"

Raskin reminded her. "More like teasing from four till midnight. This is shift work."

"Let me make sure I've got this straight. The two of you will teach me how to draft stuff, and how to read these big thick boring-looking books. And when I've learned all that, then you'll send me out to show people your designs?"

"Something like that," Erik replied.

"And they're going to listen to someone my age tell them how my husband is going to design their building?"

"I think you'll be a bit older by then."

"Well, how long's all this going to take?"

"Perhaps two years."

"Two years?"

"Think of it as working toward a degree without the need to go to school every day with a bunch of freaked-out hippies," Raskin said. "Nobody shoving flowers up your nose, making peace signs in front of you and chanting, 'Love, love, love,' all day long."

"Yeah," she said. "Working toward a degree by coming upstairs every afternoon to sit here with a couple of weird Ivy Leaguers."

"Oh, now," Raskin said. "You really want to watch what you say, Risa. Princeton and Yale are only rivals on the football field. We might gang up on you if you impugn our establishment educations."

"I'm going down to organize dinner. Let me know when my drafting table arrives." With a kiss on Erik's chin she sailed out. At once, she popped back through the door to waggle her finger, saying, "Don't you dare start talking about me before I'm all the way downstairs." Then she laughed, and went out again.

Raskin lit a cigarette, propped it on the lip of the ashtray, then said, "What d'you think, Erik?"

"I think she'll do it and be very good at it."

"So do I."

To himself, Erik thought she'd come along to salvage his entire life, including a career he wanted badly to keep. "I'm grateful for the suggestion, Raskin."

"It was nothing. Forget it."

* * *

"She's taking to it like a duck to water," Raskin was telling Kitty. "It hasn't been six months and she can knock off a drawing in no time flat and it'll be flawless every time. She finds the specs boring, but that's understandable. She'd rather be reading a novel."

"Who wouldn't?" Kitty agreed.

"Erik's very excited about the new job. Funny, but it's about the last thing in the world I'd have thought he'd accept, let alone be excited about."

"Then you've missed the point altogether," she said tolerantly. "Designin' an office building for a group of doctors is just the kinda thing that would excite him. It gives him a chance, I'd imagine, to correct every last thing that bothered him as a child about places like that."

"Jesus! You're right. I never thought of that."

"All kinds of things you've never thought of," she said. "Like how you keep on turnin' up here, regular as a six-foot clock. I'm not sure I know what-all to make of this."

"I told you, but you didn't believe me."

"I surely didn't, and I don't know that I'm entirely happy with it."

He shot her a look, his jaw going tight.

"Don't you go gettin' mean-lookin', Harold Raskin!" She pointed a brightly polished finger at him. "I'm only speakin' the truth. And the truth is, I get the impression every so often you're tryin' to make yourself indispensable to me, the way you done with Erik."

"Are you implying I have dishonorable motives?" he asked sharply.

"I'm not implyin' diddly. I'm sayin' I don't know if I want you bein' indispensable to me. I go let myself get reliant on you, you're likely as not to up an' disappear for good 'n' always. I only slept with you that first time 'cause what you said was the truth. I was lonely, missin' Cam. Now it's gettin' on for nine months and I see more of you than I do of my girl."

"What's your point?"

"I guess I want to know where I stand."

"Right now, you're not 'standing' anywhere," he quipped.

"Don't play smart with me. I asked a question deserves a civil answer."

"What kind of answer, civil aside, d'you want me to give?"

"Well, I'll tell you," she said, reaching for her drink on the side table and recrossing her legs before returning her attention to Raskin, who was sprawled on the sofa, fully aware he was admiring her legs and watching her every move. "I'd like to know who it is I've been takin' to my bed all these months. And I'd like to know your intentions, if you got any."

"If you were a man, I'd say you were getting ready to propose." He laughed.

"Oh, fuck you, honey!" she said calmly. "You're the biggest hard-ass I ever have known. 'Ceptin' when it comes down to the crucial moment, and then you're the saddest, scaredest young fella ever did cross my threshold. You don't fool me none, Harold. I've seen you hard and I've seen you soft, and I'm still willin' to talk with you, and I haven't yet heaved you outta my bed, so don't try duckin' me. Just answer me straight."

"I like you," he said, sitting up. "You're the only woman I've ever *really* liked. If you ask a lot of questions, Kitty, you might get answers you won't care for."

"There isn't one thing you could tell me that'd come as a surprise. And that's the honest truth. I know you've done some truly terrible things in your young life."

"How do you know that?"

"You got the marks on you, and I'm not referrin' to your war injuries. It's in the way you make yourself real gentle when you come into my bed 'cause you've got a killin' ability and it scares you. I remind you of someone, don't I? Or is it that somethin' about me makes you remember somethin' from way way back?"

"I don't suppose you'd consider coming over here?" he asked.

"I don't mind." She got up and went to sit beside him on the sofa.

"How come you're not afraid of me?"

"I'm too fond of you to be afraid. And anyway, I know you'd never harm me. There's some you would, and likely some you did. But not me. I used to wonder, you know, at your workin' and livin' with Erik the way you do. Handsome young man closed away most of the time with poor Erik. But not anymore. It makes good sense to me now. The only difference 'tween the two of you is his wounds show. Yours a person has to guess at.''

"How will you feel if I leave and don't come back?''

"I reckon I'll miss you and be sad for a time. But I won't be callin' you up on the phone like them others. And I won't be waitin' home nights for you.''

"I wasn't threatening you,'' he explained.

"I know that. It's just your way. You're not a real trustin' soul. I guess you've got cause. Lord knows, most of us do.''

"I suppose it's only fair that I tell you,'' he said. "Mind if I put my head in your lap?''

"I don't mind.''

He lay down, took hold of her hand, then told her about his family. She didn't interrupt or say a word until he was finished, but smoothed his hair throughout the telling. Then all she said was, "Don't tell me how you killed him. I don't want to know. Okay?''

"That's fine.''

"Bastard deserved to die,'' she said feelingly. "And so did the other one.'' She sighed and reached for her now watery drink. "Lord, but the world treats its children badly.''

"Not you, though,'' he said, taking the glass from her and setting it on the coffee table. "You treat all your children well.''

She laughed. "You ain't no child of mine, fella!''

He ran his hand across her breasts and said, "You don't know how glad I am about that.''

"So,'' she said, "I guess this means you'll be comin' back.''

"You could say that.'' He sat up and turned her to face him. "I like your face,'' he said. "I like the way your nose tilts up at the tip. And I like your mouth.''

"Don't let it go to your head,'' she said softly, "but I go around hot all the time, thinkin' about you.''

"Come take a bath with me!''

"I don't need a bath."

"Of course you don't," he told her. "But I want to soap you with my bare hands, then rinse you off, towel you dry, then rub oil over you while you're still warm."

"Yeah," she laughed. "And after that you'll coat me with whipped cream and eat it off."

"That's not a bad idea."

"Let's skip the soapin' and rinsin' and towelin' and go direct to the main event. What say?"

"I knew there was a reason why I like you."

"Ah, Harold." She smiled and pinched his cheek. "You're such a sweet young fool. You *love* me, but it scares you to death to think it."

"You're right. It does."

"Don't worry about it none, honey. It don't scare me one little bit."

19

MANY NIGHTS WHEN HIS SMALL HOUSEHOLD LAY PEACE-
fully sleeping, Erik went silently down the stairs to the
music room where, for hours, amid the wavering candle
flames, he paced about, sometimes listening to tapes he'd
made, or to albums, but as often as not accompanied
only by the almost audible turning of his thoughts. His
head frequently felt like an overcrowded tunnel jammed
full of vehicles with racing engines and honking horns,
stalled for an eternity, while their exhausts pushed out
noxious fumes that threatened to smother him.

For an entire year, Marisa had lived, in apparent contentment, inside his home. She lived beside him, the evidence of her presence was everywhere—a book left open
face-down on one of the living-room sofas, one of her
fashion magazines forgotten on the kitchen counter, her
hairbrush on the rim of the bathroom sink, or some piece
of her clothing draped over the arm of one of the bedroom chairs. Coming into a room soon after she'd va-
cated it, he'd walk unknowingly into a cloud of her
fragrance and stop abruptly, his head tilting, his hands
lifting open as if in the hope of collecting this cloud into
a package he might carry around with him. Or he'd enter
a room' when she was unaware, to have the pleasure of
watching her unguarded actions as she lifted a pot from
the stove, or sat on the kitchen counter paging through

some cookbook, or being fortunate enough to see her in the midst of dressing or undressing.

All of it seemed like some fabulous film being screened exclusively for his delectation, and so gripping was it that he lost any sense of time or of himself. At moments when he heard her voice in some other room, or the echo of her laughter as she chatted with Raskin, he experienced a happiness so intense and so foreign he wasn't altogether certain it wasn't merely another, new variation of pain.

As a seven-year-old with fractured thighs and a crushed pelvis, an arm torn halfway out of its socket and a head swathed in layer upon layer of thick bandages, he'd lived for some months in a cocoon of drug-induced amnesia, where only occasionally did either memory or physical pain intrude. He recalled those months as a time memorable solely for its absence of externalized events. Faces and voices drifted to and fro, hands were gentle, and ghostly nursing sisters were kindly emissaries from heaven. He was obliged to do nothing, only to rest and regain his strength while his sturdy little bones knitted themselves back together with the help of splints and pins and pounds of plaster and contraptions that elevated some parts of his body but not others; all of this in a small white room, in a narrow white-sheeted bed, while light gushed in through an elongated window from which he instinctively averted his eyes.

On subsequent return visits, alone in the night before his scheduled surgery, he'd lie in the dark and sing to keep the phantoms at bay, to keep himself safe from harm. Through the nights, while his fingers plucked at the bedclothes and his restless body shifted this way or that, the small boy sang every song he'd ever known, and some he'd never known. Music was all that stood between him and a world of sharp-bladed instruments, all evil-smelling anesthetics, and the blinding overhead lights of the operating theater.

Now it was many years later and he hoped he wasn't behaving as that child had, instinctively averting his eyes from the things he ought to be seeing. But as difficult as his life had been until the day Marisa entered it, it was a hundred times more difficult now because his desire to keep her happy at all costs required him to think and to do things that did not come naturally. He was obliged to pay close attention to her every word and facial expression in order to satisfy himself that she was saying what she meant; he was constantly evaluating his own behavior in order to be sure he gave her nothing less than everything within his means. And even making love to her, a glorious experience that each time surpassed his most spectacular dreams, he was watching and listening and taking care to ensure that nothing went unnoticed, no word unheard. His vigilance, while entirely voluntary, was nonetheless exhausting. Perhaps he was trying too hard. Perhaps he wasn't trying hard enough. To be wedded, to have put into writing one's commitment to love another, was an all-consuming, ceaseless enterprise. There wasn't a day when he didn't wonder if he'd answered too abruptly or too slowly some question she'd asked, when he didn't fret over the possibility that he and Raskin were pushing her into a career when she'd have been quite satisfied to continue as before, with her visits to Kitty, her shopping trips into Manhattan, and her foraging expeditions through the local supermarkets. The logistics of the life-style he and Raskin had long since established sometimes defeated her. Who made his suits, his shirts? Where did he get his shoes? How did the laundry get his shirts so white? But if he had a tailor, didn't he have to go there at least once, sometime, to be fitted? And the same for the shirts and the shoes. He'd had to sit down with her to explain that there had been legendary agoraphobics who'd lived for years on end without ever leaving their homes while managing to dress and eat and survive quite nicely. He, at least, did leave the house. He simply didn't do it, unless it was unavoidable, during the day. And the tailor came to the house; so did the man who made his shoes. Wasn't she aware of the convenience money could buy? He was touched by how unspoiled she was, by how much she was of the world he'd long ago rejected. She'd never thought to connect money with power, never realized you could pay people to do practically anything.

"I don't know why," she confessed one night, "but I

saw the two of us together, shopping for things. Anything. Just together. And I thought perhaps we might sometime go dancing. I'd really love to do that. But you're right," she said bravely. "I wasn't thinking clearly. And I'm happy to dance with you here, in the music room. I don't mind. I really don't."

It was one of those times—his eyes felt like camera lenses, recording the little facial tics that betrayed her—when her mouth put out words that directly contradicted what her eyes, and cheeks, and chin, said. His daylight child wanted and needed light. Could he not bear it for her sake? Didn't he owe her at least a few excursions into the outside world? He could, to secure her happiness, do that much. Couldn't he?

Couldn't he? Dear God! The thought alone of that funeral and the dozens of Cameron's friends willing him dead and gone with their eyes, as dead and gone as poor dear Cameron, without even so much as speaking to him, let alone making any effort to discover whether or not he was indeed human. *Who is that creature?* Why did they hate him so? Total strangers, supposedly educated people, they despised him and wished him erased from the face of the earth—because he no longer looked human. Had he grown up safe and sound with Philippe and Lavinia, had he known the luxury of a social life with girls and dating in his teens, to arrive at his manhood intact, would he have wished some other benighted bastard dead, gone, and, above all, out of his sight? Possibly. But *he* was the benighted bastard, and the others who'd socialized and dated and married their childhood sweethearts sought to cover their women's eyes, pulling away in revulsion as if he were evil incarnate. He had dared to come out into the heartless blood-heating light, and they wanted him gone from their sight, removed from the immediate arena of their sensibilities because he was the living embodiment of their every secret fear.

Yet his wife, this child he'd so recklessly taken to his heart, longed to go out with him in public. For all her sympathy and understanding she had no true notion, no innate comprehension of how trifling, how truly paltry, was the hatred of strangers when compared to his own. For this *face*, this grotesque mockery of a human face.

Every day, on her behalf, he surrendered a little more of himself. What would happen when he'd grown tame and unprotected? Would he feel scooped clean, gutted like some fresh-caught fish with the hook still implanted in his cheek? Would he feel, constantly and never-endingly, the lance of happiness piercing the chambers of his heart with its purifying thrust? Or would he, blind and defenseless, be led by the hand by this child only to find himself abandoned in the desert without water?

She was so much a part of him it felt she'd passed into his very veins and arteries, where she swam in happy communion with the platelets and red and white cells. She was his life, its meaning. Could he venture beyond the walls of this house? Was he willing, for the sake of Marisa's profound belief in a state of ongoing happiness, to subject himself to the unwarranted hatred of strangers?

He prayed for the courage to walk through crowds with his wife.

Just over a year after she'd started carrying specifications about with her to read in her spare time, Erik was asked to submit drawings for a proposed condominium complex in Southport, and she was able to go with Raskin to assist, and to learn the fine points of a presentation. She enjoyed it, and was determined to be the one who'd oversee the next submission.

But it took far longer than she'd imagined. The condo project was a big one, on a fairly lavish scale, that kept them busy for more than two years. Erik had, through Raskin, to do battle during the entire construction phase, closely supervising the primary contractor to keep him from skimping on costs by using materials other than those specified. Halfway through, with nine of the twenty units completed, Erik was forced to fire the contractor for installing substandard furnaces and for failing to make the upgrade changes requested and paid for by individual owners. This necessitated not only many conversations with the builder but also entailed bringing in bids from other construction companies that were interested in seeing the project to completion.

Night after night, Erik and Raskin drove off to make site inspections, to be sure the new contractor was following the specifications to the letter. By the time the two men returned home, Risa, having spent the evening either alone or with Kitty, would be asleep. She'd get up to wander through the house in the mornings, or to sit outside on the terrace while she waited for the men to appear and for the work to continue.

During the morning hours she spent on her own, she thought about having a child. She thought about it, too, every time she went to the supermarket and encountered either pregnant women or those with infants in carry seats propped in their shopping carts. She couldn't resist the babies, and made such a fuss over them, she wondered if the women didn't think she was a bit crazy. They seemed tolerant and even pleased by her one-sided conversations with their offspring, and usually smiled at her as they pushed their carts off down another aisle. Risa watched them go, keenly envious.

She was working herself up to another discussion with Erik when he announced he'd been asked to submit drawings for a new project. "And you will present this one," he told her. "You'll be involved in this from the outset so that by the time we're ready to show the design, you'll know it as well as I do. We'll work together on this job."

She sat beside him and watched the building take shape beneath his hands. It impressed her mightily that he could visualize something in its entirety and then reproduce his vision on paper so quickly and with such ease. He'd been asked to design a private residence on an outcropping of land situated on the Sound in Westport. The owner of this land was a young Wall Street wizard with a wife and three small children who wanted light, airy open spaces in an all but indestructible dwelling.

Erik created a splendid environment, with rounded exterior walls and a two-story living room with an outside deck cantilevered over the rear lawn, which sloped down to the Sound. The design incorporated six bedrooms, a playroom for the children, an enormous kitchen with both eating and sitting areas, as well as another deck, and fireplaces in the living room, master suite, and den. It also took advantage of the setting by offering Sound views from most of the rooms and using the existing trees to provide summer shade. The budget was immense; the client wanted the best of everything, including a sauna and five bathrooms, three with built-in Jacuzzis; he also wanted a suite for the maid and live-in nanny and garage space for four cars. He was prepared to spend at least two million dollars. He'd seen several of Erik's buildings, and wasn't at all bothered by the idea of an architect he'd never meet, just so long as this particular architect, who'd been written up in Ada Louise Huxtable's column in *The New York Times*, was the one who designed the house.

Raskin went along with Risa to meet the client and to provide moral support and backup should she need it.

"If I start repeating myself," she said en route to the city, "jump in and save me. Okay?"

"It'll be a piece of cake, Risa. The guy's already made up his mind. At most, he might want modifications here or there. Just go nice and slow and cover everything point by point."

"What if he takes one look at me and decides I'm too young and couldn't possibly know what I'm talking about?"

"Never happen. I told you: This one's in the bag." Besides, Raskin thought, the client would likely be so busy staring at the architect's wife he wouldn't even notice the drawings. He'd be so impressed by the fact of Erik's having such a beautiful young wife he'd okay the job just for the sake of running into her again, maybe, at the site.

"You think I'm dressed all right?" she asked nervously. "Maybe I shouldn't have worn a dress. A suit would've been better."

"You look fine. Stop worrying."

"Easy for you to say. You could do this in your sleep, but if I screw it up, I'll never forgive myself."

"You're not going to screw it up. Guaranteed."

They were shown at once into the client's office, and

the young man shot to his feet as Risa came in carrying her portfolio, with Raskin behind her.

"I'm Marisa D'Anton," she introduced herself, shaking the man's hand. "And I'd like you to meet Hal Raskin, my husband's associate."

As Raskin had predicted, the man was so bowled over by the sight of Risa he scarcely glanced at the drawings. "It looks great!" he said several times. "Exactly what we want. Great!"

Risa couldn't persuade him to look at the budget.

"Leave it with me. I'm sure it's in order. All I need is a starting date and an occupancy date. The rest is up to you . . . to Erik." He went behind his desk, pulled a checkbook from one of the drawers, and dashed off a check, saying, "This'll get things rolling," and handed it over to Marisa as if he thought she'd go directly from there to Bergdorf's to spend the money on furs and evening clothes. Which he wouldn't have minded at all.

As they were driving out of the city, Risa exploded. "That man has no idea what he's buying. None. How can he say it's great when he didn't even *look* at Erik's drawings?"

"So, he's a schmuck," Raskin said. "Don't worry about it. What counts is the project, the house. And he'll be happy as all get out with it."

"I don't know if I want to do this again," she said, in no way mollified. "I felt like some idiot Barbie Doll, for God's sake! Like one of those dumb-ass girls on TV who do the weather and are forever waving their pointers at Seattle when they're talking about the weather in D.C."

Raskin laughed. "You ought to feel complimented, not angry. If I had the effect on women that you had on that guy, I'd be set for life."

"What're you *talking* about? You *do* have that effect. Or you used to, anyway, before you went goofy for Kitty."

"Goofy?" He shot a look at her.

"Well, what d'*you* call it? We never have to wonder where you are anymore because you're always over there."

"You sound pissed off about it."

"I don't know about that. I love Kitty, you know, and

I hate the idea you're going to dump her one day because you decide it'd getting too heavy.''

"Is that something you've heard from her?''

"No. I'm telling you my personal feelings.''

"You must think I'm a complete shit.''

"No, I don't, Hal. I just think you could do something like that. You wouldn't do it intending to be mean or anything. You'd do it because maybe people were seeing you out with her too often or something.''

"And what if I tell you you're dead wrong?''

"Am I?'' she challenged.

"I don't know.''

"Kitty and I have never discussed you, Hal. She's not someone who'd do that. She and my father were involved for *thirteen years* before I knew a thing about it. And I only found out by sheer accident. I'm not saying you're a bad person, because I don't think that. I guess I'm asking you please not to hurt her.''

"How did we manage to get from the client to Kitty without missing a beat?''

"Because I'm a good dancer,'' she answered obliquely, which made him laugh.

"Listen,'' he said, a cigarette clamped between his teeth while he pushed in the lighter on the dashboard. "It's not my plan to hurt Kitty or anyone else. I'm not in the habit of explaining myself, and I don't enjoy it. I know how you feel about Kitty. But you don't have a clue how *I* feel about her. And I'm not about to discuss it with you. The truth is, it's none of your business, Risa. I like you a hell of a lot, but every so often you want to get into things that don't concern you. This is one of those times. For the record, so you know there's no hard feelings, I'm happy with Kitty. I trust her. And that's a hell of a lot more than I've ever felt for any woman. So, do us all a favor and leave this alone.''

"Fine!'' she snapped. "Then you do *me* a favor. Don't tell me it's nothing, it's unimportant that some sexist jerk pays more attention to me than he does to something Erik slaved away at for weeks! So the guy thinks I'm good-looking. Big goddamned deal, Hal! My looks don't have a thing to do with Erik's design, and I'm offended by what that jerk did. Okay? I worked for over three years, closer to three and a half, to be able to make that presentation, and all that asshole did was make goo-goo eyes at me. I'm not just a goddamned *face*! I'm a person who went there to do business, not some bimbo my husband sent out on an errand because I'm cute! And furthermore, when you pat me on the head and patronize me and tell me it's no big deal, you're being as much of a sexist chauvinist asshole as that guy!''

There was a silence while Raskin got his cigarette lit, then returned the lighter to the dashboard. Finally, he said, ''I'm sorry, Risa. You're right. He *was* a moron. You *did* work damned hard. And it was a put-down—by both of us. I wasn't seeing it from your point of view.''

''I'm sorry too,'' she said. ''I was interfering.''

''None of it happened. Agreed?''

''Agreed. But I think Erik should turn the job down, send that fool back his check.''

''I think you're right. You want to tell Erik that?''

''Damned right I do!''

''I'll back you up all the way.''

''Thank you. God, Hal! How am I going to *explain* this to him?''

''He'll understand.''

''Maybe. But he wanted this job, and in a way it's my fault he's going to have to pass.''

''Nope. It's the moron's fault. Not yours.''

''Shit!'' she sighed. ''Are we friends again?''

''We never stopped.''

20

ERIK LISTENED CLOSELY TO WHAT RISA HAD TO SAY, AND to Raskin who supported her every word and even assumed some of the responsibility by admitting to the sexist attitudes he'd espoused. When they'd both finished speaking there was a lengthy silence while Erik sat motionless, his eyes on the portfolio Risa had placed on his drawing board along with the check.

He'd temporarily forgotten them as he pictured the scene, imagining some moneyed cretin salivating over Marisa while ignoring altogether the work they'd so carefully prepared. His lungs began to heave. With a cry, he jumped off the stool, took hold of it with both hands and sent it crashing through the stained-glass window at the near end of the room. The blood was roaring so deafeningly inside his head that he failed to hear Marisa's scream, or to feel Raskin's hands on his arm. He wanted to drive into the city and kill the man, beat him senseless with his fists, for defiling both his wife and his work.

"Erik!" Risa put her hands on his face, seeking to bring him back.

Raskin decided the smartest thing he could do was to go to the liquor cabinet for a glass of something that would calm Erik down before he did any more damage.

"*Erik!*" Risa cried more loudly, alarmed by this new

view of her husband. "It doesn't matter," she said ineffectually.

"*Of course it matters!*" he ranted. "*You know it does!*" His fists clenched and unclenched. The muscles in his arms and shoulders bulged against his sleeves. Some fool slobbering over Marisa, ogling her while she forged ahead with the presentation. He'd destroy him, pulverize him. His eyes seemed filled with blood.

"I had to tell you, Erik. I didn't want you to waste a wonderful design on someone like that. He didn't deserve to live in that house."

"Don't you think I *know* that?" he said, glaring at her.

"What should I do?" she asked helplessly. "I was only trying to do what was best for all of us." She turned to look at the fragments of colored glass strewn across the floor, seeing again the way he'd lifted the stool to fling it through the window. She hadn't known he was capable of such rage. "Perhaps," she said quietly, "you'd like to throw me through the window, too."

He gazed at her tapering back, at last realizing she'd thought his behavior, his anger had been directed toward her.

"I'm not angry with you," he said in a more temperate tone. "Do you think I blame you?"

She turned to look over her shoulder at him, gave a little shrug, then stooped to pick up some of the larger pieces of glass. She wasn't being as careful as she should have, too upset to pay close attention. And suddenly blood was welling from a gash across her palm and, seeing this, Erik dropped to his knees at her side and wrapped his handkerchief around her hand. He was recognizably Erik once again, and she touched her free hand to his cheek, saying, "I'd give anything if it hadn't happened. I know how much you were looking forward to this job. But, Erik, I resent being treated that way. And I resent having your hard work ignored. Am I supposed to go along with people like that, with situations like that? I can't. I don't know how."

"There are dozens of jobs, hundreds. I couldn't cope with the idea . . ."

"Why even think about it? He made me mad, Erik,

but he wasn't worth any of this." She looked over at the ruined window. "We'll never be able to replace that, and it was so lovely."

"Come, let me tend to your hand."

He lifted the pieces of glass from her lap and dropped them in the wastebasket.

"You wanted to kill him, didn't you, Erik? Because of me, or because he didn't pay attention to your work?"

"Both," he said fervently. "Both."

"It's not worth your energy. I'm not harmed. And there'll be someone else for that design."

"When someone diminishes you, he diminishes me, Marisa. Perhaps I was wrong to ask this of you."

"You weren't wrong!" she argued. "I *wanted* to do it, and I still do. God! I never dreamed it would blow sky-high this way. I suppose everything would be fine if I didn't have a brain. Then some asshole like that could make goo-goo eyes and I wouldn't even notice. I'm not sure if anything's worth all this."

"Please, let me look after your hand!" he begged, seeing the blood saturating the handkerchief.

She let him take her downstairs to the master bedroom where he sat her on the edge of the tub while he opened the medicine cabinet for disinfectant and some bandages. She sat holding her dripping hand over the tub, watching the way his concern for her turned his movements concentrated.

"Erik," she said very low, feeling dizzy, "you really frightened me, the way you did that. I've never seen anyone get so angry."

Assembling his equipment on the counter beside the basin, he said, "I apologize. It was not my intention to frighten you."

"What was your intention?"

"I didn't have one. I was simply furious."

"I wish you could know how frightening it was, Erik. It makes me hope to God I never inadvertently do anything to make you furious."

"I cannot conceive of anything you could do that would."

She almost said, *I can*, but thought better of it.

"I've made us all good stiff drinks!" Raskin called from the hallway, on his way up to the office with the stool he'd retrieved from the lawn.

Risa called back, "Thank you. We'll be down in a few minutes," then turned to Erik, who had her hand under the cold-water faucet and was sluicing out the gash.

"This is nasty," he said. "You might need stitches."

"Just tape it up. It'll be fine."

He knew from her tone the discussion was not yet over. She was apprehensive and angry now herself.

Turning off the faucet, he bathed the cut in disinfectant, then began winding gauze around her hand. "There is nothing," he said, "not a think in this world you could ever do that would inspire that sort of anger in me, Marisa. It was an ungoverned moment, not the first, but I will endeavor to make it one of the last. I am truly sorry."

Stroking his hair, she said, "I sometimes wonder if I'll ever see you happy, Erik. We go for days and weeks, we have our routines, the things we do every day, every night, and you seem so glad of our life together. Then something happens, like today, and I can't help thinking maybe I'm deluding myself, that I don't have any special talent for making people happy, for making *you* happy. We've been married almost four years, and it's gone by so fast, with both of us busy, each inside our own heads, me worrying about you, and you worrying about me. When do we stop being separate?"

"Don't give up on me!" he implored her, as suddenly abject as he'd turned wild. "I am trying so very hard."

"I know you are," she said, drawing his head against her breast. "I know. And I love you more every day, because I do know. I just want us to be at a point where there are no more questions. But maybe that's kid stuff, storybook stuff. Maybe nobody ever gets to that point. I know how hard you try, Erik. And I know you were upset. It's all over now. We'll forget about it."

The events of that day so impressed themselves upon her that she put aside the idea of discussing their having a child. She dreaded ever doing anything to reawaken Erik's formidable anger. In spite of what he'd said, she felt it could be triggered by some less than well-thought-out comment or suggestion of hers. Not that he'd ever harm her. He was incapable of that. She simply hated the thought of ever again seeing him go so out of control. And, besides, the incident notwithstanding, she loved their life together.

When they weren't working, the two of them would spend hours at the piano in the music room, or listening to music together. They might sit quietly for a time, then rise precisely at the same moment and, with a laugh, begin to dance. There were evenings when they lit a fire in the living room and sat with books, glancing over at one another every so often to smile. There were all kinds of books and authors Erik recommended to her, dozens of performers he wanted her to hear. He'd often look up from the tiny circle of light cast on his book by the Tensor light he used for reading and say, "You must hear this," then read a line of poetry, or a paragraph from some book.

They cooked together, sometimes with Hal and Kitty, too. Some evenings Kitty telephoned to announce they were all expected on Butlers Island for dinner. And sometimes Risa and Kitty went off to the movies together, or into the city for a day's shopping. The cleaning was done by a team that came twice a week and went through the house from top to bottom—except for the office, where Erik remained with the door locked until they left. Hal took in and picked up the dry cleaning, and saw to the servicing of the cars. Risa did the grocery shopping, the laundry, and tended to her houseplants. And every day there was work to be done in the office.

There were new clients, and Risa went on to present Erik's work without further incident. Then, on the eve of her twenty-fourth birthday and their sixth anniversary, Erik told her he'd made reservations for a dinner out. With Kitty and Raskin they went to a local steakhouse and had a genuinely festive evening. Their waitress was a young woman of about Risa's age who didn't turn a hair at first sight of Erik but pleasantly took his drink order and gave them exemplary service throughout the evening.

Before shifting to the lounge to dance, Risa and Kitty set off for the ladies' room and encountered the young waitress in the reception area. She stepped forward to put a hand on Risa's arm and said, "My younger brother Tony had to have a lot of grafts, too. I really admire your husband's guts. It's been twelve years now and Tony, he's twenty-two, he won't set foot out of the house. I hope you're having a real nice evening."

Dumbfounded, Risa thanked her.

"Do you think I should mention that to Erik?" she asked Kitty in the ladies' room.

"No, I do not," Kitty replied. "Erik knows what to-night means for all concerned. Keep lettin' him go at his own pace, Risa. Don't start pushin'."

Risa found this evening out very encouraging because it meant Erik might be losing some of his resistance to a number of things, including the idea of a baby. She thought she'd wait for exactly the right moment before mentioning it again.

The moment she chose was late Christmas Eve after Raskin had gone to escort Kitty home. Raskin's use of the word "escort" was his way of telling them he'd be spending the night with Kitty. After they had gone, Risa and Erik sat in front of the fire in the living room admiring the tree they'd decorated with red and silver bows. She sat on the floor between his legs with her back to his chest and his arms around her and said, "Erik, this would be so wonderful to share with a child."

Instantly she knew she shouldn't have introduced the subject. He tensed. His breathing underwent an audible change. His voice pitched deadly deep, he said, "Can you imagine an infant gazing up from its crib into this face? Can you imagine a child of yours doing battle every day to defend a parent with *this face*?"

Shifting toward him, she said, "Actually, I can imagine all those things. Erik, you'd be its *father*. That child would *love* you. To that child, you'd be beautiful, the way you are to me." She wondered why she was debating the issue when she knew she'd already lost. "I want us to make something out of the love we have for each other,

Erik. There has to be someone to come after us. There has to be a point to our having been alive in the world."

"I thought there was a point," he said in that ominous voice. "I thought the point was our being together."

"A baby wouldn't change that."

"You would have a child, and you would have no qualms about raising it in this house, this dwelling that has precisely one 'normal' room in it? You would give birth to an infant and put it into my arms to teach it fear at an early age? You would expect a child to comprehend our somewhat bizarre domestic arrangement?"

"Yes, yes, yes, to all of it. A child of ours would understand. An infant in your arms would only know its father. And there's nothing abnormal about this house, Erik. It's a fine house, with fine things in it. And the people who live here love each other."

"I've failed, haven't I?" he said, his tone shifting to one of defeat. "I thought I was making progress, but I haven't succeeded. I'm not enough. I should have known I couldn't be enough for you."

"Of course you are. I love you with all my heart. You've done wonderful things for me. I'm *very* happy with you. I just want to share what we have with a child. I want to have your baby. I want to be someone's mother, Erik. And I want you to be the father."

"With Raskin and Kitty as nursemaids, no doubt."

"Don't be that way! This has to do with me and you, and the feeling I have every time I see some woman's newborn. Or I take the train into the city and I see pregnant women walking around, and I want to be one of them. I want everyone to know how much I love you, how proud I am to be your wife."

"There's nothing I could ever deny you, Marisa. But I cannot do that. If you could even begin to conceive . . . I can't! Please don't ask for the one thing I can't give you. I'm not able to contemplate the horror I might see on the face of a child of mine. Please, don't ask me! *Please!*"

To her sorrow, he crossed his arms over his face and began to weep. Slowly, keeping his face hidden, he fell back to the floor.

"I thought you might have changed your mind," she said, devastated by his tears. "I had no idea you were so . . . that you had such strong feelings on the subject. It doesn't matter, Erik. I'll never mention it again. You have my word. We'll go on as we have been, and nothing will change." For the first time she didn't rush to comfort him, but sat on her heels watching and waiting as his tears subsided. She was almost twenty-five. She'd lived this long without a child. Undoubtedly she'd survive another twenty-five years without one, and, with luck, twenty-five more after that. By which time, she'd be far too old even to remember having wanted to hold a baby in her arms.

At last, she bent to tug his arms away from his face. Then she dried his tears. "We'll never talk about it again. I hate to see you suffer this way, Erik. I hate the times when something separates us and it feels as if we'll never be able to bridge the sudden terrible distance between us."

Still choked, he drew her down on his chest and held her, mortified by his weakness and by the spectacle he'd made of himself.

"Don't be angry with yourself," she said presciently. "I know you couldn't help it, any more than I could help saying what was on my mind. I'm sorry you feel that way. I wish to God you didn't, but I do understand."

"They stripped me of my clothes, then stood in a circle laughing and pointing," he whispered. "They threw pebbles and small stones and called me names, as if I were the village idiot. They shouted obscenities about my parents, who had to be monsters too. Then, when one of the masters came to break it up, he treated me as if it were all my fault. He collected my clothes from the grass and threw the lot at me, saying, *'Get dressed,'* in a voice clotted with contempt, and an expression on his face of sheer repugnance.

"There was no one to tell, no one who wished to hear, except for Henry, to whom I was forbidden to speak because he was merely a servant. And when I came to America, I thought perhaps it would be different—a new life in a new country. It was no different, only subtler.

College students don't strip one naked in the quadrangle
and pelt one with stones. They simply cross over the
grass if they happen to see one coming along the path.
They exclude one from their groups, and pretend one is
invisible in their classes. Yes, there are people here and
there—you and your father, Raskin and Kitty are examples, as was that waitress—who go on about their business and have no difficulty allowing one to go about his.
But in the end, it's infinitely less painful and humiliating
simply to do one's business in the darkened privacy of
one's home.

"I wish I could be strong enough, or hard enough, or
sufficiently thick-skinned to go out with you and not give
a damn, Marisa. I wish I could take the hatred and the
stares in stride, but I can't. I wish I could say to hell with
the rest of the world, you and I will do as we choose.
But can you picture the scene, visualize the reaction of
the hospital staff were I to take you in for the delivery of
a child? Likely as not, they'd be so involved with the
horror of their fascination they'd forget you altogether. I
wish love were enough to work the miracles you so want
to believe it can. It's not the way reality operates, Marisa. It's not the way *I* operate. I need you to forgive me
for my cowardice, and not despise me for being unable
to give you something you want."

"You break my heart every time you describe one of
those scenes, Erik. There's nothing to forgive, and I could
never despise you. No matter what happens, I'm always
going to love you. Do you believe that?"

"Yes."

"Then please, stop making yourself miserable. When
you suffer this way, I suffer with you. Do you know
that?"

"You're angry."

"No, I'm not angry. I'm tired. Let's go to bed."

Panic sent adrenaline surging through his system. She
was growing tired of him, tired of his lengthy tedious
explanations and his irrational behavior.

"I will try harder," he told her. "We will go out
more."

"Erik"—she sat up and pushed her hair back over her

shoulders—"stop beating yourself up. I'm here because I want to be, because you matter more to me than anyone else. You even matter more to me, Erik, than I do to myself. *I* wish you'd finally believe that. I'll know it when it happens, you know. You won't have to say a word or do anything. I'll just know. Now, let's please go to bed. Come keep me company, talk to me while I have my bath."

He went along after her, convinced he'd not only made a complete fool of himself but that he'd created a small but permanent rift between them.

21

THERE WAS NO OBVIOUS ALTERATION IN RISA'S BEHAVior toward him. She was as loving and giving as she'd ever been, but there were nuances, slight hints of her mounting dissatisfaction. Erik could see it in the way she'd sometimes pause and sit chewing on her pencil, gazing at the replacement stained-glass window he'd had made and installed in the near office wall. He could tell from the fractionally inward curve of her shoulders and the angle of her head that she'd gone away from him, and was continuing daily on that voyage. He feared that unless he did something to halt her progress, she'd eventually slip away from him altogether.

Inspiration came to him as her twenty-sixth birthday was approaching. He and Raskin and Kitty made the arrangements. And on the morning of her birthday, Erik roused her to say, "There's someone I want you to meet."

Groggy, she pushed the hair out of her eyes. "Who?"

"Come downstairs, and you'll see."

"Let me just go to the bathroom, then I'll be down."

He watched her get up and walk across the room, admiring the flex of her long thigh muscles and the shift of her buttocks as she went. She'd stopped wearing nightgowns soon after they'd married and often moved about their bedroom nude and apparently comfortable, perhaps

213

unaware of the ongoing effect the sight of her had on him. He was incapable of not watching her when they were in the same room together, driven to study her in all her aspects. He lived in a state of perpetual fascination, never finding her anything less than astonishing. At moments, with his eyes on her, he'd think, My wife, and feel an overpowering sense of pride.

He tried never to be obvious about watching her, correctly suspecting that it could be cause for tension. Clearly, if he so loathed the weight of others' eyes, it was only logical and reasonable that to some lesser degree others, and in particular Marisa, would find it stressful to be constantly observed.

She came out of the bathroom tying on her robe, asking, "Who'd come here first thing in the morning? Why do I have the impression you're up to something?" She stood smiling at him from the foot of the bed, then launched herself, landing on top of him with a triumphant little exclamation. "What're you up to?" she asked, brandishing her hands before his eyes in mock menace. "I can tickle it out of you if I have to."

All pretended innocence, he replied, "I am up to nothing. You have a suspicious mind."

"Me? Never. Who's this person I have to meet?"

"Come along downstairs and find out."

"This better be good," she warned, pinching both his cheeks before giving him a minty kiss.

"I hope so."

She went with him down the stairs, certain he and Raskin and Kitty had cooked something up for her birthday and their anniversary. No one but Kitty would dare to come to this house first thing in the morning. As it was, the only people who came at all were service people of one variety or another: Erik's tailor, his shoemaker, the blind man who tuned the piano, the gardener who never actually entered the house but simply toiled patiently on the grounds, the crew of men who came to collect the trash, and the cleaning people.

Raskin was standing by the kitchen counter, and turned when he heard them coming.

Erik said, "I would like to introduce you to Prince

William,'' and Raskin put the six-week-old cocker spaniel into Risa's arms.

She held the silken, curious puppy, looked into its liquid brown eyes and felt something overturn inside her. She laughed softly, bent to put her cheek to the puppy's golden coat, and burst into tears.

For a moment, Erik was terribly afraid he'd done the wrong thing. Instead of taking her mind off her longing for a child as he'd hoped, he'd offered a poor substitute and she was in tears over the transparency and imbecility of this sophomoric attempt to placate her.

But she hooked an arm around his neck, the other arm holding the dog secure, and said, ''I love him, Erik! This is so wonderful. I've wanted a dog all my life. Dad would never agree because he was bitten once when he was a small boy and was afraid of them after that. He's so adorable. Are you hungry, Prince William, or have they remembered to feed you?''

''He's been fed,'' Raskin told her. ''And so will you two be in about ten minutes. I'm waiting for the bacon to finish, then I'll be dishing up the celebration breakfast in the dining room, if you and the pooch would care to relocate there. I would like to point out, by the way, that he's not one hundred percent housebroken and has a tendency in moments of extreme excitement to let loose wherever he happens to be. You might want to take along some newspaper.''

Risa carried the spaniel to the living room, where she sat with him on the sofa, positioning him in her lap so she could pet him with both hands, then picked him up to receive his eager kisses. ''You are totally adorable, Willie. I know you're royalty, but I hope you won't mind if I call you Willie. Do you mind? No, I knew you wouldn't.''

Relieved to see her so immediately taken with the puppy, Erik sat on the facing sofa and watched her play with it.

''There isn't anything you could've given me I'd like more,'' she said happily. ''Come sit over here with me and get to know him. He's so sweet, Erik. Here''—she put the puppy into his arms, exactly, he thought, the way she'd have presented him with a baby—"see how darling he is."

Timidly he accepted the animal, as she said, "Don't be afraid of him, Erik. He only wants to love you."

"I, too, have never had a pet," he confided, tentatively holding the puppy in the air. All trusting, the dog held Erik's eyes, waiting to be returned to safety. He let the dog settle in his lap, where it wound itself at once into a small furry knot and went to sleep.

Risa leaned over to kiss him. "You are the cleverest man alive. I absolutely love him. Maybe this afternoon I'll go to the pet shop in town and get him a bed and some toys."

"Actually, we did get a bed, as well as a blanket and some rawhide strips. I didn't do anything about a doghouse. I wasn't sure what you'd want to do."

"I don't know. Do dogs prefer living indoors? Or are they happier outside?"

"We'll play it by ear, shall we?" he said, somewhat thrown by the unconsidered aspects of pet ownership. "As long as you're pleased."

"I am, very very pleased." She tucked her legs under her and rested against his arm, running her fingers over the sleeping puppy's pelt. "At night, when I take him out for a walk, you can come with me. It'll be our nightly outing—the D'Antons taking their constitutional."

"Frightfully domestic."

"Thank you, Erik." She wrapped her arms around his arm. "I'm afraid my gift to you is very mundane, even boring after this. God! I can't wait for Kitty to see him! She'll probably go mad over Willie."

"They've already met. She and Raskin went together to the breeder to pick him out."

"You're all so secretive. I had no idea, none. I was actually trying to figure out who'd be coming here at eight-thirty in the morning. What a bunch of sneaks you all are!"

"I prefer to think of us as devious. Sneaky has such nasty implications."

She laughed and pulled his head toward her to kiss him.

"Breakfast is served," Raskin announced, coming in to scoop Prince William from Erik's lap. "The prince can sleep in his bed while we chow down."

Risa got up to kiss Raskin's cheek. "Thank you for going to so much trouble. This is one of the best birthdays ever. What's for breakfast?"

"Broiled sheep's eyes and sautéed lizard entrails."

"Oh, yummy! My favorites!"

Laughing, the three of them went into the dining room. Erik, bringing up the rear, felt his lungs expanding with relief; even his hands twitched with the loss of his many reservations. He'd done something right. Marisa was positively aglow with happiness.

Risa fell into the habit of walking Prince William in the early morning, most days making her way to Butlers Island to have coffee with Kitty before returning home to start the day. Perhaps because of the early hour, or perhaps because their prior mother-daughter-like relationship had evolved into a close bond between two grown women, their conversations had new dimension and maturity.

During these visits, while they sat in the breakfast area Erik had created years before, they confided to one another the intimate details of their lives. While the dog dozed in the sunlight, or chewed at a bone or a piece of meat Kitty had set aside for him, Risa allowed herself the luxury of giving voice to some of her most private thoughts. Her greatest concern, aside from her secret ongoing desire for a child, was what she perceived to be her failure to make Erik completely happy.

With surprising heat and energy, Kitty defended him. "You can't expect the man to change the habits and fears of a lifetime just like that, Reese. You can't expect him suddenly to go round smilin' all the day long. That's not the way things work. These things happen gradual-like. And you've worked wonders with him. Think about how he is now, and the way he was back when he first came here."

"I know that. It's just that I wonder how long it's going to take before he trusts me enough to . . . relax, I guess."

"Some people never do, you know. Some people live out their entire lives on the wire. I'd rather have someone like that than some fella asleep at the switch half the time. Try not to dwell on it," she counseled. "I never in my life saw anyone try harder to please someone than Erik works to please you."

Risa looked away, unable to explain the uneasiness she felt. "It's hard sometimes, Kitty, having someone pay such close attention, work so hard to do things to please you. It feels, every so often, as if I'm on a slide under a microscope. I get so self-conscious. It's inhibiting. At first, at the beginning, it was incredibly exciting to have him watch so closely, take such care. Lately, it's been starting to feel . . . I don't know . . . claustrophobic." Looking back, she said, "That's partly what I mean about getting him to relax, to trust me, so he'll lie back and close his eyes and not worry that I won't be there when he opens them again."

"It'll come," Kitty said. "Besides, it's not like he's doin' it for reasons you don't know about, not like he's spyin' on you."

"No. It's more like he's taking a doctoral degree in Risa Behaviorial Theory."

Kitty laughed. "We should all be so lucky. Most men're far more interested in bein' the object of attention. You don't wanna let anybody hear you complainin' your husband loves you too much, Reese. You might get yourself murdered your next trip to the supermarket."

"I guess." Risa smiled, then asked, "Did you ever want to have a child, Kitty?"

Kitty took a long draw on her Kool before answering. "I grew up thinkin' I'd be somebody's mama, you know. And when I got married, I figured it'd be the next step in the proceedin's. But I married a child. You understand? A sweet fella, but a child. So when I got pregnant, I thought a good long time about what I'd do. Did I want to get tied to this fella for life because of a baby? Or was I gonna be movin' on, the way I knew I'd have to almost from the day we married? And I knew I could never do it. So I went to this woman I'd heard tell of who got rid of babies on her kitchen table if you had the hundred dollars to pay her. I took my savin's and laid myself down on that table and looked at the flypaper hangin' from the ceilin' while she took away the baby.

"It went bad, and I ended up in the 'mergency room of the hospital, with Billy there scared silly, not knowin' what I'd done. When they took me inside, I begged the doctor not to tell Billy the real reason I was hemorrhaging. He was a decent man, told me I was a foolish girl to do what I had, but no, he wouldn't go tellin' Billy. Then they put me under and tried to fix me up, gave me a lot of blood and so forth. When I came to he told me the woman had stuck her knittin' needle, or whatever it was she used—I never did see, I kept my eyes on that flypaper—she'd gone and put it right through my uterus, ripped it up good. So all's he could do was take it out. But I'd be good as new, 'ceptin' I wouldn't be gettin' pregnant no more.

"It's kind of why your daddy's ad reached me the way it did. I thought if I couldn't have a child of my own, I'd have me second best and do right by some other poor woman's baby. And I like to think I've done a first-class job with you. You turned out to be a woman any mother'd be proud to call her own."

"You've been a first-class mother," Risa said feelingly. "Kitty, I feel so . . . I don't know . . . strange. I'm twenty-eight years old. I've been taking those pills for more than ten years and now, all of a sudden, things seem to be happening. I've got these brown marks on my face and neck. I'm all swollen and I've gone up an entire bra size."

"You better make yourself an appointment to see your gynecologist. I've been reading how it's no good to take those pills for years on end. They can cause strokes and Lord knows what else."

"What if taking them all this time has done something so I can't ever have a baby?"

"Oh, I'm sure nothin' like that would happen. And besides, I thought you told me the two of you've agreed you're not gonna have any kids."

"Erik doesn't want one, but I do. I can't stop thinking about it, can't stop hoping he'll change his mind."

"Listen to me, Risa! I can understand how you feel, and I can sympathize. But have you ever thought that maybe it really is askin' too much? Before you came along, that man had nothin' to lose. He had his life and he had things sorted out so he was gettin' by. Then you come along and you turn him on his ear and all of a sudden he's got plenty to lose. I'm willin' to wager there's not a day of the world when he's not scared half to death he'll lose you. You have a baby, and there'll be somethin' more he's got to fear losin'. Some people just can't take risks, and he's one of them. Riskiest thing he ever did was stakin' his claim on you."

"But he's not going to lose me," Risa argued. "And a baby would guarantee that once and for all."

"You're a smart woman, but not so smart as you could be. Try to see it from his side, Reese. He managed, in spite of everything, to get himself a beautiful young wife. The man's forty-three years old and you're expectin' him to change in big ways for you. It's not gonna happen. And maybe it's not fair of you to be hopin' for it. You can't agree to somethin', girl, while you're holdin' your fingers crossed behind your back like a child, intendin' to do some serious mind-changin' on the man later on. You can't go askin' for more than people are capable of givin'. And the most he can give to anyone he's givin' to you."

"I know," Risa said quietly. "I do know that."

"Then deal truthfully—with him and with yourself, and stop pinin' away for somethin' that can't happen. You got a whole helluva lot more than most women ever get. And if I had someone who loves me the way Erik loves you, I'd thank the Lord every night before I went to sleep; I'd count my blessin's, and I'd shut the hell up."

"Hal loves you."

"Hal would eat ground glass 'fore he'd ever admit to lovin' anyone," Kitty stated. "That man knows he's his father's son, and if you think Erik's got fears, they're nothin' compared to how truly terrified Harold is that he might one day haul off and start poundin' on me with his fists."

"But he'd never do that."

"Yeah, well. You know that, and I know that, but I doubt anything's ever gonna convince Harold of that. To his mind, love equates to killing. You figure that one out and I'll see to it you get the Nobel Prize. He's got a lifelong anger, and all kinds of fear. All kinds of it."

"So why do you keep on with him?"

Kitty gave a sheepish little laugh. "It's real funny how things work out," she said, pouring them both fresh coffee. "Seems I've grown attached to the man. I'm used to the way he comes and goes, prowlin' around like a hound sniffin' out some small animal. But he's gentle as can be when he comes to my bed. I kinda like the contrast."

The gynecologist said, "These are common reactions to prolonged use of the pill. I think it's time we took you off it."

"But what will I do for birth control?"

"We'll fit you for a diaphragm. We can do it right now, if you like."

"I guess we'd better."

He gave her a brief show-and-tell lecture, inserted the diaphragm, then suggested she go into the changing room and try inserting it herself. It was, she thought, like trying to fold a small greased basketball hoop and then force it inside herself. Chuckling, she succeeded in positioning the rubber shield, and returned to the examining table so the doctor could check to make sure she'd done it properly.

He said, "Good girl!" and patted her on the knee. It irked her.

"I am not a *girl*," she told him. "I am a grown woman with a small basketball hoop inside me."

He laughed hugely. "Get dressed and I'll see you in my office, give you a prescription."

She stopped at the pharmacy on her way home and emerged with a large brown paper bag filled with supplies. It seemed like an enormous amount of gear, and she couldn't imagine how she'd be able to deal with the jelly and the powder and maintaining the diaphragm, let alone stopping in the midst of lovemaking, or having to hold Erik off should he spontaneously approach her as he so often did, while she took herself off to the bathroom to insert the thing. But she was determined, and spent close to twenty minutes in the bathroom that night before finally climbing into bed.

"Are you all right?" Erik asked. "You were gone for quite some time."

She explained to him about the side effects of the pill and about the diaphragm and he grew progressively more concerned as she spoke. "I'll get the hang of it," she told him. "Don't worry."

But when they began to make love, she found that it hurt. Erik's body seemed to be forcing the rim of the diaphragm higher and harder into her. She tried to ignore the discomfort, but couldn't. Finally, she confessed, "Erik, it hurts."

Instantly he stopped and, distressed, sought to console her. "Perhaps," he said, "I should look into having a vasectomy."

"No!" she cried, horrified by the prospect. "I won't let you do that! I'll find something else. I'll call and make another appointment, get an IUD or something. But I want you intact! You have to promise me you'll never, ever again, even consider such a thing!"

"Of course I promise, if you feel so strongly on the matter."

"I do! I feel *very* strongly. I don't want you mutilated."

He had to laugh. "In view of everything else, it's hardly mutilation."

"No! Just no, okay?"

"Yes." He backed down in the face of her strenuous objections. "All right."

The following day she returned to the gynecologist for an IUD.

"This should take care of everything," the doctor assured her. "I'm sorry the diaphragm didn't work out. It's the perfect solution for a lot of women."

"Oh, that's okay," she said with grim humor. "I'm thinking of buying a hamster, and the hamster can use it for a trampoline."

"The pigmentation blotches should fade pretty fast," he said. "A couple of months and they'll be gone. You might have a little staining for a few days, but it's nothing to worry about."

She thanked him and went home to Erik. "Everything's taken care of," she announced. "We've gone from trampolines to fishhooks."

22

FOR QUITE SOME TIME, LIFE WAS SETTLED, HARMONIOUS, and productive. Work got done in the attic office. Risa and Raskin oversaw the running of the household. The dog got walked twice a day. And Erik gradually drew ever deeper breaths, the passage of time convincing him as nothing else could that he'd managed to escape notice by the Fates. They were occupied elsewhere, and paying little attention to the goings-on inside the house on Contentment Island.

To celebrate Risa's thirtieth birthday and their twelfth anniversary, Raskin and Kitty took over the kitchen, telling Erik and Risa to stay away until eight o'clock that evening.

"That's cute," Risa said. "We're supposed to walk Willie for two or three hours."

"We will have pre-celebration festivities in the music room," Erik told her. "This is an important birthday."

"It's an important anniversary."

"Is it?"

"I think so. Twelve years of wedded bliss."

"Are you being sarcastic?" he asked, unsure.

"It's been sheer agony. I've hated every moment of it. I don't know *how* I'll survive the next twelve. God!" She laughed, winding her arms around his neck. "*When* are you going to believe I like it here, that I intend to stay,

224

that I don't have a full set of bags packed and ready to go hidden at the back of my closet? Sometimes, you're such a dolt.''

"One must never take anything for granted," he said, only half joking.

"You've never taken anything for granted in your life. Why would you start now?"

"I wouldn't."

"Right! Now come downstairs and sing some of those songs you wrote ages ago, when I used to sneak over here every night. You hardly ever sing for me anymore."

"I thought perhaps you'd grown bored . . ."

"When you sing," she said, her arms going tighter around him, "I think God whispers in *your* ear. Do you know that? Sometimes, when you're upstairs working with Hal, or I go down to the music room early in the morning while you're still sleeping, I put on one of your tapes. I play it at top volume and it feels as if I'm inside your mouth, as if I'm in this huge cavern, but it's your throat. I sit and listen and my entire body turns to jelly. I listen and tell myself, That's Erik. That is my husband, Erik. I play it so loud I can hear every breath you take, and it makes my hair stand on end when you drop your voice very low for a phrase, and then, suddenly, you're shooting up to a note I can't believe you can reach, let alone sustain. But you do. You take the words and the music and you make them so personal, you fill them with so much hope and pain and meaning, that I drown in you. There I am, sitting perfectly still, but sinking lower and lower into this deep warm pool. I'm drowning, and I'm glad. It makes me want you every time. I have to force myself to stay where I am and let you sleep, because I want to come up here to wake you, so I can touch you, hold you. I could *never* be bored by anything about you. My God! I don't know how you could think that. If I happen to be feeling blue, you come along and make silver dollars appear in my hair, or you pull fifty silk scarves out of the air and make a rainbow. I love you, Erik."

"Then, of course, I must sing for you. Come with me."

He took her hand and for a moment she felt as she had

years before when he'd come for her in the boat and, pulling alongside the dock, he'd held his hand out to her. She'd gone with him every time full of a sense of dangerous excitement. She felt it again strongly now as they hurried down the stairs.

The candles were already lit. A bottle of burgundy and two goblets sat on a tray between the two black-and-gilt chairs. On top of the piano was a gift-wrapped package.

"How is it you manage to surprise me every time?" she asked him upon entering, as he turned to bolt the door. "I'm never prepared, never expect it, when you do things like this."

"That is why I do them. Shall we have the wine first, before you open your gift?"

"No. Sing for me."

"As you wish."

They sat together on the bench and he asked, "What would you like to hear?"

"Anything."

"Ah, anything." His fingers extended themselves over the keyboard, whispering over the keys before the left hand lowered itself to begin. He sang *"La Vie en Rose"* in French. She sat with her head on his shoulder, her eyes closed, feeling the side of his thigh against hers as he worked the pedals, his arms grazing her side. And she sighed, thinking how perfect it was, how utterly perfect to be with him, to be engulfed in his music, to be the focus of his considerable love. When he'd finished, she remained where she was for a few moments longer, then got up and went to put on a cassette.

Erik shifted on the bench to watch her, galvanized when she turned and began to undress. As if she'd forgotten him, she attended to the removal of her clothes. And then, when she'd dispensed with everything, even her jewelry, to stand wearing only her wedding ring, she at last looked at him. With the Haydn cello concerto sobbing into the room, she came back to stand in front of him.

"This is what I want for my birthday," she said, her hands on his face as she climbed into his lap. "Everything else, my dear, is icing."

His appetite for her in no way diminished either by

time or familiarity, he was wildly excited by her accessibility. No matter how many times they made love, he invariably wanted her more. She fascinated him endlessly. And each time they touched was, for him, as thrilling as the first time.

"This may be your birthday present," he told her, reveling in the slippery softness of her flesh, "but I consider it my anniversary gift."

"Just a part of it. There's more to come. Let's get you out of these clothes," she said, unknotting his tie.

He stood up holding her and slowly turned in a circle so that her hair swung out in a graceful arc. She laughed softly, saying, "You make feel like a little girl, as if I'm not more than eight or nine and weigh about sixty pounds."

"You weigh scarcely more than that."

"I weigh a great deal more than that. But of course to a man who can lift grand pianos, what's the weight of one oversized woman?"

"Oversized? Never."

"Take your clothes off, Erik." She began undoing his shirt buttons, then slipped her hand inside. "I'm getting dizzy."

Keeping hold of her, he bent lower and lower until she was on the floor. Then, like one of his sleights of hand, he vanished for a moment into the shadows and returned undressed.

"Come here." She held her arms out to him, and he descended into her embrace like someone dreaming.

After, they lay naked together on the carpet and drank the wine. Finally, she went for the box on the piano top. Inside, delving past layers of tissue, she found a set of keys.

"What is this?" she asked, dangling the keys in front of him.

"They will unlock your gift, which, at this very moment, is waiting out of doors."

She began to laugh, and he wanted to know what she found so amusing. Knee-walking over to the pile of her discarded clothes, she fished in the pocket of her skirt and came out with an envelope.

"The driveway must look like a supermarket parking

lot," she laughed, giving him the envelope, which he opened to reveal another set of keys.

"What is this?" he asked, holding the keys in front of her nose.

"It's too silly!" she declared. "I think we'd better get dressed and go take a look."

Facing each other on the circular driveway were a new Mercedes 380 SL and a new black Rolls-Royce Silver Wraith. Erik and Risa looked at each other and laughed.

"You see me as more sedate in my middle age?" he asked her.

"I was thinking more of my comfort. I'm getting a little tired of riding along feeling as if I'm only three inches above the road. And what about you? Are you trying to encourage me to start speeding?"

"Not at all. It's a wonderfully engineered automobile with a certain rather racy appeal to it." He looked at the Rolls. "Marisa, that's a great deal of money to spend on a gift."

"You should talk!" she countered. "And you didn't get a seven-figure check today."

"Oh, of course. The balance of your father's estate."

"Henderson went to great pains to point out my father's farsightedness and acumen when it came to the market. He told me more than anyone could ever want to know about Dad's cleverness in buying Xerox and IBM and GE and half a dozen other stocks. I figured we might as well spend some of it, rather than have it sit in a bank getting dusty."

Raskin and Kitty were standing in the doorway grinning.

"I gave Raskin last year's sedan," Erik said.

"I gave Kitty the Buick."

"It's everyone's party!" Kitty called. "Come on in, you two, and eat. It's perishin' out here."

They'd cooked up a fabulous dinner, starting with Scottish smoked salmon, a main course of brandied duck, and a dessert of a three-layer chocolate cake festooned with candles. After the meal, they retired to the living room for coffee and Armagnac, all complaining they'd eaten far too much.

Raskin looked at his watch just before twelve-thirty and said, "Come on, Kitty. Let's throw everything in the dishwasher, then go for a spin in one of our new cars."

"Leave it," Risa said. "We'll clean up. After all, you two did all the work."

"That's right," Kitty said. "We did. So we're goin' for a ride in Harold's smart new vee-hicle."

They left and Risa said to Erik, "I'll make you a deal. Take Willie out for his walk while I clean up. Then we'll go upstairs and make love for three or four hours. I'm not the least bit tired."

"Three or four hours," he repeated. "I'll be dust and ashes if we keep on at this rate. I'm not sure I care for being used in this callous fashion."

"Oh, sure," she scoffed, laughing.

"I'm also not sure I enjoy being quite so predictable," he sniffed.

"You are the least predictable human being I've ever known. Now, go walk Willie before his bladder explodes."

"A very pretty image!" he said, going for the leash.

They hadn't been in the car for five minutes, heading down Tokeneke Road into the center of town, when they heard the whine of a siren and behind them came the flashing lights of a police cruiser.

Raskin muttered, "Shit! I'm not five miles over the limit."

"Just be calm, Harold," Kitty said. "Don't go arguin' with the man. Take the ticket and say thank you very much."

"Right!" He pulled over to the side of the road and reached for his wallet as the police officer approached the car. Raskin pressed the button on the center console to open the window on the driver's side as the officer put one hand on the side of the car, leaned down and said, "Good evening. May I see your license, please, sir?"

Raskin removed it from his wallet and passed it out through the window.

"And your registration, too, please?"

"I've only got a temporary," Raskin explained, open-

ing the glove compartment, knowing it wasn't in there.
It was back at the house on the kitchen counter. "I
must've left it at home."

"Just a moment, please," the officer said, and went
back to his cruiser.

"It'll be fine, Harold," Kitty said, her hand on Raskin's thigh. "It's only a speedin' ticket, no big deal."

"If it's no big deal, maybe you can explain what's
taking him so long?" Raskin looked into the rearview
mirror to see the policeman talking into his radio.

"You know how they do it," she said, wondering about
that herself, but determined to keep Harold calm. "They
gotta call it in to the computer to see if you're a wanted
man."

"Don't joke about it!" he barked. "I've got a criminal
record."

"What's that got to do with anything?"

"You'd be very goddamned surprised."

The officer returned to the car, one hand on his holster.
Standing a good six feet away, he said, "Will you get
out of the car, please, sir?"

"Fuck!" Raskin muttered.

"You, too, please, ma'am."

Kitty got out to see the officer slam Harold against the
side of the car, turn him around, frisk him, then begin
handcuffing him.

"What're you doin'?" Kitty demanded. "Why're you
doin' that to him?"

"Now, ma'am, you stay right where you are." When
he finished with Raskin, he reached into the Mercedes,
turned off the lights, pulled the keys from the ignition, then locked the car. "Right this way, please," he
said, pushing Harold from behind and taking Kitty by
the upper arm toward the cruiser.

"I do not believe you can do this!" Kitty protested.
"You cannot pull people outta their cars without an explanation and put them in handcuffs."

"Get in, please, and watch your head."

Once they were in the back of the car, separated from
the officer by a mesh grille, trapped inside by doors with-

out handles, the officer made a jargon-filled call on the radio, then started up the car.

Upon arriving at the station they were herded into a small room where Raskin's handcuffs were removed and they were told to wait.

"Just one damn minute!" Kitty said, becoming very angry. "You have no right to be doin' any of this!"

"Yes, ma'am, we do," the officer assured her, and went out, locking the door behind him.

"What the *hell* is going on?" Kitty wondered aloud.

Raskin lit a cigarette, took a hard drag on it, then said, "This happens every so often, Kitty. I'm sorry."

"How come you've never once mentioned it?"

"Maybe four times in the last fifteen years they've stopped me for some asinine traffic violation, like going two miles over the limit. And when they run me through the computer, they come up with a flag or some fucking thing on my MVD record. Then they accuse me of every unsolved crime for the last fifty years, push me around some, then finally turn me loose. This time, they'll probably try to make me for stealing the car. No registration, see."

"Surely to God it's not their right to do that," she said angrily.

"They think it is. I have to work hard to keep cool, because I'd like to beat the shit out of these arrogant assholes who think they're superior because they're fucking cops."

"But, Harold, you were acquitted of that crime. Why're they still holding it against you?"

"I was convicted with suspended sentences two other times," he admitted. "Assault, and assault and battery. Both when I was twenty-six. There were extenuating circumstances, but the judge said if he ever saw me again in his court he'd make sure I did hard time. So I enlisted to save us all the trouble. But I've got a record. I guess I should've told you."

"I guess you should've. But I still don't see why things that happened years ago should keep interferin' in your life now."

He shrugged. "That's the way it goes."

The door opened and a plainclothes officer came in. A

tired-looking man in an ugly green polyester suit, he identified himself as Detective Raines and asked, "Either of you want some god-awful station-house coffee?"

Both declined, and he said, "Smart," as he pulled over a chair, turned it backward, then straddled it. "Who belongs to the car, Harold?"

"I do. It was transferred to me yesterday."

"Who by?"

"My employer."

"Where's the temporary reg?"

"At home on the kitchen counter."

"Your employer gonna verify that, Harold? Or did you help yourself to the vehicle?"

"For Chrissake! Why don't you have one of your flunkies drive me home. I'll show him the registration and we can get this crap over and done with."

"No can do, Harold. We're gonna have to have your employer vouch for you. You wanna give us a name and number?"

Raskin didn't want to do it. Seeing this, Kitty said, "Erik D'Anton," and rhymed off the number, facing down Raskin's glare, saying, "Don't be a fool. Erik will be glad to vouch for you."

"I'll be back." Raines got up and went out, locking the door again.

"Why the *fuck* did you do that?" Raskin rounded on Kitty.

"Why shouldn't I?"

"Because they'll make Erik come down here to ID me and the car, that's why not."

"Oh, hell!" Kitty said softly. "I'm sorry. I never thought of that."

"If you'd stayed out of it, they'd have taken me to the house, I'd have shown them the temporary registration, and that would've been the end of it. Fuck!"

"I'm sorry," Kitty apologized again and opened her bag for a Kool. "Damn! I'm really sorry, Harold. I just wasn't thinkin'."

"Never mind," Raskin relented. "How were you to know?"

"I wasn't, I guess. Damn!"

Marisa answered, then said, "Erik, it's for you. A Detective Raines."

Erik took the receiver and said, "Erik D'Anton. What is it?" then listened. Risa jumped up, convinced there'd been an accident. The moment the call ended she asked, "What? What happened?"

"They seem to think Raskin's stolen the Mercedes. They want me to bring the registration and identify him."

"Where's Kitty?"

"They're holding both of them."

"Erik, let *me* go."

"You can't. I must go in person."

"Then I'll come with you. Why would they think that?" she asked, going next door for some clothes.

"Because Raskin has a record. He doesn't know I'm aware of it, but this has happened several times over the years. They've telephoned me to confirm his identity and employment. I've asked them each time not to inform him they've contacted me. This is the first time I've been requested to come to the station."

"What kind of record?" she wanted to know, pulling on a pair of jeans as she came back into the room, a sweater tucked under her arm.

"He was involved in some brawls when he was in his mid-twenties. He broke one young man's arm and gave another several broken bones as well as a concussion. The fights were a result of Raskin's taking exception to the treatment young women were receiving—once in a bar, and once, apparently, in the back of a parked car."

"Poor Hal." She dragged the sweater over her head. "He must be so upset that they'd call and ask you to come down there."

"Yes," Erik said slowly. "I suppose so."

Without even glancing at the two new sports cars standing in the driveway, they automatically climbed into the Lamborghini. As they were heading along Tokeneke Road, Risa spotted the Mercedes.

"Have you got the spare key, Erik?"

"It's on the ring."

"Let me have it. I'll hop out and follow you, so Hal and Kitty'll be able to get home."

"Good idea."

They entered the station and went to the desk where Erik said, "Your Detective Raines rang and asked me to come down. My name's D'Anton."

The duty officer raised his head, looked at Erik and blinked rapidly several times. His mouth opened and closed but no sound emerged.

"Excuse me," Risa said to the man, who now turned to stare blankly at her. *"Hello?"* She rapped her knuckles on the top of the counter. "Anyone home? We want Detective Raines."

Without a word, the officer picked up the telephone, dialed a single digit, then said, "People out here for Raines."

"Let's wait over there," Risa put her arm through Erik's and drew him away from the desk. She could feel her anger building.

Raines came out from an inner office, saw Risa and started toward her with a smile forming on his lips. Risa tugged at Erik's sleeve, and Erik turned, causing Raines to halt in his tracks. Recovering himself, he advanced, saying, "Mr. D'Anton?" and looked up at Erik with a not-quite-formed expression that was somewhere between defensiveness and belligerence.

"Yes," answered Erik.

Raines decided to opt for belligerence. "You wanna show me some ID?" he asked. The sight of this D'Anton's face made his insides twist in anger.

"What for?"

" 'Cause I asked is what for." That face offended the hell out of him.

"Just a min—" Risa began, but Erik's hand on her arm stopped her.

"Where is Mr. Raskin?" Erik asked. "And why have you detained him and Miss Hemmings?"

"He's driving an unregistered vehicle." Who the hell did this guy think he was?

"That is not so. I'm certain Mr. Raskin explained that the registration was changed yesterday morning."

"You got the paper?" Raines couldn't meet the man's blazing black eyes.

Erik was losing his temper. "Of course I do! I think it would be wise of you to get Mr. Raskin and Miss Hemmings now." He stared at Raines, and the smaller man was suddenly overheated and a little nervous. Undergoing a change of attitude, he said, "I'll get them," and went back through the door he'd come from.

In less than a minute, he returned, pushing Raskin ahead of him. Grim-faced and furious, Kitty followed. Raskin looked both humiliated and outraged. He moved toward Erik, set to apologize, but Erik silenced him with an upheld hand.

"You wanna ID this guy?" Raines asked, less cocky now.

"Why did you push him?" Erik asked tonelessly.

"Pardon?" Like a small child, Raines knew all at once he was in trouble.

"I asked you why you pushed Mr. Raskin."

"Oh, I . . . uhm. Look, can we just get on with this?"

"We've already done it. Very obviously, this man is who both he and I have said he is."

"Okay, okay. Show me the papers!" He made one last stab at authority.

Risa felt the air between her and Erik suddenly fill with vibrations. Moving very deliberately, Erik reached into his jacket pocket and brought out the temporary registration form. Raines took it, gave it a glance, then waved it in the air, waiting for Erik to take it back. With the tips of two fingers, Erik removed the paper from the man's hand and returned it to his pocket.

"Okay, you can clear on out of here," Raines told Raskin, then turned to go. His hands were wet and his mouth was dry. He knew he'd gone too far.

"*Raines!*" Erik said in a sharp whisper that stopped the man cold. He turned back. "Have you ever heard of harassment, Raines? Or perhaps malicious persecution? Have you ever heard of good manners, Raines, or politeness? If any of your officers ever again subject my colleague to this sort of humiliation, I shall institute a lawsuit against this station and its employees that will cost every last one of you your jobs, not to mention personal injury suits against each of you individually that will ensure you end your days as welfare recipients. Do I make myself perfectly clear?''

Eyes wide, Raines nodded. If he wasn't very careful, this guy would kill him.

"You will now apologize to Mr. Raskin and to Miss Hemmings. You will also tell the officer who perpetrated this travesty to present himself at once so that he, too, may make his apologies.''

Raines nodded again, then mumbled barely audible apologies to Kitty and Raskin before rushing off to get the young officer. The man was arguing with Raines as he came through the door but went silent at the sight of Erik. He hitched up his uniform trousers, and said, "You got some problem?''

"No," Erik said. "You have a problem, as does your associate.''

"I think you're mistaken, sir.''

"No, I think *you're* mistaken. I suggest you go home and read up on the law. You will discover you have no grounds whatever for the actions you've taken tonight. My wife and I''—he reached for Risa's hand—"do not appreciate being pulled from our bed in the middle of the night in order to come here and be bullied. And my friends have done nothing that warrants the treatment to which you've submitted them. I have told Raines, and now I will tell you.'' Erik's whisper turned lacerating. "You will cease and desist your harassment of my colleague, and you will advise each of your associates of that. I will see to clearing the Motor Vehicle Department computer. Now, I believe you have something to say to Mr. Raskin and Miss Hemmings.''

"I, uhm, my mistake. Sorry.'' He glanced at Erik who, still not satisfied, and in the grip of outrage, as well as suffering under the fluorescent station-house lights, stepped close to the young officer to say, "You're playing games with the lives of people I care about. If you want a future, of any kind, I suggest you give it up. Do you understand?''

"Yes, sir.''

"Good!'' With that Erik turned to Raskin and Kitty to say, "We've brought the car for you.''

Outside, Kitty moved to speak to Risa as Raskin went over to Erik who, still caught in his anger, was visibly trembling. Both women turned to watch.

"Erik," Raskin began. "I can't tell you . . . Shit!" He threw his arms around Erik and hugged him, murmuring, "Thank you," then broke away, grabbed Kitty's hand and hurried her into the Mercedes.

"You were . . . I'm so proud of you," Risa said to a now stupefied Erik, who was watching Raskin drive off. "Why are you so surprised, Erik?" she asked, threading her fingers through his. "Did you think he didn't care? You're his mother, father, and brother all rolled into one. And you fought for him. Probably nobody else ever has. God!" she exhaled tremulously. "That was horrible. Are you okay?"

"Not really," he admitted as they climbed into the Lamborghini. He held his hands out to show her. They were shaking badly.

Risa took hold of them. "What you did was wonderful," she declared.

He shook his head. "I so dislike the world out here," he whispered, gazing through the windshield. Slowly he pulled his hands free in order to start the car. "It is so filled with fools."

"It's all right," she said. "Let's go home now."

As they headed down the Post Road, he said, "I wanted to destroy that place and those people. I wanted to bring it crashing down on them. I hate feeling that way."

"It's all right," she said again. "You handled it perfectly."

"You honestly think that?" He glanced over at her.

"Yes, honestly. Sometimes, you know, Erik, anger's a damned good thing."

"It didn't frighten you?"

"No." She smiled at him. "This time it only frightened you. Let's get home and finish what we started. 'My wife and I do not appreciate being pulled from our bed.' " she quoted, and then laughed. "You were magnificent!"

Somewhat shyly, he turned to smile at her.

23

WHEN SHE'D FIRST STARTED TAKING THE BIRTH-CONTROL
pills, Risa felt she had some direct control over her life
and her body. It was up to her to remember to take the
pills; a conscious daily decision that compounded her
commitment to Erik. But with the IUD in place killing
off any possibility of a baby without her actively having
to do anything, she began to feel she'd allocated control
of her body to others—to the gynecologist, and to Erik.
No matter how she tried to reason it through, no matter
how well she understood Erik's fears, she couldn't make
herself stop wanting a child. If anything, she wanted one
more daily. She'd dream she was giving birth, clinging
to the sides of a delivery-room table while her body split
like an overripe melon, and with no pain whatever,
there'd be her child. In her dreams she repeatedly delivered babies, then nursed them at her breasts; she held
their small sweet bodies in her arms and felt an extraordinary well-being. But nowhere did Erik figure in these
dreams. She was always alone giving birth and, afterward alone with the infant. She'd look around the vast
white emptiness of the birthing place of her dreams and
wonder where he was, why he didn't come to see the
beautiful child they'd made.

Her dreams were so real they seemed to transcend into
her waking world, leaving her with empty arms and a

belly that, despite its so-recent swelling, was remarkably flat. She'd go about for hours after rising with a sense of loss so acute, a feeling of emptiness so profound she didn't think she'd survive without locating the child she'd somehow misplaced. It had to be somewhere, but she couldn't remember where she'd left it.

She had dreams where she ran though endless empty rooms, following an infant's wail, drawn forward by the cry of the child she knew wanted its mother. She ran, doors slamming shut behind her, growing weary, knowing she'd never get to the place where the baby lay crying. And she never did. These nightly marathons ruined her rest; she awakened feeling drugged and enervated, as if she'd actually spent the seven or eight hours of the night sprinting along some country track.

As a result, even her emotions seemed no longer to be entirely under her control. One night at the climactic point of her lovemaking with Erik she began sobbing and couldn't stop, nor could she offer him an explanation.

"There must be something," he insisted, holding her while she wept. "Is it something I've done? Something that's happened? Please tell me. I can't bear to see you this way."

What could she say? The truth, she knew, would start *him* weeping. All she'd accomplish by telling him was to upset him. So she kept repeating, "It's nothing, nothing," and at last she was able to stop. But she could see Erik had serious misgivings. She knew he was reviewing every last thing he'd said or done for months in an attempt to pinpoint the problem. It revived her claustrophobia and made her want to scream at him. This was one of the times when she hated that feeling of being on a slide beneath a microscope into which Erik was peering.

"Erik," she said, suppressing her sudden and considerable anger with him, "why do you *do* that? You're lying here trying to figure out what sin you've committed. I don't think you realize that everybody, every last living one of us, is locked up with our own thoughts, *just the way you are*. I'm as trapped as you by what I think and feel. You are not the only one who wishes he could read minds and thoughts. I wish I could, too. I'm not some perfect toy without a brain, Erik. I've been working all these years, just as you have, to know and to understand and to care about and to anticipate the things that'll make you happy or that'll upset you. You are not the only one who *feels*, Erik! I'm up here''—she pressed the heel of her hand against her temple—"imprisoned up here, *just like you*!"

"But I know . . ."

"Sometimes I don't think you *do* know. And sometimes the things I feel have nothing to do with you; they have to do with me. But sometimes, *sometimes* you're so involved in your pain and fears and the stuff inside your head that you forget I've got all those emotions, too. Just because I'm not you and don't reveal myself the way you do, you think nothing's going on in my brain."

"What have I done to make you so angry?" he asked.

"Nothing! You haven't done anything!"

"But you're simply livid, and since there's no one else in the room, what am I to think but that you're angry with me? I'm confused," he confessed, his hands agitating as if with a need to take flight.

"I'm not livid. I know you're confused." She took hold of his hands, willing both of them to calm down. "I'm sorry. I'm getter older very damned fast," she said, her voice reedy with emotion. "Time's flying away from us, and soon it'll be too late. I'll be past the point where I'm able, should you ever change your mind."

"Ah!" he said, at last understanding. "We are discussing babies again."

"No. Yes. Yes! You want the truth, I'll tell you. I can't stop the wanting, Erik. I've tried everything, but it won't go away. I know it can never be but I want that baby just as badly as you want the face you should've had. I mean, it's positively amusing in this age of female emancipation that all I can think about is being a goddamned mother, but there you have it. It's never going to happen, but by Christ I think about it. I don't blame you. I understand your feelings, and I don't want to change you. I love you the way you are. I always have and I always will. I've just got to figure out some way to stop wanting. It's taking me longer than I thought it would, that's all. I know it hurts you,'' she said sadly, ''and I'm sorry. I hate hurting you. But I'm tired of walking around with this need festering inside me; I'm tired of dreaming of babies every night. I know, I know! We thrashed this out a long time ago, and I accepted the terms. I still do. I do,'' she wound down. ''I'm sorry.''

''You're unhappy.'' He looked mortally wounded.

''No, I'm not,'' she said, beyond upset now and primed to feel guilty. ''I love my life with you. I love you.''

''But you would love me more if I consented to a baby.''

''No. Maybe. I don't think I *could* love you more. It's different, Erik. It's something else, something maybe only women feel.''

''You know if I could possibly face it I would do this for you, Marisa.''

''I do know that,'' she said, saddened as she put her arms around him. ''I know you'd do anything for me. That's what makes it so damned hard.''

''Do you want to be free of me?'' he asked, terrified that she'd say yes.

''No. And don't make it sound as if you're holding me captive. I *want* to be here with you.''

''I wish . . .''

''Don't say it! I know how you feel, Erik. I do!'' She put a hasty end to the conversation by engaging him in a long searching kiss, suddenly frantic to lose herself in lovemaking. She had to use her body to distract both of them from an unresolvable issue. And she succeeded.

For Erik, however, from that night in January a few weeks prior to her thirty-second birthday, the countdown had begun. Somewhere, a huge clock had begun ticking. And there was rarely a day when he didn't all but hear the grinding of its massive wheels and feel the push of its inexorably moving giant hands. He could do nothing to stop it.

''I think your girl's gonna crack up,'' Raskin told Kitty.

''What's that mean?''

"It means what I said. She's showing serious signs of wear and tear."

"Why? How?"

"Why I can't say. You'd probably know that better than me. How? I'll give you an example or two. The other day I'm driving her over to pick up her car from being serviced, and we're talking, you know. And out of nowhere she starts asking about my family, what were they like, did I have brothers or sisters. Kitty, she knows all about my family and has for years."

"Maybe she forgot."

"Not likely, but I'll give that one the benefit of the doubt. Here's another. She's coming back one morning last week from walking Willie. I'm in the kitchen making coffee and she climbs up to sit on the counter the way she always does and starts in on this big plan she has to breed Willie with another spaniel so she can have the pick of the litter. There's only one small problem: Willie was spayed six months after she got him. You want more examples?"

"No," she said, going to the bar to refill her glass.

"It's kind of obvious to me, to be truthful," he said. "Is it as obvious to you?"

"I guess so," she said, returning to her chair. "I'd been hopin' all that was settled long ago."

"Well, it isn't, not by a long shot."

"What about Erik?" she asked.

"What about him?"

"Has he noticed? How's he behavin'?"

"Has he *noticed*?" Raskin laughed dryly. "Erik's behaving like that guy in Greek mythology chained to a rock while the buzzards come every day and tear out his liver. I think you should talk to her, Kitty. On the surface, everything's the same as always. But underneath, things are simmering. I don't blame either of them and I wish to hell there was something I could do. But I can't do one damned thing except watch it happen."

"Harold," she said, "d'you ever wonder how all this came to be? I mean, I sure never thought when I answered that ad years back I'd be takin' on a child for life. I don't mind, understand. It just strikes me strange, every once in a while. And you. Did you think you'd be signin' on for life when you came to work for Erik?''

"I didn't think about it," he answered honestly. "I'm not sorry."

"D'you ever miss all them women?"

"D'you ever miss those guys you used to pick up, you and Freed?"

"Don't you try makin' out like I was your female counterpart, Harold. If I live to be two hundred and forty, I'll never get through as many men as you did women. And besides, I didn't sleep with 'em all like you did."

"What if I told you I never slept with any of them?"

"I beg your pardon? Are you telling me none of those stories was true?"

"No, I'm asking you if you'd believe that."

"Frankly, I would not believe that."

"Well, it's true."

"I do not believe you, Harold."

"I don't care if you do. Yes, I used to hang out in bars most nights. And yes, I used to leave with women most nights. But I'd just walk them to their cars, or give them a ride home, or sit and talk with them somewhere."

"But what about all those stories you told me you used to tell Erik?"

"I made them up. He needed to hear, and I suppose I needed to tell them. Mostly, it was just one story with hundreds of variations. There were a few women I saw when I was at Yale, but I could never connect. I'd go out nights and have a few drinks, eat the free peanuts or popcorn or whatever, and talk to whoever was nearby. I never met so many lonely people as I did in those bars. And I saw the same ones over and over."

"That don't explain all those women phonin' up for you all the time," she said, her eyes narrowed.

"Sure it does, Kitty. I was nice to them. They liked me. They wanted to get something going."

"Why're you tellin' me this now?" she wanted to know.

"I don't know. I guess because I'm going to be forty-seven years old in a few weeks and it's time to come clean. Or maybe I'm tired of trying to live up to those old stories. I didn't lie to you that night when I said we were both lonely. It was the God's honest truth. And I'd never met anyone else who didn't either bore me stupid or irritate the hell out of me. I liked you. You were sharp and sexy, good-hearted and good to look at.''

"You just liked my chest, you liar."

"That, too." He smiled.

"It's a real shame it's fallin' into my lap these days."

"Horseshit."

"You always did make me feel real good about myself." She smiled over at him. "How're you gonna feel in a few years' time bein' out with a sixty-year-old woman?"

"Probably the same way I feel now: just fine, thank you. You're the best-looking old lady I know. And you don't look a day over forty."

"Lord, what a sweet liar you are!"

"Nope. Truth."

"You don't aim to make any changes, huh?"

"Nope. Do you?"

"A bit late for that, wouldn't you say?"

"I'd say that. Talk to Risa, Kitty. I'm worried about both of them."

"Come walk Willie by here and have coffee with me," Kitty said. "I've been missin' you lately."

"Okay, in the morning."

"You okay, Reese?"

Risa sighed. "I'm fine, just tired. We've been working like crazy to get the specs and drawings finished for this new job."

"You get a good sleep and I'll have the coffee ready when you come by."

Kitty didn't even have to ask. Risa turned Willie loose to roam about the back lawn, let herself in, sat down by the table, lit one of Kitty's Kools, then put her head down on the table, and began to cry.

"I don't know what to do, Kitty. I can't let it go. All I think about day in and day out is having a baby. I'm harming Erik. He's starting to go back to the way he was when we met. He's unhappy, and I can feel it, touch it even, but I can't make myself stop. I keep thinking maybe I should go away somewhere, be miserable by myself.''

"You gotta pull yourself together," Kitty said, picking up the cigarette Risa had lit and left to smolder in the ashtray. "You're gonna wreck the only good marriage I've ever known about."

"I don't *want* to go anywhere, except maybe to the doctor's office to have this goddamned IUD taken out."

"You plan to trick Erik, get yourself pregnant, then surprise him with it?''

"I couldn't do that. I want him to want it, Kitty. Why can't he want it?''

"I'm sure you know all his reasons."

"I know every last one of them.''

"So, then, why're you askin' me?''

"Because I can't ask him. It's a dead-end street, and I'm in this car going a hundred miles an hour headed right for the brick wall at the end, but I don't know how to stop.''

"Turn off the ignition," Kitty suggested.

"What?'' Risa sat up and stared at her.

"You hear me. Just turn it off. You can't have a baby. The man you love can't deal with one. You haven't the heart to trick him. So turn it off, Risa, before you wreck somethin' beautiful. Let me tell you somethin': You've got yourself a first-class, grade-A, champeen obsession, fixation, whatever you want to name it. There's not a reason in this world why you can't be happy with what you've got—which, I'll remind you, is about a thousand times more than most other women've got. But you've fixed your brain on this one thing and you're lettin' it rule your life. It's the very same way it was years back when you nagged and nagged at your daddy, wantin' him to get you a dog. It was all you ever talked about. You went bringin' up the subject every chance you got until you near drove the poor man crazy. There wasn't one occasion for years when you didn't make him feel like the meanest bastard on earth 'cause he didn't give you that dog you were so set on for your birthday, or for Christmas. And now, here you are, doin' the same damn thing again, this time to Erik. Truth to tell, it's wearin' a little thin. Years now, you've been goin' on about babies. Grow up, Risa! Every last one of us makes compromises, but you're actin' as if you think you're exempt. I've got news for you, girl. You're not. Seems to me lately Erik's the one been doin' all the work in this marriage, and you've been settin' back lettin' him do it, punishin' him for not givin' you that baby you want. Just like you did with your daddy. I gotta tell you, I thought you were bigger than that. I thought you cared more for Erik than that. I love you better'n anyone, Reese, but you're actin' a fool over this baby business. You had your answer to this question about fifteen years ago when you married Erik and the two of you discussed it then. You keep wonderin' when he's finally gonna trust you the way you want him to. Well, I'll tell you when that'll be: when you grow up and disabuse yourself of the notion you can have somethin' you just can't have. I'd be perfectly happy to have had your life, and that's the truth. Because to be loved the way Erik loves you is a rare and special thing. *You can't have it all*, Risa. You just can't. I'm sorry to take such a hard line with you, but maybe I've been wrong to let you go on for so long without sayin' what I been thinkin'.''

''You think I'm spoiled and selfish. You think I always have been.''

''No. I think you're fixated, and it's ruinin' everything. Is that what you want?''

''Why is it wrong of me to want a baby?'' Risa asked her.

''It's not wrong to want a baby, Risa. It's wrong to want somethin' just 'cause you know you can't have it. I'd bet anythin' you'd care to name if Erik had started out from day one sayin', 'Let's have us six kids,' you'd have made one hell of a fuss. Give it up!'' she repeated.

''I can't!''

''Then you'll destroy the marriage. And you'll kill Erik.''

''You're overstating things.''

''Honey,'' Kitty said quietly. ''I'm *under*stating things.

You go ahead and keep on with this and you'll kill him sure enough.''

"How can you *say* such a cruel thing?" Risa began crying again.

'' 'Cause it's the truth, and you toyed with it yourself a while back when you got here and set yourself down and started moanin' about babies. Either go home and let him live in peace, or keep on the way you are and you'll have the pleasure of watchin' him die. And he will, you know, Risa. He'll die. You can't come into the life of a man like Erik and then, when he's placed his heart and soul in your keepin', try to cut them out with your fingernails 'cause he can't give you the one thing you've decided you have to have. I'll say it one more time: The only reason you're carryin' on this way is 'cause you know it's impossible. You want the man to be Christ on the cross for you. And I think what you're doin' is the true cruelty."

"Oh, God! Is that what you really think?"

"Sure looks that way to me."

"I have to stop," Risa said feverishly. "I have to. I wouldn't want a life without Erik in it. I wouldn't want to live if anything happened to him."

"You think about that the next time you're tempted to punish him a little more by draggin' your butt around the house, or mopin' in front of the window where you're sure he can see you."

"Now I feel even worse than I did before."

"Good! Maybe it'll smarten you up some. And in case you start forgettin', just think how well you managed to live most of your whole life without a goddamned dog."

"I have to put things back together." She reached for the Kools again, but Kitty slapped her hand away, saying, "You don't smoke. Stop messing with my cigarettes. Blow your nose, and drink your coffee. Then you get Willie and go on home to your husband."

"Has it really showed?"

"Yeah, it's really showed."

"*God!* You're right. I'm so ashamed." She reached over to the table to squeeze Kitty's hand. "Thank you for telling me. I'll get it right. I'll start paying more attention to Erik, put everything else out of my mind.''

"You do that."

"I think I'll go home right now and have my coffee with him."

"Nice idea." Kitty smiled. "Go on ahead."

Risa stood up, feeling suddenly better and lighter than she had in a very long time. Giving Kitty a hug, she thanked her again, then picked up the leash and went out the back door calling for Willie.

24

SHE HURRIED UPSTAIRS CARRYING TWO MUGS OF COFFEE, but when she opened the bedroom door and looked inside, it was to see that the bed was empty. Erik was in the bathroom; she could hear the shower going. Setting the mugs down on the dresser, she quickly shed her clothes, then tiptoed over to the door to stand on the threshold for a moment allowing her eyes to become accustomed to the dark. Erik never turned lights on in any room except the office, where he was forced to use the angled lamp clipped to his drafting table.

Steam was billowing out the top of the shower enclosure. She darted forward, pulled open the stall door and was inside in a moment, with the door closed behind her. Erik started in surprise. Whirling about, he automatically took a step back. She closed the small space between them and leaned against him, feeling a powerful resurgence of her caring for him. As he'd automatically stepped back in an instinctively self-defensive move, he now just as automatically brought his arms around her. She could feel his heart pounding from the fright she'd given him. There were times, like now, when she knew how totally the man he'd grown to be had been shaped by the boy he'd once been; a damaged, frightened, neglected, and abused boy. Even after all these years, a part of him still expected to find himself in the midst of a stone-throwing crowd.

She knew him. She knew his past and his present, and the majority of his fears. She also knew the broad breadth of his chest and the tapering of his hips, the hard solidity of his thighs and upper arms. She knew the smooth hairless expanse of his chest and belly, the touch of each of the fingers and both thumbs of the two hands that enclosed her with perennial care as if fearful of holding her too tightly or too long. She knew the sturdy column of his neck and the bones of his jaw, the taste and texture of his lips and tongue, even the ridges of his teeth and the sweet interior of his mouth. Her fingers were well acquainted with the varying textures of the skin behind his ears and at the back of his neck and along his shoulders; the flesh over the wide cage of his chest, even the darker, responsive tissue at his nipples. She was most familiar with the flat planes of his haunches and the inward curve at the top of the backs of his thighs. She knew the length and depth of the scar that started at the corner of his mouth. Her tongue traced its length to the rim of his ear. She knew the sound of his accelerating breathing, and best of all, most reassuring and always exciting, was the rise of his body into her hands. She knew he would respond to her with immediacy and pulsing pleasure.

She'd come back to him. Standing there with the water beating down on them, he could feel right through to his marrow that she'd returned, that she'd reconciled her differences, settled matters to her satisfaction; she was home. No need for fear, no need to contemplate a vast desolate future. He could open the doors of his mind and let it all leave him, like starlings taking flight from a disused belfry. He embraced her, his relieved tears concealed by the downpouring water.

Standing with her, both of them wrapped in one bath sheet, he laid his cheek against the top of her head, so grateful to have her back again—he could feel the completeness of her homecoming and its lack of reservations—that he offered up silent prayers to thank the Fates for this reprieve. Then the towel fell away and he carried her, with her arms and legs wound around him like a child's, to their bed.

"I came to have coffee with you, but I was too late. You were already up."

"I'm glad," he said. "I'm very glad."

"Erik, I'm sorry. I've been awful. We'll start again as if the last few months never happened."

"They never happened," he echoed, crouched over her.

"I love you. You're all I want."

"I love you. You're all I want," he parroted.

"Stop that." She smiled up at him.

"I have stopped." He gave her a smile of beatific radiance. It reinforced everything Kitty had said. She had no right to take chances with Erik, to treat him as if he were ordinary and therefore subject to pressures like an ordinary man. This was Erik, the man who lived in shadows, the dark side of her star, and she'd loved him on sight. It was unfair, wrong of her to try in any fashion to manipulate him. It was neither something he was equipped to comprehend nor that he deserved.

"Erik, I don't want to do the presentation tomorrow. Let Hal go. I want to stay home with you."

"If you'd rather not, of course."

"Touch me," she whispered, her hands in the small of his back urging him down to her.

His hands went to her waist as her legs rose on either side of him.

"I'll keep you locked inside me forever," she said. "I'll never let you go."

She directed his mouth to hers, at the same time lifting to pull him deeper, then deeper, until there was no space left, even for thought.

Of course Kitty was right, she marveled. Why had she been making herself and Erik miserable for so long? They had no need for anything more. They required only each other. Wasn't Erik's immediate retreat from beneath that shroud of sadness that had started slowly settling back around his shoulders proof of that? It was time for her to demonstrate in no uncertain terms that he was what she wanted, that this was where she wanted to be. The first thing she planned to do something about was her room and the environment she'd created with the idea of inducing Erik to grow accustomed to the light in her company.

With her hair tied up in a scarf, wearing an old shirt of Erik's, a pair of jeans, and sneakers, she closed herself into the room and began stripping the paper from the walls. Then she ripped out the carpet, rolled it up, tied it with a rope, and got Hal to help cart it downstairs to be picked up by the Goodwill truck. Then she went off to order new wallpaper, a copy of a Victorian print with small red flowers on a charcoal background, and carpeting so dark a red it was almost black. While she waited for the paper to arrive, she painted over the bright green trim with glossy black, and removed the plants to a corner of the kitchen, where they'd get the morning sun.

Out went the white linens and wicker furniture. In came low sleek Italian furniture in black lacquer with gold trim, and two very modern armchairs with appealing rounded lines upholstered in soft dark-gray wool. She had glossy black vertical blinds made for the three windows, and then set to work putting up the wallpaper prior to the arrival and installation of the carpet.

When the room was done, she closed the shades and stood barefoot on the new carpet, admiring her handiwork. Then she went up to the office to get Erik.

"You have to close your eyes," she told him, "and keep them closed until I say so."

He obeyed and she led him by the hand into the room, closed the door, then said, "Okay. Now look."

He opened his eyes to take in the details of the room, which she'd illuminated with tall black candles in heavy brass candlesticks. "It's superb," he said, "simply superb."

"Now we can sit here together. This will be our new den."

"I'll bring up some of my books," he said, and eagerly went off to do that at once.

It seemed to her highly symbolic: There were now no unused, meaningless rooms in their home. And it had taken very little to set everything to rights.

* * *

"Perhaps," Erik said, "you might be interested in doing some volunteer work."

"What?" Risa looked up from her book.

"Greenwich Hospital needs volunteers. I thought that might possibly be of interest to you."

"Why would you think that?" she asked, setting her book aside.

"It's merely a thought, in the event there isn't enough to occupy you here."

"Are you trying to get rid of me?" she teased. "Are you trying to clear the decks so you can sneak other women in while I'm out?"

"Ah, you've caught me. And I thought I was being so very clever."

She laughed as he performed a brief pantomime of hiding behind his hands only to have the hands pushed away by a powerful unseen force, revealing a guilty expression.

"No, seriously," she said, scooting over to his chair to straddle his lap. "Do I seem bored? Do I appear to be dragging?"

"Not in the least. We'll forget it. It was a bad idea."

"Yes, we will. You know what I wish?"

"What do you wish?" His hands enclosed her hips.

"I wish we could go away somewhere together."

"We could take a cruise," he said, remembering the crossing he'd made years ago with Raskin when he'd remained inside his stateroom throughout the entire trip.

"Erik! That would be wonderful! I haven't been to Europe since I was fourteen, when Dad took me along on a business trip to London. I spent most of the time waiting in offices with the secretaries of the men he was meeting. But we did go to the theater, and to Kew Gardens. And we took a terrific boat ride down the Thames to Hampton Court. There are so many places we could go, all kinds of places I'd like to see. Venice. Scotland. So many places."

"I'll tell you what. After the presentation in July, we'll take a holiday."

"You'd do it?"

"I won't promise I'll play shuffleboard, or spend my afternoons in a deck chair, but I think I could manage it."

"We'll make it your fiftieth-birthday celebration."

"Good God! Don't rush me! That's not until September."

"Okay, but the point is, I'll take you. This will be my advance birthday present to you for attaining the incredibly advanced age of fifty."

He groaned and let his head fall back against the sofa. "Entering my decline," he said dramatically. "Starting the grand slide toward oblivion."

"That's right. And when we get home, I'll have a wheelchair and a walker for you. What else? Maybe some of those smart diapers you old people have to wear because the bladder control goes."

He snorted with laughter. "Might as well have me fitted for a truss while you're at it."

"We could take Hal and Kitty with us. What d'you think?"

"It sounds delightful. They can help carry my wheelchair and the walker."

"God! It'll be so great. Will you dance with me on board?"

"Quite possibly, provided the light level is reasonable."

"Will you stroll around the deck with me after dinner?"

"Only provided my diapers aren't slipping."

She laughed and punched him on the arm. "Be serious for a minute. You know it's going to mean meeting people in the daytime here and there."

"I am aware of that. We'll try to hold it to a minimum."

"You're absolutely sure?" she asked.

"I believe so."

"Fantastic!" She gave him a kiss, then said, "I'm going to call Kitty right now. This is wonderful!"

A week before the presentation was due and three weeks before they were scheduled to sail from New York, some kids decided to investigate the potential for mischief on Contentment Island. It was just after ten, and Risa had let Willie out prior to their nightly walk. Erik had gone back up to the office directly after dinner. Raskin and Risa had finished clearing the kitchen when they heard Willie barking, followed by a muffled bang, then the spinning of tires on the gravel accompanied by a loud engine roar as a car went speeding off up the driveway.

Raskin and Risa glanced at each other, then ran through the house and out the front door. Raskin pressed the remote control to open the gates and Risa ran ahead. When he caught up to her, she was lifting the whimpering, injured dog into her arms.

"They blew up the mailbox and ran over Willie!" she cried. "We've got to get him to the vet right away!"

"I'll get the car. You wait!"

Erik came running up, asking, "What is it? What's happened?"

"They ran over Willie!" she wept, holding the bleeding spaniel tighter to her chest. "He's suffering. It's awful, Erik. He's badly hurt. Hal's getting the car. We'll take him to the vet."

"I'll come with you," he offered.

"No, you go back. We'll take care of it. I'll call and let you know how it goes."

Raskin brought the car, jumped out to open the rear door and Risa slid into the back with Willie. As Hal was getting back in, he said, "Call the police, Erik; report this. They blew up the goddamned mailbox with a cherry bomb, then backed their fucking car over the dog."

Erik nodded and Raskin sped off.

The policeman to whom Erik spoke said, "We've had half a dozen complaints already tonight. We've got cruisers out all over town. We'll catch 'em. You gonna press charges, if we do?"

"I will. They've badly injured our dog."

"That's rough. I'll keep you posted, Mr. D'Anton."

Less than an hour later, Risa telephoned to say, "They had to put him down, Erik. Willie's dead. We're coming home now."

Erik had coffee and brandy ready when they arrived.

Risa came in, her face blood- and dirt- and tear-stained, her clothes saturated with blood.

"Come, I'll draw a bath for you," he said, taking her hand. "I've made coffee," he told Raskin. "Everything's on a tray in the kitchen."

"I need it. Thanks."

Like a zombie, Risa let Erik lead her upstairs to the bathroom, where she stood dully waiting while he started the bath water running. She couldn't seem to assist when he began stripping her out of her ruined clothes.

"Those bastards ran him down on purpose," she said wretchedly as he pulled the combs from her hair. "He was barking. They heard him. It wasn't enough fun to blow up our mailbox. They had to kill our dog to make their evening complete. Erik, it was so horrible. The vet just looked at poor Willie and shook his head. Hal said, 'Willie isn't going to make it, Risa,' and I knew it was true, but I couldn't believe it. The vet let me stay while he gave him the shot. It only took a few seconds and it was over. I *loved* that dog, Erik."

"I know. I'm terribly sorry. You're cold. Get into the tub."

She looked at the bath, then at Erik. "Why would they *do* that to a lovely little dog? Why?"

"I don't know. It defies explanation."

At last, like someone of greatly advanced age, she slowly climbed into the tub and lay back with her head resting on the rim. "Did you say you'd made coffee?"

"Shall I fetch you some?"

"Please? I've got the shakes and it must be eighty degrees outside."

"Shock," he explained. "I'll just be a moment."

When he'd gone, she squinted at the heap of clothing on the floor. In the dark she couldn't see the blood. Knowing Erik, the clothes would be gone before she emerged from the bath. Just like Willie. Gone, her dear sweet Prince. For nine years he'd been her constant companion, there day or night to play with or take for walks or merely to cuddle. She'd never dreamed he would die—especially not in so cruel and painful a fashion.

"I thought he'd never die," she told Erik when he

returned with two cups of coffee; one he set on the side of the tub for her, the other he held in both hands as he sat on the floor with his back against the wall.

"He was a fine animal with many years left, and I was very fond of him. It's most unfair."

"I've never felt so awful. When my father died that was . . . different. This was murder. They *murdered* Willie, Erik."

"They'll be caught and punished."

"A slap on the hand and a warning," she said bitterly.

"More than that, I should think. I was told they'd done a great deal of damage tonight."

"That's an understatement if ever I heard one." She took a sip of her coffee, then looked over at Erik. "I don't think I'm going to be in the mood for a vacation."

"Let's wait and see, shall we? You may find it's just what you need. We still have a few weeks."

"I'm not going to want to go, Erik. Maybe we should let Hal and Kitty go on their own."

"We'll wait," he said judiciously. "Now is not the time to make any decisions, not so soon after such an upsetting experience."

"Are you as calm as you seem?" she asked him.

"Not in the least. I simply don't know what to do, except be with you, talk about it. There are certain situations for which I have no precedents. This is one of them. Is there anything you'd like me to do for you?"

"Yeah," she said softly. "Tell me you love me, and promise me you'll never even *think* of buying me another dog."

"I love you very much, and you have my promise."

She put her head down on her knees and wept.

Three days later, although she'd finished a period less than two weeks before, she started bleeding. Only a little, but it was bright-red, not menstrual, blood. And it scared her. She called the gynecologist's office and got an emergency appointment for the following day.

"It has to come out," the doctor told her. "This happens sometimes, especially with women who haven't had children. These devices seem to work best with women who've had successful deliveries.''

"I can't use the diaphragm, and now you've got to take the IUD out. What am I supposed to do about birth control?''

"You've got a number of alternatives, everything from vaginal suppositories to sponges, to a tubal ligation, if you want to be done with the problem once and for all.''

"What happens with a tubal ligation?''

"Very simple. It's done through the navel, a short procedure under a general anesthetic. The tubes are tied off. You can do it as an outpatient, come in in the morning and be home by afternoon.''

"Well, maybe that's what I'll do.''

"We can have Liz set up an appointment before you leave. For now, let's take care of this.''

She made an appointment to have the procedure in a week's time. That way, she'd have a week or so to recuperate before she and Erik left for their vacation. Not, they'd assured her, that she'd be incapacitated in any serious way. Just a little groggy from the anesthetic, and a bit swollen in the abdomen for a day or two. Then she'd be able to get up and go on about her business.

She planned to tell Erik about the removal of the IUD and her scheduled surgery, but by the time she got home she was so tired—still in the aftermath shock from Willie's death—that all she wanted was a nap. Erik and Hal were upstairs in the office, so she thought she'd lie down for an hour or two and at some point during the evening she'd let Erik know her news.

It was one of those occasions when he popped down to the bedroom to get something, saw her asleep, and couldn't resist lying down beside her. She came awake to his touch, gave him a sleepy smile, and opened her arms to him. Slowly, without haste, the embrace changed shape, acquired heat and rhythm. It wasn't until the moment when Erik shuddered in her arms, inside her, that she realized it was the second time ever that they'd made love without any precautions. She was so stunned, and so immediately guilty, as well as fearful of the anger with which he might respond, that she simply couldn't bring herself to tell him.

Holding him, she promised herself she'd explain everything after dinner, or perhaps in the morning. But what if seeds were joining together inside her at that very moment and the damage was already done? *God!* Without intending to, she'd done the one thing she'd sworn never to do. Guilt fell over her like a gauzy curtain.

Erik dozed at her side and she tried to think of ways to tell him, rejecting each one. It wouldn't matter, she decided finally. In a week's time she'd be neutered, rendered sterile for all time. Even if by some chance seeds were dividing and multiplying, the finished product would never see the light of day.

She had the presentation to do in the city in a couple of days. And then, next week, she'd go down to the hospital for the day and when she came home the question of babies would have been answered once and for all. But still she felt acutely, sickeningly guilty. It hadn't been planned; it hadn't been intentional. But it had happened. And maybe the surgery would be too late. They'd tie her tubes only to find out after the fact that they'd neutered someone who was already pregnant.

She told herself to wake Erik and confess, but she couldn't do it.

And, finally, she fell asleep again, her thighs sticky with the evidence of her inadvertent betrayal.

25

SHE COULD NOT COMPREHEND HOW SHE'D MANAGED TO get so thoroughly trapped in her dishonesty. She was positively imprisoned in it, and wanted to get free, but she kept finding illogical reasons why the time wasn't yet right to reveal to Erik not only what she'd already done but also about the surgery she intended to have in less than a week's time. Repeatedly she asked herself what she was waiting for. Repeatedly she failed to find an answer. And to compound both her offense against Erik and her mounting guilt, she made love with him several more times during the next few days.

All at once he was like some narcotic she craved. As it had been at the very beginning, she was again stricken by a ravening sexual need she could barely contain. She thought hungrily, constantly, of his caress, of his broad powerful white body that had never known exposure to the sun. She was so single-mindedly obsessed with her need that she actually wondered if it might not be possible to expire simply from the heat of her ongoing lust for him. And Erik responded, as he always did, with an intensity that matched and even surpassed her own. She drew him into her arms, into the churning interior of her body in a desperate frenzy. And he too willingly submitted himself to the perpetual astonishment and exultation she inspired in him.

What was she doing? she wondered, appalled by her silence and by her actions. This had to stop; she had to tell him. But every time she opened her mouth to speak, she kissed him instead, or lay mutely wanton beneath him, in the grip of something she neither understood nor was able to control.

In the car, headed for the turnpike, on the day she was to make the presentation, she vowed she'd confess to Erik that evening. She loathed feeling as guilty and deceitful as she did. And if she was pregnant as a result of these few days of obsessive lovemaking, she'd do the honorable thing and abort the child. Having at last arrived at a decision, she felt a bit better.

The weather was unbearable. They were in the middle of a heat wave, into the eleventh day of temperatures in the upper nineties, and it was predicted that it would be at least another week, mid-July, before anyone could hope for some relief. As she drove along, she imagined the clogged streets of the city, and the half-hour or so it would take her to get across town to the client's office, as well as the additional time she'd spend looking for somewhere to park the car. The thought of all that traffic and hassling in the overwhelming heat and humidity was suddenly more than she could handle. She'd leave the car in the lot at the Darien station and catch the 10:45 train.

She had ten minutes to spare after buying her ticket, and went to stand on the shaded part of the platform, surprised at how many other people were waiting. She thought quite a number of them had probably had the same idea: to leave the car and avoid the traffic jams and frayed tempers this kind of heat provoked.

Standing on the platform, she planned how she'd confide everything to Erik as soon as she arrived home that evening. He'd understand. He'd believe she hadn't set out intentionally to trick him. He was bound to be convinced of her sincerity when she learned of the surgery she'd have in the coming week. The procedure would eliminate this contentious issue from their lives forever. Then, after that they'd be going off together for the first time on a splendid holiday. Nothing she'd done was so extreme that it couldn't be remedied.

When it finally came, the train was ten minutes behind schedule and packed full, with people standing in the aisles and entryways. Carrying her portfolio, she made her way to the front, to stand beside the engineer's compartment where she could look out the window. It made her feel like a child again, to gaze out at the tracks as they rushed down the line toward Noroton Heights, where more people pushed on board, and then on to Stamford, which would be the last stop before 125th Street.

Putting the portfolio down so that it rested between her knees and the outside wall of the train, she looked out, pleased with this singular opportunity to watch their progress as they sped toward the city. And she was relieved in advance at the prospect of telling Erik the truth. He'd forgive her. He wouldn't be angry; he wouldn't fling some piece of furniture through the nearest window. He'd listen, and forgive. Then they'd go off as planned. He'd been wise to discourage her from canceling their reservations. The trip would take her mind off everything, especially Willie and his piteous cries as they'd placed him on the vet's examining table.

The train hadn't reached top speed. It was going perhaps only thirty miles an hour as it approached the station at Port Chester. Risa looked out at the people waiting on the platform for the local that would be along in a few minutes. The majority were clustered in the shade of the overhang in the center of the platform. But ahead, at the extreme far end, a man stood alone. There was something odd about that. It didn't feel right to her, for some reason. She kept her eyes on him as the train proceeded through the station, and then, as they were nearing the end of the platform, the man stepped to the edge. She opened her mouth, her hands going to the glass separating her from the outside. She cried, *"No!"* as the man jumped, collided with the front of the train—collided somehow with her—before falling beneath the wheels. There was a monstrous crunching noise as the carriage went over him; then the train came to a sudden stop. Swallowing the rush of acrid fluid in her mouth, she shut her eyes and sagged against the window, hearing again that noise. "Oh God, oh God!" she whispered, under her breath, seeing him jump, watching him fall, hearing that *sound* over and over like a short loop fixed instantly in her brain.

The door to her right opened. The engineer peered around the edge to look at her. His face was filled with horror and disbelief, glazed with perspiration, as he whispered, "You saw!"

She nodded, then covered her eyes with her hand, concentrating on not being sick. "We're gonna be here for a while," he said, placing his hand on her arm in a gesture of commiseration and fellow-feeling. "Damnedest thing, huh?" he murmured. "Goddamnedest thing."

Again she nodded, keeping her eyes concealed.

He swore softly, almost reverently, under his breath, then ducked back into his compartment.

She could hear people talking, speculating on why the train had stopped, but all she could see and hear was that man leaping from the platform and the snapping of his bones beneath the wheels. Images of Erik kept getting mixed in with that recurring scene. She'd push one away, the other would come back. "God God!" she whispered. What would make someone so miserable, so desperate for an end, that he'd wait at the end of a platform for a train that was already late, in order to put a stop to his life in such a hideous and violent fashion? Her shoulders turned inward. The sound of it! The nightmare *sound*. And the look of determination on his face as he'd taken flight from the platform. *Why?* Had he set off intending to go to his job in the city and decided upon arriving at the station that there was no point to living anymore? He'd shaved that morning, dressed himself with care; he'd put on a clean shirt and carefully knotted his tie, all for the purpose of ending his life. He had to have felt the pain, the unthinkable agony on impact; the severing of his limbs . . . She winced, shivering, her ears hurting from the looping sound track, her eyes unable to shut out the inescapable visuals. She'd see it and hear it for the rest of her life. She'd feel her body pressing forward, her mouth opening to cry out as a stranger's life ended inches away from her. She'd wanted to stop him; she'd put her hands out instinctively to stop him; she'd cried out to stop him. But he'd jumped.

She wiped her face with unsteady hands and stood with her back to the other passengers, partially concealed by the open door to the engineer's compartment. More than anything, she wanted to get off this train. But her car was parked back at the station. The clients were waiting in Manhattan, and she wasn't going to make it. The train might be stopped here for hours while the police investigation got underway and statements were taken. The clients wouldn't know what had happened to her. They'd call the house when it got past the scheduled meeting time. And Erik would be frantic, because everyone believed she was driving into the city. But she'd decided to take the train, this one time, something she rarely did, and now a man was dead, and her eyes were filled with the image of his blank eyes and his grimly set mouth and his determined look as he threw himself out in front of her—an instant of concussion when he'd been held like a magnet on the other side of the glass, and her hands had tried to keep him safely in place there—and then he was gone. Why did Erik keep sliding between these images, confusing and alarming her, tricking her into feeling somehow that it was Erik who'd surrendered his life, Erik who'd lost his urge to live, Erik who'd gone from her?

"Are you all right?" someone asked.

She'd lied; she'd had every opportunity to tell the truth, but she hadn't. She'd dishonored both of them. If he never forgave her he'd be well within his rights. She knew his feelings on the matter; knew his feelings on all matters; knew how readily he was moved to tears and how this fact distressed him because he viewed tears as a sign of weakness.

"Are you all right?"

She opened her eyes, but couldn't speak. Just then a voice came over the Public Address system to say, "Uhm, ladies and gentlemen, we're sorry to say this train is going to be delayed indefinitely. We uhm . . . Unfortunately someone jumped in front of the train. We'll keep you posted."

Shocked murmurs raced through the car, strangers

turning toward one another to comment. Some stayed concealed behind their *New York Times*, or paid especially close attention to their paperback novels or magazines, or the crossword puzzles they were having trouble working.

"Sit down here," the voice said, and at last she looked to see who was expressing such concern.

The voice belonged to a tall man in his late thirties, with the most beautiful face she'd ever seen. His hair was thick and Scandinavian blond; his eyes were the same shifting blue-green as sea water; his features were so perfect they might have been sculpted from the finest Italian marble; the planes and dimensions of nose, cheekbones, mouth and jaw were the living embodiment of clean-lined symmetry.

"Take my seat," he told her. "Sit down. You've had a hell of a shock." His hands propelled her into his aisle seat. Then he squatted in the aisle at her side, saying, "You look as if you're going to faint. Better put your head down."

She did as he said, grateful to have someone take charge. But the instant she closed her eyes and lowered her head, it all happened again, and she began to quake, trying to push away the images by shaking her head free of them. *Why* hadn't she told Erik the truth? What was wrong with her?

The man in the aisle didn't say anything more for a time, but remained by her side with his hand over the back of her neck, keeping her head down. She felt alternatingly cold, then hot; she had to keep swallowing the bitter fluid that filled her mouth. She held her hands together over the handbag in her lap while she tried not to see or hear. Perhaps ten minutes later one of the doors slid open and a uniformed Metro North officer climbed into the car, followed by a Port Chester policeman.

The two spoke first in undertones to the engineer, then wanted to talk to Risa, seeking confirmation of the engineer's report. She was able to lift her head and answer their questions in a barely audible whisper. "He was waiting at the end of the platform. I thought it was odd that he was standing alone so far away from everyone else. As we got to the end of the platform, he threw out his arms"—She had to stop to catch her breath, gasping for air. "He threw out his arms, and he jumped. *He jumped.*" She shook her head again, trying to escape that dismembering sound.

The officers apologetically asked for her name, address, and telephone number, and she recited them mechanically. It didn't occur to her to open her bag and give them one of the business cards Erik had made up for her. She could scarcely think, but concentrated on answering their questions. At last, they solemnly thanked her, said they were very sorry, and left the train.

For an hour and ten minutes the train sat on the track while officials climbed on and off, and several of the conductors came through to talk to the engineer who, at one point, declared in a voice shot with distress, "I told them I wouldn't move this train until the local police give their okay, and that's the way it's gonna be." His eyes were round with shock, his skin waxy.

At last another announcement was made. "Ladies and gentlemen, we apologize again for this unfortunate delay. We're going to back the train up to the station, where you'll be able to leave through the rear carriage. For those of you continuing on to Grand Central, there's another train waiting."

"It's going to take a while for all these people to get off," her companion told Risa as he got to his feet, his hand on her shoulder keeping her in the seat. The other passengers began folding their newspapers, closing their books and magazines, preparing to disembark. There was talk about missed meetings, and of forgetting about going into the city altogether because the day was blown, but little or no mention of the reason for this unscheduled stop.

"They don't care," Risa said, looking up at the man who'd befriended her. "They're pretending it didn't happen."

"They don't know what else to do," he said, "so they're doing ordinary things to make themselves feel better."

People left their seats and began crowding into the

aisles, anxious to get off the train. The man who'd been sitting beside Risa said, " 'Scuse me," and climbed past her to join the crowd in the aisle. Risa moved over to make room, and her companion sat down.

He said, "I heard you give them your name. I'm Stefan. It's too ironic, you know. I never take the train, but I had to come into town today for a meeting and to pick up my car."

"I hardly ever take the train either," she said dully. "And I've missed a very important meeting."

"Luckily," he said, "mine's not until two-thirty."

Erik would be so terribly worried. He was fearful every time she set off in the car to go anywhere; he worried if she was merely out of his sight. No matter what else he might be doing, he was always thinking about her, wondering about her, living his life through her, tormented by the idea that some misfortune might befall her. Was this why she kept seeing him leap from the platform instead of that other man, the one in the gray pinstripe suit? She knew that at that very moment Erik would be pacing back and forth in the office, or the bedroom, or in the music room, fretting over her failure to show up at the meeting. His big body shoving the air aside, his hands sending their silent cries into the atmosphere, he'd be barely breathing as he enumerated his fears, as he anxiously contemplated any harm coming to her. All at once she felt suffocated by the sheer enormity of her obligation to him. She was back to being the specimen on the slide beneath the microscope, with not one but three sets of eyes examining her. Hal would've been the one to take the call from the client. And after telling Erik that she hadn't shown up, Hal would immediately phone Kitty to let her know, too. God! She had to get to a telephone and let them know she was okay to free herself from the claustrophobic sense she had of being too closely watched—especially now when she was so guilty of dishonesty.

"They'll understand when you explain why you're late," Stefan was saying when she tuned back in to him.

"I'll have to call the client from the station, tell him I'm on my way." The client would then call the house and Erik would know everything was all right. Except that nothing was all right. She felt as if she were coming apart, small pieces of her falling on all sides every time she made the slightest move.

Stefan laughed, drawing her attention back to him. "They'll be lined up from here to next Saturday waiting to use the platform pay phones. You'll do just as well to call from Grand Central. Otherwise, you'll miss the train that's waiting."

"Yes," she agreed, her face contorting as it all rushed back at her again. Her stomach was lurching; her hands were cold and stiff, her fingers rigid like frost-bitten twigs. She looked down at her hands, recoiling from the sight of them.

Finally there was movement as the other passengers began filing out through the far door of the car. She got up to go. Stefan hurried after her, saying, "Hey! You've forgotten this!" and she turned to see him holding her portfolio.

She thanked him and started off again. He came right along behind her, saying, "I think you need someone to look after you today."

She had nothing to say to that, but doggedly kept going forward, absently noticing the empty coffee containers and abandoned newspapers littering the floor. She stepped from the air-conditioned train into the stupefying heat of the platform, her feet and legs moving with their own impetus, taking her through the crowd. Then, without thinking, she glanced to her right, only to see the body on the tracks; part of it concealed by a gray blanket, a severed arm not quite covered by a piece of cardboard.

She gasped and averted her eyes, holding her right hand like a blinder to shield her from the grisly sight, staggering as, yet again, she saw the man fly from the platform, and she heard that sickening sound.

"Come on." Stefan took her arm to lead her onto the ramp that had been set up to allow passengers to board the train on the outside track. "In here." He directed her to a seat in the first car.

She leaned heavily against the sun-warmed window, closed her eyes and hid them with her hand. A bunch of reckless children in a souped-up car had murdered poor Willie. She'd held him in her arms while his life had drained away, pouring out in sticky streams over her chest and arms. She'd five times made love with her husband without benefit of protection, and had failed to inform him of this fact. Something that might seem inconsequential to anyone else but which, to her husband, would constitute an immense transgression. And now! Now, a desperate man had chosen to end his life in the most hideous possible way. How badly he'd wanted to die! How he had to have lusted after it—just as she'd lusted after Erik's engorged flesh. That wretched man had so yearned for his death; he'd courted and wooed it like a lover. He'd wanted to be absolutely certain there was no possibility of surviving. And he'd succeeded.

She pictured a cruiser pulling into the driveway of a pleasant-looking house; she saw two officers climbing from the car and going up the walk to knock at the door. The door opened and a smiling woman stared inquisitively at those two young men, wondering what on earth they could want. Perhaps they were collecting for the Benevolent Association, or selling tickets to some raffle. And they had to tell her then, stumbling over the words, that her husband was strewn in pieces all over the tracks at the Port Chester station, where an assembly of ghouls stood gaping down at his remains. The woman shrank, her hands flying up as if to fend off this unbelievable tale delivered by two strangers. Then she went past denial into belief, on to horror at the knowledge that the man she'd lived with, likely for some years, had secretly harbored an immense and terrible love for something other than her or their children. He'd had an ongoing, clandestine date with death. Was it because of something she'd said or done, or failed to say or do? She'd probably never know. She'd live out her life periodically tortured by questions to which there could be no answers.

And there sat Risa, with the blazing sun beating in on her through the glass, on her way to an already late meeting in the city. There she sat with Erik's seeds swimming inside her receptive body, while she had an appointment already made for voluntary neutering. Willie was dead;

a man lay dismembered on the tracks. Were these omens? Was there something she was failing to see? She glanced at her watch, her eyes widening. It wasn't running. It had stopped at 11:07, the precise time that profoundly despondent man had stepped out into space.

"My watch stopped," she said with fear, looking into the sea-water eyes of the man beside her. "It stopped at the precise moment it happened."

"No kidding!" He took hold of her wrist, looked at the face of the watch, then tapped it with his finger. At once, the second hand began its sweep around the numerals. She looked at the watch, then at his finger, and finally at the man. How had he done that? Was this, too, an omen?

"Look," he said. "Why don't you let me give you a ride back from the city? You'll go to your meeting; I'll go to mine. Then I'll grab a cab uptown to the garage, pick up the car, and meet you wherever you like."

"That's very kind of you," she said, intrigued by the way his lips moved when he spoke. It was like seeing a painting come to life, a work by some massively talented Old Master. "I don't think I'd be able to ride the train again today."

"Okay, then." He smiled and showed her his even white teeth. "Tell me where and when."

She couldn't think, and looked again at her watch.

"You'd better set that to the correct time," he told her, and consulted his own watch. "It's twelve-forty now."

"Twelve-forty," she repeated, and adjusted the Piaget wristwatch Erik had given her one Christmas; she couldn't recall what year. When had it been? God! Why couldn't she remember?

"Now, where and when?" he prompted.

"Yes. Four o'clock? I should be finished by then, if I can reschedule the meeting. Where?" *Why* couldn't she think? "At Grand Central?" she asked, unable to come up with anyplace else. "At the driveway on Vanderbilt?"

"Fine. I'll be there at four."

"It's very kind of you," she said again, drawn once more to look at his remarkable blue-green eyes and at his well-shaped mouth, which was, for some reason, smiling at her.

"That was the client," Raskin said. "Risa didn't show up for the meeting."

Erik slowly turned, putting down his pencil.

"They were wondering if there'd been some change of plans," Raskin went on.

"But she left here at twenty past ten. She couldn't possibly have been caught in a traffic jam for more than two and a half hours."

"I'll make a few calls, see if I can find out anything."

Erik turned back to his drafting table. There was a low humming in his ears, and his hands were writhing about together on the table in front of him. He prayed nothing had happened to her. Please, let her be safe! He stared at his anguished hands while, behind him, Raskin called the state police.

26

SHE FLEW FROM THE TRAIN, THE PORTFOLIO SNUGLY tucked under her arm. She'd go directly to the client's office, not stop to call. She didn't want to waste any more time. She was an hour and fifty minutes late, but perhaps the client would still be there. If he wasn't, she'd explain to someone on his staff, and then ask to use a telephone to call home and talk to Erik.

At the receptionist's desk, breathless and soaked through with perspiration, she said, "I'm Marisa D'Anton. I had an appointment at twelve, but I took the train this morning, and someone jumped in front of it. We sat on the track for over an hour. There was no way I could let you know. Is it still possible to see Mr. Simmonds?"

"You poor dear!" the receptionist said. "That's awful! Let me call through and see."

Risa paced back and forth in front of the desk, the air-conditioning raising goose bumps on her wet skin.

"You're in luck," the receptionist told her. "He'll see you in a few minutes."

"Thank you. D'you think I could use this phone?" Risa asked of the extension in the waiting area.

"Sure. Just dial 9 for an outside line."

"It's long distance, but I'll use my credit card."

"No problem."

She sat on the edge of the sofa and picked up the phone.

"It's me," she said when Raskin answered. "I've only got a minute."

"Hold on," he said, picking up on her urgency.

Erik came on, asking, "Marisa, what's happened?"

"I decided at the last minute to take the train, not bother with the car. Erik," she lowered her voice, cradling the receiver with both hands, "I was standing right at the front and as we were going through the station, a man jumped. It was so awful."

"You *saw* it?"

"Everything. I can't talk now. I'm at the client's. He's going to see me in a minute. I know you were worried and I'm sorry. I'll be home late. We'll talk then. I have to go now." She hung up as a secretary came over to show her into Simmonds' office.

"I'm terribly sorry about this," she told the woman, following her down the carpeted corridor.

Simmonds looked angry.

Risa went directly over to him with her hand out, saying, "I am most terribly sorry, Mr. Simmonds. I took the train, and as we were going through Port Chester a man threw himself in front of it."

Simmonds was at once sympathetic. "Please get Mrs. D'Anton a drink," he told his secretary. "Some brandy, I think. Do, please, sit down. You actually saw it?" he asked, echoing Erik.

She nodded, wondering if she looked as decimated as she felt. "There was no way to contact you. I do apologize. I know how valuable your time is, and I have everything prepared."

"Just relax a minute. You'll have your drink, then I'll get Trudy to order some lunch. As luck would have it, my afternoon's free. I've got plenty of time to see the renderings. Christ! What a thing to have happen."

"I keep hearing it," she confided. "It was the most nightmarish sound."

Trudy brought Risa a large glass with a fair amount of brandy and gave it to her with a kind smile.

"Trudy, be a sweetheart and order something up from the dining room for Mrs. D'Anton."

"Certainly," said Trudy and went off to her outer office.

Risa took a sip of the brandy. At once she felt the burn of the alcohol, then its spreading warmth. "Thank you," she said to Simmonds. "That helps." The man was watching her closely, as if he could see she might disintegrate in front of him. "I'll be all right. It was just such a . . ." She couldn't finish. She didn't know how to describe the effects on her of the suicide; she wasn't even sure she knew what they were. Primarily, she felt disengaged and at a distance from everyone and everything. An image flashed before her of that sprawled mutilated form on the tracks and she shook her head, pushing the image away as she reached for the portfolio.

"Erik's very excited about this," she said. "We hope you will be, too."

Somehow she got through the presentation. Halfway into her description of the ways in which Erik planned to use the acreage, Trudy returned with a tray, which she put down on the coffee table. Risa dared not look at it; if she so much as smelled food she knew she'd be sick. Instead, she sipped away at the brandy and accepted one of Mr. Simmonds' cigarettes, glad to have something to do with her hands.

Simmonds loved the design, had no immediate qualms, felt the budget was definitely in line, and wanted, if that would be acceptable, to study the drawings and figures for a few days before contacting Erik with his final decision.

She said, "Of course," and got to her feet, again offering her hand. "I very much appreciate your understanding, and I'm sorry to have upset your schedule."

"Not at all," he said jovially. "*I'm* sorry you had such an unpleasant start to your day. I like the proposal very much. Please tell Erik that. And I'll be in touch shortly."

Carrying the empty portfolio, leaving behind the untouched tray of food, she left the office and got all the way to the lobby before she thought to consult her watch. Three-ten. She had almost an hour before she was to meet Stefan at Grand Central. It was far too hot for window-shopping. She definitely wasn't hungry. Another drink would be one too many. What could she do? She had an hour to kill. What was nearby? Saks. She'd wander around the store for a while. It'd be cool. And the air on the main floor was always pleasantly perfumed. She'd walk up and down the aisles and look at pretty things until it was time to go to the station.

"What happened?" Raskin wanted to know.

"Marisa took the train. She saw a man commit suicide."

"Shit! How did she sound?"

"Very upset, as one would expect."

"I'd better call Kitty, let her know everything's all right."

"Yes," Erik agreed, somewhat dazed with relief. His imagination had painted a series of pictures so bleakly detailed that their abrupt departure left him gazing inward at a glaringly blank screen. He lit a cigarette and leaned over the table, exhaling with slow gratitude. How truly frightful for Marisa to have been a witness to such a thing! She'd sounded shattered. He hoped she'd take some time after the meeting with Simmonds to do something to take her mind off the event, perhaps see a film—which she sometimes did on her afternoons in the city—or go shopping, buy something frivolous and completely removed from the horror of the morning.

Raskin completed his call to Kitty, and Erik said, "I think perhaps I'll drive over later to meet her. I don't expect she'll stay late in the city."

"Hold on a minute," Raskin said. "I've got a schedule here." He looked it over and said, "Peak trains come in at 4:59, 5:33, 5:54, 6:26, 7:09, and 7:24. She might be planning to take any one of those," Raskin said. "You could be hanging around the station for up to two and a half hours."

Erik consulted his watch. "She said she'd be late. Usually, she's back on the 3:07 out of the city when she takes the train. So I wouldn't think she'd come much before 5:54. But just in case, I'll be there to meet the one that gets in at 5:33."

"I don't mind going," Raskin offered, knowing how apprehensive Erik had to have been to be volunteering now to wait at the station.

"I'll go," Erik said decisively. "She'll be glad not to have to drive home alone."

"Okay," Raskin backed off. "Whatever you think's best."

At five-fifteen, Erik got into the Rolls and drove to the station. He found a parking place opposite the platform and backed in between a van on one side and a large station wagon on the other. From there, he'd have a clear view of the trains as they pulled in, as well as of the arriving passengers. He could also see Risa's car down at the far end of the lot. He planned to sit in the car until he saw her on the platform, then he'd get out and go across the lot to surprise her.

To have the benefit of the air-conditioning, he kept the motor running and sat back to wait with a cigarette.

At 5:35, two minutes off schedule, a train pulled in. Quickly stubbing out his second cigarette, he scanned the people on the platform. No Marisa. The platform cleared quickly. He sat back again, tuning in WJAZ in Stamford. Coltrane. Good.

At 5:58, four minutes off schedule, the next train arrived. He switched off the radio, opened the car door and stood looking up and down the platform. No Marisa. He got back into the car and turned the radio back on. Woody Herman. Not bad.

At 6:12, a white late-model Mercedes cruised into the lot. A man was driving. And in the passenger seat Marisa was pointing toward the end of the lot. Ducking down, Erik watched the car go to the far end and stop. He didn't move, except to turn his head to watch.

The two sat in the car for a few minutes, talking. Then Marisa got out carrying her portfolio and a Saks shopping bag and went over to the SL. While she busied herself opening the door, Erik put the Rolls into gear and drove directly out of the lot, racing toward home. His hands gripped the wheel so hard his arms ached. Upon arriving at the house, he went directly to the music room and bolted the door.

Raskin, on his way down from the office, saw Erik sail through the front door alone and head directly for the basement stairs. Where was Risa? Raskin wondered, opening the door to look out. The Rolls sat alone at the top of the driveway.

Erik dropped down on one of the black chairs and sat with his head in his hands for several moments. Then he got up and walked across the room, stopping a foot or so away from the piano. His hands plucked at his trousers, at the lapels of his jacket, and, finally, at the mask. He removed it and allowed his fists to grind into his eyes. Then he went back and sat on the chair in the dark with his head in his hands. He sat motionless, yet he was sliding down a long chute, a tunnel of total darkness, slippery-sided and miles long; his descent was so rapid and so prolonged that the air howled against his ears and his hands flailed uselessly, searching for something to catch on to, something that might slow this sickening downward plunge.

As she was running along Forty-ninth Street, ten minutes late, she realized she was a little drunk from the brandy she'd had in Simmonds' office. Things seemed to spin outward from her field of vision, so that everything she saw was distorted, as if viewed through a fish-eye lens. Running in the high heels she'd never have worn if she'd known she was going to take the train and therefore do a lot of walking, she felt as if she were caught inside something with the transparency and density of a paper-weight. She was hurrying toward a meeting with a man she didn't know. If she slowed down and let more minutes get away, he'd give up and be gone by the time she got to the station. But she'd agreed, she'd said she'd be there. And meeting him meant she wouldn't have to ride another train today.

He was waiting and with a welcoming smile he leaned over to open the passenger door as she came running up. Apologies spilling from her lips, struggling to get herself and her things in the car, she had the strange idea that she'd been catapulted into another universe, a world that somehow traveled parallel to the one she'd always known, but one in which everyone—everything—was just the slightest bit skewed.

The cool interior of the car was shocking after the intense heat outside. It took her some moments to settle, while Stefan pulled out into the traffic and started across town. He didn't remind her to do up her seat belt—something Erik always did automatically—and it wasn't until they were crossing Second Avenue on Forty-second Street that she remembered to do it, experiencing a guilty pang as she fitted the two parts of the belt together. She hadn't said a word about this man to Erik; she'd omitted him altogether from her cursory explanation of this morning's events. Erik would assume she was planning to come home on the train. And she'd told him she'd be late. He knew she didn't like staying alone in the city after dark. That meant he expected her to be no later than nine, which was when the 8:07 got to Darien. He'd be waiting at home to hear her relate the full story of her day, and to comfort her if she required it. But his instinct to comfort her would evaporate altogether if she told him about the IUD and how she'd dishonestly made love with him for the past several days. God! Her head ached.

It occurred to her that the reason things seemed so off-kilter was because, by the standards of life she'd been living since she was sixteen, they were. She and Erik scarcely lived what could even remotely be considered a normal life. She was married to a man who found it impossible to do something as mundane as meeting her in the late afternoon outside a railroad station. For Erik this would be a major, and alarming, event. For Stefan, it was not in the least unusual and certainly in no way menacing. She'd lost touch with the everyday things other people did.

Stefan asked how her day had gone. "I hope it improved after the bad start this morning."

"Things worked out," she answered, turning to look at him. He was incredibly handsome. "This is very kind of you."

"So you keep telling me." He smiled over at her, his right hand fiddling with the radio until he found a station to his liking. Nondescript music poured from the speakers and he quickly lowered the volume. "Relax and enjoy the ride," he told her. "It's all over now, and you're on your way home."

"I do appreciate it," she said unnecessarily, and looked out at the cars keeping pace with them as they bounced over the rutted surface of the FDR Drive. It had taken them nearly an hour to get this far in the rush-hour traffic.

"What was your meeting?" he asked after a time. "Are you in business?"

"I had to make an architectural presentation."

"Oh!" His eyebrows lifted; he was all set to be impressed. "You're an architect?"

"No, I'm a draftsman." She would not and could not bring Erik into the conversation. It felt wrong to discuss him—even obliquely—with a stranger. "It worked out fine. What do you do?" she asked to deflect the conversation away from her private life.

"This and that," he said casually. "Marketing, for the most part. I'm on my own, do consulting work out of my house mainly."

They were both folding the truth into origami figures, she thought, relieved. She could keep the whole truth safely to herself, and she didn't particularly care if this man chose to do the same. After all, he was just someone she'd encountered on the train who'd opted to be concerned about her. He was easy to be with, though, and she was glad of that. She went quiet, and he allowed the silence to hold for quite some time.

"You left your car at the station, didn't you?" he asked as they were approaching Greenwich. They were now running into local rush-hour traffic.

"That's right, I did. But you can drop me anywhere in town and I'll walk over." She'd never dreamed it would take almost two hours to drive home.

"Don't be silly. It's no problem to take you to your car."

"Thank you very much," she said politely, thinking she sounded like a child out with some grown-up family friend, and wishing they could go faster.

"Would you have dinner with me?" he asked as they left the turnpike at the Darien exit.

It threw her. "Oh, I don't think so." She sat up straighter.

"Why not?" he asked pleasantly.

She couldn't think of a reason. She knew she should've been able to come up with dozens of them right off the top of her head, but all she could think was how nice he'd been. She didn't feel claustrophobic in his company; there was no need to explain her every thought and deed. And he'd been there this morning; he knew what she'd seen and how she felt about it. "I don't think it would be a good idea," she said lamely.

"I think it would be a terrific idea," he disagreed. "Let's say tomorrow night. Give you a chance to recover from today," he said as he made a turn before the railroad underpass, and drove into the station lot.

"My car's at the far end," she pointed. "The red sports coupe."

When he pulled up behind her, he reached into his pocket for a business card and a pen, to write his home address and telephone number on the back. "Let's say seven tomorrow," he said, giving her the card. "I'm a good cook. I'll fix something you'll like."

Doubtfully, she glanced at what he'd written. "I really don't . . . ."

"I'll be very disappointed if you don't come." He gave her a coaxing smile.

"Yes, well, thank you again for the ride." She got the door open, climbed out, then opened the rear door to get the portfolio and the Saks bag from the back seat.

"Tomorrow at seven," he said, before she closed the door. And smiled again at her.

She hoped he wouldn't be too disappointed when she didn't show up, she thought as she fumbled in her bag for the car keys, then climbed into the SL. The car's interior was almost molten from an entire day's baking in the sun. She put the air conditioner on full blast, then started toward home, driving slowly in order to organize her thoughts. She was going to have to tell Erik about the morning, and about the meeting with Simmonds, and about everything else she'd done. But she felt too drained—seeing that man jump again, hearing the wheels crush him—and too upset to talk to anyone about anything.

She was surprised Erik wasn't in the living room or the kitchen. Whenever she was delayed, which wasn't often, he always remained close by the door waiting for her. But not this time. Raskin was nowhere to be seen either. For a few moments she stood expecting Willie to come bounding out from the kitchen, his ears flopping and tail waving with excitement. Then she remembered Willie was gone.

With a sigh, she looked at the mail Hal had left for her on the kitchen counter. A registered envelope from the French Consulate in New York. Their passports had finally been returned, after three weeks, with the French visas. Raskin had removed his and Erik's passports, leaving hers in the envelope. She put it in her purse, glanced at the several bills and left them on the counter to be dealt with later. The house was utterly quiet. Carrying the portfolio—she'd forgotten the Saks bag in the car— she stepped out of her shoes, picked them up, and went upstairs.

She left the portfolio on the landing before going into the den to get some fresh clothes. She badly needed a shower and, possibly, another drink. She didn't know if she'd be able to eat. What she most wanted was to get into bed in the air-conditioned darkness and go to sleep. No talking, no explaining, just oblivion.

She used the shower off the den, with the light on. She'd never fully mastered the art of bathing in the dark, although she did it without hesitation for Erik's sake. Since he often came in to keep her company and to chat while she was in the bath, she usually left the lights off. But there were times when she really wanted to see herself in the mirror while she brushed her hair or toweled it dry; times when she wanted to study her full-length reflection to take note of the changes in her body. And lately the changes were becoming more obvious. Somewhere along the line, she'd lost that scrawny look she'd thought she'd have for life. She only weighed four or five

pounds more than she had at sixteen, but the distribution
of her weight had altered once she'd reached her thirties
and she thought she looked more rounded, even possibly
somewhat excessively, especially on the undersides of her
arms and her inner thighs. Erik laughed when she made
observations like this, insisting she had absolutely no idea
how she looked. She was, to his eyes, consummately
beautiful. She had no flaws. And of course she had no
wrinkles. She definitely didn't look her age. If anything,
he insisted, she looked seven or eight years younger.
"Twenty-six or -seven at most," he said regularly. "Certainly not a woman approaching the deathly age of thirty-
five."

This evening she thought she looked closer to fifty.
There were dark circles around her eyes and her mouth
had a stern-looking set to it. She was standing with her
shoulders drawn forward like an old crone. Throwing her
shoulders back, she stared at herself, seeing clearly the
signs of age: the softening of her jawline, faint lines fan-
ning out from the corners of her eyes, and parenthetical
ones around her mouth. She thought of Stefan, that impossibly handsome man and wondered why he'd been so
insistent on having dinner with her. She'd been at her
worst, sweaty and disheveled, upset and non-
conversational. It had to be, she concluded, a further
demonstration of his kindness and ongoing concern for
her. He'd heard it, too, that horrendous *sound*. He'd mentioned that at some point on the train, although he'd only
talked about her day during the ride back from the city.
He hadn't actually spoken of his own reactions to the
morning's suicide. He'd been deferential. Knowing it
would distress her, he'd elected to steer clear of the subject.

When she came out of the bathroom, Erik was sitting
in one of the armchairs, his hands spread over the arms,
legs crossed. To anyone who didn't know him, he'd have
appeared quite relaxed. But she knew better. He was
coiled tight as a mainspring; his hands were the give-
away. They were positioned like birds of prey, hovering,
ready at a moment's notice to fly off to a kill.

She stopped, looked at him and then over to the bed,

where she'd laid out fresh underwear and a loose cotton dress. She said, "Hi," and went to the bed for her underwear.

"Would you care to tell me about it?" he asked softly, his hands delving into his jacket pocket for cigarettes and the Dunhill. He held these items while he waited for an answer.

"The train was absolutely packed, people standing everywhere. So I went to the front of the first car." She pulled on silk tap pants and a matching camisole. "It was fun, like being a kid again. My dad used to take me to the first car when we went by train into the city, so I could look out the window. I was thinking what a good idea it had been not to drive, how wonderfully clever I was. No sitting for ages stuck in traffic, no endless searching for a garage. And then it happened. He waited until we were right in front of him, and he jumped." She held her hands over her ears and closed her eyes.

"Dreadful," Erik said, and lit a cigarette. Holding the filter end between his teeth, he returned the pack and the lighter to his pocket, then removed the cigarette from his mouth. "How unfortunate for you to witness such a thing."

"It was the sound of it that bothers me the most," she told him, reaching for the dress. "I keep hearing it over and over." She stood holding the dress, looking at him. He was large, solid; a powerful shadow seated before the window. They weren't touching. There had never been a time when they'd been apart that they didn't touch upon being reunited. Still holding the dress, she walked over to where he was sitting and positioned herself in his lap. With a sigh, she rested her head against his shoulder and breathed in his scent. One arm went around her, but he turned his head to take another puff of his Sobranie. Something was wrong. She knew his gestures, his reflexes and automatic moves as well as she knew her own. She kissed his cheek. He accepted it but didn't respond.

"What's wrong, Erik?"

"Not a thing," came his uninflected whisper. "I had an uneventful day. You, on the other hand, have had a truly ghastly day, and I am sorry for that."

"You seem angry with me about something." She sat away from his shoulder.

Not angry, he thought. Terror-stricken would have been a more accurate assessment. "No," he lied. "Not at all. I can't begin to imagine how you must feel having seen such a terrible thing."

"I can't begin to tell you," she said, remaining on his lap for another moment, waiting for his touch. If he embraced her, if he drew her close, she'd tell him how she'd allowed him to make love to her as if there were no risk when all the time she'd been as dangerously activated as a mine field. He drew again on his cigarette, then put it out. She got up and stepped into the dress, feeling chilled. Tell him! she told herself. Tell him about the doctor, about Stefan! Clear the air and tell him everything! She opened her mouth, prepared to do just that, when he suddenly rose from the chair and she thought arbitrarily he was the same height as Stefan, but of a considerably sturdier build. He was quite a bit older than Stefan, too, and of infinitely greater consequence. *Tell him!*

"I have some work still to do," he said, standing close to her for a moment.

She put her hand on his arm, willing the words to come, but he said, "I'll leave you to rest for a bit. I expect you're quite worn out. We'll have a late dinner." And then she was alone, slowly breathing in the fragrance he'd left behind of tobacco and of cologne with an underlying essence of sandalwood.

27

IMMEDIATELY AFTER DINNER, ERIK CLAIMED HE HAD more work to do, excused himself and returned to the office. Risa sat on at the table while Hal began clearing the dishes. There'd scarcely been any conversation during the meal. Risa had described the suicide from beginning to end, feeling no more eased by the repetition. Both Erik and Hal had listened closely, with rightful expressions of horror. Risa kept looking at Erik, but he'd seemed unwilling, for some reason, to meet her eyes.

While he was loading the dishwasher, Hal asked, "Have you talked to Kitty yet?"

"No. Why?"

"Why don't you give her a call?" he suggested. "We were all pretty worried about you today. I mean, I've filled her in vaguely, but I think she'd like to hear from you."

"I thought I'd leave it until the morning."

"Call now," he said.

"You're treating me like a child."

"Of course I'm not. I'm just saying I think you should talk to her now."

"All right," she sighed, and got up to bring the extension over to the table.

"How are you?" Kitty sounded very concerned.

"Exhausted and upset."

285

"Why don't you come over and talk with me awhile?" Kitty invited. "Have a drink and tell me about it."

Risa looked over at Hal who was wiping the countertop with a sponge, and said, "Okay. I'll be there in a few minutes."

She put the receiver down, her eyes still on Hal, who had his finger on the dishwasher button. He'd been waiting for her to finish her call before starting the machine. "What's going on?" she asked quietly.

"What d'you mean, what's going on? Nothing's going on."

"No," she said. "I may be the one on the slide, but I've got eyes, too. I can see everyone looking through the microscope at me."

"Pardon?" Raskin looked bewildered.

"Nothing. Never mind. I'm going to see Kitty. I won't be too long. Will you tell Erik?"

"I'll tell him."

"Okay. Thanks."

Picking up her keys, she went out to the car in the still overhot air.

"You want a drink?" Kitty asked, leading the way into the living room.

"I don't think I should. It'll put me into a coma."

"C'mon, sit down," Kitty said, dropping into Cameron's old chair.

Kitty hadn't changed a thing in the house since Cameron's death. The furniture looked shabby, the carpets were wearing out. The place was immaculate, though. And Kitty looked better than ever. Her face had thinned with age, so that her bone structure was more obvious, and eyes seemed even larger. She still wore her high heels, and manicured her nails once a week. Nowadays, she wore her hair in a twist at the back of her neck, and it suited her, made her seem taller.

"So," Kitty said. "What's happenin'?"

"Hal told you about the suicide."

Kitty nodded.

"I can't stop thinking about it. I feel as if I'm going to be seeing and hearing it for the rest of my life."

"It'll fade in time. Tell me what's goin' on, Risa."

"I don't know what you mean."

"There's things you're not tellin'."

Guiltily, Risa stared at her. "What things?"

"I don't know. That's how come I'm askin'." Kitty kept her eyes on Risa's, waiting. Hal had telephoned her earlier to tell her how Erik had gone to the station to meet Risa, and that he'd returned home alone to lock himself into the music room. He'd only have done that if he'd seen or heard something to distress him. Obviously, Risa was unaware Erik had gone to the station to meet her.

"I have absolutely no idea what you're talking about," Risa insisted.

Kitty picked up her drink and downed half of it in one swallow before plonking the glass back on the table. "Talk to me, Reese," she begged.

"About what?"

"About what is goin' on."

"Nothing. Is. Going. On," Risa said strongly.

"Reese, you're the worst liar who ever lived. You have absolutely no talent for it. It's written all over you that you're lyin'. And I'd like to point out that if I can see it, so can Erik."

Risa wanted to scream. They were *all* doing it to her; the three of them scrutinizing her every word and move. "I haven't lied about a thing," she said, knowing whatever she said to Kitty would be communicated back to Hal, who without doubt, would report it to Erik.

"Okay," Kitty said. "Then you're *omittin'*. What's goin' on you're not admittin' to?"

"Jesus Christ!" Risa exploded. "A man kills himself right in front of me and I come back to abuse? I simply don't *believe* this!"

"Tell me what else happened." Kitty lowered her voice. "There's more and I know it. Sure as God I know it."

"Sure as God?" Risa gave a small unpleasant laugh. "Since when are you omniscient, Kitty? All-seeing, all-hearing, omniscient Kitty! I'm going home to bed. I'm tired and I'm not in the mood for an inquisition."

Kitty followed Risa to the door where she stopped her,

her hand on Risa's arm. "I know I'm right," she said sadly. "Whatever it is, please don't do it. You'll destroy everything. You don't know enough about the world to play its games, Reese. You've spent your whole life sheltered from the harder truths the rest of us've had to live with. You're a baby when it comes to what's out there." She indicated the front door and what lay beyond it. "Don't be foolish, girl. You can't deal with a world you've only visited part-time. There are people here who know you and love you. Don't put it all at risk."

"Kitty, you're imagining things. And you're forgetting that I love you, too."

Kitty released Risa's arm, saying, "If you knew how badly I want to believe you. If you could know how it feels standin' on the outside. It's the same as your bein' at the front of that train and seein' that man jump. Only for me, it's more like standin' behind barbed wire watchin' you runnin' toward the edge of the world."

"It's been a long bad day and we're all tired." Risa gave Kitty a kiss. "We'll talk tomorrow and everything'll be fine. There's nothing going on, so stop fussing."

Kitty stood at the door, watching her get into the car and drive away. At last, she closed the door and went to call Hal, to say, "I'm even more worried now. She's holdin' somethin' back, somethin' important."

"Leave her be," Hal counseled. "Things'll settle down."

"Not this time, Harold," she predicted. "This time it's serious. And you know it just as surely as I do."

Risa waited until midnight for Erik to come to bed. Then she pulled on her robe and went up to the office to get him. She opened the door to see him sitting at his drafting table with his head in his hands and the work light out.

"Come to bed, Erik." She went over to put her arms around him from behind.

"I still have work to do," he said, his back unyielding. "Go ahead. I'll be down shortly."

"I want you to come with me."

He sighed and sat up, the movement forcing her to release him. He reached for the mask and fitted it on before turning to face her, taking hold of her hands. He tried to get himself to speak, but couldn't, and instead felt beneath his fingers the long bones of her hands and the pads of flesh at her palms and the tips of her fingers. He willed her to speak to him, to identify for him the man in the white Mercedes, to explain her being with him. Tell me! he pleaded mutely. When she merely stood watching him, he bent his face into her hands and remained that way for a long moment before straightening. "Go to bed, Marisa," he said. "I'll join you soon."

"All right," she agreed, too exhausted to argue. She pulled her hands slowly from his, then turned and left him.

The instant she was gone, he wrapped his arms around his chest and began to rock back and forth over the pain.

Throughout the next day she debated telephoning Stefan to say she wouldn't be coming, he shouldn't expect her or go to any trouble preparing a meal. As she stuffed clothes into the washer, as she absently wiped down the countertops, as she went downstairs to shift the wet clothes from the washer to the dryer before going back up to the kitchen to make a fresh pot of coffee, she deliberated.

Erik hadn't come to bed at all. She'd awakened in the morning to find his side of the bed undisturbed. And when she'd gone searching through the house for him, he was nowhere to be found. Hal had only said, "He can't have gone far. Both cars are still here."

"But where is he?" she asked.

Hal simply shrugged.

The music room was empty. So was the office. Where had he gone? Why was he hiding from her? He'd never before done anything like this, and it both angered and disturbed her. Just when she'd geared herself to the point where she was ready to tell him everything, he went into hiding. Nothing made sense.

Without consciously deciding, she went upstairs at five-thirty and laid out the clothes she'd wear that evening: a

simple short black skirt, a smart black Emmanuelle Kahn
top, and suitable lingerie. Then she closed herself into
the bathroom and locked the door, fully expecting Erik
to be there when she emerged. But he wasn't. Now even
angrier, she marched over to flip on the ceiling light in
the den before getting dressed. She returned to the bathroom to put a bit of concealing cream under her eyes and
some color along her cheekbones, some lipstick and
mascara, and she was done. She was about to leave when
she went back to the dresser for her mother's tortoise-
shell combs. She pushed her hair behind her ears,
jammed in the combs, turned off the light and went
downstairs to the kitchen for her purse and keys.

Hal was at the stove pouring a cup of coffee.

"If and when Erik decides to reappear, tell him I'm
going to the movies in Greenwich. I need to get out for
a few hours." With that, she snatched up her bag and
the keys and left. She'd been through one of the worst
weeks of her life, what with Willie's death, and the IUD
business, the suicide, and then the disagreement with
Kitty. On top of that she'd had a night when her sleep
was haunted by images of men leaping before fast-moving
trains. And if all that weren't enough, Erik had decided
to cut himself off from her, hiding out somewhere. Everyone was behaving as if she'd done something of truly
heinous dimensions. Her claustrophobia had reached unbearable proportions. She simply had to get away and
spend a few pleasant hours with someone who understood what she'd been through and who was sympathetic,
not to mention plainly eager for her company.

As she drove off, Erik sat up from behind the wheel of
the Lamborghini and turned the key in the ignition. He
waited until she reached the main road, then put the car
in gear and followed, staying well behind. Over the intercom he'd heard her tell Hal she was going to the movies in Greenwich, and he hoped to God she'd been telling
the truth. He promised himself that if she took the on
ramp to the turnpike, he'd turn around and go home. But
she drove right past it, heading through town. He
amended his promise: If she got on the Merritt, he'd fol-

low, and if she took one of the Greenwich exits, he'd turn around and go home. But she drove past the Merritt Parkway entrance on Route 124, heading into New Canaan.

She took a right turn before the center of town and he followed. She slowed, obviously looking for a number on the mailboxes, and he held back. When her indicator showed she was about to make a turn into one of the driveways, he pulled over, left the car running, jumped out, and ran through the bushes to where he'd have a clear view of her destination. She parked, got out, went to the front door of an unprepossessing ranch house, and rang the bell. After a moment, the door opened and the man Erik recognized from the white Mercedes in the parking lot stepped out, took Marisa's hand, kissed her on each cheek, then led her inside.

His heart racketing noisily, the breath leaving his mouth in a steady low whine, Erik tore back to the car, reversed into the nearest driveway, and shot off at top speed back toward Darien. His hands opened and closed in a death grip on the steering wheel and the gear shift. Taking corners and sharp curves at well over seventy miles an hour, he was home in ten minutes, flying out of the car and into the house up to the bedroom. The door closed behind him, he stood with his back to it, panting. *She'd lied!* His beloved traducer was, at this very moment, with another man; a young, *handsome* man. She'd found someone whose beauty complemented her own; someone whole and in no visible way impaired.

Falling to his knees, he bent until his forehead touched the floor, his hands knuckled against his chest in a useless attempt to beat down the pain. It wouldn't go. Wound into a knot on the floor, he wept into his fists, then tore at his face until it bled into his raging hands. And finally, gradually, he grew still. His hands, tacky with blood, twittered slowly against the air, like dying prehistoric creatures. It occurred to him as he lay on the floor that there was more to come. Perhaps this was merely the beginning of what would be a lengthy ongoing betrayal. "Why?" he asked into the deep pile of the carpet. *"Why?"*

Ah, but he knew why. He'd taken charge of a child who'd at long last discovered there was an entire world beyond the darkness of this house. And she craved its brilliance, its brightness, its garish lure. It was to be expected. She'd stayed far longer than he'd dared to hope she might. And it was ending now. That giant clock had stopped ticking. He could no longer hear the turning of its immense wheels or the insufferable shift of its razor-honed blades. All was silent.

He got up and went into the bathroom, pausing to turn on the light. Removing the mask, he approached the mirror and stared at the abhorrent blood-drenched apparition there. And then he began, quite uncontrollably, to laugh.

Risa was very nervous, and kept telling herself to turn around and go home. What on earth was she doing, going to some man's house for dinner, as if she were single and free to accept casual invitations? But she wanted to talk to Stefan about the suicide, to review it in the company of someone who'd participated in the horror. She was also curious. He seemed so very kind, so concerned about her. Besides, what harm could come of it?

What harm? Maybe she really was crazy, as Kitty had been implying. Harm of every conceivable variety could come from this. But somehow she couldn't turn around and go back. She did regret having told that silly lie about going to the movies in Greenwich. Why hadn't she told the truth? Because none of them would have understood, particularly Erik. Hal and Kitty and Erik had spent so many years with her as their focal point that they seemed to have forgotten she had a right to life and a degree of independence. But since yesterday it had felt as if they'd been trying to control even her thoughts.

Erik didn't have to know about this. One night, one small lie. She'd have dinner with Stefan, then go home. It was nothing, a couple of hours, a chance to air some of her acutely upsetting reactions to the previous morning. She'd talk with the man, eat a meal with him, then go away, and it would be forgotten.

He greeted her so effusively she was taken off-guard, especially by the kisses he placed on her cheeks, as if he'd known her for years and had long since earned the right to offer her affectionate greetings.

"I knew you'd come!" he said, and hurried her inside just as the telephone rang. He excused himself saying, "Make yourself at home. I'll get rid of whoever that is."

She stood for a minute or two in the small entryway, then ventured to look into the living room, which had obviously been decorated by a woman, with a lot of chintzy fabric and brightly colored pillows. Somewhere a stereo was playing, that same tedious middle-of-the-road music he'd tuned in on the car radio. Clearly, he knew nothing about music. But at least the place was clean and cozy. And something was cooking that didn't smell too bad. She sat on the sofa and waited for him to come back, which took almost ten minutes.

He came hurrying in, apologizing. "Sorry about that. Couldn't get them the hell off the phone. Let me get you a drink. What would you like?"

"Nothing, thank you."

"Oh, come on." He stood and smiled at her. "You look lovely, but I should've told you this would be casual."

"This is casual." She looked down at herself, and then at him. He meant she should've worn something that would've been more in keeping with his polished-cotton pants, Izod polo shirt, and Topsiders.

"What'll you have?" he persisted. "Scotch, gin, rye, vodka, what?"

"Some mineral water, if you have it. Otherwise, nothing. Thank you."

"You don't drink?" He seemed astounded by this concept.

"A little wine now and then."

"Well, you'll have some wine with dinner, won't you?"

"Sure. That'd be great."

"Let me get my drink, then we'll talk."

He went off to the kitchen and returned quickly with a half-empty glass of what looked to be Scotch. With another smile, he sank down rather too close to her on the sofa and shifted around to face her squarely. "So," he said, "what kind of lies did you have to tell to get away tonight?"

"I beg your pardon?"

In answer, he reached across to lift her left hand, pointing out her wedding band.

"Oh! I said I was going to the movies."

"And he *bought* that?" Stefan laughed. "He really must be slow."

"I think," she said, reaching for her bag, "I'd better go. This was a mistake."

"Wait a minute! Don't get offended. We'll forget I said that. Okay? It's gone; it didn't happen. Are you hungry? I'm kind of ahead of myself. Everything'll be ready in a couple of minutes. I hope you brought your appetite."

"Actually," she began just as a timer went off.

He jumped up, saying, "Back in a minute," and went off to the kitchen again.

She sat for a minute, then thought, What the hell am I doing here? I shouldn't be here. Get up and walk out the door right now, while he's gone!

She reached for her bag and was ready to get up and leave when he came back saying, "Come on. Kind of a rush job, I know, but dinner's ready, so we might as well eat."

She had no alternative, really, but to get up and go with him.

28

As Stefan wolfed down the meal he'd cooked—a rather wet meat-loaf suspiciously red in the middle, with lumpy mashed potatoes, and frozen peas of an impossible emerald green—Risa toyed with the food on her plate, intrigued and repelled. She simply couldn't understand why she hadn't left. It had something to do with good manners, with the training her father and Kitty had given her from a very early age to respect others and to honor obligations and commitments. She also couldn't understand why she'd thought this man to be so beautiful. Now that she looked more closely, she could see that his eyes, although of a wonderful color, were quite bloodshot; there were blackheads around his nose; his fingernails were bitten to the quick; his eating habits appeared to have been learned at truck stops. He talked with his mouth full so that she had to look away. She told herself she was being hypercritical. He'd been kind and considerate yesterday, while almost everyone else around them had either actively ignored the situation or pretended it hadn't happened at all. How could he have displayed such positive qualities yesterday and seem so dissolute, even decadent, today? Or was it her? There was no question that her perceptions were out of kilter. She admitted that. But was there something wrong, as well, with her ability to see things clearly?

295

"I can't stop hearing it," she said, looking at the black wrought-iron candlestick in the center of the table. It had a thick coating of dust, and a substantial build-up of wax spills.

"Hearing what?" he asked around a mouthful of mashed potatoes.

"The sound yesterday, when the train went over him."

He paused to swallow, his eyes on her. For a very beautiful and obviously wealthy woman, she struck him, at that moment, as being almost childlike in her refusal or inability—he couldn't tell which—to let something go once she got her teeth into it. "Hey," he said. "Let's forget that, huh. File it under the heading of 'Jumping to Conclusions.' " He laughed heartily at his own macabre humor. She was quietly scandalized that he could make a joke about something tragic that had so strongly affected her. She drank a little of the not unpleasant California Cabernet Sauvignon, abandoning her attempt to eat. The sight and smell of the food was making her queasy.

"You're not going to eat that?" he asked, pointing his knife at her plate.

"I'm afraid I'm not very hungry. I'm sorry. It really is very good."

"No wonder you're so skinny," he said, scraping the contents of her plate onto his own. "What d'you do, take pills?"

"Pardon?"

"You don't eat, right? So you take pills."

"Why would I do that?"

"To stay thin," he said patiently.

Mystified, she said, "I eat. Quite often, as a matter of fact."

He found this funny, and laughed again before going back to eating at an amazing pace. She was transfixed by the sight. In only a few minutes, he'd consumed everything in sight and was lifting the bottle of wine to refill their glasses.

"We'll have coffee and dessert in a little while, okay? Take a breather now, and let things settle." He patted his stomach, then picked up both their glasses. "Come on. We'll take a break, listen to some music, talk, get to know each other.''

He led the way back to the living room, where he set the wineglasses on the coffee table before going to the stereo to raise the volume. An insipid bass-heavy orchestral rendition of a Beatles song blared from the speakers at either end of the room. It made her ears throb, and she thought it was a crime that anyone would ruin a good song by stretching the melody line thin as thread and then destroy the composer's intent altogether by throwing a full string section into the background to distract the listener entirely from the theme.

"I really can't stay too long," she said as he turned from the stereo.

"What's your rush? It's early. Movies last at least a couple of hours. Sit down," he said. "Relax."

Relax? She couldn't imagine what he meant. In what way did he intend her to relax? She sat at the far end of the sofa and took a sip of her wine before carefully positioning the glass on the coffee table. She felt woefully out of place, out of her depth, and was glad to have moved from the dining room because it brought her somewhat closer to the door.

"I knew you'd make it tonight," he said with a smile, sitting down in the center of the sofa. "I would've made book on it."

"Why do you say that?"

"I'm never wrong," he said with preening self-confidence.

"About what?" The longer she spent with this man, the more convinced she became that she'd made the mistake of a lifetime in coming here. As Kitty would have said, the man was common as mud and twice as thick.

"About turned-on women," he said. "About Darien and New Canaan and Greenwich and Westport housewives who get bored and like to play away from home once in a while." He took a gulp of his wine, then returned the glass to the table. "I know all about you."

She had no idea what he was talking about, but suspected he was making veiled sexual references. It heightened her nervousness. When he slid over closer to put his hand on her shoulder, saying, "Nice top," her nervousness began edging into fear. And yet she was still very curious. It was like visiting some alien culture, one she'd never guessed existed.

She said, "Thank you," and shifted away, coming up against the arm of the sofa. She crossed her legs tightly, and tugged the skirt down over her knees.

"You're so antsy," he said, moving closer still, smiling to reveal bits of food between his teeth and at his gumline. "It's probably your first time off the ranch. Right? Relax, sweetheart. It won't be your last." His hand descended once more to her shoulder.

"I'd prefer you didn't do that," she told him.

"Do what?"

"Put your hand on my shoulder."

"Oh!" With an exaggerated movement—pretending her shoulder was hot and he'd burned himself—he held his hand to his mouth and blew on it. "Ooops! Hey! You're not drinking your wine. You don't like it?"

"No, it's very pleasant, thank you."

"Very pleasant," he repeated. "Christ, it's cute the way you talk. What were you, raised by nuns?"

"I'm not Catholic."

He laughed. "You're adorable, flat-out adorable. I could eat you up with a spoon."

She looked at her watch, then said, "I really should be going."

"Take it easy," he said, his voice dropping. "Once you get started, it'll be okay."

What *was* he talking about? She looked at him blankly, about to tell him she was leaving, when he put his hand over the back of her neck and glued his wet open mouth to hers. She jerked away from him, protesting, but he ignored her, muttering something about ". . . the ones who want to but just don't know how to get it going."

"Stop it!" she insisted, swatting at his hand, which was busy with the buttons of her top.

"Relax!" he said maddeningly, giving up on the buttons and pushing his hand down the front of her blouse over her breast.

"I *asked* you to *stop*!" she said loudly, pulling back

while, with both hands, removing his hand. She was astonished that he was disregarding everything she said. "Just be quiet now!" he told her, then fell heavily on top of her. She shoved against his chest to no avail. His tongue was worming around in her mouth, his hand over the back of her neck preventing her from escaping this obscene invasion, while his free hand pushed between her thighs. Very frightened, she clenched her fist and hit him on the temple as hard as she was able. Instantly, he went motionless. Then he smiled and said, "Like that, huh?" as his hand flew out and he hit her back, twice, very quickly. For a few seconds she was stunned by the blows and overcome by bursting panic. If she didn't get out of there, he'd beat and rape her. And she was unprotected. If he raped her, he might make her pregnant. The idea of being raped was terrifying in itself; the thought that a pregnancy could result from it sent her nearly demented. He was so involved in his determination to complete this sexual act that he scarcely seemed aware of her. Frantic, she glanced around, looking for something to use to defend herself. There were only the two wineglasses on the coffee table. He was pulling at her clothes, exposing her, his hand working its way up her thigh, and she was trying, one-handed, to fend him off. She extended her left hand, her fingertips meeting the edge of the table. He was dragging her skirt up around her hips, then ripping at her panty hose. A pause. He unzipped his fly. She wanted to scream, terror racing through her bloodstream. Her struggles of no concern to him, his knees were pushing her thighs open. Her hand closed around the stem of the glass. She overturned it, spilling the wine and shattering the glass so she was left clutching a jagged spike. He was pushing harder, higher. Getting a good grip, she drove her weapon into his upper arm. He let out a howl of pain, his left hand immediately going to his wounded right arm as he reared back in agonized surprise.

Instantly, she grabbed her bag and went running through the house and out the door toward the car, fishing for the keys as she went. She found them, got the car open, threw herself inside, pressed down the button to lock the doors, then, with a violently shaking hand, tried to jam the key into the ignition. It wouldn't go in. He came charging out of the house, blood streaming down his arm, his face contorted with rage, shouting.

"Oh God, God! Go in, go in!" She got the key into the ignition, turned it, released the hand brake, threw the shift into drive and floored the accelerator as his hand closed on the passenger-door handle. He hung on, pounding on the window with his fist, until the speed of the car threw him aside.

Quaking in the blast of the air conditioner, she drove madly back along Route 124, until she came near the entrance to the Merritt Parkway. She pulled over where the road widened before the entrance, put her head down on the steering wheel and sobbed, her chest heaving with accumulated fear and anguish. She felt sick and dirty and rabidly ashamed. Opening her bag for a tissue, she wiped her mouth over and over, trying to rid herself of his imprint while her body twisted in revulsion, feeling his hands all over her. She sat mindlessly wiping her mouth, staring blindly out the window, loathing herself and that despicable pig. How could she have gone to that place? How could she have done *any* of the insane things she'd done?

She'd lied to everyone; she'd been colossally disloyal to Erik; a strange vile man had dared to put his hands on her. He'd put his filthy fingers inside of her. She cried out and pushed her hands between her thighs, feeling as if a snake had crawled into her vagina. "Oh, God!" she moaned, unable to control her shaking. What was she going to do? She felt so dirty, so utterly, atrociously soiled. What could she do?

Slowly, a bit of reason seemed to return. She put out her unsteady hand to adjust the climate control and cut off the push of gelid air. Then she looked down at herself. He'd ripped her top, torn the strap of her camisole. Her panty hose were shredded. And there was blood all over her left hand. Crying out again, she tried wiping it off with the tissue. But it just flaked, remaining imbedded in her pores. She spit on her hand and rubbed it with the tissue. Then she opened the window and threw out the stained tissue.

What else? Her joints seized up, her muscles cramped with residual fear, she opened the lighted mirror in the sun visor to look at her face. Her entire cheek was discolored, starting to bruise. The mascara had run, leaving black rims beneath her eyes. She couldn't possibly let anyone see her looking this way, especially not Erik.

At the thought of Erik, she folded her arms over her breasts and began weeping again. He'd never want to touch her if he knew about this. He'd be as disgusted with her as she was with herself. What to do? Kitty! But, no. Kitty would tell Hal; Hal would tell Erik. And Erik must never know! God! He'd never forgive her for this. She'd been a fool, an incredible fool. She could see herself saying, "This is casual," and wanted to murder that imbecilic woman.

What was she going to do?

Run!

Where?

Her open handbag on the passenger seat caught her eye. The envelope with her passport was still in it. And the Saks bag was on the back seat. She had a wallet full of money and credit cards. She'd go away somewhere, stay away until she recovered from the self-loathing, the engulfing aversion she felt for a woman so stupid she'd go to the house of a man she didn't know, thinking he'd invited her out of sympathy and fellow-feeling. You silly pathetic bitch! She swore at her mirror image. You're too stupid to live. She shoved the mirror closed.

Run!

She'd deceived Erik; lied to him. She'd behaved badly with Kitty; she'd smugly gone out to put herself in the soiled hands of a woman-beating rapist. Kitty had been right. She was mentally and emotionally retarded when it came to the harsher realities of the outside world. What on earth had made her think she could deal with strangers, with all their unknown and inexplicable drives? She'd been vain and arrogant and, above all, extraordinarily stupid.

Run!

It was the only thing she could do.

She started up the car and followed the ramp onto the parkway, intermittently turning her head to blot her face on her sleeve. If only she'd never got on that train. She wouldn't have witnessed that poor man's death, and she would never, as a direct result, have met that beast she'd thought so handsome. All she'd done for days was tell lies and behave offensively; she'd even driven Erik to hide from her. Erik knew she'd done something; he'd always sensed her moods and thoughts and feelings. He'd hidden himself in order not to have to see or speak to her. How could she have *done* that to him? She'd broken every promise she'd ever made, dishonored everything between them.

Remembering trips years ago with her father, she automatically followed the airport signs until she found herself taking the exit for the British Airways terminal. She'd been to England several times. It seemed far enough away. She parked the car. It wasn't yet nine o'clock. They'd all hate her for the things she'd done. She'd done exactly what Kitty had said she'd do: She'd destroyed something beautiful. Now she had to go away, to hide.

Using the mirror from her purse, she cleaned her face as best she could, then tidied her clothes. She reached over the back seat for the Saks bag, took the keys and got out of the car.

"Hal, I need to talk to Erik!"

"Hold on a minute, Risa."

Hal got on the intercom to say, "Risa's on line one, Erik. Says she needs to talk to you."

Numbly, Erik said, "Yes," and pressed down the button. "Marisa?" He was very afraid of what she might say.

"Erik!" She broke into tears at the sound of his voice. "I know you'll never forgive me. I don't blame you. I'll never forgive myself. I'm sorry. I'm so sorry. I'm going away. I need time to think. I have to get away. Please, try to forgive me. The car's in the British Airways lot.

You can arrange to have it picked up. I can't talk. I just
wanted to tell you I'm sorry."

"Wait! Don't hang up! Where are you going?"

"Just away. I have to go!"

"Please, don't go," he pleaded. "Please don't! Let
me come get you! Let me come with you!"

"I don't want you to see me, Erik. I have to go now."

"*Wait!*" he implored her. But she'd gone. She'd severed the connection, cut them apart.

Slowly he put down the receiver, feeling deadened. He
had hoped he might have more time, another chance. But
she had to get away. *Now.* So soon, with so little warning. From the start of one day to the end of the next,
everything he'd loved and lived for had ended. She'd left
the house yesterday morning planning to be gone for a
few hours and now she would be gone from him for all
time. Perhaps she was running away with that handsome
young man. Perhaps it was something that had been going on for a long time, but he'd been too busy, or too
preoccupied to notice. It was of no consequence, not
anymore.

He picked up the photograph in the heavy silver frame
and held it to his chest, his eyes closed, his impossible
heart beating and beating. After a time, he returned the
photograph to the dresser and walked leadenly to the
closet to push aside the clothes. He entered the secret
room and closed the door behind him. Going at a lei-
surely pace—he had all eternity now—he lit several of
the candles with the gold Dunhill lighter she'd given him,
then sat down and put the lighter on the table next to the
candle there.

For a time he simply listened to the sound of his own
breathing as he reviewed scenes of their marriage, of the
many nights he'd gone hurrying to fetch her in the car or
the boat just to be near her, to hear her sing, to be close
enough to study the sweep of her eyelashes, the delicate
tracery of veins in her eyelids, the dainty cleft in her
chin.

At last, he reached for the box that had for so long sat
at the back of the table, and positioned it on his knees.
He drew back the lid to look at the oily gray surface of

the gun. His hands removed it from the box and opened the chamber. Full. Then, keeping hold of the gun, he returned the box to the table.

Such a long lovely dream it had been, so filled with sound and sensation, so charged with emotion and quiet excitement. A dream beyond his dearest hopes, a dream of cherished moments revolving around a beautiful child who had, as he'd always feared she would, led him deep into the wasteland of his own ravaged emotions only to abandon him there. He couldn't blame her. She'd given him far more than he'd deserved. She'd sung for him; she'd taught him to dance; she'd shown him how to smile, and even to laugh. And now the time had come for her to go away. She cared enough to express sadness, even remorse, at the death of the dream; she had shed tears over its passing. And she would find consolation in other arms, another's bed. But he couldn't contemplate any of that. It revived the pain. He couldn't cope with the pain. The pain was lacerating his bowels; it was collapsing his lungs.

At last, with a deep sigh, he removed the mask and set it aside. He gazed at the gun with a certain fondness. It would save him finally, take away the pain forever. He opened his mouth and lifted the gun.

Suddenly, alarmingly, the door slid open, and Raskin cried, "Don't do it, Erik!" and dived across the few feet separating them to try to wrestle the gun from Erik's startled hands. *"Don't be a fool!"* Raskin cried as he struggled for possession of the gun.

"Get out!" Erik insisted, refusing to yield. *"Go away!"*

"I won't let you do this!" Raskin argued, grappling with the bigger, stronger man; tugging with all his strength at the weapon.

"I have to!" Erik ranted. "You can't take it from me!"

"You *don't* have to!" Raskin panted, determined not to let this happen; his determination giving him almost superhuman strength, while at the same time destroying the cool veneer that had sustained him throughout his life. *"This isn't the answer!"* he persisted, straining against Erik's mighty hold on the gun, so bent on preserving the other man's life that he was unaware of his own frustrated tears. "I *won't* let you do this!"

"I must! Leave me be! Stop this!" Erik cried, frantic as the gun began to slip from his fingers.

"I fucking won't!" Raskin shouted. *"I won't just back off and let you die!"* With a last, valiant tug, he succeeded in wrestling the gun from Erik's grip. At once, he emptied it and tossed the bullets into a corner of the room where they fell soundlessly to the carpet.

Erik sank back into the chair and buried his face in his hands.

"Weren't you *listening*?" Raskin demanded. Distraught, he tossed the gun into the opposite corner. "Didn't you *hear* what she was telling you?"

Furious at having his so-careful plans thwarted, Erik lifted his head. "Why were *you* listening?" he roared. "And what in bloody *hell* are you *doing* in here?"

Raskin laughed bitterly. "You think you're the only person in this house who knows all the hidden doors, Erik? Don't be an ass! It's my goddamned *job* to look after you."

"I am no one's *job*!" Erik barked. "And it is *not* your prerogative to cavesdrop on my telephone conversations! Damn you! *Damn* you!"

"Don't be a schmuck, Erik," Raskin said tiredly. "You didn't listen! She was saying *she* screwed up. Not *you*. Her!"

"Why is she *leaving*?" Erik asked him beseechingly, his anger departing.

"Listen to me!" Raskin dropped down in front of him. "You have a choice, Erik. You can sit here and splatter your brains all over the walls. Or you can do something about this."

"What? What should I do?"

"Go after her!"

"But she wants to be away from me."

"No, she doesn't. Something went wrong, and now she doesn't know how to face you."

"What should I do?"

"The big question is: What are you *willing* to do?"

"Anything!" he said passionately. "*Anything!* I can't be here without her."

"Okay!" Raskin got to his feet. "Okay! Leave it with me, but be prepared to go traveling."

"Just to be able to see her," Erik whispered. "That's all I ask."

"Then that's what you'll do," Raskin told him, impatiently wiping his face on his shirt sleeve. "Forget that fucking peashooter and pull yourself together. And why the hell don't you turn this goddamned room back into a closet?"

"Hal?"

Raskin stopped and turned back.

"Why are you doing this?"

"Why d'you think?" Raskin replied.

"But why should you care?"

"Oh, shit, Erik! Why the hell *shouldn't* I?" With that, Raskin went off to make some telephone calls.

29

"SHE'S ON A FLIGHT TO LONDON THAT ARRIVES EIGHT o'clock tomorrow morning local time. I've made arrangements to have her tracked from the minute she sets foot in England. You and I will be on the Concorde flight tomorrow morning that gets in at six in the evening over there. By then, we'll know where she's staying and what she's doing. And you can decide how you want to handle it."

"I want only to be near her."

"Fine. I've arranged for a car and driver, and you can do that."

"But what about.Kitty?" Erik asked.

"For now, Kitty's going to stick close to her telephone. And I've got the service set to take care of ours. They'll relay messages to us, in case Risa decides to call home. I've also arranged to have her car picked up from the BA lot. A limo'll be coming here for us at seventhirty."

"Why," Erik wanted to know, "did you listen in on our conversation?"

"Because of the way she sounded, because I was afraid something like this was going to happen, and because I knew if it ever did, you'd get it all ass backwards exactly the way you did, and point it at yourself just like that goddamned gun."

307

"She saw another man," Erik confided. "He was young and very handsome."

"He was probably a schmuck. Most of them are. Of course, she wouldn't know about that, in view of the fact that the only man she's ever known or cared about, outside of her father, is just a little bit different."

Erik smiled wryly. "You've picked an odd time to become cautious with your turns of phrase."

"Let's not play games here. I've known Risa almost as long as you have. I've seen her grow up, and I've seen her change. And I'll tell you something: She's taught me a few things, fixed a few of my attitudes. I know what she's given up to make a go of your marriage. And I know what kind of work you've had to do, too. Shit, Erik! Don't you get it yet? You *did* it. You went ahead and got what you wanted and made it work, in spite of everything. There's not a fucking thing wrong with this face"—he pointed to himself with a stabbing finger— "but I've never had the guts to go after what I wanted. Now, instead of working at it a little more, for a little while longer, so you get the goddamned happy ending that comes with the fucking fairy tale, you're going to shove a gun in your mouth and blow your brains out. You can't give up just when you're winning! She loves you, stupid. The thing is, she's a kid in a lot of ways. Just the way you are. So she looked at another guy. So big deal! She gave it a try and it went sour; she didn't like it; it wasn't what she thought it'd be, wasn't what she wanted. Would you want her to blow *her* brains out if you made one mistake? Of course not. I'm like the fucking referee in this marriage, or the keeper of this particular zoo, or something. The point is, I *like* what goes on in our house. It feels like a *family*, Erik. And in view of the fact that the only family I ever had turned to ratshit, I'd kind of like to keep this one. Purely selfish, but there you are, I get to see one decent marriage, to experience it vicariously, even to be a part of it. Believe it or not, you're my goddamned role model. You set me such a good example, I've been gearing up maybe to try it myself sometime soon."

"You'd marry Kitty?"

"I'm trying to get up the nerve to let her know I care that much about her. But first we've got to get this house back in order."

"Twice now you're rescued me," Erik said humbly.

"Oh, hey! You can forget that garbage. Okay? I can't even *count* how many times you've saved my ass. Look, Erik! We're friends. We have been for a hell of a long time. But you've got this one small problem: You're even worse than I am at knowing what name to put to what situation. Risa's your wife, and that's your marriage. I'm your friend, and this is your friendship."

"Why are you shouting at the poor man?" Kitty asked, letting herself in the back door. "You leave him alone, Harold! He's had a rotten couple of days. Come here, Erik," she said, and drew him into her arms, standing on tiptoe to embrace him. Then, stepping back, she said, "The two of you better keep me posted every single day. You hear? I want to know where my girl is and what she's doin' and what condition she's in. And Erik, you listen here to me. This don't have one single thing to do with babies. Not one thing. This has to do with a bunch of hooligans runnin' down poor Willie, and then seein' a man die in front of her eyes. And I'll wager my eyeteeth it has somethin' to do with some fella standin' close by watchin' and waitin' to take advantage. Now, she's gone runnin' off, and it's likely because she learned herself a hard lesson tonight. It's only 'cause she's ashamed of herself, Erik, and can't stand to look you in the eye that she's gone off to hide and lick her wounds. You understand? That girl's loved you since the day she first set eyes on you, and as soon as she gets herself put back together she'll be callin' you up to say she wants to come home. She's gone and got herself traumatized, like they say on the TV. But she's sensible, and she's resilient. It might take her some time, but she'll come around. Now, what in heaven's name have you done to yourself?" she asked. "Lord, but you're a mess. Harold, go get me somethin' to clean up Erik's face, and some antiseptic. Erik, you sit right down here and let me tend to you. I've never *known* anyone so liked to punish himself for every little thing."

Hal went off to do as she'd asked, and Kitty pulled over a chair, pushed Erik into it, then sat down close to him, holding his hands firmly in her own. "I'm gonna give you some advice," she said. "Stay back from her, Erik. Don't go crowdin' in on her. Don't go nowhere near her until she lets you know it's time."

"Kitty, twice I saw her with another man."

"It don't mean nothin'," she said flatly. "I slept with her daddy for better'n fifteen years and I looked at plenty of other men. But I didn't go off with none of 'em because he was the one I cared for. There's no sin to lookin', Erik. It's the leavin' part that's worrisome. I have to confess I'm surprised this didn't happen a whole lot sooner. But you can't blame yourself, because it don't have a thing to do with you, and that's the truth. You're what's constant in her life, and it'll go back to bein' that way again. This was somethin' that was bound to happen, and now it's out of her system. You're a dear, sweet man, and she loves you. So I want your promise you won't go hurtin' yourself anymore. D'you promise?"

He nodded.

She leaned forward and kissed him lightly on the lips. "We all love you, Erik, especially Reese. Everything's gonna be okay. So don't you cry anymore. Everything's gonna work out fine."

The Saks bag contained two dresses she'd bought the previous afternoon. As soon after takeoff as it was allowed, Risa closed herself into one of the lavatories. She stripped naked, pushed the panty hose and the ruined clothes into the waste bin, then fastened the torn camisole strap with a safety pin. She filled the basin, took one of the small squares of soap and a washcloth from the tidy stack, and began scrubbing herself from top to bottom.

It took ages. She had to change the water four times. But at last she felt somewhat cleaner. She pulled on the camisole, stepped barefoot into her shoes, and put on one of the new dresses. Then she tried to do something about her face with the concealer stick from her makeup bag, but she couldn't camouflage the darkening bruise. The concealer only drew attention to it. She washed off the makeup, then picked up her hairbrush only to see there was just one comb in her hair. With a pang, she realized she'd lost it, perhaps in that man's house. It made her start to cry again. She stood cradling the remaining comb in her hands, convinced she'd betrayed everyone, even her long-dead mother.

She wrapped the comb in several tissues and tucked it into her purse before at last returning to her seat, undone by the loss of the comb. It struck her as so pointed an illustration of her overall stupidity that she had to wedge a fistful of tissues against her mouth in order not to make any sound that might either disturb the other half-dozen first-class passengers or call their attention to her.

She'd have given anything not to have been so supremely foolhardy, and not to have lied to Erik—about anything—or to have allowed that repugnant rapist to refer to Erik even indirectly. She'd ruined everything by not telling him about Stefan at once. It would have been so simple to tell Erik about the man on the train who'd been so kind to her. But no. She'd hoarded her experiences with that fiend like some fuddled teenager with a crush on a rock star. If she had mentioned him she'd never have gone to his house, and none of this nightmare would've occurred. But she had gone. And now, coupled with her recurring auditory and visual experience of the suicide, was the cringing self-hatred she felt at that man's thrusting his tongue into her mouth while his filthy hands invaded her. Squirming, she longed to bathe properly and rid herself of the impression his brutalizing hands had made on her body. She kept reliving that moment when she stabbed him, the sound of rending flesh as she'd driven the glass deep into his arm, wishing it could have been his eyes, or his heart, or his groin—someplace where the damage would have been permanent and crippling. She had visions of driving back to that dreary house and murdering him in his sleep, slashing his throat with a butcher's knife, or severing his penis with a pair of gardening shears. He'd *dared* to strike her! He'd hit her twice, hard, and she could feel the resultant swelling, the throbbing ache in her head. She could never face Erik after having done all that, and feeling, as she did now, such a raging need to commit mayhem. She could only believe Erik would be as repelled by her now as she was by herself.

Throughout the flight she reviewed the suicide, and Stefan's attack. The garlicky reek of his breath was like a foul coating on her skin and in the interior of her mouth. She dug her fingernails into her palms to keep herself from screaming as she felt again his knees forcing her legs apart, his fingers pushing up into her.

In the morning, wearing her sunglasses and carrying the Saks bag, she went through immigration and out the "Nothing to Declare" customs exit. She got into a cab and told the driver, "I need a hotel."

"What kind and where, my darlin'?" he asked over his shoulder.

"A good one, in the center of the city."

"You might like the Park Lane," he told her. "Right near Green Park, very nice it is."

"That'll be fine."

"Right you are, my lovely," he said cheerily, and they were off.

Anywhere, she thought. As long as there was a bathroom where she'd be able to begin trying to scrub herself clean.

Erik was smoking a cigarette in the narrow seat at the rear of the slim supersonic plane, with Raskin dozing beside him. So far, despite their being forced to travel during the day, the trip had been uneventful. No one at the Concorde check-in had been anything less than friendly and helpful. Luckily, there had been only a handful of other passengers waiting in the lounge, and he and Raskin had found a quiet corner at the far end of the room where they sat to drink some of the complimentary coffee while looking out the glass wall that separated them from the plane sitting on the tarmac beyond the windows.

Raskin was worn out from a sleepless night and from the many telephone calls he'd had to make in the course of it. Well before takeoff, he folded his arms across his chest, tucked the small airplane pillow between his head and his shoulder, and fell into a heavy sleep.

Erik had watched his friend sleep for a time, then lowered the window shades, and waited, holding his hands together in his lap. As soon as the ''no smoking'' sign went off, he lit a cigarette, and began to study the scenes that played on the screens of his closed eyes.

He could see, in vividly graphic detail, every failure of his life with Marisa, every last occasion when he'd neglected to be fully aware, to be more open to her needs. In order to win her back he had no choice but to collect what courage he had and put it to good use. His only hope was that he hadn't left it too late.

Marisa, he told her mutely, I was dishonest when I said there was nothing I wouldn't do for you. I withheld and withheld because I didn't dare believe what you insisted was true. I denied you and deprived you because my fears were greater than my love for you. Come home to me and I will make amends. I will lay myself at your feet and give you everything within my power to give. I don't care what you've done, or what you think you've done. I don't care where you went, or what was said, or to whom. None of it matters. If I must spend the rest of my life lurking in doorways only to have a glimpse of you, it will be just punishment for my errors and omissions. To be able to see you, regardless of where you are, regardless of how distant, will be enough to sustain me. There is no point to a life without you in it, without the sound of your laughter, without the feel of you next to me in the night, your head resting lightly on my shoulder as we make our music, your breath sweet and slow as you trust me to transport you to safety. Come home to me and I will devote myself to the care and shaping of your days and nights until the last breath leaves my body. Come home to me and I will try with all my heart to open doors and windows, to tolerate the bludgeoning light. Anything. Just, please, come home.

A small nattily dressed man with a fedora was waiting for them outside the arrivals area. Erik stood to one side, with his hat brim pulled low over his face, smoking yet another cigarette—he'd been chain-smoking since his confrontation with Raskin in the secret room—while Raskin conferred with the man.

"She's staying at the Park Lane," Raskin came over to report, as the small man took charge of their luggage and led the way to a vintage Bentley limousine with dark-tinted windows. "We're booked into the Ritz, just up the road. It's the closest we could get. So far, she's stayed in her room, ordered one meal from room service, and asked the switchboard about good stores nearby where she can buy some clothes. She's alone, by the way, in case you haven't figured that out. We've got it worked out so her calls are being monitored, and the staff is organized to let us know the instant she sets foot out of her room."

"It seems wrong somehow," Erik said, staring out the limousine window, "stalking her this way, invading her privacy."

"You have a better suggestion?" Raskin countered.

"No, I have not."

"Okay. When we get to the hotel, I'll order up some dinner, then we'll check to see if anything's happening. Okay?"

"Yes, fine."

"You're not starting to slip, are you, Erik?"

"No. I'm all right."

"We both need some sleep. I'm getting too old to be staying up all night."

"Yes," Erik agreed, distracted. In his head, he continued the lengthy prayer he'd started on the flight over. He had the completely irrational, and admittedly arbitrary, idea that if he kept on praying, everything would come out right.

Risa spent three hours in the bathtub after being shown to her hotel room. But upon emerging from the bath she felt scummy. That foul coating still adhered to her skin. So she turned on the shower after the bath water had drained away and rubbed her skin raw for another hour. Then she inspected herself in the mirror. Not only did she have the now purple bruise on her cheek, she had additional bruises on her breast and thighs. She'd broken three fingernails below the quick and had actually cut herself on the shattered glass. There were several small deep gashes on her left hand. It relieved her somewhat to know that the blood had been her own and not that revolting rapist's. Her face was a mess, and she had nothing in the way of makeup that would cover it. She also had no underwear, only two dresses and a pair of shoes. She was going to have to go out and buy things. She was also going to have to prevail upon the hotel to give her some cash because she had no sterling. She'd persuaded the taxi driver to accept seventy-five dollars for the ride from the airport, apologizing even after he'd agreed to take her money.

She was utterly worn out, but when she lay down on the bed to try to sleep she found herself back in the chintzy living room with that man unzipping his trousers, exposing himself to her horrified eyes while his fingers forced their way into her body like foraging animals that only lived underground and were blind in the light. It drove her almost insane with self-reproach and she raked her loathsome body with her broken fingernails, despising herself so convulsively she wished she could shred her skin right off.

She got up, turned on the television set, and sat naked in one of the chairs with her knees drawn up to her chest and her arms wrapped tightly around them, to stare at some children's program hosted by a young man and woman whose vivacious energy made her feel more exhausted. She fell asleep in the chair and woke up with a jolt as she felt herself falling. She stayed awake only long enough to relocate to the floor in front of the TV set. The nap of the carpet was rewardingly rough against her skin, and as she sank into a troubled sleep she thought approvingly that it was only right for her to pay the full premium for her exceptional stupidity. She pounded her fists on the carpet, sandpapering her body against the rough fibers, grieving for everything she'd so casually, so cavalierly, thrown away.

30

FEELING LIKE A WHORE, RISA WALKED THROUGH THE lobby, nodded in response to the doorman's greeting, touched a hand to her sunglasses to make sure they were in place, and went out, following the hotel operator's directions, on her way to Bond Street. She felt as if everyone were staring at her, as if it were obvious she'd managed to get herself beaten up and very nearly raped; as if it were clear she had nothing on under her dress. It was a testament to the completeness of her absorbed self-loathing that she failed to notice the limousine crawling along, keeping pace with her to the extreme irritation of other drivers.

"She'd headed up Bond Street," the driver told them. "It's one-way, I'm afraid, gentlemen. I could circle round up to the top at Oxford Street and come down."

"No!" Erik said and, in one instant, before Raskin even realized what was happening, Erik had jumped from the car and gone darting up the street.

"I'll be damned!" Raskin said to himself, then told the driver to do as he'd suggested, to go to Oxford Street and then come down Bond.

As they headed toward Albemarle Street, Raskin watched as Erik tugged his hat brim low, slowed his pace, and followed after Risa as she turned the corner into Bond Street. Erik seemed so bent on his pursuit that he appeared unaware of the several people who turned to stare after him.

"Go do it!" Raskin cheered him on, losing sight of Erik as the driver made the turn.

Risa glanced into shop windows, determined not even to consider buying any clothes before she'd found someplace to get some underwear or panty hose. She stopped in front of the window of Fogal, backed up a few steps, and went inside to buy six pairs of panty hose from the charming, if bemused, shop manager who, when Risa asked if she could put on a pair then and there said, "Oh, but of course, madame. Please, use the office."

Feeling fractionally more secure and less whorish, Risa signed the charge slip, thanked the woman, and stepped out of the store.

From his vantage point across the street and several doors down, Erik watched Marisa come out of the shop, his hands folding into fists at the sight of the large bruise that covered most of her cheek. That bastard had struck her! She was wearing dark glasses. Was that to conceal more damage? he wondered, wishing he could hurry over, take her in his arms and console her. But he heeded Kitty's advice and waited to see which way she'd go. She chose to go on in the direction she'd been heading, toward Oxford Street. He stepped out of the doorway, adjusted the brim of his hat, and went after her.

A few doors along, she stopped to look in a shop window, and he fell back to wait. After a moment, she went inside. He reached into his pocket for a cigarette, lit it, and settled in to wait again. Farther up the street, he could see the Bentley pulling up at the curb. Then Raskin got out and came strolling toward him, asking, "How's it going?"

"She's been beaten!" Erik whispered hoarsely.

"Exactly how d'you mean that?" Raskin asked.

"I mean *beaten*. I mean that son of a bitch took his *fists* to my wife!"

"Oh, shit!"

"This is very difficult," Erik admitted. "I'm having terrible trouble restraining myself."

"Smoke your cigarette and try not to think about it. You're doing what you said you wanted to do."

"I have never done anything I cared for less."

"Yeah." Raskin smiled. "But you're doing it."

"Harold," Erik said humorlessly, "there are times when your cheerleading is something of an impediment to my progress, as well as an outrage to my sensibilities."

"Oh, now it's Harold. Soon it'll be Hal and you'll be inviting me for drinks at the Princeton Club."

"I doubt it. I'm not a member."

"Here she comes," Raskin said, stepping in front of Erik to block him from her view.

"Which way is she going?" Erik asked, dropping his cigarette and grinding it out beneath his heel.

"On up the street."

"Good," Erik said, neatly sidestepping around Raskin. "I'll meet you later at the limousine. Why don't you buy yourself a new tie, or some diaries at Smythson's?" With that, he glided away off up the street.

At one-fifteen, Risa sat down at an outdoor table in front of a restaurant on South Moulton Street. Erik took himself into a jewelry shop diagonally opposite and spent some time pretending to examine the window displays while simultaneously discouraging the young saleswoman from offering assistance. He held a quite wonderful bean-shaped gold wristwatch in his hand as he watched Marisa speak to the waitress across the way. As he went on with his mock deliberation of the pros and cons of the timepiece, the waitress brought a cup of coffee and a sandwich out to Marisa, who drank the coffee and ignored the sandwich. Then to Erik's great surprise, she opened her handbag, removed a package of cigarettes, lit one, and smoked it while she drank a second cup of coffee. He couldn't have been more taken aback if she'd injected herself with heroin. In view of her strong opposition to his and Raskin's smoking, it was nothing short of astonishing to see her indulging now in something she considered not only a vice, but a lethal one. It stated categorically the high degree of her upset.

At last, in order to justify his malingering, he purchased the wristwatch. He thought perhaps Kitty might like it. While he signed the charge slip, he kept glancing out the window, and his transaction was completed just as Marisa laid some coins on the tabletop, collected her numerous bags and packages, and started on her way down to the far end of the street.

She made no further stops but returned directly to her hotel. Erik had no choice but to go back to the Ritz— Raskin and the driver having long since given up waiting—where, as promised, he put in a call to Kitty to bring her up to date before turning the telephone over to Raskin, who'd spent the previous two hours cat-napping between other telephone calls.

A short time later, the telephone rang. Raskin answered, listened, then hung up to say, "She just phoned down to ask where she could buy something to read. She's on her way to Hatchard's, a bookstore almost across the road from the Meridien in Piccadilly. I say we sit tight on this one. It's too visible."

Reluctantly, Erik accepted this, and resumed his pacing of the suite.

Another call less than an hour later confirmed she'd returned to the hotel and gone directly up to her room.

"Time to eat," Raskin announced.

Erik gave a shrug of indifference, picked up the remote control, sank into a chair and turned on the TV set. He stared at the screen while he imagined himself driving to that house in New Canaan and knocking at the door. When that handsome young bastard came out, Erik put his gun to the forehead of the odious villain and pulled the trigger. The scene provided him with a small, savage satisfaction. It also augmented his anxiety for Marisa's well-being. God only knew what else that slug had done to her! He dared not think of it. It frightened him to feel such rampant hatred.

It helped to have several changes of clothes, as well as underwear and some makeup with which to hide her bruises. But it didn't help as much as she'd have liked. She felt unworthy of the new clothes, even of the hotel room and the staff, who responded so pleasantly and quickly to her simplest requests. And nothing seemed to hold her interest—not the television set, nor the radio, nor any of the several novels she'd bought. All she could do was review, over and over again, the events of the previous few days, and her part in them. The resulting despair and disgust so filled her, it all but seeped from every pore.

When her period started early in the morning hours of the second day in London, she was both so relieved and so distraught, she thought she really might go insane. She hadn't anything to use, and the stores would not be open yet for hours. She had no choice but to fold up a wad of tissues and stuff them into her underwear, then sit on her still made-up bed with legs drawn up, her fists tucked into her armpits, and her teeth chattering as she battled down the raging revulsion she felt for every aspect of her being. She ran down a list of the possible ways she might kill herself in this rented room, thought of that man waiting so patiently, for so long, at the end of the platform, and knew she wasn't capable of taking her own life. She just wished something, or someone else, would. It would have been better if Stefan had killed her, because between his actions and her own, it didn't feel as if she'd ever be able to live her life again. And feeling this way, she couldn't possibly consider returning to Erik, or even contemplate picking up the telephone to be eased by the sound of his voice. She'd discredited the marriage, violated the trust he'd placed in her. She'd thrown it all away with a combination of deceitfulness and foolish naivety that galled her each time she thought of it. That anyone could live to be almost thirty-five and be so ignorant of the world and the people in it was dismal in the extreme. And it certainly wasn't as if she hadn't been warned. Kitty had told her she was playing on dangerous turf, but she'd refused to acknowledge that. Instead she'd treated Kitty vilely, with none of the respect she deserved.

She banged her head hard several times against the headboard, but it didn't hurt enough, so she tried the wall, and then the door. Finally, reeling, the wad of blood-soaked tissues stuffed between her legs driving her

crazy, she threw herself face-down on the bed and managed to cry herself to sleep.

She was awakened by the arrival of a chambermaid
who, upon seeing her, said, "Oh, I'm sorry, madame.
I'll come back later."

Risa had the presence of mind to say, "Wait a minute,
please," and explained her problem to the nice young
woman, who said, "I'll fetch you something from house-
keeping," and went off to return in less than five minutes
with a box of self-adhering sanitary napkins. Risa
thanked her profusely and gave her a pound, which
seemed to amaze her. She crept out of the room quietly,
pausing as she went to slip the "Do Not Disturb" sign
over the doorknob.

When asked a short time later if she had anything to
report, the young chambermaid deliberated for a moment, decided the matter was far too personal to discuss,
and shook her head, saying, " 'Do Not Disturb' sign's
still on 'er door, ain't it?"

Erik knew it was a terrible risk, but he had to do it.
While Raskin slept, he silently left the room and flew
down the street to the Park Lane, where he slowed his
pace as he investigated the hotel's possibilities. Locating
a staff entrance, he entered the hotel and made his way
up rear stairways and along the corridor to stop outside
the door to Marisa's room. Holding his breath, he put his
ear to the door, to hear, too clearly, the sound of her
weeping on the other side. His hands at once pressed
themselves flat to the door, as he listened to the rending
sounds. He stayed for less than a minute, then retraced
his steps to the staff entrance and out to the street.

Once away from the hotel, he stepped into a doorway
to light a Sobranie then walked slowly, heavily, back to
the Ritz. He'd never imagined anything could be this terrible, or this agonizingly frustrating. But he had to trust
Kitty's wisdom. She was the only woman, aside from
Marisa, with whom he'd ever had any real connection.
And Kitty, better than anyone else, knew Marisa's ways.

He walked along the empty two A.M. street and continued his silent incantation. Call for me and I will come

to you. Just ask and I will take you home. Please, I beg you, come home.

For three days Risa failed to emerge from her room. Raskin received regular reports each time she ordered anything from room service and on the two occasions when she made outside telephone calls—one to a luggage shop to ask them to deliver a small suitcase to her COD, and another to a livery service inquiring about engaging a car and driver.

"Obviously, she's thinking of going somewhere," Raskin said. "I think you and I better get ready to take this show on the road."

"You should tell Kitty and notify the answering service."

"Yes, sir, boss." Raskin saluted and went to the telephone, saying, "I do so love these holidays abroad."

Erik turned and gave him a sharp warning look.

At once, Raskin said, "Sorry. I'm a little stir-crazy," and picked up the receiver.

Erik ignored Raskin's several calls, and sat staring at the TV screen, not seeing or hearing anything, so that Raskin had to tap him on the shoulder to get his attention.

"There's a hell of an interesting message the service took for Marisa."

"I beg your pardon?"

Raskin dropped into the chair opposite and referred to the piece of hotel stationery on which he'd made notes. "The doctor's office in Greenwich called to remind her she's scheduled for outpatient surgery in three days."

"Outpatient surgery?" Erik sat up straighter.

"I'll quote you the message. 'Mrs. D'Anton is booked at nine A.M. on the morning of the nineteenth at Greenwich Hospital for a tubal ligation.' " He looked up at Erik. "I take it this is a surprise to all of us."

"A surprise," Erik whispered. "More like a bombshell. I had no idea she'd done this, none."

"I've got a couple more calls," Raskin said tactfully. "I'll make them in the other room." He got up and left Erik to deal with his shock.

Erik used the remote control to switch off the television set, then lit a cigarette before getting up to walk the length of the room. Marisa had made arrangements to have a procedure that would sterilize her. She had taken him so literally at his word that she'd made preparations to eliminate any possibility of her ever having the child she'd so wanted.

He turned to walk the other way, pausing to tip the ash from his cigarette into the ashtray on the coffee table.

What had he done? he asked himself, flabbergasted by this additional evidence of the seriousness with which she viewed the issue of childbearing. Had he the right, he wondered, to dictate to anyone, but most especially to Marisa, the terms and conditions of her life to such an extent that she'd undergo surgery in order to satisfy those terms?

How, he thought on, would seven-year-old Erik have felt if there had been someone, regardless of what he or she looked like, who'd wanted to care for that boy? He would have loved that person wholeheartedly, gratefully, unreservedly. He would have tied himself to a lifelong bond with that person. And nothing about that person would have had meaning beyond the fact of that person's willingness to care. *I would have loved someone who loved me*, he thought, astounded by this realization. It was what Marisa had tried so hard and for so long to explain to him. It wasn't the face that mattered, but the humanity of the person to whom that face belonged. She was right, he thought, wondering why it had been so difficult for him to recognize this simple fundamental truth. I would love a child of ours. And that child would love both of us. Because we would be mother and father to someone we created out of the love we have for each other.

What a thing to come to so late in the day, and by so circuitous a route! He might have spared them both years of frustration and pain if he'd understood this sooner. It was the ultimate lesson she'd tried to teach him, and he'd failed to learn; he'd resisted learning because he'd been so mired in self-hatred that he'd been unable even to consider it. Now, suddenly, he could quite readily imagine

Marisa and himself with a child. Not that he would take
to sunlight all at once like some exotic plant. But so
many things were possible. Why not a child? He was
bound to love anything that was a part of Marisa. And
what could be more intimate a part of a woman he loved
than a child that came from her body? He'd been stubborn and infantile, he'd wept and carried on like someone demented at the very notion of impregnating his wife.
He'd behaved like a complete madman, for no valid reason.

If she would consent to come home; if she decided she
wanted to come home, he would never again deny her
anything. He'd been made to see all too clearly how little
time there was. He was no longer a young man, but he
had a young wife who could bear children. He'd been
insufferably selfish to deny her. How lucky to realize this
now, before the irreparable surgery! It really wasn't
too late. If she'd just ask to come home; if she'd only
consider returning home.

On the morning of their sixth day in London, the telephone rang soon after seven.

"We're on our way," Raskin said. "The car she's ordered is picking her up in forty minutes. She just phoned
down to ask them to get her bill ready. I'll get on the
phone and tell them to do ours, then zip down and take
care of it."

"No. I'll go down and do it. You ring our driver. I
don't want to waste any time."

Filled with urgency and fearful of losing her for any
reason, Erik went downstairs to pay the bill, ignoring the
glances of the reception staff and of the several early-
rising guests in the lobby. He really didn't have the time
or energy to concern himself with anything but his fer-
vent need to see Marisa, to remain as close to her as he
was able.

When her car and driver pulled up in front of the Park
Lane, Erik and Raskin were in the Bentley a short way
ahead. Peering out through the dark-tinted rear window,
they saw her come out of the hotel followed by a bellman
with her suitcase. She tipped both the bellman and the

doorman, who held open the door to her hired limousine, then disappeared into the rear of the Rolls.

As the liveried chauffeur cruised past them, their driver allowed two cars to get ahead of them, then swung out into the traffic to follow.

"It's a magical mystery tour," Raskin said, then waited for Erik to get angry.

Erik chose to be philosophical. "I suppose it is," he said, his eyes never leaving the car just ahead.

They drove through the day, stopping only when the Rolls did—to fill up with fuel outside Birmingham, for Marisa to go to the ladies' room once, and once mid-afternoon when her chauffeur went into one of the roadside restaurants to buy food.

Erik couldn't even think of eating, but drank several containers of not bad coffee, and smoked Sobranies until he'd given himself a headache.

"The only problem I can see we're going to have," Raskin said, "is finding accommodations when she decides to stop."

"We'll manage," Erik said, closing his eyes for a moment. "Have you any aspirin?"

"Headache?"

"Yes."

"I've got some somewhere in here," Raskin said, digging around in the leather satchel Risa had given him on his birthday a few years before. "You don't have anything to take them with."

"It doesn't matter." Erik popped the tablets into his mouth and chewed them up, then closed his eyes again.

"That," Raskin declared, "is probably the most impressive thing I've ever seen you do. How the fuck can you chew aspirin?"

"You should see me do razor blades," Erik replied. "*That* is impressive."

"Jesus! Maybe you should try to cut back a bit on the cigarettes."

Erik opened his eyes and turned to look at Raskin. "When I am sitting somewhere with Marisa and she has agreed to return home with me, I will go back to smoking the occasional cigarette. Until then, my choices consist of alcohol, cigarettes, or narcotics. Since I don't believe on principle in the use of narcotics, and since I wish to remain in full possession of my so-called faculties, I will continue to smoke.''

''Right,'' Raskin said, and looked out the window. He hoped to hell this wasn't going to go on for too long. He and Erik would wind up at each other's throats. On top of that, he missed Kitty. This was the first time they'd been apart, and the separation pains he felt were an unpleasant surprise. He missed their telephone conversations, their arguments, and, most of all, their lovemaking. She'd started talking a lot about her age lately, the difference in their ages, and he'd been using up all his energy telling her it didn't matter a rat's ass to him how old she was. But now that they were apart, he could see he'd been less than convincing because he could never get himself to say he loved her. And she was such a proud and feisty woman she'd keep her tongue between her teeth forever rather than be the one to say it first. ''What a fucking jerk!'' he muttered, disgruntled.

''Are you speaking to me?'' Erik asked quietly.

''No, I'm speaking to me. But you qualify, too. A pair of first-class jerks, that's what we are. You because right when you're standing at the end of the rainbow in front of the fucking pot of gold you decide maybe it's all just a sham, and me because I don't have the balls to break down and tell Kitty I love her. What the hell are we doing, Erik?''

''We are working to get my wife back,'' he answered. ''And when we have succeeded at that, you're going to get on the telephone and tell Kitty to come—wherever we are—on the next available flight.''

''Yeah!'' Raskin said. ''That's a damned good idea.''

''And then we will have our holiday, as planned.''

''You're starting to believe it'll all work out, huh?''

''I have no choice,'' Erik said fatalistically.

Risa's car left the M-6 fifty or so miles south of the Scottish border.

''I think we'll be stopping soon,'' their driver told Erik and Raskin. ''It's getting late.''

"We'll see where they go, then find a place nearby," Raskin told the driver, then said to Erik, "She must've made a reservation, but I'll be damned if I know how. The Park Lane switchboard didn't know a thing about where she was going or where she planned to stay."

"Perhaps," Erik offered, "she saw a travel agent and we're not aware of it."

"I'd say perhaps you're right," Raskin said.

Risa's car stopped at the Old England Hotel in Windermere. Erik and Raskin were able to obtain rooms for themselves and their driver at a smaller hotel up the road. A couple of quick calls ensured the cooperation of several staff members at the Old England, then Erik and Raskin took a short walk to stretch their legs.

"This is going to wind up costing a small fortune," Raskin said, as they looked at the choppy surface of Lake Windermere under the last of the setting sun.

"I don't care how much it costs," Erik stated. "I thought you realized that."

"Just checking. It's not my money, remember, and I've been playing fast and loose with it, paying people off right, left, and center, not to mention the agency in London and the staff at the Park Lane."

"If it costs every last penny I have, it will be well worth it. I think we should return to the hotel now, in case there's news."

After a room-service dinner at which she picked, Risa decided to take a walk through the town. She strolled out into the balmy night air, noting that a number of the shops were still open and quite a few tourists were out and about despite the lateness of the hour. Grateful for the darkness, she went along the winding streets, her hands jammed deep into the pockets of the cashmere cardigan she'd bought in London, looking down at the Ferragamo walking shoes she'd also acquired there. She felt fractionally better, less crazy, than she had even the day before. And the bruise on her face was beginning to fade.

Looking up, she wished suddenly that Erik were there with her, walking along at her side. This was such a pretty place. Had he been there, she'd have been able to point out the quaint little house across the way that leaned slightly to the left. And they might have gone inside to investigate some of the souvenir shops. She missed him suddenly, intensely, most painfully. She thought of that night he'd come to dinner, when, before he'd gone hurrying away, she'd kissed his cheek. And his shocked reaction. No one had kissed him, at that point, in twenty-five years. Thinking of it now, she felt a sharp pang, missing him so acutely she had to stop all at once and begin retracing her steps to the hotel. She couldn't bear to be out on the street, playing at being a tourist, when she'd ruined something rare and wonderful. She felt like a murderer. And, God only knew, if she'd really wanted to, she could easily have been one. All it would have taken was directing that broken wineglass to some other, more vulnerable, part of that filthy bastard's body.

Seeing her suddenly stop and turn around, Erik darted into a nearby doorway, crowding close to a rough brick wall, as, on the far side of the street, Marisa, head down, went walking quickly back in the direction of her hotel.

He watched her, a tall black-haired woman hastening toward shelter as if something he'd failed to see had menaced her. He longed to tell her not to be afraid, not to run away. He was there to see no harm would come to her.

A moment. Then he slipped back onto the street in order to keep her within his sight until the last possible moment.

31

After one night at Windermere, Risa was off again, this time heading north and west into Scotland.

"This could get tricky," Raskin said. "Depending on where she finally ends up, we could have serious problems getting a hotel anywhere close by."

His hunch proved right. Risa had booked herself—somehow; they still had no idea when or how she'd made her travel plans—into a very small and exclusive hotel on Loch Linnhe. There was no hotel nearer than four miles away. They had no choice but to book into that other hotel, where Raskin, struck by inspiration, at once got on the pay phone in the lobby.

"I've done it!" he told Erik excitedly. "I've hired a boat. Since there's no way we can get close to her by land, we'll do it by water."

"But how will we know her movements?"

"Easy. Our driver's already enlisted a chambermaid at her hotel, and he's talking to one of the waiters right now."

"I wonder," Erik mused, "if she can sense any of this."

Since the hotel was so small, there was no room service. Risa would have to present herself in the dining room for meals or go hungry. The only concession the hotel would make to room service was the offer of a tea tray in the afternoon in one of the two small adjoining rooms that served as lounges. Both had peat fires going that first evening, and the aroma was exquisite, as was the view from both her bedroom and the dining-room windows, of the sun setting over the loch, with the mountains beyond tangled in low-hanging gray-white clouds.

Fortunately, she was given a small window table that allowed her to sit with her back to the room and her eyes on the view. She ordered without interest, and was startled into positive response by a first course of succulent fresh langoustines, followed by a fillet of wild salmon in the best hollandaise she'd ever tasted. She wasn't able to sample the dessert offerings, having eaten far more than she'd imagined she would, but the filter coffee was dark and strong and served with heavy cream. One of the waitresses poured the coffee, then asked if Risa would care to sample the tablet, which turned out to be a sugary confection rather like fudge.

She was able to drink her coffee in the seclusion of the glass-enclosed but still chilly sitting area beyond the hotel's entryway. She wondered if the owner's wife who, she'd been told by the waitress at dinner, was also the chef and an award-winning one at that, would consider revealing the secret of her superb hollandaise. She thought Erik would adore it. Erik would love this place altogether. If she ever managed to stop hating herself, and if he could somehow forgive her, perhaps they might one day come here together. The air was crisp and bracing, and she was actually sleepy. She stayed looking out the windows for a half hour more, until the sun had long since set and the view was lost to darkness, then she rose and went up to her room.

For the first time since she'd run away, she slept through the night and awakened early the next morning feeling less frazzled, more relaxed, and even slightly optimistic. The sun was shining, she saw, looking out the window at the white Victorian cottage across the way with its splendid wildflower garden. She bathed and dressed and went down to the dining room for a breakfast

of fresh-squeezed orange juice, thick savory oatmeal por-
ridge, and several cups of the excellent coffee.

Her driver was waiting out front with the car, but she
said, "I think I'll take a walk down to the port, have a
look around."

"Shall I follow with the car, madame?"

"No. Why don't you wait here. Go inside and have
some breakfast. I'll come back in an hour or so, then we
can drive through the countryside."

"May I suggest Fort William, madame? I think you
might enjoy that."

"Fine. We'll go there," she said, and set off to follow
the single-lane road the quarter mile to the port.

There were all kinds of boats moored here and there.
She walked out onto the long pier to stand in the wind,
breathing deeply the salt fresh air. It might have been
paradise, she thought, lifted by the great natural beauty
of the place, by the lighthouse to the left and, beyond,
in the distance, the castle standing on a small island at
the far end of the loch. Fields ran on either side of the
water, with bluebells, primroses, and wildflowers whose
names she didn't know growing in profusion. If only Erik
could see this, she thought, pushing the hair out of her
eyes. There was no one about to disturb him, no one
among these gentle, good-natured people who'd dream
of taking pointed notice of him. She wanted so much to
call him, to try to explain, but she didn't yet feel clean
enough, or sure enough of her emotions to risk speaking
to him.

While she stood there, she remembered the first time
they'd made love, the veneration with which he'd touched
her; his trepidations had moved her almost as much as
his touch. He'd been so shy, so terribly fearful of showing himself to her. And she could feel even now her own
fear at first sight of his naked body, the fear she'd refused
to acknowledge because she'd always believed Erik would
never hurt her. It had, of course, hurt. But she'd wanted
that pain; she'd guided him to the apex of her thighs
knowing in advance that joining with him would demonstrate as nothing else could the strength of her love for
him. She'd somehow needed that pain; it was emblematic

of his meaning for her. She might never deliver a child
out of her body but eighteen years before she'd taken one
in; she'd brought him home inside her, and had never,
since that first day, even considered refusing him access
to his rightful place within her. Yet just a matter of days
ago she'd said and done things that had closed him out,
robbed him of the home she'd vowed always to keep for
him.

Erik, I'm sorry, she thought, narrowing her eyes
against the sun as she gazed out at the loch. I promised
never to hurt you, but it's all I've done for such a long
time now. And there was never anyone who deserved less
to be hurt than you, never anyone less equipped to handle
the pain. Forgive me. I'm so very sorry.

From the boat anchored halfway between the pier and
the lighthouse, Erik watched through binoculars as Marisa walked out onto the cement pier and stood looking
around. She stayed for quite some time, not moving, just
gazing soberly at the view, every so often pushing the
hair out of her eyes. The binoculars brought her so close
his hand actually rose to touch her. Then, catching himself, he reached for a cigarette, and went on watching.

Think of me! he willed. Wish for me! Within moments
I'll be with you.

Raskin came to stand beside him. "She told her driver
she'd be back in an hour. They're going to Fort William.
Our waiter overheard him telling one of the waitresses.
Our Ned's waiting to pick us up."

Reluctantly, Erik lowered the binoculars, saddened to
have to lose sight of her again. He gave the glasses to
Raskin, put out the cigarette, then picked up his hat.
"We'd best be on our way," he said.

As she walked head-down back along the road toward
the hotel, she stopped and turned, looking around. It
wasn't possible, she knew, but she could have sworn Erik
was nearby. She took a deep breath and thought
there was the faintest hint of sandalwood on the breeze.
She stood a moment longer, then continued on her way.

* * *

For three days they followed her about the countryside, to Fort William, where the driver showed her Glen Nevis and then Ben Nevis, and then down to Oban, where she walked along the waterfront, glancing into shops and even occasionally going inside but emerging empty-handed every time. On to Kilninver, Kilmelford, and Arduaine. She stopped now and then to drink a cup of coffee, or to look admiringly at the roughly beautiful scenery in the uniformly sunny days. Often she left the car to walk; often Erik was unable to follow and had to be content watching her through the binoculars.

On the morning of the fourth day, word came that she was on her way again, and they rushed to stay with her, heading south, back into England. The weather had turned foul overnight, and they drove throughout the day in a torrential downpour that resolved into a fine mist as they left the main highway heading—their driver guessed, and correctly—for Grasmere.

"I reckon you'll have to chance it, see if they've any rooms at The Swan, because you wouldn't want to stay anywhere else. There's too much chance of missing her if and when she takes it into her mind to leave. With luck, though, she need never know you're in the same hotel."

It was risky, but Erik wanted to try. After she'd gone inside with her chauffeur, who was carrying both their bags, they pulled into the parking area across the road from the hotel and waited half an hour before sending Ned in to ask about vacancies. The small dapper man came running back through the mist with a smile on his face to declare, "Luck's holding, gentlemen. They've had two cancellations, as fate would have it. And the lobby's empty now, it being near to dinnertime."

Raskin got them registered while Erik waited outside. Then they sprinted up to their rooms, the driver at one end of the floor, Erik and Raskin sharing another at the opposite end. Their room was immense, with a pair of double beds, a sofa, and an armchair. There were welcoming complimentary glasses of sherry on the desk, as well as a hospitality tray with coffee, tea, and hot chocolate, a small electric kettle, a teapot, and a ceramic jar containing bars of chocolate and locally made ginger-bread.

Raskin went around investigating the contents of the drawers and closets, announcing, "Even hot-water bottles if our tootsies get cold! Nice place. That's another one for our Ned."

Erik wasn't listening. Marisa was so near he could feel her. He looked at the walls, then at the ceiling, cocking his head to one side as if he might hear her speak.

"I'll go arrange for some food," Raskin said, and left Erik to himself.

In the middle of undressing to take a shower before dinner, Risa stopped and stood very still. It was the oddest thing, but again she had the powerful feeling that Erik was somehow close by. Her guilt, she decided, was starting to turn her peculiar. Erik was at home in Connecticut. And as if to prove this to herself, she went to the telephone, said she wished to make a credit-card call, gave the number and waited for the operator to call her back. When the phone rang, she snatched up the receiver nervously, wetting her lips as an overseas operator said, "Your number's ringing."

It rang four times and then a woman came on saying, "Answering service," and Risa slammed the receiver down, her heart racing, to sit staring at the telephone, wondering what this could mean. The only other time Erik had resorted to using the answering service during the day—they often let the service take calls at night—was when he'd so suddenly gone away years and years ago. Had he gone away now? And if so, where? And why? Had she made such a mess of things that he'd left altogether? God! It frightened her. She put her hand out to the telephone thinking she'd call Kitty and ask her. Kitty would know. But she pulled her hand back. She couldn't do it. She didn't have the nerve to call Kitty, not yet. She didn't want to hear Kitty say Erik was gone and that no one knew when he'd be coming back, if ever.

With a final look at the telephone, she got up and went to take her shower.

* * *

"She just placed a credit-card call," Raskin said, hanging up the telephone. "Are you listening to me, Erik?"

"Sorry. What?"

"Risa just called home."

Erik's face began to brighten. "She did?"

"Yeah. But when our service answered, she hung up."

"Oh!" Erik's features drooped.

"Hey! Don't go all down in the mouth! It's a damned good sign."

"Yes." Erik looked back at the television screen.

In the dining room, she was given a booth overlooking the rain-drenched garden with its varicolored rose bushes and its thatch-roofed birdhouse. She nibbled at overdone roast lamb with bottled mint sauce and stared out at the misty hills across the way, then at the garden slowly losing its color as an unseen sun sank behind the clotted clouds.

She drank two glasses of wine with her dinner, then lingered in a corner of the lounge afterward curled up in a window seat with a cup of coffee. She smoked several cigarettes, one after another, as she continued to stare blankly out the window, completely unmindful of the cloaked figure hidden by shrubberies, who stood out in the rain and, immobile, watched as she got through her dinner and then shifted to see her inside the lounge as she drank coffee and persevered with her new cigarette habit.

He was perfectly reconciled to stand perhaps ten feet away, totally concealed, and yet with an optimum view. He stood for close to ninety minutes, his eyes on Marisa, his treacherous hands safely clasped behind his back. When she let her head come to rest against the window, he very nearly reached out to her, but he kept the control, and remained stationary. And when at last she uncurled herself and left the window seat, he remained outside another five minutes on the off chance she might come back. But she didn't. It didn't really matter. He'd been closer to her for those ninety minutes than he had in what felt like years.

* * *

By six the next morning, Erik and Raskin were back in
the Bentley with Ned at the wheel, the car parked half a
mile up the road at a point Risa would have to pass on
her way to the M-6. They knew that she was now en route
back to London because the Swan receptionist had
booked a reservation for Mrs. D'Anton at the Park Lane.

Raskin wanted to know why they didn't just get a good
head start and beat her back to London.

"I want to keep her in my sight," Erik said, and that
ended the discussion.

By that evening, he and Raskin were again in their
suite at the Ritz and, according to the Park Lane staff,
Risa was ensconced in a suite of her own.

"She started to place another credit-card call," Raskin
told him, "then changed her mind and canceled it."

"Did she give a number?" Erik asked, hope-filled.

"She didn't even get that far. Started reciting the
credit-card number, then said, 'Never mind,' and hung
up."

"Oh!"

"Don't keep deflating that way, Erik! Who the hell
d'you think she'd be calling, if not you?"

"I don't dare take anything for granted."

"That's not taking for granted. That's plain logic and
common sense."

"So you say," Erik said, and toyed with the remote
control, flipping through the channels on the TV set.
"I'm beginning to think this may take a very long time."

"Why d'you say that?"

"I'm tired, Harold. I've never felt so tired."

"Well, hell! I wonder why! Let me think. What could
it be? Could it be because of the couple of hours you
spent standing in the rain last night? Or could it be maybe
a solid week's worth of chasing all over hell and gone,
sneaking around back alleys, hiding in doorways, creeping through bushes, hiking on and off boats, in and out
of limos, sneaking around hotels? What d'you think? Or
maybe it could have something to do with the week *before* that, chasing all over London. D'you think that could
have anything to do with why you're tired? Erik, go the
hell to bed and get some sleep. Of course you're tired.

I'm amazed you're still *conscious*, for Chrissake! I'll order up some food. You'll eat, grab a shower, then hit the sack.''

"And what about you?" Erik wanted to know.

"I've got to talk to Kitty, bring her up to date."

"Tell her you love her, Harold. Learn something from the mistakes I've made."

"What mistakes might those be?"

"Too numerous to mention. Do it! Perhaps you should even consider going home. I know you're missing her."

"Better yet, why don't I tell her to come over? It's still early back home. If she hustled, she could get on a flight tonight and be here in the morning."

"Do that," Erik told him. "I'm going to take your suggestion and have a shower. If I'm still awake when the food arrives, come fetch me."

In the dark bathroom, Erik wearily got out of his clothes and turned on the shower. He did feel exceedingly tired. He also felt very middle-aged and somewhat flabby. His hair was thinning, he was getting jowly, too; as if his face weren't bad enough already. He needed to get reading glasses but hadn't so far summoned up the grit, or been sufficiently hampered by his increasing far-sightedness to see an eye doctor. Fortunately, his teeth were still good, and his flexibility in general had diminished only slightly with age. But he was incredibly tired. He wanted Marisa to make the move that would mean he could go to her, reclaim her, take her into his arms, and return her home. He stood under the shower willing her to pick up the telephone in her room and make good on that credit-card call. Please! he urged her. It will take so very little. All you have to do is say you want me.

Risa walked back and forth through the rooms of her suite, each leg of her circuit bringing her to a halt before the telephone. She'd pause for a moment or two, then turn and start walking again. Thirteen days, thirteen nights. It was the longest period of time she'd ever spent entirely alone. It felt much longer.

For an hour she paced. Then suddenly she had to stop and stand very still. She was overcome by a driving need for Erik. It was a longing so intense it almost bent her double. She had to try; she had to hear his voice at least. She had to tell him how sad and sorry and ashamed she was.

She pounced on the telephone before she had time to change her mind, and rhymed off the credit-card and house numbers, then hung up and stood wringing her hands, waiting beside the telephone for the operator to call her back.

"Your number's ringing," the overseas operator told her.

And then the damned answering-service woman came on the line.

"I want to leave a message for Mr. D'Anton," Risa said hotly.

"Yes, ma'am?"

"Tell him Marisa wants to come home!" She recited the hotel number, then said, "Have you got that?"

"Yes, ma'am, I do."

"Good! Make sure he gets the message," she snapped, then threw down the phone. "Damn, damn, damn!" she muttered, and went back to pacing.

Erik had just fallen asleep when Raskin came bursting in, crowing, "She called! I've got a message for you, Erik!"

Erik sat up, instantly awake, his heart drumming. "What is it?"

"She said to tell you Marisa wants to come home! She called, and she wants to come home!" Raskin did a mad little dance.

"Thank you," Erik said thickly.

"You're welcome. And Kitty'll be here in the morning. If it's okay with you, I'm going to go out to Heathrow to meet her."

"Of course. Thank you," Erik said again.

Raskin stood for a moment, a bit confused by Erik's subdued reaction. Then he went out and quietly closed the door.

* * *

Erik waited alone during the morning for the call from the Park Lane. When it came, he thanked the caller, then went hurrying from the hotel.

Risa walked along, crossed Piccadilly, and strolled toward Covent Garden. She turned off into the first small street in the environs of the Garden, looking in shop windows. Cutting through smaller and smaller streets, she emerged suddenly right in the main body of the Garden. She couldn't understand why Erik hadn't responded to her message. Maybe he'd gone away somewhere. Maybe she'd screwed up so badly that he no longer cared what she did or where she went. But no. Erik cared. He had always cared. She'd been the one who'd been sidetracked for a short time. First there was that business about babies. Another subject on which Kitty had been absolutely right. She'd only carried on about it the way she had because Erik was so set against having a child. Well, that was scheduled to get taken care of. She'd missed the appointment, but she could always make another. A baby simply was no longer earth-shatteringly important to her. But Erik was.

Erik was her heartline, her source of life-sustaining nourishment. He'd married a child, and she'd stayed a child for far too long. But all that was over now. Whether she'd wanted it or not, whether she liked the form her transition to adulthood had taken or not, she was no longer a child. She'd had a large dose of the real world, as Kitty liked to call it, and it didn't taste all that good. But it hadn't killed her. And she'd taught that moron Stefan a lesson he wouldn't forget in a hurry. She was damned glad she'd stabbed him. She wondered if he had any idea how lucky he was that she hadn't killed him.

Leaving the Garden after an hour or so, having looked in most of the shops and seen nothing she cared to buy, she walked back in the direction she'd come, crossing streets to go down a meandering laneway that led to a charming restaurant with a huge skylight and dozens of thriving green plants positioned in and around the tables. It was nearly noon, and she was hungry. The hostess directed her to a table beneath the skylight and opposite the door.

She sat down, lit a cigarette, and picked up the menu, the sun pleasantly warm on her hair. As she reached to put the cigarette on the lip of the ashtray, a hand whisked it from her fingers, and it vanished. A moment, and a pink rose lay before her on the table. She looked up to see Erik seated opposite, smiling at her.

"I understand that you would like to come home, Marisa," he whispered.

"Erik!" She put her hands in his, shaking her head in wonder at the sight of him, sitting smiling in the spread of sun beneath the skylight. Her heart gave a tremendous leap against her ribs and she lowered her head for a long moment, holding fast to his hands. Then she raised her eyes to ask, "Can you forgive me?"

"Only if you forgive me," he replied, the heat from the sun soaking into the top of his head, his shoulders, his arms, scalding him. He tried to ignore it.

"There's nothing to forgive you for, Erik. I'm the one."

"There's a great deal."

"No," she disagreed. "I was a fool. I did such stupid things."

"It doesn't matter."

The waitress came to the table, looked at Erik, then looked quickly at Marisa.

Her arms still extended across the tabletop, her hands linked with Erik's, Marisa smiled at the young woman and said, "My husband and I would like to see the wine list, please." She turned, smiling, to Erik. "My husband knows a great deal about wines."

The waitress went off, craning to look back over her shoulder at the dead peculiar pair at table twelve.

Marisa had to ask, "What are you *doing* here, Erik?"

"I have been here all along," he answered, drowning in the heat and the light, but determined to withstand their effects.

"I've never been anywhere without you," she said, holding tight to his hands, unwilling to let go of him.

"Are you all right?" he asked.

"I am now. Please, could we forget the whole thing, forget any of it ever happened?"

"Forget what?" he asked, straight-faced.

Again she lowered her head, her grip going even tighter on his hands. He was so unutterably good, so very kind, so remarkably forgiving. "I'm not hungry," she said, returning her eyes to his. "Are you hungry, Erik? What I really would like is to hold you, make love. Wouldn't you much rather do that?"

"Now that you mention it, I think that's an excellent idea. Why don't we go back to your hotel?"

"What an excellent idea!" she declared, beaming at him. She released him only long enough to grab her handbag and the rose before taking hold of his hand to go rushing out of the restaurant with him. "Let's take a taxi," she said, scanning the street outside. "We'll have to make a stop at a drugstore on the way, though."

"Why?" he asked.

"Because the IUD had to be removed," she answered. "I don't know why I didn't tell you. Somehow, I just couldn't."

"Well," he said, "I'm afraid I really have no interest in making any side trips. I'd prefer to go directly back to your hotel."

She stood looking at him for a moment, then she threw her arms around him and hugged him. "Erik! I'm so happy to *see* you!"

And without giving it a thought, he held her and kissed her, right there on the street.

> "And . . . and . . . I . . . kissed her! . . .
> I! . . . I! . . . I! . . . And she did not die!"
>
> *The Phantom of the Opera*
> *(Le Fantôme de l'opéra)*
> Gaston Leroux